PRAISE FO

"There are storytellers who seem to come to us fully formed. Bards who create worlds and characters that captivate us instantaneously. Eryk Pruitt is such a storyteller, and *Something Bad Wrong* is such a book. A kaleidoscope of Southern Gothic traditions seamlessly combined with an incredible murder mystery, all told with Pruitt's unique, indomitable style. *Something Bad Wrong* is some very, very good writing."

—S. A. Cosby, bestselling author of *Razorblade Tears* and *Blacktop Wasteland*

"*Something Bad Wrong* hits on every cylinder—expertly plotted, deliberately paced, deeply human, incredibly relevant, and just utterly absorbing. This is a golden example of the genre."

—Rob Hart, author of *The Paradox Hotel* and *The Warehouse*

"I still can't believe *Something Bad Wrong* wasn't written specifically for me. A gripping page-turner about a cold case murder with a gutsy true crime podcaster as a main character. It's the most devourable mystery novel I've read in years."

Brooke Cain, *Raleigh News & Observer*

"*Something Bad Wrong* is more proof that Eryk Pruitt is one of the most original, dynamic, and powerful voices writing today. While his uncanny flair for language and acute observation set him apart from his contemporaries, it's never lost that, foremost, Pruitt is a natural storyteller—the kind of person quietly telling a story to a group of people at a table in a restaurant, and by the end of the evening, the entire restaurant is listening, rapt. At a time when contemporary crime fiction is putting out outstanding title after title, *Something Bad Wrong* belongs on a bookshelf among the best of the best."

—E. A. Aymar, author of *No Home for Killers*

"A rising crime-fiction star, Eryk Pruitt is at the height of his powers with *Something Bad Wrong*, a page-turning story of people caught between truth and lies, justice and corruption, and life and death. Pruitt utilizes his experience as an (excellent) true crime podcaster to expertly plot a narrative that weaves two timelines, rich with twists and mystery. Above all, Pruitt has the crime writer's greatest gift of being able to slice into the human heart so he can show you its darkest, bloodiest chambers."

—Jordan Harper, Edgar Award–winning author of *She Rides Shotgun* and *Everybody Knows*

"Eryk Pruitt has crafted a nail-biter of a crime novel, a slice of the American South populated by unforgettable characters and peppered with dialogue so razor sharp it would make Elmore Leonard nervous. It dances deftly across the years, equal parts gasp inducing and profound, a warning that although past evil may fade from our memory, some bad things ought never be forgotten. Perfectly paced from beginning to end, *Something Bad Wrong* is a propulsive runaway freight train of a story that will grab you by the throat and hang on until the very last page."

—J. G. Hetherton, author of *Last Girl Gone* and *What Lies Beneath*

SOMETHING BAD WRONG

ALSO BY ERYK PRUITT

Townies: And Other Stories of Southern Mischief

Dirtbags

Hashtag

What We Reckon

SOMETHING BAD WRONG

A THRILLER

ERYK PRUITT

This is a work of fiction. Names, characters, organizations, places, events, and incidents are either products of the author's imagination or are used fictitiously. Otherwise, any resemblance to actual persons, living or dead, is purely coincidental.

Published by Thomas & Mercer, Seattle

www.apub.com

ISBN-13: 9781662507052 (paperback)
ISBN-13: 9781662507069 (digital)

Cover design by Caroline Teagle Johnson
Cover image: © Richard Nixon / plainpicture

Printed in the United States of America

For Carolyn and Tim

God gave us memory
so that we might have roses in December.
—J. M. Barrie

PRELUDE

[END MUSIC CUE]

JESS KEELER: When we first began investigating the Lake Castor Christmas Eve Murders of 1971, it was easy for us to become mesmerized by what few sensational aspects were available to the public. Such lack of detail often serves as an aphrodisiac for true-crime junkies like myself. Newspapers reported that on December 24, 1971, Linda Harris and Steven Hicks vanished after attending a small gathering with colleagues and friends, only to be discovered two weeks later.

For nearly fifty years, their killer, or killers, has never been identified.

It would be easy for us to describe for you, in lurid detail and living color, the gory nature of the crime scene photos or the autopsy reports. Even easier to relay four decades of rumor and conjecture, then parse them down until they are accepted as fact or discarded. Since nothing has ever been documented to the public about this case, anything we produce could be declared complete and substantive.

But it will never be complete.

No matter how many original or current investigators we interview, no matter how many stories from family members or friends of the victims we record, and no matter how many suspects we name . . . this story will always be missing two vital ingredients: the victims.

Linda Harris and Steven Hicks are unable to tell their story. Their lives were brutally cut short nearly fifty years ago, and we will never know if their love would have endured. Would they have broken up during college, as so many young lovers often do? Or would they have grown up to be married, have children, and perhaps even grandchildren?

Instead, all we have are stories. The accounts from those closest to them. Their friends and family. Or those who ruthlessly pursued their killer. The surviving, original detectives who worked the case back in 1972 and those who still ruthlessly track their killer today.

We also have three suspects who were never ruled out and who will be publicly identified for the first time in this podcast.

Throughout our investigation, we came to realize that these people—the victims, their families, the investigators—are not simply characters in a story, and this is not simply a story. Fifty years is a lifetime and, for many, is how long this murder has been left unsolved. What we present is the story of the people who have lived that lifetime, as well as those who did not.

This is the story of the lives touched by the murders of Linda Harris and Steven Hicks.

PART I

CHAPTER ONE

Jess Keeler

Present Day

Jess Keeler located her target on the third stool from the end of the bar. His shoulders hunched over what had to be his third or fourth bourbon. Head low so the couple canoodling in the corner might not recognize him. At least a week's worth of growth yet to be shaved from his face. Not looking up—not even once—save to signal for the bartender to pour him another.

"Excuse me," she said, "but you look familiar."

He side-eyed her and smiled tight before returning to his whiskey.

"I'm serious." She wasn't used to high heels and wobbled as she neared him. "Do we know each other?"

"I'm not from around here," he apologized. "I just moved to Lake Castor last mo—"

"Oh my God." Jess widened her eyes. "That's where I know you from: you're Dan Decker."

Decker flinched at the sound of his own name. He checked over both shoulders, as if someone might have heard.

Jess gushed. "*Dan Decker at Six and Eleven.* That's you, right? Oh man, you were a big deal in our house. My husband—ex-husband, that is—only ever watched Channel Ten because he said you were an honest anchorman. 'A face you can trust' is how he'd put it." She inspected him closer. "I can see that now."

Of course, her husband had said no such thing. After she had dropped out of school to raise their son, Benjamin, Philip had finished his business degree and launched into one grand plan after another until finally settling on real estate. The only current events he cared about were sports scores. However, Jess had done her research and knew Dan Decker could be played like a fiddle by appealing to either his ego or his sex drive.

"It was you who first told us about the virus," she continued. "It was your voice that talked us through the quarantines and told us everything was going to be okay."

Decker's eyes landed on his near-empty cocktail.

Jess leaned on the stool next to him. "The entire time we were married, you could count on two hands the number of things we actually agreed on. But I'll say he was right about one thing: you were a true, old-school *journalist*. A dying breed. Most TV reporting today is done by *personalities*. Instagram influencers passing themselves off as real reporters."

A wounded smile crossed Decker's lips. "They put microphones in the hands of reality-show wannabes and instruct them to fetch man-on-the-street reactions to world events. They wonder why it's called *fake news*."

"Precisely." Jess motioned to the stool. "May I sit?"

Decker looked over his shoulder. The bartender polished bottles with a mildewed rag. The old drunk in the corner kept his eyes on the television set. The young couple busied themselves with each other in the back booth.

"Sure," he said. "Be my guest."

Jess climbed onto the barstool. Her forearm brushed against Decker's.

"What are you drinking?" she asked.

"Bourbon."

Jess raised two fingers to the bartender.

"Could we get two more of these?"

The bartender obeyed. Decker motioned for the drinks to land on his tab. He was still an attractive man, Jess thought. She could trace the troubles of the past year in the lines beneath his eyes or in the fleshiness of his stubbled cheeks. However, he'd managed to keep fit, and his eyes harbored a vulnerability she found incredibly sexy in an older man.

"What would your husband say," Decker asked, "if he found out you were having a drink with his favorite former anchorman?"

"*Ex*-husband," she corrected. "Although he'd probably wonder why I didn't ask for an autograph."

"Let's not disappoint the unlucky bastard." Decker plucked a fresh cocktail napkin from a stack of them. "Who do I make it out to?"

"Jess." She offered her hand. When he took it, she did not let it go. "Jess Keeler."

"Where are you from, Jess Keeler?"

"I grew up right here, in Lake Castor."

"Like I said earlier, I just moved here. I lived the past ten years up in Tucker, but I was born in—"

"You were born in Toledo, Ohio." Jess tried to hide her delight when Decker's jaw dropped. "Your first job was at the Cincinnati network affiliate as a street reporter. Then Biloxi. One brief gig in DC, but the majority of your career has been spent delivering news to southern Virginia."

A shadow crossed his face, and Jess drew a breath. Perhaps, she feared, she might have overplayed her hand. Everything slowed down except for the steady rhythms of the room. She held her breath and waited for Decker's inevitable reaction.

However, instead of suspicion, all the interaction seemed to have sparked within him was possibility. He snaked an arm around her hip and drew them closer together.

"And now I'm right here, right now," he whispered. "What gods have I pleased to deliver such great fortune? I find myself recalling literature invoking love at first sight."

"Nice. Shakespeare?"

"I'm more into Nabokov."

Decker moved in for the kill. His lips were aimed for hers and might have landed, had Jess not braced him with a stiff forearm.

"That's not a good idea," she said evenly.

"Why not? Because of your husband?"

"*Ex*-husband."

"So what am I missing?"

Jess motioned with her eyes over his shoulder. Decker followed her glance to the corner booth. The young couple had their eyes on them. The young man showed his date something on his phone while she snapped a pic with hers.

"See?" he said to his date. "It's totally *him*. I told you."

Decker composed himself. His hands retreated to his own jacket pockets.

"Are you familiar with those new condominiums they built in the old mill building?" Decker asked her.

"Monstrosities," she said.

"I just bought one. What do you say I show you? It's got a great view of the river. At night, you can see clear to the—"

"I think it's nice right where we are." Jess touched his arm lightly to keep him engaged. "There's plenty of bourbon, and it will give us the opportunity to talk."

Decker's face soured. "Talk?"

"You might find this hard to believe, but I've wanted to bend your ear about something for quite a while."

Decker reached beneath the bar and rested his hand on her thigh. "And I want to listen."

"Really?"

"More than anything in the world."

"Good." Jess motioned for the bartender to bring another round. "When is the last time you've done a long-form piece?"

"Beg pardon?"

"A long-form deep dive. True investigative reporting?"

"I don't follow."

"Not some thirty-second segment on the news or some ten-inch article in the local fishwrap. I'm talking about a deep exploration."

"The only thing I want to explore right now is that perfume you are wearing. It's intoxicating."

"I'm not wearing any."

"I may have a heart attack."

Jess rolled her eyes. "A man your age shouldn't joke about that."

The drinks arrived. Decker lifted his glass and waited for her to join him in a toast. Once the glasses clinked, he took a sip. "That's what I'm talking about," he said. "Now, where were we?"

"You were about to tell me the last time you investigated a story."

"I can think of so many other things I'd rather do with our mouths."

"The answer: You haven't done any true investigative work in nearly twenty years. Not since the piece you did on Judge Menkin. That got you promoted to anchor, where I heard you insisted on writing your own copy for the first couple of years. But after that . . ."

"I love it when you talk about me," he said. "Keep going. Tell me more."

"From that point, you got fat and happy."

"I never got fat," he said between light and tender kisses along her neck.

"No, you certainly didn't. In fact, if you had worked half as hard on real journalism as you did on your looks, then it might not have been so easy for the station to part ways with you."

Decker moved his creeping hand into position. He breathed whiskeyed humidity into her ear.

"I assure you," he whispered, "my parting ways with that station had nothing to do with the quality of my work."

"Oh, I know. It had more to do with your behavior with interns."

There.

She had said it.

Decker zipped his lips. He leaned back from her, as if to make sure he had heard her correctly.

"All that was *he said, she said.*"

Jess stirred her ice with her pinkie. "More like five *she saids*. Or was it six?"

"Are you seriously bringing this up right now?"

"I told you I wanted to have a conversation with you."

Decker shrank back to his barstool. He crossed both his arms but didn't take his eyes off her.

"Do I know you from somewhere?"

Jess brought her glass to her lips and fought the urge to inform him that they had indeed met once before. When he was a young reporter just starting his career at Channel 10, he'd visited State to deliver a lecture on journalism. She'd stayed after to speak with him. He'd told her he couldn't determine if he liked her eyes or her lips better and asked for an opportunity to further investigate. However, she saw no point in reminding him and opted again for a softer approach.

"I have a strong online presence," she told him. "Perhaps you recognize me from that."

"Social media?" He rolled his eyes. "I canceled all my accounts after . . . *you know.*"

"I enjoyed some traction on Instagram during COVID, but for the past six months, I have been developing content for a website focusing on civic resources."

"What kind of resources?"

"Advice. Connections. Experiences. Recipes."

"Hold the roll—just a second." Decker placed both his hands on the bar top. "Are you telling me I nearly went home with a *mommy blogger*?"

"In all fairness," said Jess through clenched teeth, "I merely asked you for a conversation. And the proper nomenclature is *content creator*. My website is not a *mommy blog*; it's the *Piedmont Sundial*, and it has nearly six thousand subscribers." It was her turn to cross her arms. "It's a start-up."

"Either way," Decker growled, "you're writing a hit piece. And for what? I paid my dues. I apologized on air. I lost my job, I lost my wife . . . I lost *everything*. What else will you people demand of me? When will you feel like I've suffered enough? When will you move on to the next poor son of a bitch? Did you hear they found black plague in Nevada? *Black plague*. Yet does anybody talk about that? Hell no. All they want to talk about is where I had the poor sense to stick my—" He stopped himself, took a deep breath, and then grabbed his jacket off the back of his stool.

"Dan," she said, "where are you going?"

He stood and slipped into his jacket. "I thank you for your charming company," he said, "but the last thing I need right now is to have anything to do with a takedown written by a mommy blogger."

"Oh, Dan," she said, "I don't want to write about you. I want to write *with* you. I'm onto a big story, but I need someone with more clout to help give it the splash it rightfully deserves."

Decker blinked. He blinked again.

Jess motioned for him to return to his seat. Once he did, she asked, "Have you ever heard of the 1971 Lake Castor Christmas Eve Murders?"

CHAPTER TWO

James Ballard

1972

Ballard couldn't remember.

He sat in the front seat of his county cruiser for nearly ten minutes, wondering which route he had taken that morning to the Waffle Hut. Had he driven the farm road, which skirted the Deeton County line, or had he come up the interstate? Or instead, had he chosen the bumpy back roads upon which he had lived his entire forty-seven years, minus the tours he'd served in Korea? Not that it mattered, because he'd reached his destination—and how he had gotten there would otherwise be unremarkable, except for the fact that he'd already forgotten it.

What else had he forgotten?

Ballard couldn't remember.

These spells had become more frequent. What had started as a lost set of keys or misplaced paperwork or failure to conjure an old friend's name had lately given way to incidents of greater consequence. Two weeks ago, Ballard had forgotten where he'd hidden his daughter's Christmas presents. Last week, he'd gotten lost driving a neighborhood that he'd patrolled nearly half his life.

As was custom during these spells, Ballard struggled to keep his cool. He dabbed sweat from his brow with a handkerchief. He counted inhales and exhales until his heartbeat steadied. He repeated the names of those closest to his heart—

My wife, Cora Ballard.

My daughter, Samantha Ballard.

My wife, Cora.

My daughter, Samantha.

—until he felt assured this passing phase had indeed passed. He weighed what he remembered against what he might possibly have forgotten, then assumed—for the moment—that all again was well.

But all was not well, Ballard reminded himself. Once again, that morning, he'd snapped awake obscenely early for work, his mind too wired and electric for any hope of slumber to return. Rather than continue his usual ritual of staring at the ceiling, running over every disappearing option in his head, he slipped silently out of bed and dressed for work. Quietly, so as not to arouse Cora, he tucked into the kitchen for coffee and a quick peek at the newspaper.

Instead, he found his daughter foraging through the fridge.

"Sam? What are you doing home? Is everything okay?"

Samantha rolled her eyes. "I told you a hundred times already, Dad: Christmas break doesn't end until Monday. I'll be out of your hair soon enough."

Ballard gently pulled her from the refrigerator and into his arms. He held her tight. He never wanted to let go.

"Jeez, Dad . . ." She bucked a little, but not much. She was his daddy's girl. She always had been and always wo—"What's gotten into you?"

Ballard released her, then went for the cabinet. He opened one door, then closed it. He opened another.

"Have you seen my . . ."

"It's next to the coffeepot." Samantha pointed to his favorite blue mug sitting on the counter. "Where it always is."

She watched him with wary eyes as he set about the process of brewing a pot.

"Put a little whiskey in it," she said.

"Huh?"

"Hair of the dog."

Ballard narrowed his eyes at her.

"It helps," she told him. "It's one of the many things I'm learning in college. When you tie one on, you can chase away the hangover by having a little more of what you drank the night before. They call it the hair of the dog that bit you."

"I didn't *tie one on*, hon."

"Really?" Samantha padded her way silently on stockinged feet to the trash can, then reached inside. She came up with an empty whiskey bottle. "This was full when you came home yesterday."

Ballard pretended to ignore her, but the words landed. It would explain some of the thick cobwebbing of his brain and give justification to any failure to recollect anything from the previous night. Why his mouth was so dry and his arms and legs were filled with sand.

It offered him odd comfort because if this was merely a hangover, then maybe everything would be okay with a little *hair of the—*

"I'm worried about Mom." Samantha said it casually, as if it were a thought shared by the two of them that needed no further explanation. "She sees it."

"Sees what?"

Samantha shook the empty bottle in her hand, then dropped it into the trash.

"Has she . . . ?"

"She hasn't said anything," said his daughter. "She doesn't have to."

"It's the holidays, sweetheart." Ballard kissed her on the forehead, then poured the coffee into his cup. "It's just a drink or two. It's nothing to worry about."

But was it? Ballard had no idea. He could remember pouring the first one. He could also remember reaching for the bottle again but not whether it was the second time or the third—or even the fourth or . . . one memory crashed into another until all he could see was concern scratched across his daughter's face. The holes in his memory gaped like the jaws of a beast. They infected. They multiplied. As he struggled to get his hands around one image, it slipped away and took others with it.

There were things he remembered and remembered well. Like the first and only time he'd ever shown up to the office before the sheriff. How the other deputies at the time had been giants, men like Cappy Jenkins and Ernie Bass. They'd hooted and howled at him, and Ballard had spent the rest of his shift shamefaced. How for years—*decades*—after, it had become an initiation rite to tell the following generations of Red's Seven, "Red likes his men to show initiative. Show up at the office before he does." A man's mettle could get tested during one of Red's dressings-down. He could remember like yesterday the latest prank, pulled this time on Ennis Worthy, the only Black man to serve as a Deeton deputy—how he had not fallen for it. Worthy seemed to divine when it was proper to zig as opposed to zag. Ballard and the boys had lain in wait for his every mistake, only to find themselves waiting in vain. How this boy managed to dance between the raindrops was well bey—

"Breakfast this morning, Jim?"

Ballard blinked the world into focus. He'd entered the Waffle Hut, stood before the cigarette machine where he'd normally park his hat. The waitress crossed the room with a coffeepot, from a booth full of farmers to another filled with mill workers.

"Eggs over easy with some bacon." Ballard sat on a stool two seats from a trucker. "You got a newspaper, Rosie?"

Rosie pointed with her eyes over the top of her glasses to a far spot on the counter. Ballard reached to fetch it. The front page: Nixon announced his campaign for reelection. More soldiers killed in Vietnam, despite plans to decelerate troops. The two missing kids from Virginia had yet to be found.

NO NEW LEADS.

"That's a shame," said the waitress, over his shoulder. "I heard somebody spotted a couple who looked just like them down in Raleigh."

"Said they were shopping for wedding rings," said the trucker. "I heard that one too."

"Somebody saw them at a filling station in Blacksburg," said old Tom, the short-order cook.

"What about it, Big Jim?" The waitress dangled the coffeepot off her pinkie and leaned in. "What's the word?"

"I'm never surprised one bit when things go ass-over-tits up there in Lake Castor," Ballard said. "If you ask me, those two kids will turn up when they're ready."

Having said all he planned to on the matter, Ballard fingered past the headlines—past the sports page, past the advertisements—until he came to the crossword puzzle.

"You mind if I take this?" Ballard asked.

"Help yourself, Jim."

He did. He worked it with his ink pen. Confident in his choices yet frightened that he had to make them. *Exercise your mind,* the doctor up in Lake Castor had told him. *Challenge yourself with crossword puzzles.*

Also recommended: the little green notepad Ballard kept in his uniform's shirt pocket.

Written by his own hand on the front page of it:

TELL YOUR WIFE.

Ballard could not tell her. He had sat in the room with her for an hour the previous day yet still had not worked up the courage. He'd watched from the sofa as his wife and daughter had carefully plucked ornaments from the Christmas tree before wrapping them in newspaper and packing them away. All the while, he'd turned that notebook over in his hands.

TELL YOUR WIFE.

He stared at the words until fire burned in his eyes and he felt the stirrings of a slight palsy in his hand. He flipped the page. What he found there offered him no comfort.

YOUR NAME IS DEPUTY JAMES W. BALLARD.

Ballard had lost so many things lately. Things like memories—or time. For instance, he had no idea when he'd been joined by Bobby McCoy and Tim Doody but found his two fellow deputies on either side of him, sipping coffee while Doody told the story, yet again, of how he had failed to slap handcuffs on the wrists of a local bootlegger named Jem Fosskey. As was his custom, Doody told the long version of the tale rather than the short.

"No sooner do we get close to old Fosskey," Doody was saying, "than does he slip the noose. Before we can catch his trail again, we get sucked up by a mess of bureaucratic bullshit."

"What do you mean?" Ballard asked. He had continued to diligently work his crossword puzzle, had completed two-thirds of it. He looked up to see if Rosie was any closer to delivering his breakfast. "What kind of bullshit?"

"Red told us to take time off our case to check farmhouses along the northern edge of the county. Said we got to ask folks to look in on their barns and outbuildings."

"Why for?"

"In case those two missing kids are holed up in there."

McCoy snuffed out his cigarette in the ashtray before he lit another. "Said they've searched all over Lake Castor but turned up nothing."

"No surprise there," said Doody. "Lake Castor boys can't find their own assholes with an asshole detector and a head start. You knew it was only a matter of time before they came asking for help."

"If you ask me," said McCoy, "it's a waste of everybody's time and resources. Those kids will turn up. They either ran off to get married or they're halfway to California to join some hippie cult."

"They ain't alive," Doody argued.

Ballard scratched in another answer on his puzzle. "You don't think?"

"You see the size of that old boy?" Doody pointed to the picture of the male victim on the front page of the newspaper. "Steven Hicks was a hoss, man. Captain of the Tucker football team that year they went to the semifinals. Lost to Danville. You remember that? My brother's kid played against him their senior year. Said that Hicks boy got on him like a prom date. What is he? Six-one? Six-two?"

"He was a big old boy—that's for sure."

"That's my point." Doody waited for Rosie to refill his coffee. "Boy that size has plenty of fight in him. There's no way he's letting anything happen to that girl of his. The only way he's coming out of that fight is on top or laid out. Now, I say since it's been, what, two weeks since they went missing . . ."

"Either way," said McCoy, "I think Lake Castor should have sent their boys down here to do the rooting around in barns and outbuildings. I don't care for the smell of Virginia water, much less cotton to carrying it."

Rosie arrived with the breakfast. Doody and McCoy dove right in. Ballard, on the other hand, cocked his head and stared at the food on his plate.

"This isn't what I ordered."

Through a mouthful of eggs, Doody asked him, "What'd you get?"

"I got two eggs and some bacon." Ballard pointed at his plate. "That ain't what I ordered."

McCoy waved Rosie back to the counter.

"Get y'all anything else?" she asked them.

"This ain't what I ordered."

"Like hell it ain't, Jim." She looked at him over the top of her glasses. "Two eggs over easy with some bacon. That's exactly what you ordered."

Ballard's smile was tight. "Rosie, I ordered a waffle."

"No, you didn't."

Ballard opened his mouth. He second- and third-guessed his every tumbling thought.

Rosie stuffed a fist into her apron. She came out with the carbons from her ticket book. She thumbed through them until she came to one that read *FLOP TWO / BACON*.

"See? That says eggs over easy with bacon."

"I don't care what it says." Ballard's tone grew pinched. "It ain't what I ordered."

Rosie looked from Doody to McCoy.

"What's the big deal?" McCoy asked him. "Those eggs look just as good as any waffle old Tom can cook. Why not just—"

"Don't do that, Bobby." Ballard's eyes could cook chicken. "Don't you dare do that."

Doody shrugged. "Hey, Rosie . . . it's a busy morning. Maybe you got your signals crossed and you—"

"I haven't written down the wrong order in twenty-seven years, Tim Doody. If you think for one second that I—"

"Listen, goddammit!" Ballard slapped the counter in front of him and nearly rattled off the salt and pepper shakers. "I ordered a waffle."

The whole of the diner hushed. No more scraping of forks against plates. No more casual din of conversation. Instead, there remained only a silence louder than bombs. Ballard retreated further inward. How did he know whether he'd ordered a waffle? Could he even remember? He couldn't, which frightened him to no end, because if he couldn't trust himself . . .

How could anyone else?

"Rosie," said Doody, "be a sweetheart . . ."

"Fine, Jim," said Rosie, her words filled with resentment. "You ordered a damned waffle."

Rosie left them to fetch it, and folks slowly returned to their breakfasts, their small talk. By the time she dropped the waffle in front of Ballard, folks had mostly forgotten it. Doody and McCoy made short work of their meals, but Ballard's appetite had disappeared. Instead, he stared hate-fire at the waffle, as if the entire thing were its fault. He wanted more than life itself to be able to pitch the plate against yonder wall and thought he might do exactly that, if not for the terrible palsy bubbling up in his right hand.

No, goddammit.

Not now.

Ballard dropped both hands beneath the counter. He steadied his shaking right with his left. He looked to both sides to see if either of his fellow lawmen might have noticed. They had not, and he opened his mouth, opened it wide, to tell them just how scared he—

"Telephone," barked Rosie. She pointed to the far wall. "It's Lois. She says the sheriff knows you all are here and it's an emergency."

McCoy slouched off his stool. "I got it, I got it."

Once they were alone, Tim Doody, his old friend, leaned closer. "Hey, Big Jim . . . is there something you ought to be telling me?"

There was, Ballard thought, but that moment had passed. He brought his right hand above the table and found it eerily still.

"I'm fine," he said.

"Cora. Is everything okay with you two?"

Ballard poked at the waffle with his fork and tallied in his head all the things that *weren't* okay. He tried to run back his thoughts to the single moment when everything had gone south but kept coming up empty.

Ballard couldn't remember.

Finally, after a long moment, he said, "Tim . . . what if I told you I was—"

"Come on, boys; it's time to go."

Words spoken by Bobby McCoy. He had already collected his hat and jacket.

"I just got off the phone with Lois down at the station," he said. "She said a surveyor found two bodies in the woods off Gilmore Road. Said we need to get out there pronto."

Rosie appeared over their shoulders. "It's them two kids from Lake Castor, ain't it?"

An electric hum buzzed beneath the noise of the diner. Ballard refused eye contact with anyone as he dropped money on the counter, then gathered his coat and hat. He could feel it, though; he knew what they'd find in those woods.

McCoy lit another cigarette. "You boys ready?"

"Let's go."

Behind them, the speculation of the farmers and mill workers reached a fever pitch. *Is it them? I told you they were dead. I knew all along that they*—all those voices became one as the three deputies marched single file out of the diner. The morning-traffic noises mingled with the memory of the excitement, and Ballard almost didn't hear Rosie flagging him down as he crossed the parking lot.

"Big Jim," she hollered, "you forgot something."

Horror shook Ballard by the shoulders as he saw what she held in her fingers: his little green notepad. He narrowed the distance between them in three, four steps and quickly snatched it from her.

"Thank you," he said, head down.

"I knew whose it was because of that page," she said.

Ballard thought he might turn sick. He knew which page she talked about without even looking.

That Lake Castor doctor had stood over him and waited for Ballard to write it with his own trembling hand.

YOUR NAME IS DEPUTY JAMES W. BALLARD.

And the page before that . . .

TELL YOUR WIFE.

CHAPTER THREE

Dan Decker

Present Day

There was a time when a story like the 1971 Lake Castor Christmas Eve Murders would have earned more than a raised eyebrow from Dan Decker. When he was a young-buck reporter back in Cincy or Biloxi, he would have killed to sink his teeth into an unsolved double homicide, especially one with such little ink. So why, after being pitched it by a woman in a low-cut dress, did he still hesitate to show further interest?

Perhaps it was because since that time he'd spent in the journalistic trenches, he had interviewed one on one with three presidents, two popes, and one of the world's leading terrorists. He'd traveled to Cuba, Beirut, and Beijing. He'd climbed Mount Everest.

If a story such as this one had passed across his desk after he had been promoted to anchor, he would have, no doubt, passed it along to a junior reporter. Or quite possibly to an intern, if she exhibited enough promise.

Jess Keeler showed him such a spark, and it raged like a wildfire behind her eyes as she sifted through her material. She'd kept everything inside two overstuffed file folders jammed inside a Trapper Keeper notebook. All of it she laid across the table of the greasy-spoon diner just outside downtown Lake Castor. Handwritten notes, microfiche newspaper articles, printouts of social media posts and chat rooms. Her voice took a fevered pitch as she described the nuances of the case and the lengths she had gone in order to track down what little information she had found. She communicated a startling intensity, a fiery devotion, and an absolute admiration for the search of truth, but Decker heard none of the words she spoke. Instead, he found himself distracted by her thigh, which disappeared beneath the cut of her dress. While he had placed her in her late twenties under the low lights back at the Armory, the hard fluorescents at the All-Niter and the way she spoke made her a solid thirty-eight. Thirty-nine, tops. Either way, the years had certainly been incredibly kind to her legs. They had a shapeliness to them that was often first to go on a woman, as they had been for his own wife—*ex*-wife, rather—Cassandra. The flesh around Keeler's legs had very little give, and she had the cutest lit—

"Dan?" Jess's face was flat. "Are you listening to me?"

"Yes . . . ," he said, perhaps a bit too quickly. "But hit me with the briefest of summaries."

"On December 24, 1971," Jess began, "two young lovers named Steven Hicks and Linda Harris went missing from a lovers' lane in Lake Castor. Two weeks later, their bodies were found tied to a tree across the state line in Deeton. Fast-forward fifty years, and still no one has ever been publicly named as a suspect in their murders."

Jess pointed to a photocopied microfiche article from the *Lake Castor Times*. The accompanying black-and-white image showed two suited men in hats standing in the woods and pointing to the base of a tree.

"Using what scant details I could find in these articles," she said, "plus some other notes I've been able to find—"

"Where?"

"I'll get to that in a minute." She smiled. She proudly reached for a yellow notepad filled with neat and precise handwriting. "Here is a bit of copy I've cobbled together about the crime scene."

It had been a cold winter, even by North Carolina standards. Linda Harris and Steven Hicks had been missing for two weeks, and every indication suggested that they had been killed on Christmas Eve, the night they went missing. However, the frigid temperatures—which dropped as low as 29 degrees the morning that Alvin Stapleton discovered their bodies—preserved them from the elements.

When Deeton County deputies cleared the leaves from their corpses, they found a young man and woman, each individually bound at the wrists and ankles. A rope had also joined them at the waists and throats, although these ropes had been loosened in order to lay them down and cover them with leaves.

Aside from the ligatures at their throats, there also appeared to be small puncture wounds in each of their midsections. According to Deputy James Ballard, the lead investigator, these wounds appeared to be postmortem.

Decker set down the pages and found her waiting expectantly.

"Well?"

"Well what?"

She rolled her eyes. "Tell me what you think."

"It's raw," he said, "but it's good. There are a lot of holes you'll need to fill."

"I could do that no problem if I had a look at the case file."

Decker knew from experience how unlikely that was to happen. "Have you asked the detective in charge of cold cases with the Lake Castor police?"

"Oh, Dan . . ."

"What?"

Jess shook her head. "Did you really read any of the copy you spouted from behind that news desk in fourteen years?"

Decker, still, was lost.

"The Lake Castor Police Department was decommissioned back in the aughts," she explained. "The county handles law enforcement."

"Okay. Did you ask the sheriff?"

Jess shrugged. "They said they retained no records from LCPD."

"How is that possible?"

"One time they blamed a fire in the property room," she said. "Another time it was flooded after a hurricane. Either way, they claim not to have them."

Decker was quite familiar with the long and dark history of Lawles County. It had done wonders for his career. "That's too bad," he said. "It doesn't look good for your story."

"Au contraire," Jess said. "The kids were kidnapped out of Lake Castor, but their bodies were found on the other side of the state line in Deeton County."

Decker reckoned she was the type to slow roll a winning hand in poker. He finished the rest of his coffee and wished to replace it with bourbon.

"What happened when you called Deeton County?" he asked.

"The detective has yet to return my calls."

Decker was losing interest. He scanned the empty diner for the waitress, who had yet to give a shit.

"That's why I need your help," Jess said.

Decker felt icy fingers tickle the sides of his gut. He blamed it on the lack of alcohol, then reached across the table for the uneaten cheeseburger on Jess's plate.

"That's all very interesting," he said after taking a bite, "but what do you expect me to do about it? Back when I was behind the desk, I *might* have been able to get this story a thirty-second recap before weather or maybe a slick reenactment and a tip hotline. But now . . ."

"If Deeton County won't return my calls," she said, "maybe a fire will be lit beneath them when *Dan Decker at Six and Eleven* drops them a line."

"Ahh." Decker finally got it. He leaned back in the booth. "To what end?"

Jess made a face like she didn't understand.

Decker tried again. "I mean, what's my in on this?"

"You're asking what's in it for you?"

"In other words."

Jess leaned forward and set both her elbows on the table. "I'm proposing a redemption story."

"Beg pardon?"

"Dan Decker's big comeback."

Decker stopped chewing. "With a blog post?"

"I'm not talking about a blog post," said Jess. "I'm talking about a *podcast.* A true-crime podcast about the unsolved Lake Castor Christmas Eve Murders."

Before he could react, the waitress finally appeared with the coffeepot to freshen their mugs. The old newspaper headlines on the tabletop caught her eye, and she pointed to them with her free hand.

"I remember that," she said. "I was a little girl when it happened. It's all anyone could ever talk about."

"If someone did a story about it," Jess asked her, "would you be interested?"

"Everybody around here would. We always wondered whatever happened to those two and why they never caught the one who did it."

Jess arched an eyebrow toward Decker and smiled like a dog who'd just shit the carpet.

Decker saw her challenge, then raised her.

To the waitress, he asked, "Tell me: Do you know what a *podcast* is?"

"Do what?"

"It's like a radio documentary, but they broadcast it over the internet."

She set the check facedown on the corner of the table. "Sounds like something I ain't got time for," she said, then walked away.

Rather than gloat, Decker asked, "Why me?"

Jess stacked her newspaper headlines into a neat pile, then arranged their corners. "Like you said: I'm only a blogger. A divorced, middle-aged, single mother with too much time on her hands. I didn't even graduate journalism school because I got pregnant and dropped out to raise my son. You, on the other hand, bring *clout* to the project. Sure, it's *damaged* clout, but it's more name recognition than I could swing on my own. And besides"—she shimmied her shoulders and pouted her lips—"those bourbon-soaked pipes of yours would add credibility and texture to the audio."

Decker dropped the burger, then leaned back in his seat. "This is a hard sell, and you've certainly pulled out all the stops."

"Thank you."

"But nobody's going to buy it."

"I beg your pardon?"

"There's not enough for the audience to dig into."

"Into an unsolved mystery? They're all the rage right now. There's literally a television show with that very same title. The demographics alone will—"

"I'm talking about us."

"Us?"

"You and me." He enjoyed the expression on her face a beat, then continued. "This union you propose of a canceled news anchorman and a J-school dropout. Audiences are going to want to connect with us, and I'm afraid there's not enough for them to inspire a connection between us and this case."

Jess smiled. "I was hoping you would say that."

She moved aside the half-eaten burger in front of him, then opened a second file folder. He watched her thumb through the papers until she found a photocopied picture of a man in uniform.

"This was the lead investigator on the case," she said. "His name was James Ballard, and he was a deputy for the Deeton County Sheriff's Office."

Decker snatched the photograph and eyeballed it skeptically. "Yeah?"

"He was my grandfather."

A wry smile spread across Decker's face. "Will he talk on record about this case?"

"No," she said. "He died long before I was born. But that's the connection your audience is going to want."

Decker considered it while he flipped through more of her photographs and press clippings. Something deep down in him tingled, like the woman might actually have something worthwhile in front of him. However, he was far from sold. Finally, he set them all down and leveled with her.

"I'll admit it sounds somewhat promising," he said, "but you are going to need more than a familial connection to the deceased detective. You'll need more than microfiche. You'll need access, and based on my experience, cops aren't likely to hand over case files. Have you thought about what happens when you are denied access by law enforcement? You'll have nothing. You'll have nowhere to go."

"Not necessarily."

Decker crossed both arms over his chest and waited for her to continue.

"When I moved home after the divorce," she said, "I took up residence in the house where my mother grew up, over in Deeton. She rents it, but it was vacant. With my son, Ben, back in school, I wouldn't need much room. While I was clearing space in the attic, I found an old box of my grandfather's things."

Decker leaned forward. "You found the case file?"

"Not quite," she said. "But I found something nearly as good."

Decker perched at the edge of his seat while he waited for Jess to rummage through her knapsack. When finally she emerged, she produced not another file folder but instead a tattered and faded green notepad.

She flipped it open to the second page.

YOUR NAME IS DEPUTY JAMES W. BALLARD.

CHAPTER FOUR

Red Carter

1972

"No lawman in my county should ever feel one ounce of affection for Lake Castor. It is a bastion of sin and iniquity. It is the long-term result of what happens when the politicians turn their back on law and order. While its textile mill may be a boon to the local economy, I can find ten crooks, prostitutes, or perverts for every decent, honest worker over there."

As the county cruiser made the final turn onto Gilmore Road, Sheriff Red Carter's face turned sour. He didn't bother to hide the disdain in his voice. He said these words to the man driving the car. Ennis Worthy was the latest recruit to Red's seven-man fleet of deputies and therefore tasked with a year of "shadow shifts" with the boss.

"Most the time somebody dares pull something out here in my county, you can trace it back to Lake Castor." Red motioned for Worthy to pull the car over to the side of the road. "The rest of the time, you can trace it right here to Gilmore Road."

Worthy parked the car, but Red stayed in his seat. He watched out the window. His men worked in the cold. Tim Doody stuck his head in the trunk of his county cruiser, came out holding two flashlights. Bobby McCoy had hold of a cigarette in one hand and the arm of a short fellow wearing a puffy coat in the other. Big Jim Ballard stared ashen into a long, unpaved lane that disappeared into the blackness of the woods.

Red had a feeling this might be his last moment of peace for quite some time.

"When the press shows up," Red said to Worthy, "and by God, they are going to show up earlier than we want them to—I want you to steer clear of the cameras. If my hunch is correct and it turns out to be those two kids from Lake Castor, then this is going to be a big enough mess without those vultures twisting it into a story about the color of your skin. Will that be a problem?"

"No sir."

"None of them other boys are giving you any sass, are they?"

"Nothing I can't handle, sir."

"There ain't no name-calling?"

Worthy's jaw tightened. "They call me Mr. Tibbs."

"Like the movie?"

Worthy nodded.

"That better be all they call you." Red hopped out of the passenger seat. He approached his men.

"Bobby McCoy, do not think for one minute that I can't see an unironed uniform beneath that jacket." To the others, he said, "What do we got down there? Is it them? Tell me it ain't them."

"It's them," said the short man in the coat. "I just know it. I saw them and knew right away it was those two missing kids from Lake Castor."

"Who the hell is this?" Red asked.

Big Jim Ballard read from a little green notebook. "This is Alvin Stapleton. He's a surveyor working for the county. He was called out to mark a property line. He was doing so when he came upon the bodies."

"At first I thought it was a mannequin," the surveyor, Stapleton, said. "You'd be surprised how many of those get dumped in the woods these days. But this weren't no mannequin. It was a man and a woman. Y'all need to hurry on down there and see."

"You said they're dead?"

"Without a doubt."

"Then what the hell is the hurry?" Red stepped away and motioned for Ballard to follow him. To him, he asked, "Anything we need to know about this surveyor fellow?"

"I don't believe so. He says after he found the bodies, he drove straight to the trailer park up the road and asked to use the phone so he could call it in."

"Where are they?"

Ballard pointed into the dark maw of the thicket. "Bottom of the hill there. Just off the road. He said it looked like they had been tied to a tree."

"You ain't taken a look at them yet?"

"No sir. I figured if it really was them, you'd want us to wait until you got here."

Red appreciated that, truly; but to be honest, he wished his hands to be clean of it. He'd have given anything for Ballard to say he'd already descended the hill, ID'd the bodies, and found a written, signed confession from the killer. Even better would be if the two dead kids had been planted three hundred yards to the north of them, just on the other side of the state line.

"Goddammit." He sighed to himself.

"Sir?"

The sign that read **Deeton County Line** rocked in the breeze created from the phalanx of Red's remaining deputies approaching in their county cars.

"Of all my shitting luck."

◆ ◆ ◆

Red was no stranger to death.

Two years in Europe during the war and a lifetime of law enforcement after had rid him of any notions of immortality. He'd seen carnage in its every manifestation, from the mortar in a foxhole to the sudden ends of a drunken Saturday-night joyride. Suicides. Domestic abuses. Whatnot. As Red mulled retirement, he wondered if he would be followed by the images of the unthinkable things that mankind could do to one another.

By those respects, he reckoned those two kids had gotten off easy.

Red removed his hat. All seven of his deputies did the same.

No one spoke a word.

Once Red's eyes adjusted enough to the dark, he took in specific details—the girl's pretty yellow dress had been hiked to her hips; her boyfriend's self-winding watch had stopped at 12:14; the young man had caught a lick in the mouth, and the wound showed evidence of insect activity—before he allowed himself to swallow the entire macabre scene.

They'd followed a two-rut lane a couple hundred yards into the thicket. The surveyor had led them to where it dead-ended, then pointed his flashlight to the east.

A male and a female lay back to back, separated by a tree trunk about eight and a half inches in diameter. Ropes slackened between the couple that connected them at the chest, then again at the throat. They had been bound individually at the wrists.

They had also been covered with leaves, and judging by the thickness of the cover, it had most likely been deliberate. The winter had been cold, by Carolina standards, and the foliage might have helped keep them dry. For those reasons, the bodies had been somewhat preserved and showed little signs of decomposition.

Her skin, only recently emaciating. Lips, pulled back over her gums and exposing two buckteeth. The rope had torn grooves into the flesh around her throat. Her eyes were closed. Red noticed she wore no nylons and immediately felt embarrassed for her.

"Ennis, turn around."

"Sir?" Worthy asked but did it anyway.

Red reached and pulled down the hem of her dress. He pointed his flashlight over to the male.

He wore a pair of checkered dress pants. A pink collared shirt. No jacket, as it had been found in their vehicle, which had been abandoned at the Lake Castor lovers' lane.

On his left hand: a Tucker class ring.

Class of '69.

"Shit."

Ballard asked, out the side of his mouth, "What do you think, Red?"

At the top of the hill, a mess of cars came to a screeching halt, and there rose a commotion of voices. The popping of flashbulbs.

"I think," Red said, "we're about to be in a world of shit."

Red moved fast. He slapped his hat on his head and grabbed hold of Deputy Bill Gentry.

"Bill, get your ass up that hill, and stop those reporters from coming any closer."

Gentry obeyed.

Red removed the Lovera cigar from his shirt pocket and pointed it like a pistol at McCoy. "Bobby, I want you to run up to Yellowfinch Corner and call this in on the pay phone. Give Lois the news, and tell her to get Doc Wilson down here. Don't say nothing about it over the phone; just tell her Red said she was right. She'll know what that means."

McCoy obeyed.

"Which one of y'all got the camera?" No one moved quick enough to his liking. "Goddammit, did nobody bring the shitting camera?"

Up stepped Deputy David Garrett. "I got it, sir."

"Then why the hell aren't you taking pictures yet?" Red kept at him while the young man dropped to his knees to assemble his gear. "I want pictures of the road leading in. I want to see where it is in relation to that damned trailer park. Trees, clouds, cigarette butts. Even if you don't think it looks viable, I want a picture of it. It's not for you to decide what's viable and what's not viable at a crime scene. If you see it, I want a picture of it."

Garrett obeyed.

Red hitched a thumb over his shoulder at Deputy Michael Howard, who had yet to take his eyes off the bodies or replace his hat. "The second Garrett snaps those pictures, I want you to document them. Scoop those cigarette butts, and bag them. Tag them. And for Christ's sake, do *not* use your bare hands again. I don't want another deal like the one we had in Huckleberry Heights. You got me? Gloves, son."

Howard obeyed.

"Where the hell is Ennis Worthy?"

"Right here, sir." Worthy bent at the waist to closer inspect the male victim.

"I don't want you to leave my side. They are going to scrutinize every—what the blood-covered hell happened here?"

Red's flashlight caught sight, for the first time, of the condition of the forest floor at the dead-end turnaround. The skinny road leading into the woods was packed solid with rusted pine needles. However, the base of the hill had recently been destroyed and muddied. Red's flashlight tracked the destruction to its source: the surveyor's truck.

"Son, what the hell did you do to my crime scene?"

Stapleton shrugged. "I told your deputy that first I thought it was a mannequin. When I got up the road some, I thought maybe it wasn't. So I came down to take another look. I saw it wasn't a mannequin, but maybe they weren't dead. So I came back down again to see. After that, I left to run and call it in, but I reckoned maybe you might want my truck back down here so you could . . . well, come to think of it, I don't know why I was thinking you might want that."

"So much for tire impressions." Red slapped the side of the surveyor's truck with his hat. "You didn't enter my crime scene, did you?"

"No sir."

"So the only footprints my boys are going to find will belong to somebody who had something to do with killing those kids?"

"Well . . ."

"Spill it, son."

The surveyor shuffled his feet. "Okay, I went over there. But it was to only, you know, make sure they were . . ."

"Did you touch anything?"

"Of course not. You don't think I'm an idiot or nothing?"

Red didn't answer. Instead, he turned the flashlight back on the woman's body. The man's. Something he remembered.

"That wound on her leg there looks fresh."

"Oh," said the surveyor. "I'm afraid that was me. I poked her with a stick."

"You did what?"

"I told you I thought they was mannequins."

"You told me you didn't touch them."

"I didn't. I used a stick."

Red closed his eyes. Counted to ten. "Tim Doody, would you take this man and—"

Doody obeyed.

Something at the top of the hill caused a clamor. The reporters grew excited. Red turned his attention in that direction, which reminded him of something else.

"Ennis, you and me are going to need a list of every resident at Shady Village. If there's trouble to be found, I reckon it to turn up at that trailer park."

"Yes sir," said Worthy.

"Where do you want me?" asked Big Jim Ballard.

Red glanced at his longest-tenured deputy. His right-hand man. A soldier who looked like he could use a good night's sleep. Red didn't see the point in mentioning that it might be a while before either of them enjoyed one.

"Something tells me I'm going to need someone to help me run interference with our guests from Lake Castor."

"What guests, Red?"

Red pointed up the hill and out of the thicket at the congregation of rubberneckers, which Deputy Gentry struggled to contain. Flashbulbs popped at a frenzy. Before them all stood two men in suit coats who muscled their way around the deputy and began their descent into the darkness.

Lake Castor detectives.

"Those two are going to be a handful," said Red. "I need you to keep them out of my hair and out of my crime scene."

Red recognized Hank Dorritt, a Lake Castor lieutenant who had been on the job long enough to know better. Less educated was his partner, the young sergeant Jack Powers, who had been all over the TV news since the two kids had gone missing. That one was a big old boy and stood about eye to eye with Ballard, which was no small feat. Red watched his deputy brace the two approaching lawmen, and he watched the big old boy blow him off. Dorritt and Ballard called after Powers as he stomped angrily down the hill toward the crime scene, which Red had specifically directed was not to be encroached.

"Hank," Ballard called out, "you better tell your boy to get his ass back here and not to step one foot in Red's crime scene."

"Dammit, Jack," called Dorritt. "Get on back here, and hear what Red has to say."

Powers didn't like it any. "Who the hell is Red?" Powers shouted back up the hill. "And how the hell is it *his* crime scene?"

Red cut him off at the pass, stood between the detective and the bodies.

"I'm Red, son," he told him. "And I am the duly elected sheriff of Deeton County. You are standing smack dab in my territorial jurisdiction."

Powers followed Red's finger to where it pointed, all the way over to the green sign reading **Deeton County Line.**

"Like hell."

Dorritt caught up with him. "It's true, Jack. I'm afraid we're on the Carolina half of Gilmore Road." Dorritt turned to Red. "Howdy, Sheriff. Why don't you level with us? Is it them? What do we got down there?"

"A damned shame is what it is," Red answered. "A real damned shame."

"Red, this is Sergeant Jack Powers. We've had him working on this thing for the past—"

"Yeah, I seen him all over the TV news more than Walter Cronkite. You sure talk an awful lot, don't you, boy?"

Powers narrowed his eyes. "What did you say to me?"

"Go easy, Red," said Dorritt. "It's his first case."

"A hell of a one to cut his teeth on, ain't it?" Red turned to Dorritt. "And you're the ranking detective they assigned to him? Ain't you teach him not to make all those promises he can't keep?"

Powers stepped forward. "Sir, with all due respect, I have no plans to let this go. I look into that family's eyes every day, and I—"

"Save it for the cameras, son."

"Come on, Red," said Dorritt. "Me and Jack have been on this thing every day for two weeks. We respect that we're in your jurisdiction, but this is our *case*."

Red didn't like it. "The case you two biscuit-eaters are working is a missing persons. This right here is a double homicide, and it so happens to be, what, three, four hundred yards on my side of that sign. It's my crime scene, and I say who gets a look-see at it and who can go fuck themselves right back to the top of that hill."

Dorritt tossed his cigarette. "You got the crime scene, but you don't have the crime."

"You had your chance, Hank. Both of you had your team of Virginia jackhammers crisscrossing three states, chasing nothing but your own damn tails. Lake Castor is known for a few things, but not one of them is good police work. I'm not itching for people across the state line to get it in their heads that they can come into my county to dump their trash. So do me a favor, will you, and throw your cigarette butts into your own crime scene."

The popping of camera bulbs up at the top of the hill momentarily distracted Red. He took advantage of the moment to let his blood cool. Red could read the younger detective like a book, which only added to the resentment. Had Red ever been that green? Could he remember the first time he'd had to tell a loved one that a victim would not be coming home?

Red lowered his head and shook it. "This is how it's going to work, gentlemen," he said. "My boys are just about done documenting everything, so I'm going to give you two some time to take a look. Doc Wilson is on his way, so that should give you about five, ten minutes. Sound good?"

Powers didn't wait for Red to change his mind. He was halfway down the hill before anyone else could breathe a word to stop him. Red watched after him and wondered how long it would take before that passion and commitment would be sucked clean from the sergeant.

"Both of you tread careful," Red said to Dorritt.

"He's young," Dorritt said. He lit another cigarette. "He doesn't see the lines yet, Red. All he sees is those two young kids and a handful of opportunities he may or may not have had to stop what you and I both know is coming."

CHAPTER FIVE

Jess Keeler

Present Day

Jess Keeler was in a hurry. She couldn't find her left shoe, so she hobbled frantically throughout the house with a single bare foot in search of it: beneath the couch, behind the coffee table, under the bed. Twice she considered abandoning the hunt and choosing instead her red pumps, but both times she reminded herself that, for this visit, she would best appeal to their subject by wearing something sensible.

Previously, she had spent weeks trying to earn an audience with a single ranking member of the Deeton County Sheriff's Office, only for her every call to remain ignored. For Decker, it merely took a single phone call. An appointment with the sheriff was scheduled for the following day.

"You got to know how to talk to these good old boys," Decker had told her.

Jess knew better but had very few other options to entertain. Since finding her grandfather's notebook two months prior, she'd had little more than a stack of photocopied newspapers for content. She'd mined each and every article for names of potential sources to track down, but each time turned up nothing but more questions.

Her grandfather, James Ballard, had, of course, died long ago. Sheriff Red Carter had passed in the early seventies. The surveyor who'd found the bodies had lived until 2003. Many of the news articles written in between the kidnapping of Linda Harris and Steven Hicks and the discovery of their bodies had quoted Sergeant Jack W. Powers of the Lake Castor Police Department. Jess had searched high and low and had found no information on the former detective. All exhaustive Google searches could produce was that a man with that same name had been checked into a retirement home on the coast in 2018, but no one there would confirm or deny that he still lived there or if he had died.

Every which way Jess had turned, she'd slammed face-first into another dead end. No possible leads to take this story. None, that was, save for one thing:

Her grandfather's notebook.

And even that, she told herself, *is no sure thing.*

Since moving into her mother's childhood home after her own divorce, Jess had wanted to write something of substance, to contribute more than reporting on Lake Castor's annual Hog Day or the *Sundial*'s "Hometown Hero" segment. When she'd found the green spiral notebook in the attic, she'd felt her fortunes change. She'd known immediately that what she was holding was a time capsule, and it might be the key to deciphering the missing pieces of a puzzle that could catapult her work into uncharted territories. So far, however, the notebook had only provided more questions than answers.

Jess feared she might spiral herself into endless frustration, were she not distracted by the search for her shoe. Even still, she was on the verge of giving up. Then the doorbell rang.

"I'm almost ready, Dan," she called to the direction of the door. "It's unlocked. Come on in."

There was no movement. Jess poked her head around the corner and into the foyer.

"Dan?"

The door opened, just a little. Her own mother filled the frame.

"I don't know who *Dan* is, but I don't like the fact that you'll just allow him into your house." Although Samantha Bowen had grown up in the house, she still eyed the threshold like it might require disinfectant. She made no move to enter. "Jess, sweetheart, I only came by because I need—where are you going dressed like that?"

"Like what?" Jess looked herself over. She'd intentionally chosen a smart skirt and blouse. One that might offer an air of gravitas. Still, only one shoe. "Mom, I don't have time for this. I'm running late. I have someone picking me up, and he'll be here any minute. Could you please . . ."

"You know I'd prefer to never again step foot inside this house, Jessica. Don't you thi—"

Jess hobbled down the hallway. Peeked her head inside her home office. The guest bedroom. Back through the house to the kitchen. She could hear her mother behind her but could not make out the words. The old woman had horrible timing.

Nothing had changed.

"Mom, I'd love to talk, but I'm afraid that I—*aha*!" Jess pounced upon the missing shoe, which had somehow found its way between the wall and the refrigerator. "Mom, please. If you'll just—"

"I wanted to sell this house years ago." Samantha stepped one toe into the house. When the ground didn't open up to swallow her, she stepped in the other foot. "Your father insisted . . ."

"I'm glad you didn't, Mom." Jess slipped into her shoe with both hands on the kitchen countertop. "These online articles don't pay near enough to afford those ridiculous rents in Lake Castor."

"Who is this man you are meeting?"

"His name is Dan. He's the guy I told you was helping with the story I'm writing."

Jess blew into the living room and past her mother in a bluster on the way to the hall bath. There, she checked her makeup in the mirror for the fifth or sixth time. She realized only then that she wasn't necessarily trying to look good in order to impress the sheriff; she was terrified of losing Decker's attention.

"I don't like you busying yourself with another man," her mother called from the living room. "Not while you and Philip are on the mend."

"We're not *on the mend*, Mother. Phil and I are *divorcing*. Don't pretend you don't know anything about it. You've been married three times."

Jess stepped briskly back into the kitchen and grabbed her water bottle. She filled it from the tap.

"I'm still holding out hope that the two of you will work things out." Her mother's voice inched slowly closer to the kitchen. "If for no other reason, then for Benjamin. He needs both his parents."

"Benny is twenty-one. He doesn't need anything from me. And if anything at all, I'm doing it *for* him. When they closed the college during the lockdown and he had to move back in with us, he started asking what the point was and talking about dropping out. How could I criticize him for throwing his education away when it was exactly what I had done?"

Samantha finally breached the kitchen. She stopped at the doorway, then pitched furtive glances every which way at the ceiling, the stove, the countertops, as if trying hard not to attach herself to any particular memory.

Jess felt sorry for her. Not just in that moment but in several collections of moments. Although she never talked about it, Jess only imagined her mother's childhood had not been ideal. For that reason—as well as many others—she appeared even more on edge when she was inside her childhood home.

Which was perhaps half the reason why Jess had rented it.

"You didn't *throw away your education*," Samantha said. "You gave birth to a son. You raised a family. I was proud of you because that was something I nev—"

"Mom," she sighed. "Can we talk about this later? I've got a lot going on today, and I don't want to rehash any Phil drama. If anything, I'd like to—"

"What the hell is this?"

The shock in her mother's voice spun Jess around to find Samantha staring, slack jawed, at the papers that Jess had left strewed across the kitchen table.

Dammit . . .

Jess moved quickly, as if to shield Samantha from them, but it was too late.

"Is this . . . ?"

Samantha had found Jess's files, left open to the spot where Jess had fallen asleep taking notes the previous night. The stacks of yellow notepads filled with Jess's scribble. The microfiche headlines, the black-and-white photographs. The Google satellite images and printouts of addresses that might or might not belong to surviving persons of interest. Jess stood at the opposite side of the table and could not make eye contact with her mother.

"What . . . what is all this?"

"Mom, can we—"

Samantha reached for the papers and parted them, revealing more and more, all of which compounded her shock and revulsion. When she sifted through to the bottom of the pile, she came upon a single photograph that caused her to quickly draw back her hand, as if perhaps it had burned her.

It was a photograph of James Ballard.

"What are you doing with this?"

Jess swallowed thickly. "I told you I was writing an article."

"You said you wrote stories on the computer about recipes and creative uses for almond milk," Samantha spat. "You didn't say anything about . . . about *this*."

Jess had feared the day she'd have to explain it all to her mother. Several times she'd tried to get her to talk about any memories of the Christmas Eve murders and her father's investigation, but Samantha had refused to utter so much as a single word about James Ballard. Jess had felt it would eventually all come out but had hoped that *someday* would still be a bit further down the line.

"I write blog articles for a local civic resource and manage their social media," Jess explained, "but that's not why I went to school all those years ago. I wanted to do real journalism. You remember? But all that had to be put aside when—" Jess cut her eyes to the high school graduation photo of Benjamin that was stuck to the refrigerator door. "I've been reevaluating my life even since before Benny went back to school. I promised myself during that damned lockdown that if I had one more chance . . . I wasn't going to be an empty-nest housewife. I'm more than that. More than a woman picking up a man's socks every day. And I promised I would spend my time doing something more worthwhile than *blogging*."

"That case destroyed our family," Samantha said behind clenched teeth. "It ruined my—it changed your grandfather forever."

"How?" Jess pleaded. "Please tell me."

Samantha closed her mouth. She could not seem to bear looking at the scattered pile of Jess's research. Jess thought more than once about covering the photograph of Ballard but decided against it.

"Why won't you talk to me about him, Mom? Why won't you tell me about your father?"

Samantha shut her eyes. "We had everything," said Samantha in a weak voice, "and then one day we had nothing. All because of that *case*. Whoever did that . . . they killed more than that nurse and her boyfriend. They took our family and tore it apart."

Jess realized this was the most her mother had ever spoken about her past. She felt icy fingers grip her stomach and hold it tight. She wanted to say nothing, for fear of losing the moment, but she had so much she wanted—no, *needed*—to ask.

"What was he like?"

Samantha looked up from the table. "Who?"

"Your father. James Ballard."

She pointed to the newspaper clippings. "What do those tell you?"

"Absolutely nothing. He's quoted here and there. Sometimes they don't even spell his name right."

"I'm told he was a good deputy." Samantha's tone turned chilly.

"What else?"

Samantha clenched her teeth. "Why are you putting me through this, Jessica? So you can have more material for your little story?"

Jess let out the breath she'd been holding. She'd thought she'd lost the ability to pity her mother years ago. Apparently, she'd been wrong.

"My life is not your entertainment," said Samantha. "That murder is not *content*."

"Mom, I'm not writing about you. This has nothing to do with you."

Samantha's eyes bugged. "This has *everything* to do with me. If you're writing about those murders, then you are writing about *him*. And if you are writing about him, then you are—"

Outside, a car honked.

"Who is that?" her mother demanded.

"That's my ride," said Jess. "But wait, Mom. I want to talk to you. I do."

The car honked again.

Samantha rolled her eyes. "He hasn't the decency to ask for you at the door?"

The moment was over. Once again, her mother had conveniently avoided engaging with Jess about her past. Jess sighed and gathered her notes. She stuffed them into her knapsack, then turned to her mother. Samantha's eyes remained on the table, as if the papers were still there for her to read.

"Stay as long as you like, Mom. Lock up behind you."

"The last thing I want is to stay here." Samantha ripped herself away from the kitchen and swayed uneasily into the living room.

"Can we please pick this up when I get back?"

Again, Decker honked his horn.

"Just go."

Jess knew from experience that the last thing she should do was hug her mother. Still, she tried anyway. She was cut short by the sound Samantha made as she peeked out the window.

"Who's that behind the wheel?" she asked. "Oh my goodness . . . is that . . . is that the man from the news? The one who . . . ?"

Decker rolled down his window and leaned out his head. "Let's get a move on, Keeler," he called. "Neither of us is getting any younger."

Jess had never seen that particular expression on her mother's face. She looked like she might need to sit a moment.

"Mom, it's not what you think. He's . . . he's just . . . he's helping me with the story."

Samantha still would not face her own daughter. Jess threw up her hands.

"Let's talk later, Mom."

Jess stepped quickly out the door before her mother could say anything further. She did not look back, not even once, as she made her way down the sidewalk and into the passenger seat of Decker's SUV.

"You sure you're ready?" Decker asked.

"Yes," she answered. "Let's go."

"I mean, we can go back inside and make sandwiches, unless you're—"

"I said *let's go*."

Decker got the hint. He slipped the car in gear and stepped on the gas. They rode the rest of the way to the sheriff's office in silence as Jess replayed the interaction with her mother over and over in her head and lost count of all the missed opportunities.

CHAPTER SIX

James Ballard

1972

Ballard drew his jacket tighter and blew hot breath into his hands. The morning grew long, and the sun had yet to pierce the gray curtain overhead. The shadows of the forest had begun to scatter, but the air had turned no less cold. Furthermore, what he had once assumed to be a typical morning's headache had twisted into a full-blown hangover. Perhaps Samantha was right: maybe he had drunk a bit too much the night before.

The sickness began to creep in on him like a hungry pack of wolves, pacing terribly through his stomach until moving on to his bloodstream, separating, and then spreading out to his extremities. Soon the wolves had settled into the whole of him, and his mouth became cotton. He turned damp beneath his hat, beneath his arms. His body ached all over. He couldn't seem to get enough air in his lungs. He thought he might sick up his breakfast, then remembered he hadn't had the chance to eat it.

Ballard felt every one of his forty-seven years. In fact, he felt even older. He felt like each of his individual parts had betrayed him and left behind a sum of rapid decline. But what he felt most was the need for a drink.

Hair of the dog.

When Samantha had said it earlier that morning, nothing had sounded like a worse idea. Ballard had never been much of a drinker. He didn't thumb his nose at it the way Red did, but outside of a cold beer here and there, Ballard had never had much need for it.

But after that visit with the doctor in Lake Castor . . .

Now it seemed to be the only thought that calmed him down or offered him any comfort. A couple of splashes of corn in a hot cup of coffee. A bottle small enough to fit inside his coat pocket. Give his hands something to do when they started to tremble.

In this moment, he could attribute the despair and loneliness and anxiety to the hangover. In a couple of hours or later tonight or as the week dragged on, then where might he lay the blame?

Again, a clamor arose at the top of the hill. Ballard lifted his head, curious, and found that Doc Wilson had arrived. The county coroner had brought with him two young assistants with twin gurneys. They maneuvered the stump-strewed hill as flashbulbs popped at their backs.

The two Lake Castor detectives, Dorritt and Powers, had spent nearly twenty minutes examining the two bodies. As the coroner approached, they abandoned that post and rejoined Ballard in the small roadway.

Dorritt arrived first. "What can I say?" he asked. "It's them."

Powers said nothing. His face had taken on a ghastly pallor. Ballard's wartime experience told him the man was shell shocked.

"I really hope this damned deal doesn't turn out to be one of those Manson-type things," said Dorritt. "That's the last thing we need right now is to have one of those sickos running around Lake Castor."

"I'm sure y'all have looked into other couples gone missing?" Ballard chased another thought but let it go.

Dorritt strained the muscles of his face. "We've looked into that and then looked into it some more."

"We've looked into everything," Powers insisted.

"If you ask me," Dorritt said, "the trouble started at the hospital. That's where I think the key to this whole thing is."

"Oh?"

"All those nurses." Dorritt lit a cigarette. "Where there are nurses, you will find all kinds of creeps and weirdos hanging around and messing with them. You know how many times they've called police on some yahoo peeking in windows or showing off his pecker?"

Ballard asked, "What about her personal life? Outside the hospital?"

"Her personal life was the boyfriend," said Powers. "We asked everyone, and they all said that he was her everything."

Over their shoulders, Ballard could see the coroner and his boys lifting the female victim from her grave of leaves, then slipping the body bag beneath her. They fit her carefully into it, then zipped it up.

Ballard asked, "Any ex-boyfriends?"

Powers shook his head. "We looked. We checked into anybody that ever had anything to do with her. She had a pen pal, and we had him tracked down. He's got an alibi as solid as anyone ever did. I've got a file on each of her ex-boyfriends going back to first grade. Zilch. Anybody who graduated Whitfill High School with her, just in case they turned out to have a grudge or may be the next Richard Speck. Nothing."

"By all accounts," Dorritt added, "these two kids were squeaky clean. No enemies, no grudges, no nothing. Smoked occasionally, drank only socially, and no mention whatsoever of any drugs. Neither of them were involved in any of those hippie-dippie antiwar movements or civil rights marches . . . just all-around good kids from good families."

"We got nothing."

Ballard removed his hat and wiped his brow. His mind drifted again to *hair of the dog*, then brushed that thought away. His concentration fringed at the edges. He squinted to better focus.

The coroner and his boys next went to work on the male. He was larger, so Red hollered for two deputies to assist. Ennis Worthy and David Garrett stepped up to the task. Together with Doc Wilson's boys, they lifted him off the forest floor and laid him gently inside the second bag.

As soon as it was zipped tight, Red began his ascent up the hill. Powers dashed down to meet him.

"Sheriff Carter," he said, "I respect that this is your jurisdiction, but I have lived and breathed this case for the past two weeks. You need me on it."

Red shifted his Lovera cigar from one side of his mouth to the other. "The only thing I need, son," he said, "is coffee in the morning and my wife's cooking at night. What I don't need is two Virginia shit birds mucking my murder investigation."

"We've got a two-week head start. We'll share information."

"What information have you got that I might possibly want?" Red's smile made Ballard uncomfortable. He knew what was coming. "Tell me, boy: Can you point me toward any viable suspects? What about the cul-de-sac where they went missing? Was it processed? Did you fingerprint the car?"

Powers hung his head.

"That's right. You didn't even fingerprint the goddamn car."

Dorritt said, "We thought they eloped, Red. Why would we fingerprint a car when we thought these two kids ran off to get married?"

"That's my point exactly." Red turned his back to Powers. "The two of you farted around, playing to the TV cameras while these kids rotted in the damned leaves. I highly doubt I need either of you for a shitting thing."

Powers lunged for the sheriff. Ballard could not get there in time. Powers shoved Red in the back with both hands, nearly knocking them both to the ground. Red turned around and, before he could square his footing, went for Powers's neck. There was a commotion at the bottom of the hill with the deputies, as well as with the reporters at the top.

Ballard might have been the only man with the strength to separate the sheriff's hands from the detective's throat. Dorritt caught hold of his boy, and again, the two men were separated on opposite sides of the road.

Ballard pointed up the hill. "We got an audience, boss."

Red couldn't catch his breath. Red faced, he blew steam. His eyes burned hot.

"Get those sons of bitches out of my sight, Jim. Do it before I have Tim Doody haul off and shoot them."

Ballard kept his head. He jerked his chin toward the top of the hill, where the reporters gathered like birds on a line. He leveled with his sheriff.

"They'll turn it into a contest," Ballard said. "They'll make it look like we're at cross-purposes with Lake Castor. One of us will have to be the villain so they can sell more newspapers."

Red's eyes narrowed. He didn't like it one bit. He scowled and grimaced. He puffed out his chest. Ballard knew it was all for show. When Red finally composed himself, the two of them turned to face the Lake Castor detectives. They found Dorritt approaching them slowly, his palms outstretched.

"The last thing we want," he told them, "is to step on anyone's toes."

"I'll step on more than his toes if that son-bitch ever crosses my sight again," Red growled.

Dorritt nodded. "Jack's got that boy's daddy every night on his front porch when he gets off duty. That's another two hours he's on the case, sitting up with that man while he cries out his eyes over his boy. He's already thinking about how he's going to break the news to him. We owe it to both those families to find out what happened to their children."

"We want the same thing, Hank," Ballard said.

"Let's work this together," Dorritt said.

Ballard heard Red wince but nothing else. He knew that meant the old man was thinking on it. After a moment, Red pulled Ballard by the elbow so that he could talk soft in his ear.

"I don't mind y'all swapping notes," Red said, "but if those boys say the sky is blue, I want you to verify. This is *your* case. *You* are in charge, not them."

Ballard felt his windpipe close like a fist. Sweat spackled the inside of his shirt.

"Me?" He nearly choked the words out of his throat. "No, Red. Not me. Not now."

"This here is a big one, and I can't think of no one else to run point on it. First thing I want you to do is follow Doc Wilson back to the cooler and be there when the families come to ID the bodies. We're going to want to talk to them first thing. I want you to be the point of contact."

"Red, I *can't* . . ." Ballard fought the urge to vomit. "Can't you get Tim Doody on it? Red, it's not . . . I can't . . ."

"Hell no, I can't get Tim Doody on it. Not after last time. This situation is going to require diplomacy and tact, which means I'm going to need my best guy. I need someone I can trust to handle things. That's you, boy."

"You don't understand . . ." Ballard wrestled with a tic forming in his left cheek. "Right now is not a very good time for me."

"What it ain't a good time for is you deciding to quit doing what you are told."

Ballard got it.

Loud and clear.

"And another thing," Red said. "When duty calls you into Lake Castor, I want you to pack a lunch. Just because I got you keeping an eye on those two, that don't mean I want you to spend a plug nickel in that damned county."

Ballard nodded. He drew a breath and held it as he noticed Doc Wilson leading a parade up from the bottom of the hill. Behind him were Red's deputies and Wilson's boys, each flanking the two gurneys as they carefully rolled them toward the road.

Not a word was spoken as the bodies rolled past them. Ballard removed his hat and held it to his chest. He pinned both eyes to the dirt and thought over and over about how cruel and unfair this life could be.

CHAPTER SEVEN

Jess Keeler

Present Day

"My name is Jess Keeler, and I'm here to see the sheriff."

The receptionist at the Deeton County Sheriff's Office couldn't have been any older than thirty, but she'd already mastered the glance over the top of her eyeglasses.

"I'm afraid the sheriff is quite busy today," she said. "If you'd like to make an appointment . . ."

"I already have an appointment. It's for eleven thirty. Jess Keeler."

The receptionist tapped her long fingernails on her mouse and stared at the computer screen. Her expression remained flat and gave nothing away.

"We made the appointment yesterday. He said he would—"

Decker shouldered his way around Jess and leaned across the counter as far as the bulletproof window would allow. "Perhaps the appointment is under my name. Try Decker. Dan Decker."

The receptionist registered recognition with an arched eyebrow. "Like the newsman?"

"Exactly like the newsman." Decker's smile could have sold Cadillacs. "What's your name, sweetheart?"

The second eyebrow joined the first. The rest of the receptionist's face fell. "Take a seat over there," she said, pointing to a bank of metal chairs against a far wall. "The sheriff will be with you as soon as he is available."

Jess followed Decker across the small lobby to their seats. No sooner had she landed in her chair than she began to unpack and inspect, piece by piece, her sound equipment from her knapsack.

"What the hell is that?" Decker asked. "Holy . . ." His jaw dropped. "Is all that really necessary?"

"I bought this on eBay." Jess showed him the handheld recorder, which several review sites claimed was the best within her budget. She then produced a shotgun microphone on a collapsible pole. "I had to buy this one new, but it's wireless and can be controlled with our phones."

"It looks like it has enough buttons to land a small airplane."

Jess slipped a brand-new headset out of its packaging. "Our platform is podcasting. Capturing great audio will be essential to this brand of storytelling."

"How do you know how to use all this stuff?"

"I watched videos on the internet." Jess shrugged. "Why don't we test it out while we're waiting for the sheriff? Read me something you've written."

Decker's face was blank. "What do you mean? I haven't written anything."

"What do you mean, *you haven't written anything*? We agreed that we'd each write up the crime scene and choose who wrote the best copy, then record that."

"No, *you* agreed we'd do that. I haven't written my own copy since I was a junior anchor." Decker's interest shifted to his fingernails. "The deal we made was that you write, I read."

Jess watched him a moment as he considered his cuticles. For the first time since she'd set out to find him, she began to question her judgment. Was it a good idea to involve him in her investigation? Sure, his reputation was stained, but she felt in her bones that if she could make him see how exciting a story this was, he might rediscover the skills he'd once had that had propelled him to stardom. In the meantime, she reckoned, she would have to deal with casual complacency and indifference in exchange for opening a few doors with his name recognition.

"We need a strategy," she said.

"For what?"

"For our approach with the sheriff. I imagine we'll only have one shot, so we'll want to make it count. If we want a look at the case file, we'll need our ducks in a row. My suggestion is that we—"

"When we meet the sheriff," Decker said, "you should let me do all the talking. These old guys, they speak a certain language. I'd like to say I'm more than fluent in it. It's best if we take the easy approach. Milk him a little, then work our way gradually into—"

"What do you say we hit him straightaway with what we know and test his reaction?" Jess countered. "Hit him with our big bombshell?"

"Which is?"

"George Berry."

Decker blinked twice. "Who?"

"He's the number one suspect."

"According to whom?"

"The notebook."

Decker leaned back in his seat and stretched out his legs. He placed both hands behind his head and closed his eyes, as if he might squeeze in a quick nap before their meeting with the sheriff.

"I'm talking about my grandfather's case notes," she said. "Tell me you didn't really forget about them."

Just in case, she rummaged through her knapsack until she found it. She kept it wrapped in a clean dish towel for protection against the elements. She opened it carefully, then gingerly turned the pages until she found what she was looking for: the first page where the name George Berry appeared. The penmanship was precise—assured—like it was written by a man who slaved for detail.

GEORGE BERRY.

20 YO / W / M.

LINEMAN—SOUTHERN BELL CO.

ADDRESS UNKNOWN:

DATED NURSES.

NO ALIBI?

MOTIVE.

Then she turned to several pages later, where the handwriting was far more erratic and rushed, the lettering growing larger and more scattered as it neared its terminus, as if the frustrations were mounting and its author was trying so desperately hard to convince someone who might not be listening, over and over, for three pages:

GEORGE BERRY IS GUILTY.

GEORGE BERRY IS GUILTY.

GEORGE BERRY IS GUILTY.

"I didn't forget," Decker said, as if reading her mind. "Did you forget that we aren't supposed to have that notebook in our possession?"

"It's private property," said Jess. She instinctively drew the notebook away from him, as if he might try and take it. "It belonged to my grandfather."

"Maybe so," said Decker. "But if the sheriff decides to play hardball, he could tell us that it's evidence in an ongoing investigation and request to requisition it. We could be charged with withholding evidence. No, I suggest we keep it close to our vest."

"But—"

"And furthermore"—Decker spoke over her—"as journalists, we are required to double and triple confirm any information we discover. Especially if we are going to accuse someone of murder. In fact, better to *quadruple* confirm it. We're going to need more than some old notebook. Especially considering Ballard is quite unreliable."

Jess recoiled. "Unreliable?"

Decker nodded. "Think about what else we found in that notebook and how that might possibly come into play later down the road."

Jess closed the notebook and rewrapped it in the dish towel. She had to admit that she did not understand the meaning behind everything they had found written by her grandfather, but there was no mistaking that he vehemently believed a man named George Berry was guilty for the Lake Castor Christmas Eve Murders. However, beyond the markings inside that notebook, there was very little proof that George Berry had ever existed at all. Nothing had turned up on Google or any social media sites. No mention in any archived newspaper articles. Nothing in the obituaries.

"The notebook," she said, "is all we have to go on right now. Which is why we're going to need to look at that case file."

If Decker had anything to add, he kept it to himself. Jess took advantage of his silence to familiarize herself with the handheld recorder until finally the door buzzed and was opened by the receptionist.

"Excuse me," she called to them. "The sheriff will see you now."

CHAPTER EIGHT

Red Carter

1972

Big Jim and the Lake Castor boys followed Doc Wilson and the bodies to the hospital so they might get an official write-up and observe the official identifications. Red remained behind to lord over his men until everything was bagged, tagged, and photographed. Soon, it would no longer be a *crime scene*; it would return to being simply a *forest*.

Red was already forming a list in his mind of next steps. He called together his remaining five deputies at the base of the hill near the surveyor's abandoned truck.

"Well, boys," said Red. "What do y'all think?"

"It could have been a rape," Deputy Garrett offered. He blew a hot cumulus of breath into his hands.

"Her britches are still on," argued Deputy Howard.

"Maybe the killer put them back on when he was done."

"Why would he do that?"

Garrett shrugged. "To throw us off the trail?"

"Maybe the boy put up a fight, and that's what got them both killed," said Howard.

"The way the bodies are arranged," said Tim Doody, "could let on that it's one of them cult things. You read about how they have those special feast days when they sacrifice—"

"Shut up, Tim Doody," said Red. "Somebody throw something at me that I can actually work with."

"How about a series killer?" suggested Howard.

"Do what?"

"Sort of like the fella up in Chicago with the nurses?"

Deputy Howard piped up. "Wasn't the female victim a nurse?"

"She was."

"This weren't no random lunatic." McCoy gestured with an unlit cigarette between two of his fingers. "This was someone they knew. This was personal."

"The hell are you talking about?" said Garrett. "I read nearly everything there is on these two kids in the paper and whatnot. Everybody breaks their own neck to tell you how good of kids these two were."

"I agree," Howard said. "I don't make them for the type to get mixed up with Blacks, biker gangs, or whatever the hell would do something like this."

"Their killer stood over them while he strangled the air from their lungs," said McCoy. "He wanted them to suffer, and he wanted to watch it done."

"Wasn't there something like this with goddamn Billy Nickel two or three years ago?" Howard asked them. "He came back from the war all ass-backward, tied up a couple girls, and said it was how they did things over in Vietnam or some shit like that?"

"Billy Nickel raped those girls," McCoy said. "Our female wasn't raped."

"We won't know that until Doc Wilson tells us," Garrett said.

That gave the men something to chew on until Red turned to Ennis Worthy.

"You're awful quiet," Red told him. "What do you think?"

"Me, sir?"

"Yes, son. Let's hear what you got."

"It hardly matters what I think, sir."

"I disagree, Worthy. You're a college boy. Not just any college boy but a friend of Reverend Elijah P. Stallings."

The white deputies groaned at the name.

Red continued. "I can't mention your name in public without somebody saying, 'Oh, he's a smart one,' which I guess is as good of a testimony as you can ask for these days. Your damn nose is always in a book, and you've spent the past God knows how long shadowing the highest-ranking lawman in the county, which would be me. But most important, I asked for your goddamn opinion, so spit it out, son."

Worthy swallowed. "It hardly matters what I think, because what matters is what the evidence is saying. Everything else is conjecture."

"And what does the evidence tell you, son?"

Red watched the boy square his shoulders. All eyes would be on him. Red knew Worthy would not wither from the attention but would choose instead to blossom.

"It's obvious that our victims were transported by vehicle to this location," Worthy said. "They were abducted from Creechville Road, which is, what, three, four miles from here?"

"Three and a half," said Garrett. "We could assume the killer used his own car because theirs was found abandoned in the cul-de-sac where they were known to go parking."

"Were there any fingerprints on their car that didn't match those of the victims?" asked Worthy.

Red rolled his eyes and looked to the heavens.

"In that case," Worthy said, "we can assume nothing." He pointed to the destruction wreaked upon the bottom of the hill by the surveyor's truck. "Nor can we verify. But we can deduce that they were indeed transported via vehicle. It would be too difficult to march two people in here on foot. Which brings me to my next point."

Worthy stepped off the road. He shimmied in and out of the ditch to the other side. With muddied shoes, he shushed through the pine straw until he came to the tree where the bodies had been found.

"It would have been no easy task to cross the road to this here spot, even in the daylight."

"But it weren't daylight," said Howard. "Are we seriously letting this here Mr. Tibbs tell us how to work a cri—"

"Deputy Howard is correct," Worthy said. "It was *not* daylight. Our victims were last seen between eleven and eleven thirty at night, then reported missing the following morning. The self-winding watch on the male victim's wrist was stopped at about twelve fifteen. It's most likely they were taken to this tree, then tied up after dark."

"Our killer would have needed a flashlight," said Garrett.

"Correct."

Doody was still skeptical. "He could have angled the car so the headlamps gave enough light."

"He certainly could have," Worthy said. "But you yourself pointed out the size and reputation of Mr. Hicks. It would have been remarkably difficult to drag him alone to that tree and tie him up, not to mention a second victim as well."

Red smiled. He knew where Worthy was headed.

"Unless he had a gun."

"Yes sir." Worthy crossed his arms and turned his eyes to the landscape, as if he was taking it all in. "So we picture this scene at night. Maybe he has a gun; maybe he has a flashlight . . . he has that ditch to maneuver, as well as the darkness . . . he has a man of great physical prowess as well as a second person to control long enough to secure them to the tree."

"What's he getting at?" asked Howard.

"He's saying," Red told them, "that's an awful lot of trouble for one man to handle."

A silence passed among the lawmen, one more profound than any previous.

"By my estimations," Worthy said after that long, quiet moment, "this is the work of at least two men."

Red let those words sink in a bit; then he clapped his hands together. "All right, boys," he hollered, "there's nothing I can do to stop them from printing the newspaper tomorrow. But we can determine if the headlines read *Bodies Found* or *Killers Caught in Deeton County*. Two guesses which one I want to read with my coffee tomorrow morning?"

Every last man fell in line.

"Nobody asked my opinion, so let me go ahead and give it to you. I think the answer to all our troubles will be found where it normally is: at the ass-end of Gilmore Road. I got Big Jim up at Doc Wilson's with the bodies and those two assholes from Lake Castor. I want the rest of us to descend upon Shady Village like a Mongol horde. The answer to this mess is in that trailer court. I can feel it in my bones."

The white deputies wasted no time hustling up that hill. Worthy held back to shadow his superior. Red spoke in a low voice so the squirrels in the trees might not hear.

"You did good back there, son."

Worthy kept his eyes forward. "Thank you, sir."

"My boys are good boys. But it's going to take them a while. You understand that, don't you?"

"Yes sir. I do."

"I'm sure the reverend prepared you for all that."

"He did, sir."

They reached the top of the hill. The reporters clamored toward them and spoke in one crescendoing voice.

"Get the car started. I'll be there in a minute." Red pointed to the approaching reporters. "These assholes are going to want a word with me."

Red couldn't think of a single time he'd ever enjoyed speaking with the news media. Nine times out of ten, they arrived to the fringes of his crime scene with a narrative already fleshed out. All they needed was to stop him from doing his job so they could jab a microphone into his face and demand words that would be deliberately twisted to support their point of view. Their profession attracted a certain element.

There were far many more of them than Red was accustomed to seeing at his crime scenes, and a great many of them were unfamiliar faces. Two, even, from the TV news channel up in Virginia.

Red held them in even greater disdain.

They *converged.*

Chip, from the *Deeton Examiner*, asked, "Red, what can you tell us? Is it the two kids from Lake Castor?"

There were nearly a dozen of them altogether—TV and print news, their cameramen and photographers—and each of them dropped silent as Red positioned himself where they all could hear him.

"I only want to say things once." He hitched his britches. "So get yourselves situated. I have a lot of business to tend to."

They did.

Red cleared his throat. "At approximately seven thirty this morning, we received a call from a surveyor who was marking a property line, who claimed to have found what he believed to be two dead bodies. My deputies arrived shortly after and confirmed his discovery. Those two bodies have been relocated to the Deeton coroner, who most of you already know is Dr. Stanley Wilson. Anybody need me to spell that?"

Sid, from WSVA, asked, "Can you confirm that it's Steven Hicks and Lin—"

"I cannot," Red said. "I have two eyes, which can see, but those will do neither me nor you a single lick of good until I've received word that the families of the deceased have identified the remains. What I can tell you is—"

"In what conditions did you find the bodies?"

Red was not accustomed to being interrupted. He turned his head slow, like a turret on a tank, and centered his sights on a woman in long pants. She looked to be about thirty, and Red already didn't like the look on her face.

"Excuse me, ma'am?"

"I asked, In what conditions did you—"

"I did not ask you to repeat yourself. I was making sure you were a *ma'am*."

The woman's face flushed. The men around her tittered.

"My name is Olivia Crane. I'm with the *Lake Castor Her*—"

"I knew Lake Castor was bass-ackward"—Red snorted—"but when did they start letting women on the crime beat over there?"

"In October of last year, Sheriff." Crane did not smile. "I worked my way up."

"From the funny pages?"

More laughter.

"From home decor." She held Red's gaze, but he could see her pen hand shaking. "My question, however, pertains to the condition of the—"

"Most of y'all know me," said Red to the other reporters. "Y'all know I won't be investigating this crime on the front pages. I will give to you the appropriate information as I see fit. That's the way of things, and hopefully those of you who are quicker to pick up on that"—Red turned his head to Ms. Crane—"will help out those of you who might be a tad bit more slow. Let's go, Ennis."

Red and Worthy cut through the congregation of journalists and headed for his county car.

"What I will tell you," he hollered over his shoulder, "is that the two bodies were found tied to a tree. They had been there for some time."

"Two weeks?" asked an unfamiliar reporter.

"I won't know that until Doc Wilson gets back with me."

"Were they murdered?" asked another.

"Doc Wilson will have to tell me."

"Were they stabbed? Shot?" That one, asked by Ms. Crane.

"It's not the duty of the sheriff to determine cause of death in a murder investigation." Red cut her a glance and muttered, *"Home decor."*

Red reached the passenger-side door of his county car and opened it. He hiked his foot up on the interior. He reached into his shirt pocket for the moistened stub of his Lovera cigar and pressed it between his lips. All this to afford time for Worthy to start the car.

"I got work to do," he announced to the reporters, "but I know y'all do too. So I tell you what: let me handle my investigation, and I'll give you a head start on this evening's headlines."

They held their pens at the ready.

"We'll have the son of a bitch, toot sweet."

CHAPTER NINE

Jack Powers

1972

Jack Powers stacked three dimes on top of the pay phone's call box. He slid the door closed behind him, then picked up the receiver. Dialed.

He answered before the first ring finished.

"Jed," Powers said softly into the phone, "it's Jack."

Powers heard weeping through the line. Soft, mournful choking sounds that gave way to gut-wrenching sobs.

Somewhere beyond that, a woman screamed.

"My boy . . ."

"Jed, I'm so sorry."

"My boy . . ."

Dorritt waited in the car. The sedan's muffler choked steam out the back, as if it were a dragon. All the world was gray.

After Powers completed the call, he hung up the phone and stared up at the sky. Traffic lazed slowly on the highway into town. His simmer began to boil. Not a damned person back at that crime scene had invested a fraction of what he had into Steve and Linda's disappearance.

His own colleagues back at the station had treated the case like some *joke*, practice for the new kid.

"They'll turn up."

"They ran off to get married."

"Keep searching, Columbo."

But none of them came home every night—*every damned night*—to Steven Hicks's father at the front step of their apartment. Jedidiah Hicks, pleading with red-rimmed, exhausted eyes. Demanding inventory of Powers's every action that day, which he readily relinquished. Mostly out of guilt but also in the hope that something might finally break the logjam. But where Jed Hicks's grief was so visceral, so violent, it was no less palpable than the painful silence on the other end of the line when Linda Harris's mother called. Sincerely shattered, the woman asked—almost apologetically—in a frail, breaking voice: *"Have you found my daughter, Sergeant?"*

Nothing they said—nothing *anyone* said—could drown out the questions he asked in his own head. Was he missing something? What had he done wrong? Would a different detective have found Steve and Linda by now?

When Powers had gotten the call, he'd been promoted to the Crimes Against Persons division only three weeks ago. He'd been dying to catch his first case, knowing he was three away from his turn, then two away . . . then next up. When the call had come on Christmas—two kids gone missing—he'd almost been disappointed. Like everyone else, he'd assumed Steve and Linda had eloped. But Christmas had come and gone. Then the next day and the next. Dorritt had still believed the two lovers had run off, but Powers had had a *feeling*.

Now as Jack Powers stood at that pay phone, just down the road from where the two bodies had been found, he faced a crippling notion that he might never go *undefeated* in his career. The possibility existed, even, that he could go *winless*.

Unless he did something about it.

When Powers climbed into the passenger seat, he caught the last bit on the radio.

"But Deeton County officials are not confirming yet if the bodies belong to Steven Hicks or Linda Harris, who went missing from Lake Castor on Christmas Eve. We'll have more on that story in a moment, but in the meantime, let's get our afternoon rocking and rolling with the Chi-Lites and—"

Dorritt snapped off the radio. "How'd it go?"

"How do you think it went?"

"Who did he arrange to meet us there?"

"He wants to do it himself."

Dorritt closed his eyes. "Did you tell him that was a bad idea?"

"I told him several times."

"Hell, it's not even necessary. Their pictures have been splattered over every television screen and front page for two weeks." Dorritt slipped the car into gear and backed away from the phone booth. "A blind man could ID their bodies."

"He wants to do it himself."

The hospital was on the far side of Deeton, so they drove through town. Powers did the math. It would take the average person twenty minutes to drive from Tucker to Deeton. Powers reckoned Jed Hicks would get there faster.

"You got to get ahold of yourself," Dorritt said. "If you hope to have a long career in Lake Castor, you'll see plenty of death. Some of these investigations will be slam dunks, but even with those . . . you can't win them all is what I'm trying to say."

They stopped at a light. A woman with three children in tow crossed the street. Another man smoked a cigarette on a bench while reading a book.

Life went on.

So did Dorritt. "Whatever you do, don't promise you're going to catch him. You've got to quit doing that because it's so much harder on everyone when you don't."

"I will."

"Yeah, maybe. But what if you don't?"

"I will."

Dorritt sighed. The light turned, and they continued through town. Deeton was sleepy, the polar opposite of Lake Castor. Where Lake Castor had popped up overnight after the Civil War because of the textile boom, Deeton had been built before the revolution. Cars passed them in drips.

"And I'll tell you something else," said Powers. "I'm on these murders. No matter what that cracker sheriff says, I'm going to investigate it."

Dorritt kept his eyes on the road. "You'll learn quick enough that Red's the reality out here. He's the truth. There's no getting around him. If we want to play ball, it's going to be with his say-so."

"If he gets in the way . . ."

"Listen up, son." Dorritt sighed. "Do you know why you were promoted?"

"I scored an eighty-six on my—"

"Big whoop, Sergeant. I scored a forty-two. That blue boy, Chambers, who pounds patrol in the Back Back—he scored a ninety-five. I didn't ask what grade you made on the sergeant's exam. I asked if you knew why you were promoted to Crimes Against Persons."

Powers said nothing, let Dorritt continue.

"Because you're a hoss, son. What are you? Six-three? You look like you rode in on a tractor. That will scare the sin out of half the shit birds in Lake Castor. But you aren't in Lake Castor anymore, boy. Hell, you aren't even in Virginia."

Powers tried to look away, but Dorritt did not let him.

"Some things on this job, you are going to be able to change, but a great many of them, you won't. As the superior officer guiding you through this case, I'm supposed to teach you which is which. In some cases, I'm going to have to let you make your own mistakes so you can learn from them. However, in other cases, you are just going to have to trust me."

Dorritt paused until he had Powers's complete attention.

"Trust me," said Dorritt. "No amount of bitching and moaning is going to matter on that side. Things are going to happen the way Red wants them to. He's from the old school. He's been running this county for going on twenty years with only seven deputies. He pays them well, and he trains them well. His is their only recognized authority, and he can trace it all the way back to the Bible. It's his world, and we're just passing through it."

Powers didn't care. Every time he closed his eyes, he saw the image of Steven and Linda in those leaves. Bound at the wrists. Bound together for all eternity. Someone had covered them with leaves and left them in the woods to rot. A fire raged inside of him. He needed it extinguished.

"The good news," Dorritt continued, "is we drew Big Jim. If Red would have stuck us with Tim Doody . . ."

"What's the deal with Ballard?"

"He's one of Red's, no question, but he'll at least have his head on straight. He's been at the sheriff's right hand since coming home from Korea. He doesn't mess around. He'll want to see it solved, sure. I know how to talk with him."

Powers said, "I still don't like it."

"Me neither, but we can use Red's hubris to our advantage. He's not going to let it go unsolved. We have that going for us. He wants us to share information, and we'll share it, but we'll also keep our eyes on them. I have a feeling that Red doesn't plan to play fair."

The hospital appeared on the landscape before them, then grew larger until finally it filled their view. Dorritt parked them at the back, near the loading zone. Powers checked his watch. They had ten minutes, maybe, before Jed Hicks arrived.

Dorritt led the way. They hit the service entrance doors. Heads popped up to view them, but no one said a word as Dorritt and Powers crawled the bowels of Deeton County's hospital. Soon they were in the hallways among the nurses. Powers thought again of that couple, tied to a tree. Linda had been a nurse. She should be in a hallway much like this at her hospital in Lake Castor. She should be among the faceless women tending to the sick instead of burned into his mind as a corpse tied to a tree.

Dorritt talked as they walked. "The phone calls in the middle of the night, the long hours . . . that feeling that everyone is hiding something from you. That everyone is lying to you. All those things come with the job. I can do all of that while standing on my head."

They hit the stairwell. They took them two at a time to the basement. They pushed through a door to a hallway. At the end of it, Powers saw a door marked **County Coroner.**

On a chair just outside the door sat an older couple, about forty years old. The man was much smaller than he had been the last time Powers had seen him, which was only the night before.

Jed Hicks.

Powers checked his watch again. He had miscalculated. Not necessarily the distance and the amount of time to cover it but the anguish of the man behind the wheel and his anticipation to finally put an end to the uncertainty that had plagued him for two weeks.

He had brought his wife.

Powers filled his lungs with more air than he knew what to do with.

"Despite all of that," said Dorritt as they approached the couple, "*this* is the hardest part of the damned job."

CHAPTER TEN

JESS KEELER

Present Day

While there appeared to be a shortage of information on nearly every person involved with the Lake Castor Christmas Eve Murders, that did not necessarily apply to Sheriff Ennis Worthy. Jess had spent hours since booking their interview with him deep in research and found it incredibly refreshing to have access to so much information.

Ennis Worthy had been narrowly elected the first Black sheriff of Deeton County in 2000 after a contentious race with the incumbent. He had run unopposed for every election afterward. There were several Google images for him: getting inaugurated in his dress blues; shaking hands with Barack Obama; greeting a constituent in a rain poncho; receiving an award from the Black Lawmen of North Carolina; sitting behind his desk in a polo. In each and every one of them, Ennis Worthy boasted a timeworn, honest smile and a folksy demeanor. His hair frosted whiter and whiter as the photos grew more recent. One interesting datum claimed Worthy to be the second-oldest sheriff to serve Deeton.

He'd earned a law degree from North Carolina Central University. He'd married his first wife, Rochelle, in 1975, then his second wife, Tamara, after Rochelle had passed away twenty years later. Each marriage had provided him with one daughter, each of whom had borne children of her own. He attended Christ of Kings Baptist Church every Wednesday and Sunday, and his only rumored vice was a weekly game of dominoes.

Jess had committed it all to memory, but nothing could have prepared her for the moment she finally laid eyes on him. The receptionist escorted her and Decker into Worthy's office, deep within the bowels of the sheriff's station house. They were led down one hallway and up another until they reached a thick wooden door, behind which they found Worthy at his desk.

The walls were bedecked in awards, accommodations, and photographs. An American flag folded in a case. Shadow boxes filled with badges from around the globe. The desk was neatly arranged—nothing out of place—with dust-free family photographs at every corner.

Worthy himself was smaller than Jess had expected, but only in frame. He rose from his desk, shoulders stooped, and immediately filled the room with a humble gravitas. His friendly face had been sanded by years upon years of rural law enforcement. His folksy manner belied his direct, immediate nature.

He extended his hand to Jess, who quickly accepted it.

"Thank you for seeing us, Sheriff Worthy," she said. "It means so much to us."

"We'll have to see about that." He smiled, then turned his eyes to Decker. "How do you do?"

"Sheriff," said Decker, "my name is Dan Decker, and I'm—"

"Oh, I know who you are, Mr. Decker. I thought we were finally done with the likes of you in these parts."

The light caught Decker's front teeth. "You know how hard it is to keep a good man down."

Jess reached into her knapsack for her audio equipment. She had placed the recorder on her lap and was producing the microphone when Worthy stopped her.

"I hate to break it to you, ma'am, but none of that will be necessary today. I have no plans to speak on the record about this case or any other. What do you say we keep this conversation casual?"

"But sir," Jess said, "we need audio for our podcast and—"

"Ms. Keeler," Worthy said, "one thing I learned long ago is that if I don't want to get bit by a copperhead, then maybe I ought to stay out of the tall grass."

"I don't follow."

"I'd like to keep the recorders off."

Worthy returned to his swivel chair behind his desk. He leaned back and placed both arms on the rests, then waited for his guests to continue.

"We're here to speak with you about one of your cold cases," said Decker.

"Deeton County does not have any cold cases," Worthy replied. "Our investigations are only solved or unsolved. Open or closed."

"This would be an old one."

"Was it solved?"

"No sir."

"Then it's not cold," said Worthy. "It's open."

Decker took his licks, then took his seat. He motioned toward Jess's knapsack, then seemed to think better of it. He crossed one leg over the other.

"Sheriff," he said, "we're specifically talking about a case from 1972. I believe you used to call it the Lake Castor Christmas Eve Mur—"

"I know what you're talking about. We still get phone calls and drop-ins from tabloid TV producers all the time." Worthy crossed both his arms over his chest. "And no, we never called it that. All that Christmas Eve business was something ginned up back then to sell newspapers. In law enforcement, we refer to it as the double homicide of Steven Hicks and Linda Harris."

"That's the one," said Decker. "Can you confirm that it's still being actively investigated?"

Worthy shook his head. "It's not our policy to comment on an open investigation."

"Will you tell us if someone has been assigned to the case?"

"It's not our policy to comment on an—"

Jess had had her fill. "We know about George Berry," she said.

"Who?"

Decker rolled his eyes.

"George Berry," she continued. "The number one suspect in the murders."

Worthy's arched eyebrow was his only facial expression since they'd introduced themselves. "According to whom?" he asked.

"Deputy James Ballard. He was the lead invest—"

"I know who Ballard was," Worthy said. "Do you?"

"He was my grandfather."

Worthy took a deep breath, then let it out slowly. He appeared to reassess the woman in front of him, then softened his tone.

"I knew your grandfather," he said. "For a long, long time he cut a large shadow in Deeton County. I'm sure you've heard."

"My mother never talks about him."

Worthy nodded. He licked his lips. "Well, Big Jim was a good man. A fair man. He was what we used to call *a big ole boy*. But there towards the end . . ."

A heavy silence wrapped its arms around the room. Jess felt her heart rate speed up until she was certain it might beat straight out of her rib cage. She looked to Decker, only to find him glaring at her. Desperate not to have ruined their only shot, she doubled down.

"Can you at least confirm George Berry as a suspect?" she asked the sheriff.

"I cannot," he replied.

"Why not?"

Worthy shook his head.

Decker leaned forward. "Is it because he wasn't?"

"Where did you say you found that information?" Worthy asked. "Did you say it was a newspaper article or a—"

"The newspapers say very little about this investigation," Decker said. "We find that odd, especially for a crime that tapped into the very consciousness of both the Lake Castor and Deeton County communities. Aside from the initial articles when the victims went missing and when the bodies were found, there's actually very little on record about the investigation."

"Red had a very different way of doing things," said Worthy. "Let's just say his relationship with the media was *adversarial* at best."

Jess's ears perked up. "Red?"

"Red Carter. He was sheriff in Deeton back when the murders happened. We've come an awful long way since the days of Red's Seven."

"What was Red's Seven?"

Nostalgia dusted the smile on Worthy's lips. "Red once said he could run the entire county with only seven of the best men that North Carolina had to offer. 'One for each of the seven deadly sins,' he used to say. It was a big deal back then to be accepted into his seven."

"You were one of the seven?" Jess asked.

"I was. I served alongside your grandfather."

"What can you tell me about him?"

The sheriff's smile faded. "He was a good old boy, your grandfather. I wish you could have knowed him."

Decker leaned in. "Do you think he handled the investigation appropriately, or were there steps he might have missed?"

Worthy turned to Decker and said, quite frankly, "If your intention is to write a hit piece on an investigator in my office, then perhaps I should show you to the door."

"No, Sheriff," Jess insisted. "That's not what he meant. Dan, tell him we only—"

Worthy's attention turned to Jess. "If you want to know more about your grandfather, perhaps you best ask your mama. But I will not be party to speaking cross on another law enforcement officer."

Jess had no intention of dropping the subject, but Worthy was faster. He leaned forward and spread his arms across his desk.

"Rest assured," he said, "that crime was always one I wanted to see solved. I always thought it could have been, but the kidnapping took place in another county, and the bodies were found in Deeton. The relationship between Lake Castor and Deeton back then was frosty, to put it mildly. As time has passed, it's proven a mite tougher to get things done. A fire—I believe back in '92—destroyed the original medical examiner's report, and Hurricane Fran washed out the facility where we used to keep our evidence. A mess of things went down in Lake Castor back in the eighties, so their records are spotty, to say the least."

"But you have your original records, don't you?" Jess asked.

"We have some stuff in an old box," he answered. "And I'd love to open that thing back up because it's one I'd bet could still be solved. But everyday crime doesn't stop in Deeton. I don't have the resources or the man power to dedicate to a forty-some-odd-year-old crime, as much as I'd like to."

"We can help," she offered.

"Maybe, but like I said, it's not our policy to work with journalists on open investigations."

"We're more than just journalists," Decker offered. "What happens if, using our own set of resources and two sets of fresh eyes, we're able to turn up something new?"

A wry smile crinkled Worthy's face. "Two law enforcement agencies worked morning, day, and night on this thing for years, but you are going to find something we missed?"

Decker didn't blink. "Maybe so."

Worthy rubbed his eyes with his palms. When he looked up from them, Jess could see the years stacking up. He rose from his desk and once again extended his hand.

"I appreciate your interest in this case," he said to them both, "but it's against our policy to speak on the record with journalists about an open investigation. I'm afraid I'm not going to be any help to you. Now, if you don't mind . . ."

Further protests fell on deaf ears, and the sheriff ordered a deputy to escort them both to the reception area. Jess, however, felt the blood pumping through her coils so fast she could hardly wait to get to the parking lot. Once out the front lobby doors, Decker clapped his hands.

"There you have it," he said. "I told you he wasn't going to say anything, and I was right. We gave it all we had. I saw a little bar down the road; what do you say you and me—"

"He didn't say a word," Jess said, "but he told us everything."

Decker cocked his head.

Jess continued: "Did you see the way his eyes lit up when I mentioned George Berry?"

"I told you not to do that."

"It was a gamble that paid off. Just like when I told him I was James Ballard's granddaughter. He nearly had a stroke."

"Keeler, I'm not following you."

Jess turned her back to him and headed toward his car. The thoughts were flying too fast in her head for her to keep track of them.

"First thing we need to do," she said, "is go back over the notes. There's something we're not seeing. It's staring us right in the face."

"Keeler . . ."

"We need to visit the crime scene. Then we need to find out if either of the victims have any living relatives. Someone we can get to talk on tape. Maybe some of the nurses that Linda Harris worked with are still alive. A doctor, maybe. We need to—"

"Keeler." Jess heard his feet plant firmly on the asphalt. She stopped walking, then turned to face him. "Worthy told us that he won't talk to us."

"We don't need him. Besides, I think he would only lie."

"Why do you say that?"

"Because that man"—Jess pointed toward the sheriff's office—"doesn't want us looking into this case. Just like my mother, Sheriff Worthy is hiding something from us."

"Hiding something?" Decker couldn't mask his confusion. "What on earth would he have to hide from us?"

Jess's grin widened as she batted her eyelashes.

"My darling Dan," she said, "that's what we need to find out."

CHAPTER ELEVEN

James Ballard

1972

Steven Hicks could have been sleeping.

The young man, or what remained of him, lay on the table in the county morgue, and that imagined slumber might appear so peaceful, were it not for certain nagging details.

The discoloration of skin.

The early stages of insect activity inside an open wound near the dead man's mouth.

The pine needles stuck to his unkempt hair.

Other than that, Ballard might fool himself into believing that Steven Hicks was taking a nap, albeit lying naked beneath a plastic blue sheet, with his clothes cut away and preserved for evidence.

"That's him," said the young man's father, standing over him. The semblance of serenity offered him no solace. "That's my boy."

The father remained stoic. A thunderhead threatening to burst. Ballard watched him battle the tears, murmur through clenched teeth, and ball those meaty hands into fists.

Dr. Stanley Wilson, the county coroner, hunched over a desk and scribbled furiously into his notes. Dorritt and Powers flanked the father, and neither man appeared to know what to do with their hands, other than hold their hats at their belts.

"What kind of animal would do this?" asked the father. "Who would do this to my boy?"

"We're working real hard to find out," Powers said.

The father turned, as if to comment, but instead something else caught his eye: the body on the second table behind them, covered with a sheet.

"Is that her?"

Neither detective answered him.

"May I see her?"

Dorritt stepped in front of the father. He placed a hand on the man's shoulder. "Her mother is on the way," he said softly. "Why don't we—"

"Elizabeth is coming? Alone?"

Dorritt and Powers exchanged glances.

"Come on, Jed." Powers took him by the arm and led him toward the door. "Let's grab some air."

Mr. Hicks opened his mouth but seemed to either forget or disregard whatever it was he had to say. His resolve had headed for the hills sometime long ago. By the time Powers led him to the door, all the fight had quit him.

Ballard, however, kept his eyes fixed on the boy. He stared at him for such a great length that soon it was no longer the boy lying there on the slab but himself. Ballard, his pallor covered only by the sheet, his face blackened at the mouth, as if from a muzzle flash. The back of his head opened up, and—

"I won't know for sure until I get inside," Dr. Wilson was saying, "but based on what I see right now: deep ligature grooves in the neck, petechial hemorrhages on the skin of the eyelids and the conjunctivas on both sides . . ."

The doctor's voice faded into the room's echoes. Ballard no longer saw him. Instead, there stood his own wife, Cora, who could hardly stand were it not for the help of his young daughter, Samantha.

She asked aloud, "Why would he do this? Can somebody tell me that? I need to know."

Samantha said nothing. Her eyes were a holocaust from betrayal. She moved her lips but swore only silent oaths. That touched Ballard the hardest. What was she thinking? Could she not understand? Did none of them understand? Did they not realize this pain and agony were but a fraction of what they might experience if he decided to—

"Jim?"

Dr. Wilson placed a hand on his shoulder.

"You okay, Jim?"

The boy lay on the table. Ballard's own wife and child were nowhere to be seen. Instead, there was Dr. Wilson with his arms at the ready to catch the big man, were he to fall.

"I'm . . ." Ballard struggled for the word. "I can't . . ."

"It's harder when they are this young," said Dr. Wilson. "It catches me every time."

"It's not that . . ." Ballard lost any desire for further explanation. "It's . . . I can't . . ." He swallowed. "I'm going to get some air before the girl's family . . ."

Dr. Wilson waved him off and returned to his notes. Ballard turned the knob with a shaky hand and spilled into the outer corridor. He fell against the door and sucked in a deep breath, then quickly composed himself at the sight of Lieutenant Dorritt, who sat across from him in a chair.

"You got kids, right?" Dorritt seemed lost in thought and only barely considered his colleague.

Ballard wiped the corners of his mouth and straightened his necktie. "I have a daughter."

"How old is she?"

"Same age as those two in there."

Dorritt hooked his hat on the toe of his shoe. "My boy is still in grade school," he said, "but damned if I don't . . ." He blinked his eyes quickly, then changed the subject. "You ever seen anything like this before, Jim?"

"I don't know."

"I mean . . . on *Christmas*."

Ballard nodded.

"What kind of animal . . . ?"

Ballard didn't know that, either, but it was nowhere near the front of his mind. He took a seat next to Dorritt.

"Listen, Hank," he said. "I think something is wrong. I haven't told anyone this, but—"

Dorritt hopped to his feet and sprinted, as if he could stop anything that was already underway. The target of his panic: a frail woman, late thirties, already shattered. She was mousy and beige and might disappear into the walls at any minute. Her eyes belied any sanctity, as if she was quite familiar with pain and loss and being cold and knew that tragedy awaited around nearly any corner.

"Mrs. Harris," said Dorritt. "Jack was supposed to meet you downstairs."

"Is she this way, Lieutenant?" The woman continued toward the door to the coroner's examination room, as if guided by an unseen force. "My daughter, is she . . . ?"

"Let's wait out here a moment and let the doc—"

Behind her was another figure, one that brought Ballard forward in his seat. He rubbed his eyes and blinked away the stars, but there before him stood . . .

Linda Harris.

The dead girl.

"What the . . . ?"

No one else appeared to notice her. Dorritt held Mrs. Harris at bay, blocked her access to the exam-room door with his body.

"Please, Lieutenant. I want to see her."

"You really didn't have to come. We could have—"

"Lieutenant . . ."

Dorritt gave in. "Elizabeth, it's really not—"

"I'd never get another moment's sleep," said the woman. "I'd never be able to rest. I'd be looking into the eyes of every woman her age on the street, wondering if it was her. If my Linda was still alive." She straightened herself. "I'm going to see my daughter."

"Mommy?"

No one acknowledged the girl behind them. Ballard never expected them to. Not because of the intensity of the melodrama at the door but because Ballard was losing his mind. There was no girl. Linda Harris was not alive. She was not—

"Mommy?"

How much longer will all of this last?

Ballard closed his eyes, for he could no longer bear the hallucination.

"Mommy? I want to—"

"No," said Dorritt in a firm voice. "You can go in, fine, but I won't let you . . ."

Mrs. Harris bowed her head.

Dorritt crossed the hallway and lowered his eyes to those of the girl.

"You can't go in there, Lee Ann," he said to her. "I'm going to go inside with your mother. We'll only be a minute. I want you to do her a big favor and wait out here with . . ."

When Dorritt turned his head to him, Ballard felt like he might be sick. His stomach seized up cold, and his chest drew tight. He felt a throbbing in his head, and his mouth went completely dry. He thought of that empty bottle of whiskey at home and the lengths he might go to to hide the next one from his daughter.

"Jim . . ." Dorritt's eyes were on him. "Would you . . . ?"

Ballard wanted to find a dark, quiet room where he might lie down and never get up. He wanted to pull the gun from his holster and . . .

"Jim?"

"Yes." Ballard wanted it all to end. "Of course. Sure."

With that, Dorritt opened the door and led the girl's mother inside, leaving Ballard alone . . .

With *her*.

She seemed to float as she approached him. Her eyes were hollowed and dark, her fingers long and bony. He noticed how delicate her features were, how pale. She opened her mouth, and where Ballard expected the terrible wail of a banshee, he heard only a soft and sweet Carolina warble:

"I get that look all the time."

Ballard opened his mouth but could not speak.

"I'm her sister, Lee Ann," the girl said. "Linda and I are . . . we *were* twins."

Ballard fell into the chair that Dorritt had vacated. He thought he might never fill his own lungs with enough air, but he tried.

"For the past two weeks . . ." The girl took the seat across from him, next to an ashtray. "I see it in their eyes, whenever I walk into a room. I hear the collective breath and a sudden crackle of electricity. Then they see it's not her—it's just me—and they're all so . . ."

The girl bit her lip.

"My mama doesn't even look at me anymore."

Ballard didn't trust his voice to be steady enough to fill the vacuum of silence.

"What's really sad," said the girl, "is that I loved my sister. I loved her dearly. Do you have any brothers or sisters?"

"Um . . . yes. I have a brother."

"Are you close with him?"

Ballard paused. *Close?* He didn't know the answer. He couldn't remember the last time he had spoken with John. He could remember them rarely going a day without speaking when they were younger, but anything after their service in Korea was a dark spot in his memory. Had it been weeks? Months? Ballard chased after it for a moment, then suddenly realized that might be *the answer*. John had always known what to do.

Ballard should talk to John. He wrote it in his little green notepad: *CALL YOUR BROTHER.*

He looked up from his writing and told Lee Ann, "Not as close as we used to be."

She nodded. "With a twin . . ." She didn't finish the thought. She didn't have to. "I loved her. I loved her so much, but now . . ."

She raised a finger to her lips, as if she might sneeze. Ballard yanked his handkerchief from his shirt pocket and offered it to her.

"I prayed every day they'd find her," she said, taking it. "Even though I knew it meant they'd be finding her dead. I just wanted an end put to this."

Lee Ann dabbed the handkerchief in the corners of her eyes. Ballard watched her do so until the door again opened, and once more the hallway filled with great sorrow. The mother stepped out with her face in her hands.

"My . . . my . . ." She could not form the words.

"You aren't going to do anyone a lick of good in this state," Dorritt said. "Not like this. What do you think you can accomplish carrying on half-cocked? You need to keep your head. You need to be strong. For your daughter."

When Mrs. Harris looked up at him, whatever it was that he saw in her eyes made Dorritt take a step back.

"My daughter is *dead*," she hissed.

Ballard imagined the woman might have shattered, were there anything left to break. Instead, she drifted down the hall with Dorritt in tow.

Lee Ann said to him, "But there is no end to this, is there, Deputy?"

Ballard heard it in her voice, sure, but he mostly saw it in her eyes. He recognized the weight of deep, inconsolable grief because, since his diagnosis, he'd seen it every day in the mirror.

Ballard put a hand to her knee.

"There is," he said. "I assure you there is an end."

Lee Ann forced a smile. "Do you really think so?"

"I know it." He tried to squeeze her knee but couldn't muster the energy. "I promise."

"I hope so, Deputy." Lee Ann stood and let Ballard's hand fall away. She took the briefest of moments to gather herself. "I really do hope so, because the greatest tragedy would be if we were the only ones forced to pay for all this."

Lee Ann stepped away. Before she rounded the corner of the corridor, Ballard saw her turn to look back at him.

"Thank you, Deputy," she said.

The weight of her remained long after her departure. It pulled Ballard down by the ears so that he wanted so badly to lower his head into his hands. However, he refused. He willed himself to stand on rickety knees and quit the hallway. Quit the hospital. Quit the parking lot in his car, and if he could have managed, he might have quit the world in that very moment—but instead he found himself at the liquor store on the edge of town, where he hoped he might find his first and only solace.

Hair of the dog.

CHAPTER TWELVE

Red Carter

1972

"Did I ever tell you about my first murder investigation?"

Worthy shook his head. "No sir."

The distance between the crime scene and Shady Village Trailer Court was a small one, so Red knew to tell the short version.

"Three months after I signed on, I get the call to Highway 316. You know the part where it bends out by Thompson's corn? Out there, somebody had shot a motorist, and I didn't have to be goddamn Jack Webb to figure out that Henry Mitchell done it."

Worthy kept his eyes on the road. In the rearview, the reporters were either clearing out or stalking down the hill toward the crime scene for more photographs.

Red continued. "The district attorney at the time was an old hard-ass named Jeb Hargreaves, and old Hargreaves kept wanting more, more, more. He said we didn't have enough to pin this thing on Henry Mitchell and was about to let him go—except for Buck Grant, who was sheriff at the time, went after Mitchell hard for the car he'd stolen after killing the man. We couldn't get him on the murder, but we could get him on the car. Do you follow?"

"Yes sir."

"That got Mitchell five years. During that time, he earned himself another two for an escape attempt. Then another couple for a fight with an inmate or some shit like that. Next thing you know, Mitchell's got a knife in his stomach because he said the wrong thing to the wrong guy and they threw his body into a hole in the potter's field out behind the prison."

Worthy parked the car along the side of the small one-lane road leading into the trailer park. They watched through the window as Red's deputies fanned out across the property, knocking on doors and questioning residents.

"The point is that justice can be awful patient," Red said. "Even though I can't."

"Yes sir."

"McCoy and Tim Doody will already have started questioning the residents, but I'm going to want to lay eyes on everyone my own self. It's how I do things."

"Yes sir."

"Let's go make some friends."

Many of the residents of the trailer park had already caught wind of the incident down the road. They loitered on their porches or in the thoroughfare and watched with curious interest the commotion in their own trailer park. That sea of rubberneckers parted as Red led Worthy toward the front door of one of the units.

"This ain't going to be as easy as they make it look on *Columbo*," Red told him as they climbed the steps of the makeshift stoop. "Anybody who thinks the first door we knock on is going to lead us to the killer is a confounded idiot."

Red knocked.

"But one of these doors is going to turn up something. It might give us a guy who peddles a little reefer to his buddies. He doesn't want to go to jail, so he flips on one of his buddies who sells coke. That guy wants to make a deal, so he gives up his friend who one time stuck up a liquor store."

Red knocked again.

"Half the investigation depends on your gut. But a lot of it boils down to luck. All the training in the world can't replace experience, and none of that will matter a hill of beans if you don't have the right man in the right place at the right time. Somebody who will catch on to that one little detail that nobody else is going to catch and know what to do with it."

Red leaned over to the window and peeked inside. The curtains were drawn, but a small break in them revealed no furniture, save for a recliner and a small television. Other than that, the unit was empty.

"Hmm." Red hollered out to the yard behind him, "Somebody tell me who lives in here."

No answer.

Red chewed on his Lovera and considered the interior. Something about it struck him as strange, but so did nearly everything else about Shady Village.

"You got to listen to your gut," Red said to Worthy. "Maybe you'll get there; maybe you won't—but you work enough of these damn things, and it will be like you develop some sort of sixth sense. It takes a degree of—what the hell was that?"

Worthy jumped back a couple of steps. He pointed to a hole chewed through the siding along a patch of neglected scrub brush. "Whatever it was," he said, "it crawled under there."

"Was it a dog? A cat?"

"I don't know, sir."

Red didn't, either, and didn't want to be there when it came back out. He led Worthy off the property and toward the next unit. They passed a kid with no shirt on.

"Boy, it's colder than a penguin's titty at sundown," Red called. "Why you ain't got all your clothes on?"

The kid said nothing.

"Tell me who lives in that trailer over yonder."

The kid still said nothing.

Red nearly tripped over a chicken as he and Worthy crossed the yard to a neighboring trailer. They found Deputy Bobby McCoy beneath a rebel flag, already talking to a man wearing only a quilt.

"Red," called McCoy, "this here is Ellroy Fickle. He works over at—"

"Me and Mr. Fickle are quite familiar with one another," said Red. "Aren't we, Ellroy?"

"Yes sir," said the man wearing the quilt. "I reckon so."

"It's nearly past lunchtime, boy." Red pointed up to the sky, where there should have been a sun. "You just now getting out of bed?"

"I know my rights, Sheriff Carter. Y'all need to have a warrant."

"We don't need a warrant to catch up on old times, do we?"

"I want my lawyer."

Red rolled the Lovera to the other side of his mouth. "What on earth you want a lawyer for?"

"You know I work third shift up at Honey's, man. I ain't slept in—"

"Were you working at the restaurant on December twenty-fourth?"

"Man . . . what was that, like, a month ago? How am I supposed to know what I was doing on some random night?"

"It was Christmas Eve. Surely you remember what you were doing on Christmas Eve."

Fickle thought it over. "I might have been working."

"You don't sound so sure about it. Is that when you got all that mud on your truck?"

"Mud?" He looked into his driveway at the Chevy C10 like it was the first time he'd seen it. The lower half was caked in chunks of dried mud. "Man, me and George did that, oh, I don't know, maybe last Saturday. Friday?"

Red tapped McCoy on the shoulder. "That look to you like the same color mud we found down at the bottom of that wooded road?"

"That's what it looks like to me." McCoy turned to Worthy. "What do you think, Ennis? Same color mud?"

Worthy kept his eyes on the flag flying over Fickle's head.

"You got a problem?" Fickle asked him.

Red reached out, quick as a copperhead, and slapped Fickle across the face.

"Don't you speak to my deputy like that," Red warned him. "You hear me?"

"Jesus, Sheriff . . . I was—"

"When we ask you something, you best answer it." Red climbed a step closer to him on the stoop. "How often do you go mudding in your truck down yonder hill?"

"In the woods?" Fickle rubbed that cheek a deeper color of crimson. "I don't really go down there much. I do my mudding up in Blood Holler, like most everybody else. George is down there some, though. You can ask—"

"Who is George?"

Fickle squinted an eye. "What's all this about anyway?"

McCoy spit sideways onto Fickle's patch of dead grass. "You wouldn't be talking about ole George Berry, would you?" he asked.

Something at the neighboring trailer caught Red's attention. As soon as he realized what he was looking at, he snatched his hat off his head and swatted it at his knee.

"Goddamn Tim Doody," he spat. "Bobby, you stay and get Mr. Fickle's statements. Ennis, come on and help me save Tim Doody from his own damned self."

Worthy followed the sheriff off Fickle's lot and ducked beneath a clothesline full of clothes, which had crisped stiff due to the chilly air.

A German shepherd stretched the length of its chain and bared teeth at the passing lawmen, who sidestepped a toppled charcoal grill, then stood at the bottom of a porch where Deputy Tim Doody questioned a skinny redhead.

"Who are your friends?" she asked Tim Doody.

"Him? That's the sheriff."

"Not him." She giggled. "I'm talking about the other one."

"Oh. That's the new guy."

The redhead twirled one of her frizzy locks with her finger and said, "Hi, new guy. Everybody calls me Cherry."

"Her name might be Cherry," Tim Doody said, "but you have it on my authority that she is an honest-to-God peach."

Red shifted his Lovera. Tim Doody caught the change in air pressure, then abruptly cleared his throat.

"Like you was saying, Cherry," he said as he straightened his shoulders, "you remember seeing anybody going down that little road that cuts off Gilmore? Say about, oh, Christmas Eve or thereabouts?"

"So it *is* true." The girl arched her back, and Red turned his eyes so he might keep from choking on his cigar. "It's those two that got took on Christmas Eve? Oh my God! So they're . . . they're . . . they found them down *there*? Are we going to be on the news?"

"I'm afraid all of that is top secret police business," said Tim Doody. "Ain't none of us at liberty to div—"

"Shut *up*, Tim Doody," she squealed. "For real, you are too crazy."

Red grew impatient. "Ma'am, can you tell us if you saw anybody?"

Her eyes bugged wide. "Oh my God! I *do* remember. That night those two went missing . . . there was a white car driving out there real slow."

"A white car?"

"Yes." She crinkled her nose. "No, wait . . . it was green."

"White or green, ma'am?"

"Definitely green."

"Do you remember what kind?"

"Kind of like a *lime* green?"

"No, sweetheart," said Red. "What kind of car?"

Up came Bobby McCoy, ducking beneath the laundry on the line and cutting a wide berth to the German shepherd. He tipped his hat.

"Howdy, Cherry."

"Bobby McCoy. Fancy seeing you here."

"Ellroy said George Berry has been spending a bit of time out here," McCoy told her. "You happen to see him any?"

"Are you asking me as a *cop*?"

"As one of Red's Seven, yes ma'am."

"Ma'am?" She tried not to laugh. "Hold on, y'all . . . Bobby McCoy here is on *official business*. Well, Bobby McCoy, I'll have you know I am *very* familiar with George Berry. Very familiar indeed. In fact, I've known him for quite some time."

"Now, now, Cherry—"

"In fact, one night I knew him three times."

"Cherry, that ain't—"

"That was probably one of those nights you were with your *wife*. Too bad, because that was also one of those nights when I reckoned to stretch my legs behind my—"

"Dammit, Cherry." McCoy's voice rose an octave. "Could you just tell us if—"

Cherry set her sights on Worthy. "Let me ask you a question, new guy: Do you think I'm pretty?"

"Me? Uh . . . I—"

She leaned against the doorframe and draped her arm above her head. "I bet I'd look a lot prettier in those handcuffs of yours."

◆ ◆ ◆

One guy remembered a white '72 Mustang on or around Christmas Eve. His wife said it was a blue Nova. Halfway through the trailer park,

Red and Worthy were unable to turn up anything noteworthy until they came upon Mavis Reynolds. They found her on the front porch of a unit next to a fallen tree. Her hair was in curlers, and she drank from a steaming cup.

"I've been waiting for you all," she called to them.

Ms. Reynolds knew nothing about George Berry. Nor could she testify to a white, green, or blue car. Instead, she told them everything she could about Thomas Bardwell.

"And who is Thomas Bardwell?" Red asked her.

"He's a pervert; that's who he is."

"You care to add more to that, Ms. Reynolds?"

"I've seen him."

"Seen him what?"

"Be a pervert."

Red shifted his cigar. He kept his eyes fixed on her.

"I've seen him peep into windows," she told him.

This perked up Worthy's ears. "Your window?"

Ms. Reynolds appeared hesitant to address the deputy. However, she had a story to tell, and no long-held cultural beliefs were going to get in the way of her telling it. She tightened the belt of her bathrobe and looked at a spot just over Worthy's shoulder.

"He peeps in *everybody's* windows. Last week, I had to run him off from outside Cherry Winston's trailer."

Red rolled his eyes. He reckoned he would need more than seven deputies if he were to arrest every man who stood outside Cherry Winston's trailer.

"I heard he goes down into those woods," she said quickly. "I heard he goes down there to . . . you know . . ."

Worthy readied his pen at his notepad. "To what?" he asked.

"He goes down there to . . . to . . ."

"Yes ma'am?"

"To . . . ," she whispered, *"touch himself."*

Worthy frowned. "And you've seen this, ma'am?"

"Heavens, no. What kind of woman do you take me for?"

Worthy pointed down the road toward the crime scene, where the last of the news trucks and emergency vehicles were leaving. "Those woods, ma'am?"

"Yes. I've seen him coming out of those very woods, buckling his britches and—"

Red threw up his hands. "Okay now, Mavis. Thank you very much for your time. We'll let you get back to your afternoon stories."

"Sir?" Worthy appeared perplexed. His feet remained planted in Mavis Reynolds's rotting sod. "Perhaps a couple more questions? She's describing a man—a known pervert—who has been frequenting the very woods where—"

"The day I start taking Mavis Reynolds serious," Red said, "is the day I might as well pick me up one of those little Magic 8 Balls. This woman is what we like to call a *frequent flyer*."

"I don't follow."

"Mavis?" called Red.

"Yes?"

"Do me a favor. Will you enlighten Ennis here on why you called my deputies out to Shady Village last week?"

"Last week?" Mavis appeared lost for a moment. "I don't remem—"

"That thing with Skinny Wilson."

"Oh, *that*." She shook her head in disapproval. "Yes, I—"

"You said you thought he was working with the Russians."

She wagged a finger. "Well, he *is* a Communist."

"For the hundredth time, Mavis," McCoy interjected, "just because he's got a McGovern sticker on his Volkswagen, that don't make him a Russki spy. What about the time you called because you thought there were Mexicans in your—"

Behind them, a black LTD kicked up gravel as it pulled to a halt behind Mavis Reynolds's rusty Pinto. Out the driver's side door came the property manager wearing little-man's clothes. Despite the chilly climes, he mopped sweat from his bald spot and wore no hat. He bristled his bushy mustache as he approached the lawmen in a bluster.

"I just got the message from my girl. I came as fast as I—is everything okay? Have you made an arrest yet?"

Red intercepted him. "Did you bring that list we asked you for?"

"Of the residents? Yes, of course. Right here." He tugged a crinkled sheet of paper from his pants pocket.

Red snatched it and looked it over. "You have occasion to know a . . . what was the name of that fella Bobby was interested in?"

"George Berry," answered Worthy.

"Yes. George Berry. You know him?"

"When you run a business of this nature," he said as he waved a hand over his trailer park like a magician, "unfortunately types like George Berry are part of the package. I often wish that not to be the case."

"Which unit is he in?"

"Oh, no . . ." The stumpy man chortled. "Berry does not live on this property. He applied, but we've no vacancies. I guess you can count me lucky if—"

"We'll need his address."

Worthy entered the fray. "What can you tell us about Thomas Bardwell?"

"I can see you've been talking to Mavis Reynolds." The property manager flattened his mustache. "After Mavis caught him peeping, I told him it might be better if I don't see him on the property anymore."

"How did he take that?"

"To be honest, I'm not even sure if he heard me. There's something weird going on with that fellow."

Red's ears perked up. "How do you mean, *weird*?"

The property manager scratched his head. "I don't know. He served in that war, you know. Way I'm told, he was one of the last to come out of that jungle. You know how some of them are known to get."

He quickly considered the men standing before him. "No offense, of course."

"Where does he live?"

The property manager pointed a pudgy finger down Gilmore Road, to a house on the other side of the crime scene. Red couldn't believe his eyes.

Red punched a fist into the palm of his other hand. "Hot damn," he said. "We might actually get this one wrapped up by dinnertime."

The other deputies were still fanned out across the trailer park, knocking on doors and talking to the lookie-loos. Red hollered for them to wrap it up, then hightailed it with Worthy to his county car. The distance between the trailer park and the Bardwell home was scant, but still it felt to Red like it might take forever to cover it. The proximity of his first suspect's residence to the location of the murders filled Red with an immediate gratification that he should have known was premature. What they found at the edge of Bardwell's property dashed any hope of a quick resolve.

"Well, I'll be dipped in shit," said Red.

"You have got to be kidding me," Worthy added.

It wasn't the Bardwell property that sank their spirits. Oddly enough, it was well kept and tidy, with its leaves neatly raked and its flower beds already mulched for spring. Instead, what dampened their cheer was the sign that stood before them.

YOU ARE NOW LEAVING DEETON COUNTY.
WELCOME TO VIRGINIA.

CHAPTER THIRTEEN

Jess Keeler

Present Day

At first glance, the notebook would be nothing remarkable at all. It was a green spiral, developed by Mead, and one of over a million produced in the year that James Ballard would have purchased it. Nearly fifty years later, the pages had turned brittle and yellow, so much so that Jess Keeler would require the utmost care and caution when turning the pages with the nails of her thumb and forefinger. And turn them she would. Over and over until nearly every page had been committed to memory.

The ink had faded some, but not to the point where the writing would be illegible. She had inherited Deputy Ballard's habit of pressing the pen hard to the paper. His penmanship in the early days was neat and precise. The pages were clean and professional, as if they might one day serve as official documents. Certain entries were clearly written and easy to understand, such as the one that read:

BARDWELL, THOMAS.
W/M/25yo 416 GILMORE RD VA.
SUS OF PEEPING?

KNEW AREA WELL.

ACCESS TO ROPE (BYRUM'S FUNERAL HOME).

VIETNAM VET (OBTAIN RECORDS).

However, as the pages turned farther toward the back of the notebook, the shorthand grew cryptic and terse. His intentions became harder to understand. Fewer lines could be drawn to his conclusions.

GEORGE BERRY IS GUILTY.

GEORGE BERRY IS GUILTY.

GEORGE BERRY IS GUILTY.

The notebook was shoddy and timeworn. It had not been well preserved. Instead of answering any questions, the notes within its coiled binding only created more confusion. Furthermore, it was not even supposed to be in her possession.

Yet it was all she had to go on.

Why, Jess wondered to herself, was this case being kept so secret? How could a crime as sensational as the Lake Castor Christmas Eve Murders—no, she corrected herself: *the murders of Linda Harris and Steven Hicks*—go unsolved for so long, not only without resolution but also without further discussion? There were no articles in the newspaper about the investigation beyond the initial weeks after the bodies had been found. No current law enforcement was willing to discuss it with anyone. Furthermore, her own mother couldn't stand to shine any further light upon it.

What was everyone hiding?

What she found most puzzling was the mystery of her grandfather, James Ballard. Her mother remained strangely tight lipped. Jess had grown up without photographs of him around the house. In fact, the only pictures she'd found were a wedding photo in a box in the attic and a handful from scattered newspaper articles.

However, it was not only her mother who kept information on Ballard so close to the vest. Jess had scoured both the internet and microfiche for hours and still had yet to find worthwhile material regarding the former lawman. She had expected the days before Google to not be very productive but remained shocked that the only article that revealed anything—*anything*—about her grandfather was the article that reported his death.

DEETON DEPUTY SLAIN, read an article from the archives of the *Lake Castor Herald*. The article was as enigmatic as any other source involved so far. It reported that "Deputy J. W. Ballard died in the line of duty" and listed the location as "Deeton County, NC." The details were scant, and the only comment came from Sheriff R. C. Carter, who reported no arrests had been made and gave a steadfast promise to apprehend whoever was responsible.

There was, of course, no follow-up.

Jess became more determined to find out the answers. She knew they had to lie in that notebook. She considered her own notes so far and couldn't help but remark that her penmanship had declined the further she'd waded into the morass of the story, much like her grandfather's. In fact, she wondered if there might be meaning after all in that last page before the others had gone blank, where he had written across the page in a shaky hand the words—

"Where's your friend today?"

Jess looked up from her work. Her favorite All-Niter waitress stood over her with a steaming pot of coffee. Nobody else in the joint. Somehow her late breakfast had stretched well past lunch.

"He's . . . uh, he must be . . ." Jess searched for an appropriate answer. Decker had been MIA since Sheriff Worthy had shot them down. He only occasionally returned texts, and her calls had gone unanswered. "I'm working alone today."

"If you ask me, you're better off." While the waitress refilled Jess's coffee, she scanned the stacks of notes spread across the tabletop. "Any closer to cracking the big case?"

Jess shook her head. "I'm afraid not. No one seems to know anything."

"That's too bad." As the waitress turned to walk away, she said over her shoulder, "I got no idea why someone would ever want to do that to a nurse."

Jess dove back into her notes, but something the waitress had said triggered a thought, which led to another, then sent her flipping through the notebook again. Almost immediately after the entry on Bardwell, Thomas, she found what she was looking for: the list of nurses who'd worked alongside Linda Harris when she'd gone missing.

Jess snatched her phone and opened her browser. She entered one name after another, clicking every possible link until she filled several pages from her legal pad with notes on each of them. Of the nine nurses who'd worked the same floor with Linda in 1971, seven were still living. Three of them still lived in the area, while one of them—according to her social media page—still worked at Lake Castor General.

Jess gathered up her notes, left money on the table, and hit the door.

Jess Keeler craned her neck to better see the top of the building and wondered to herself how much Lake Castor General had changed since the days when Linda Harris roamed its hallways. From pictures she had studied, she could tell that several wings had been added on during the past fifty years, as well as a first-rate cancer center and helipad. The medical staff had integrated and diversified. The local population had waned, then again boomed.

She'd nearly lost herself in all the real or imagined transformations when the car behind her blared its horn. Jess held her ground. She signaled for it to go around and pass her. As it did, the driver offered her a signal of his own, followed by a string of expletives.

Jess paid him no mind. She had other things on her plate.

Namely, the stocky older woman crossing the intersection at the light. She, like the others on the street near the hospital, wore nurse's scrubs. Jess clicked on her hazard lights and leaped out of the car.

"Ms. Nelson," she called to the older woman. "Ms. Jean Nelson?"

The woman stopped in the crosswalk and pushed her bifocals farther up the bridge of her nose for a better look.

"I'm Jeannie Nelson."

"Ms. Nelson, my name is Jess Keeler." Jess approached her on the right and gently placed a hand on her right shoulder, as if to assist her in crossing the street. "I'm the reporter who has been leaving you messages on your voice mail."

"Oh shoot. I wish you had told me you were coming. I'm just getting off work, and now is not a—"

"I would have loved to tell you, Ms. Nelson, but you never called me back."

"Well . . ." Ms. Nelson looked pained. "I know why you are calling me, and to be honest, I don't really want to talk about all of that."

They reached the opposite end of the street. The other pedestrians moved as one toward a six-story parking garage. Jess stepped closer to Ms. Nelson so that she wouldn't have to shout.

"I'm real sorry about catching you after your shift. Perhaps I can take you somewhere for coffee? It's my treat."

"My feet . . . I have troubles in my ankle, and these shifts take it all out of me. All I want to do is soak my feet and turn on the tele—"

"How about a beer instead?"

Jess suggested an Irish pub up the road. They found the happy hour crowd to be lively, with several people still wearing their hospital scrubs. Jess directed her to a quiet booth in the corner, then carried over both their drinks.

"I'm not much of a drinker," Ms. Nelson apologized, "but all the young ladies on my floor talk about this place, and I've always wondered."

"It's new, I think."

"Except for the hospital, everything in Lake Castor is new." Ms. Nelson handled her martini glass like someone who knew what they were doing. "When I was starting out at LC General, this was an old feedstore. After that, somebody turned it into a pizza restaurant." She took in the walls, the furniture. "Things sure do change."

"You started out in 1971?"

"I did."

"Wow." Jess sipped her own bourbon. "You've been a nurse for a long time."

"I retire in less than a month."

Jess reached into her bag. On the way to the hospital, she had stopped in Whitfill. Deep in the stacks of the local library, she had found a high school yearbook from Linda's graduating class. When she placed it on the table between them, Ms. Nelson seemed to recoil at first before finally settling into it. Her fingers handled it like a relic.

"Oh my stars." Ms. Nelson gingerly turned the pages.

"I bet this has to feel like stepping into a time machine, doesn't it?"

"Will you look at that?" Ms. Nelson pointed to a black-and-white picture of three young women in cheerleading uniforms. "I didn't even remember I used to be that skinny."

"That's you?"

"It sure is." She turned the page again.

Only two pages to go . . .

Jess asked, "After high school, you ended up going to nursing school, didn't you?"

"I did."

"Do you talk to any of the other women you went to nursing school with?"

"Not very often, but we do keep up. There's a Facebook page where some of them get on there and give updates on who all retired and who all has passed on and such, but I don't pay much attention to it. They have reunions every now and again, but . . ."

She turned another page. Jess rocketed with nervous energy.

"Most of the other girls retired years ago," Ms. Nelson explained. "I planned to stick it out until they barred me from the grounds, but lately my ankle . . . my back . . . well, you're too young to know about such things."

"Believe me: I have my—"

Ms. Nelson flipped the page again. She saw the photo and blanched.

Jess played dumb. "What? What is it?"

Ms. Nelson reached out, as if to touch the photograph. Her hand stopped just shy as she seemed to remember where she was. She dropped that hand to her lap, where it lay useless.

Jess pretended to catch on. "Oh," she said. "Yes."

The image of Linda Harris smiled at them from the lower left corner of the yearbook page. Her eyes were wide, her smile even wider.

Her whole life in front of her . . .

"How well did you know her?"

"Linda? I—well, we graduated high school together, then nursing school. We both got on at Lake Castor General. She was so excited. Lake Castor was one of the newer hospitals then, and we thought we had it made."

"So you were close?"

Ms. Nelson was still lost in the photograph. "She just *loved* that boy."

"Steven Hicks?"

"Steven. Yes."

"It must have been devastating when you heard their bodies had been found."

Ms. Nelson snapped awake. She closed the yearbook, then leaned back in her seat.

Jess's face flushed hot. Her question had dumped cold water onto the air between them. She opened the yearbook again in an attempt to bring it back, but Ms. Nelson would no longer look at it.

"I have found seven nurses still living who worked the floor with you and Linda Harris back in 1971," Jess said. "No one will return my phone calls or emails. Why won't any of you talk with me?"

Ms. Nelson fingered the olive perched on the lip of her martini glass.

"Certainly you must have had some thoughts about who might have done this," Jess said. "I'm sure you ladies must have had some suspicions."

Ms. Nelson began gathering her things. Jess leaned forward.

"You can talk to me. I promise."

"I've spent my whole life in health care," the old woman said. "I've spent it right here in the same town where I started. It's not a very big town; I know—it's an even smaller community."

"I don't follow."

Ms. Nelson looked over her shoulder, then leaned across the table. She said in a low voice, "They never caught the man who did it."

"No, they didn't," said Jess. "But this story I'm working on will shine a light in some very dark corners, and who knows—maybe someone somewhere might remember something and finally come forward."

Ms. Nelson finished her drink in a single swallow, then placed her purse on her lap. "You'll have to do that without me. I'm not speaking to any reporters, and I won't—"

"Do you remember a man named George Berry?"

Jess felt the change in the air pressure. Ms. Nelson had pulled her keys from her purse but had yet to move from her seat. The lines in her face tightened.

"Who?"

"George Berry."

Ms. Nelson blinked. "I'm afraid I don't know who that is."

Jess felt her grandfather's notebook burning a hole in her bag. "According to my information," she said, "he used to date a fellow nurse on your floor. Do you remember Margaret Cornwell?"

Ms. Nelson's eyes dropped down and to the left. They popped back front and center.

You bet she remembers.

"Margie . . . ?"

"Yes. In 1971, George and Margaret were—"

"Wait a minute." The emotions roiled to a crescendo inside the old woman. "Of course I worked with Margie, but I don't remember anybody named George Berry."

"Are you covering for someone?"

"I beg your pardon?"

"It's just that every time I mention George Berry's name, I get the same reaction."

Ms. Nelson grew more flustered. "I don't like what you are trying to insinuate."

"I'm trying to get to the bottom of a story that no one wants me to get to the bottom of. Why won't you help me?"

"Because I can't. If I knew anything, I would have told the detectives when they came asking."

"What are you scared of, Ms. Nelson?"

Ms. Nelson opened her mouth. She thought for several beats before she spoke.

"For a long time after it happened," she said, "we were terrified. Was this some kind of serial killer who had a thing for nurses? Was he coming back to get us? Was it someone we knew?" Ms. Nelson plucked a Kleenex from her purse with a shaky hand. "We quit walking to the parking lot alone. Nobody went out parking anymore with their boyfriends. A couple of the girls transferred to another hospital."

"I'm sorry. I know that must have—"

"Over the years," Ms. Nelson continued, "when nobody was arrested for it, we started to hear the rumors. Maybe it was somebody we knew. Maybe it was somebody we saw every day. Maybe we missed something or should have seen something, or maybe even we were next."

"Did you?"

"What?"

"See something?"

Ms. Nelson dropped the Kleenex back into her purse. Her knee popped as she stood from her chair. "Honey," she said, "it's been nearly fifty years or so. I've had plenty of time to acquaint myself to the fact that the only justice that will be served for Linda is going to happen in the afterlife. But in the meantime, I have to take care of myself."

"Ms. Nelson, wait."

She would not. "Lee Ann would kill me if she found out I said this much to you."

"Who?"

Ms. Nelson tucked her chair beneath the table.

"Wait a second," Jess said. "Who is Lee Ann?"

Jess could do nothing but watch as the old woman made for the front door. After she'd left the premises, Jess retrieved the recorder from her bag. She switched the power to off. Next, she pulled out her grandfather's notebook. The ink written in his own hand, still as vibrant as if it were yesteryear:

THE NURSES KNOW.

NOT SAYING ANYTHING.

DRUGS STOLEN?

COVERING FOR SOMEONE?

Then she flipped several pages and stared at the words—

GEORGE BERRY IS GUILTY.

GEORGE BERRY IS GUILTY.

GEORGE BERRY IS GUILTY.

GEORGE BERRY IS GUILTY.

—until they ran together in her mind, creating a chaos and commotion that fevered up a din, then, as quickly as it had started, fell silent.

That was when she reached for her own yellow legal pad. On the first blank page she could find, she added her latest entry.

WHO IS LEE ANN?

CHAPTER FOURTEEN

James Ballard

1972

Determined not to repeat the mistakes of the day previous, Ballard dumped the remnants of the whiskey bottle into his coffee thermos. He was overly tempted to sneak a swallow before climbing out of his county car but instantly denied himself.

Make yourself earn it, he told himself. *Turn it—and the comfort it delivers—into a treat.*

Still, his right hand trembled as he tucked the container into the breast pocket of his jacket. He climbed out of the cruiser. Outside the sheriff's office, the pavement was icy. He stepped carefully up the walk.

Arriving inside, he realized he was late. Lois sat at the desk up front. Her stern eyes melted from concern.

"Running a bit behind," said Ballard. "Truck wouldn't start."

Lois nodded and pointed toward the back of the building. "Red has everyone gathered in the briefing room. They'll be waiting for you."

Ballard thanked her, then headed on back. He considered several times ducking into the bathroom for a quick bolt from the thermos.

Later.

He passed the deputies' desks, then the locker rooms. In the back, the door to the briefing room was closed. Ballard could still hear Red's voice booming through the door.

The other deputies' heads turned upon Ballard's entrance. Red checked his watch from behind his lectern. His face soured.

Ballard second- and third-guessed his decision not to take the drink. He took the open seat near the back and withered under Tim Doody's smirk. Careful not to drop the thermos, Ballard shrugged out of his jacket.

"Thank you for joining us," said Red from up front. "Now where were we?"

"The rope, sir." Deputy Bill Gentry stood. He read from two crisp sheets of paper. "It was a sisal rope, and unfortunately, it's pretty common. It looks to have been cut from a fifty-foot line."

"Anything on the knots?" asked Bobby McCoy.

Gentry nodded. "Yes, but I can't say what. Not just yet. They appear to be nautical in fashion, but I'm afraid I can't—"

"I'll have Cappy take a look at them," said Red. "He's an old navy boy, and tying knots is about all those are good for." Back to Gentry: "Any way to narrow down where this particular rope was sold?"

"There are two hardware stores in Deeton. Six up in Lake Castor, where those kids were took."

"And even more in Lawles County." Red threw up his hands. "Gentry, I want you and Howard to make up a list of every store that sells that type of rope, and I want you to visit every last damn one of them. Shake that bush and see what—"

But mention of Cappy's name had caught a stray thread in Ballard's mind. It sounded familiar, and he knew he should know who Cappy was. He scanned his memory but couldn't seem to catch on to that thread. In the meantime, it unraveled, and he had no idea how long he'd spent chasing that thought before Red snapped him out of it.

"Ain't that right, Big Jim?"

Unsure of what Red was talking about, Ballard nodded.

"And it's that very coroner's report that we plan to go by." Red snatched dog-eared papers off the top of the lectern and read from them. "According to Doc Wilson, the time of death reads as 12/25/71, between the hours of twelve thirty a.m. and five a.m. The manner of death for both victims has been ruled to be homicide. The male victim suffered a lick to the mouth, and the female took one to the kidney. Neither blow was fatal, because Doc Wilson has listed the cause of death to be strangulation."

Bobby McCoy raised his hand. "What about those puncture wounds?"

"Best we can tell," said Red, "the doc believes those to be postmortem and caused by that surveyor idiot."

Deputy Garrett asked, "Were there signs of sexual assault?"

"Not according to the doc. Her nylons were removed, but those were reported to have been found beneath the car seat. It's our belief that they had been taken off before they were accosted."

Tim Doody said, "Robbery also weren't the motive because the male victim still had his wallet, and the car wasn't stolen."

Red ignored him. He crossed the room and stopped directly in front of Ballard's seat. He loomed over him like a bad debt.

"All of this was available in Doc Wilson's report, which he sent over to me. Apparently you dismissed yourself from the proceedings before they were completed."

Had he? Ballard thought it over. "I . . . I, uh . . ."

"Did something more pressing come up in the middle of my murder investigation?"

Ballard thought harder. What had happened? He remembered, clear as day, seeing the male victim's body on Wilson's table. It had imprinted into his brain. Why, however, could he not remember the female? *Think: Why not her?*

"Jim, I know you weren't exactly juiced about the prospect of close proximity to Lake Castor po—"

Ballard still couldn't suss it out. After he'd seen the young man, next on the slab was . . .

Ah.

Ballard *remembered.*

He opened his mouth and tried to reflect certainty. "It was my first opportunity to observe the family, Red. I spent time with the sister of the female victim. She's her twin. She and I spoke at length."

"Turn up anything?"

"Only insight."

Red squinted at him. "You and those Lake Castor boys playing nice with one another?"

"Like a symphony orchestra."

"They cooperating?"

Ballard nodded. "I got them eating out of my hand."

"Sharing everything?"

"Everything except the size of their mama's underwear."

Red pulled the unlit cigar out of his mouth. "One hundred percent?"

Ballard didn't like the shadows crossing the sheriff's countenance. Something was amiss. He felt like he was walking blindfolded.

"What gives, Red?"

Red turned his back to him and headed toward the lectern. "If y'all are sharing everything lovey dovey over there," he asked, "then certainly they must have told you that they picked up Thomas Bardwell over an hour ago?"

Ballard felt something hot burn in his chest. No, he corrected himself; it was *cold.* Had he crossed signals with Hank and Jack? Was Red kidding with him?

Ballard saw that Red was most certainly *not* kidding.

Then Ballard's hands balled into fists.

"I'm on it, sir."

He flipped the table he was sitting at, then headed for the door.

CHAPTER FIFTEEN

Red Carter

1972

Big Jim Ballard's departure left an unmistakable echo, which rang long after he had quit the room. The other deputies bore the weight of that silence.

Red said, "Boys, I wouldn't trade places with a single detective over there in Lake Castor this morning."

Which earned laughter from the men but not from Red. Big Jim had long been one of his best men, and Red didn't enjoy making an example of him in such a way. However, he couldn't allow Big Jim to lose focus.

Not in the middle of a homicide investigation the scale of *this* one.

"Talk to me, boys," said Red to his six remaining deputies. "Tell me what the shitting hell we got."

Deputy David Garrett stood. He flattened the top of his bushy blond head with his hand and referred to the stack of notes he was holding.

"I've been following up on the night in question," Garrett said. "Our two victims met at the hospital around seven p.m. The female victim was a nurse, and her shift had just ended. The male drove her to dinner at"—he consulted his notes—"the Top Hat in Lake Castor. At approximately nine thirty p.m., they joined a group of her coworkers from the hospital and their dates at a small holiday party. Overall, there were about sixteen other people in attendance. I have spoken with three of them so far, but I have the list of the remaining thirteen. All of them, so far, claim our victims left the party no later than eleven thirty p.m. They all report that nothing unusual happened at the party."

Red thought it over, then said, "Keep on it. We've seen it all before; somebody at that party knows something and maybe don't know that they know it. I'm sure all their families and friends have been questioned by Lake Castor, but I doubt they could catch the killer even if he gave them a signed confession written in blood and witnessed by his own mama. Tell me what you got, Tim Doody."

Deputy Doody stood. "I was up all last night doing some research into the Church of the Night's Temple, which apparently is the big church of Satan out this way. They have four feast days, all of which require a sacrifice to Satan. Now, who wants to guess what one of those dates is?"

Two deputies raised their hands.

"Put your damn hands down," barked Red. "Dammit, Tim Doody. I don't want to hear another word about cults and whatnot. We got Big Jim with the Lake Castor dicks looking at Thomas Bardwell. What else did we turn up from our little visit to Shady Village?"

Deputy Bobby McCoy stood. "We heard mention of a George Berry, who is a known associate of Ellroy Fickle."

"We'll all agree Fickle is an idiot," said Red. "But I'm not too familiar with Berry."

"Neither were we." McCoy read from his clipboard. "Berry moved here in 1971 from Greenwood, South Carolina. He's a lineman on a crew that came up with Ma Bell to string wire, and he took up with one of the nurses at the hospital where the female victim worked. According to Ellroy, they like to party."

"Were they partying on Christmas Eve?" Red asked.

McCoy shrugged. "Ellroy says they sat up at Honey's all night long, that nothing was going on."

"That's *according to Ellroy*." Red soured his expression so the other men would know how he felt about it. "Of course I'm going to want that picked apart some. It smells kind of funny if you ask me. Any restaurant open all hours of the night is going to attract a class of trouble, but Honey's usually outdoes itself."

"Yes sir."

"We're going to want to take a crack at him, but I want to know him inside and out before we get him in the Box. We can't catch him in a lie if we don't know what's the truth. Do a little more digging, Bobby. See what we turn up."

"Yes sir."

"In the meantime," Red said to the men, "I want a list of anybody and everybody who had anything to do with them. I want to know the names of her ex-boyfriends all the way back to a harmless little crush in kindergarten. I want to know if he ever stepped out on her with another girl, even if it's a one-night stand with a Georgia peach during a trip to the beach with the boys. Did they have any enemies? Were people jealous of them? Who had any reason at all to do something like this?"

"Should we consult with Lake Castor?" asked Deputy Howard.

"Hell no," said Red. "We have fresh eyes. We have *sharp* eyes. Why on earth would we ask a blind man to lead us?"

Red stepped back around to the lectern. If it were any other day, he'd be talking instead about traffic patrol, civil summons, or something or the other dealing with the jailhouse. All those things still existed but would wait until tomorrow or whenever the hell he could clear these damned homicides off his plate. Regardless, he was already thinking about the drive home and whatever his wife, Lois, would be cooking for dinner.

"I also want to know who else we might like for this," said Red. "We all know somebody in town who likes to play with rope. We got Bill and Mikey out looking for who might have bought one, but who do we know that's already playing with some? Who has a history of tying people up? Thank God it's not a rape we're dealing with, but what if it was headed in that direction and the guy got spooked before he could finish? Get me a list of names of who might be up to that kind of business."

Each of the men wrote something in his notes.

Red pointed to Deputy Ennis Worthy. "Why don't you put your ear to the ground over in your part of town and see if there's any chatter? Every time I turn on the TV these days, they're talking race-war this or kill-whitey that, so maybe they finally slapped some roller skates onto this revolution they've been crowing about."

"Yes sir," said Worthy.

"One more thing, boys." Red leaned both elbows onto the lectern. He spoke slowly and solemnly to impart gravity. "Lois is up to her eyeballs in phone calls since we pulled those two kids out of the leaves. We can't tell folks who the killer is, so they're likely to think it can be *anybody*, which means everybody and their donkey is going to call in with some worthless tip or another. A high percentage of these tips are going to mean diddly-squat, which means we're simply not going to be able to run every one of them down."

The men murmured their assent.

"Y'all are a good bunch of boys," Red told them. "Ninety-nine percent of the time, y'all do everything necessary to keep the people of this county safe. I appreciate that, and so do those people out there. But what's going on now is different. They are going to be watching us. Keep that in mind while you're working this one. And for the love of a cranky God, do not let me catch you talking to any reporters. Because if I catch so much as a—"

The door opening cut him short. Everyone looked up to see Lois filling the frame. Her face had gone lily white.

"We got a phone call," she said. "Someone on the line swears they seen Charles Manson in Lake Castor on the night those two kids went missing, and they want to talk to somebody about it."

Red sighed heavier than he meant to. He reached into his breast pocket and produced one of his Lovera cigars. He stabbed the spit-soaked end into his mouth and rolled it from one side to the other.

"Okay, boys," he said. "Let's get on it."

CHAPTER SIXTEEN

Jack Powers

1972

Sergeant Jack Powers heard the cacophony from the hallway through the doors of the observation room. He had been expecting it. The only surprise was that it had taken so long to happen.

"Sir, sir . . . ," came the voice in the hallway. "You can't go in there."

"Like hell I can't," came the reply.

Powers heard the opening and closing of doors growing closer and closer until finally the door behind him opened, and Big Jim Ballard filled the frame.

"You got a lot of nerve," growled the deputy.

Powers stood in the dark. He motioned for Ballard to close the door and step inside.

"You and Hank looked me in the eye and swore to share information," Ballard said through clenched teeth. "Why did I need to hear from my sheriff that—"

Powers put a finger to his lips and hitched a thumb over his shoulder at the large picture window behind him. Through the one-way glass, Lieutenant Dorritt sat at a table, opposite a scruffy young man in coveralls. The two untouched cups of coffee sitting in the no-man's-land between the cop and the suspect had long gone cold.

Thomas Bardwell.

Powers motioned again for the deputy to step inside and close the door behind him. This time, Ballard obeyed. He moved closer to the glass, transfixed by the events on the other side of it.

Dorritt spoke easy to the young man. "You said you're very familiar with the woods off Gilmore Road—right, Tommy?"

Bardwell nodded. "Sometimes I go down to those woods. Sure."

"And what do you do down there, Tommy?"

Bardwell shrugged.

"Come on, Tommy. You can talk to me."

Bardwell stared at his shoes.

"It's either me, or I can ask Sergeant Powers to come back in here and—"

"I go down there to . . . I don't know . . . I go down there to relax."

"Relax from what? You said you dig graves for Byrum's Funeral Home. That doesn't strike me as a very stressful job. Am I wrong about that?"

"No. It's . . . sometimes, man, I just get in my head. Sometimes I just need to take a walk. Sometimes, I just want to . . . I just want it to be *quiet*."

Bardwell twisted an empty sugar packet into knots. Dorritt watched him a moment. He let the air coalesce between them. When he finally spoke, he did it softly.

"You were in the war, weren't you, Tommy?"

Bardwell's eyes glazed over.

"I was too," said Dorritt. "Two tours in Korea."

"That was different."

"That's what everybody tells me. Maybe it is; I wouldn't know."

"Me neither."

"What I do know," said Dorritt, "is that sometimes it's tough to come out of that jungle. Some people don't ever come out. Is that why you spend so much time in the woods?"

Bardwell chewed his lower lip.

"When you go down into that forest," asked Dorritt, "are you still stateside? Or are you back in the shit?"

"I didn't do nothing down there."

"Your job at the funeral home . . . you said you dig graves. Right?"

"Among other things. Yes sir."

"What kinds of other things?"

"I set up the interments. The burials. Chairs, tarps—"

"You handle a lot of rope?"

"Sure. I—"

"I bet you know how to tie a lot of different knots. Am I right?"

Bardwell's eyelids fluttered. "Sure," he said. "I can tie knots."

In the adjoining observation room, Powers could feel Ballard growing restless. The big man continuously shifted his weight from one leg to the other and drew breaths that signaled his desire to interrupt. Confident that Dorritt had control of the interrogation, Powers turned to the deputy.

"I don't think he's our guy," Powers whispered. "He said he spent Christmas Eve with his mother in—"

"Red wants to know why I wasn't called before y'all picked him up."

Powers shrugged. "We moved on him early this morning. We reckoned if there was anything interesting, we'd let you know right away."

"Bullshit."

"We reckoned you could use the extra sleep."

Ballard moved in so close Powers thought he might smell booze on his breath.

Powers waved him off. "You're telling me Red didn't keep y'all up half the night working the info you pulled from the trailer park?"

Ballard took a step back.

"Ahh." Powers smiled. "You didn't care to clue us in on anything you got from Shady Village, did you? In fact, we probably would have heard squat about Mr. Bardwell here if it weren't for that pesky little detail about jurisdiction."

"We called you first thing."

"You called us *second* thing." Powers returned his gaze through the window, where Dorritt continued to question Bardwell. "First thing you did was cross out of your jurisdiction—into ours—to knock on Bardwell's door. He wasn't home, but had he answered . . ."

"Red doesn't have to ask permission," Ballard said. "Not when he's working two Deeton County murders. You forget we have the case, and that suspect you are interrogating is ours."

"You have the Deeton County murders," Powers hissed, "but we picked up Mr. Bardwell for a Lake Castor kidnapping." He added, "But we're happy to let you *observe*."

The door behind them opened. Lieutenant Dorritt entered the observation room. Powers hadn't seen him quit the interrogation, but through the glass, Bardwell remained at the table, twisting the sugar packets.

"He didn't do it," Dorritt said. "He's another shell-shocked son of a bitch who came back from over there with his head on backwards. But that doesn't mean that he did it. If you want my opinion, he wasn't peeping in anybody's windows either." Dorritt cut eyes at Ballard. "Looks like we were operating on bad intel."

"We'll make that determination after Red's had a crack at him," said Ballard.

"If Red wants to waste his time, then by all means. We sent a man down there to analyze the rope Bardwell uses at the funeral home, and it doesn't match. I'm making the recommendation that we kick him after a polygraph."

"We'll expect a copy of that."

"We're happy to share." Dorritt's eyes twinkled. "Why don't you tell us everything you turned up at the trailer park yesterday?"

Powers had hoped Dorritt was wrong about their friends down in Deeton. Against his better judgment, he'd thought perhaps Jim Ballard might level with them. However, when they had gotten the call from Thomas Bardwell's mother saying that the deputies were sniffing around their house the night previous, asking all sorts of questions about her son, Powers had known his optimism was unfounded.

As Ballard went over the Shady Village residents list with Dorritt, Powers recalibrated his expectations. He understood he'd have to keep an eye on them. In the meantime, Ballard detailed Deeton's history with Mavis Reynolds, as well as the several run-ins they'd enjoyed with Ellroy Fickle. None of it drew much interest until Powers spotted notations made by Deputy McCoy.

"These marks here," he asked. "What do they mean?"

"It means they interviewed the occupant." Ballard pointed to the stack of reports he'd laid on the desk between them. "The significant details of the interview will be recorded there."

Powers lit a cigarette with his chrome Zippo. "And if there isn't a check next to his name, that means you didn't interview the subject?"

"That's correct."

"What about this one here?" Powers pointed to an entry near the top. "Says *nobody home*."

Ballard thumbed through his report. "Apparently Unit 114 was unoccupied."

"This list has no unoccupied units. That one is listed to a C. A. Dean."

Ballard double-checked. "You're right," he said. "According to the property manager, the unit was rented through the end of the year, but the tenant moved out over Thanksgiving."

The corners of Dorritt's mouth hung like saddlebags. "I'm assuming you have the tenant's alibi for Christmas Eve."

"In progress."

"What does that mean?"

"It means we're awaiting confirmation."

Dorritt nodded curtly. "See that I get that information as soon as you do."

Powers watched Ballard grit his teeth and wondered whether there might have been a different reaction if they had been back in Deeton.

"Jack," said Dorritt, "come take a look at this."

Powers did. His eyes widened when he saw where his lieutenant pointed on the file.

"Is that . . . ?"

"It sure is."

Powers leveled his stare at Ballard. "Tell us about George Berry."

"Who?"

Powers pointed to the interview notes.

Ballard looked over the info as if it were his first time to see it. "It appears," he said, "that he and one of the other residents enjoyed mudding their trucks near our crime scene. Also, he has occasion to associate with another of the residents. A female." He looked up from the report. "Why is he of interest to you?"

Powers kept his lips zipped. He looked to Dorritt to see if he planned on doing the same.

"Come on," Ballard urged. "We're in this together, right?"

Dorritt shrugged. "Fine," he sighed. "After the kidnapping, we got a couple of the nurses together. Linda's roommate, a few of her friends. The girls who knew her best. We asked them if she'd ever had any problems with anyone, if anybody had a grudge against her. Ex-boyfriends, classmates, a spurned lover . . . you know."

"Sure."

"We get to digging and hear that maybe she saw somebody stealing drugs from the dispensary. Nothing solid yet—just a bunch of girls whispering and gossiping."

"Trying to make sense of a senseless situation," said Powers. "Who could blame them?"

"A man working a kidnapping could and would most certainly blame them," said Dorritt. To Ballard: "We ask who might have been stealing drugs, and one name kept coming up. We had to dig and scratch to get it, but it's one nurse in particular: Margaret Cornwell. Seems she's gotten involved with a guy who likes his fair share of trouble."

"Want to guess what that boyfriend's name is?" Powers asked.

Powers took delight in watching Ballard calculate the answer. The big man's jaw fell slack, and his eyes darkened. Finally, he reached his giant paw into his shirt pocket and retrieved a green notebook, which appeared so tiny in his hands. In it, he wrote the name *George Berry*, then beneath it the words *nurse* and *drugs*.

"Sounds to me," Ballard said, "like it's high time I visit the hospital."

CHAPTER SEVENTEEN

Jess Keeler

Present Day

After her meeting with the nurse, Jean Nelson, Jess went home and moved all her furniture in the living room so that she might have more space to spread out all her notes. She laid every single printout across the carpet, starting with her grandfather's notebook. She revisited every website she'd bookmarked. She rewrote her list of each name mentioned in all the articles and compared them with any new insights she'd developed since digging deeper into the story.

It took a week and a half for her to find Lee Ann.

The name was mentioned in an archived obituary for Linda Harris's mother, Elizabeth. *Preceded in death by one daughter, Linda, and survived by a second, Lee Ann (Thompson).* In the absence of any other "Lee Ann" anywhere else in her notes, then compounded by the possibility of a surviving relative, Jess could only assume that she had hit pay dirt.

There was not a lot of available information on Lee Ann Thompson, but Jess gathered every piece of data with legal means. She had a Facebook page, although she was hardly active with it. Her friends list was populated mostly by children, grandchildren, and childhood friends. No one ever posted or commented about the murders.

Lee Ann had changed her name to Thompson following her marriage to a grocer, which had lasted thirty-two years until his death in 2005. She lived at an address in the Lawles County township of Whitfill.

Anything else Jess wanted to know, she would have to ask in person. This, she discovered, would be no easy task. Every single one of her telephone calls and emails remained unanswered. She concluded, much to her chagrin, that she would not be able to continue on her own.

Dan Decker also neglected to return any of her phone calls, so she drove into Lake Castor and refused to leave his front door until he opened it. When he finally did, all her anger melted away as she drew a breath at the sight of him.

"Oh, Dan . . ." She covered her mouth. "Are you okay?"

He looked horrible. Dark circles ringed his eyes. His normally unflappable hair looked like it hadn't been washed in days. His face appeared puffy, and his stubble had grown into a patchy beard.

"I may be going through a bit of a rough patch," he said.

"What's going on? Do you want to talk about it?"

He appeared to be on the verge of tears. "My life has been ruined."

"Come on." Her voice turned soft as she breached his doorway. "Let's get you cleaned up. We can talk about it in the car. We're going to need every ounce of your charm today."

Jess couldn't help but feel sorry for him, but to his credit, he cleaned himself up nicely. As he took the back roads to Whitfill at seventy miles per hour, he seemed a sharp contrast to the man who had opened the door only an hour earlier. Jess attempted to engage him further on what troubled him, but he insisted that she read aloud from the latest copy she'd written for the script of their podcast.

When the bodies of Linda Harris and Steven Hicks were discovered deep inside those North Carolina woods, only one question appeared to have been answered: Where were the two lovers who had gone missing from that lovers' lane in Lake Castor? However, for the members of that community, instead of answers, there were only more questions.

What had happened that night that had resulted in them disappearing from that 1969 Ford Maverick left in the Creechville cul-de-sac? Who had done this to them? Why?

When would it happen again?

It was that last question which plagued the beleaguered investigators. A crime as sensational as the Christmas Eve murders was not committed by the type of person who would simply stop. Rather, the ritualistic aspect of the murders—the tying of the victims to the tree, the patient nature of the slaying, the postmortem arrangement of the bodies—all of this seemed to signal that it was not the killer's first time, nor would it be his last.

So we looked into this. Had there been similar killings? Were other young lovers abducted from a lovers' lane, then found tied to trees?

Silence filled the vehicle, punctuated only by the sound of their car whipping past trees, road signs, mile markers. When Decker seemingly realized no more words were coming forth from the passenger seat, he turned to her.

"Don't stop now," he said. "It's just getting good."

"That's all I've got for now."

"So you don't know if there are similar murders?"

"It appears that lovers' lane killings are more commonplace than you'd imagine," Jess said, "but none around here. And certainly none which involved rope. Any killings had been done with gunfire or knives. Anyone tied to a tree had been tied alone but mostly left alive. Those mostly involved robberies or rapes."

"But nothing remotely similar to what happened to Stevie and Linda?"

"Steve," said Jess.

"Beg pardon?"

"Nowhere in any of my research has anyone ever referred to Steven Hicks as *Stevie*."

"What does it matter?"

"We're about to speak with a living relative of one of the victims," Jess said. "You should take great pains to refer to their loved ones properly."

They passed an empty fruit stand. A fallow field. A dollar store that dotted the landscape to nowhere.

After a long moment, she finally asked, "Do you ever think about it?"

"Think about what?"

"What it must have been like? For them?"

Decker smacked his gum. "What it must have been like for whom?"

"Them? Steve and Linda. To be in love, out on a date . . . to be taken and carried out to the woods. What they must have been thinking as they were tied to the tree, then that rope tightened around their—"

"Hey, kid," Decker said, his voice flat. "You're getting morbid."

"It's usually the last thing I think about before I go to bed and the first thing I think about when I wake up in the morning." She produced her grandfather's notebook from her pocket and held it before her like Yorick's skull. "But I also think about my grandfather and what he must have gone through. To know who did it and to be so certain yet have so many obstacles to finding justice. I mean, what must that have felt like to know someone did something so horrible but not be able to do anything about it?"

"We don't know that Berry was guilty."

Jess opened her mouth to speak but second- and third-guessed everything she wanted to say.

Decker continued, "We know that Deputy Ballard *believed* he was guilty. That's all we know, and like it or not, that's all we're allowed to comment about it in our story."

Jess's cheeks burned hot. She knew Decker was right. She cursed herself for allowing herself to get caught up in the story and lose sight of that. Defiantly, she returned the notebook to her pocket.

"Hopefully," she said, "all that is about to change."

The Thompson home was a nice one, neatly manicured and skirting the eleventh hole of a nearby golf course. Decker parked in front of the mailbox. Jess was already out of the passenger seat and halfway up the sidewalk before he killed the engine.

"Whoa, whoa," he called after her. He caught up with her on the porch and stopped her just shy of pounding on the front door. "What's our play here?"

"What do you mean, *what's our play*?"

"I mean, so far your number one dance move has been to barge in and ask what you want up front. I've learned etiquette can take you much further in journalism than ethics. If we're going to get Lou Ann to open up—"

"*Lee* Ann. Jesus, Dan."

"We should have a script. What do you say we—"

The screen door let fly a cranky squeak as Jess opened it to rap three times with the brass knocker. Decker's protests were cut short when the front door opened. Behind the screen stood a severe woman with features etched by tragedy. Jess drew a breath and realized she'd seen those eyes many times before, only a version less angry and sad. Eyes that glanced warily from Jess to Decker, then back to Jess.

It was that moment when Jess realized Lee Ann had been Linda's twin.

"Ms. Thompson, my name is—"

"I know who you are," Lee Ann told her. "I haven't returned your calls for a reason. I don't want you calling anymore, and I certainly don't want you showing up at my—"

"Mrs. Thompson, I just want to—"

"I know what you want. Now you listen to me: nobody in this family is interested in talking about what happened to my sister nearly fifty years ago."

Decker eased between them, arms outstretched and showing both palms. He stopped just shy of the porch.

"Trust me, Mrs. Thompson," he said, cool and easy. "I understand my colleague can be somewhat of a bulldog. It's her generation, I'm afraid. It's not like it was when we were—"

Lee Ann was not amused. "I know who you are."

"Ah. So you watch your news on Channel Ten?"

"I watch it on Four," said Lee Ann. "They talked about you plenty on there too."

Decker took it like a champ. "So you know, then, that I am a fair and bal—"

"I know what they said you did to those women, and that's all I know."

"I'm sure you also know there are more than two sides to every story. That's why we're here today: we're interested in telling yours."

Lee Ann squeezed through a small space in the door, as if she feared letting something else out . . . or in. She closed it behind her and stepped out onto the porch. She wrapped herself up in her own arms, then looked up and down the street.

"I grew up here," she said. "Not in this house but in this town. It's not a very big one." When no one interrupted her, she added, "There was a time when I was angry that it was all anybody ever talked about or thought about when they saw me. But that didn't hold a candle to how angry I was when they stopped. And they stopped, dammit. After a while, it was like nobody cared what happened to my sister and her boyfriend."

"Our plan is to change that," said Decker.

"Every three or four years around Christmas," Lee Ann continued, "we get somebody from the news station to come down and ask a few questions. They say they're going to generate public interest. They dig up a lot of pain and heartache, then run a slick forty-five-second segment on the air with a tip line. What do we get out of it? A new bunch of stares at the supermarket or the post office."

"Mrs. Thompson . . . ," said Decker. "Actually, may I call you Lee Ann?" Lee Ann did not blink. Decker continued. "Lee Ann, a lot has changed in media over the past couple of years. Technology has grown in leaps and bounds, and the internet has democratized storytelling. Back when this terrible tragedy happened, stories like Linda and Stevie's could only be told in column inches or tiny news segments. That's not the case anymore. The market has opened itself up to new and innovative methods of storytelling that will allow us to dig deeper into the actual story."

"And how is that supposed to help me, Mr. Decker?"

Decker smiled like an alligator. "Please," he said, "call me Dan."

"Mr. Decker."

Decker backed off.

Jess, on the other hand, reached for Lee Ann's shoulder.

"It's our opinion," Jess said, "that by engaging with a wider audience with a true-crime podcast, we can shine a light on this story, and maybe it might jog the memory of somebody, somewhere."

"And what good would that do?"

"It might help us solve it."

Jess regretted the words as soon as they left her mouth. Decker shut both his eyes and covered them with his hand.

"Is that what you plan to do," Lee Ann asked. "*Solve* it?"

"What I mean is—"

"For over forty years, we've had all these different detectives looking over this murder, but what you're saying is all we needed this whole time was an internet radio show?"

"No ma'am," Jess stammered. "What I'm proposing is that we—"

Jess was interrupted by the sound of a rusted pickup screeching to a stop in the street out front of Lee Ann's house. Out spilled two corn-fed Virginia boys, neither of them a hair beneath six feet tall or a stone lighter than three hundred pounds. They bounded toward the front porch from the truck. Their footfalls pounded the front lawn like an avalanche.

Lee Ann clapped her hands, as if dusting them clean. "Miss, I'm not the least bit interested in what you are proposing. Now if you'll excuse me . . ." She stepped off the porch to intercept the two approaching men. "My babies," she said. "My boys."

Decker shrank in the shadows of the two young men.

"Is everything okay, Aunt Lee Ann?" asked one of the boys.

The other asked, "Are these the ones that were bothering you?"

"Everything is all right, my babies." Lee Ann stepped between the two giants and looped her arms around their tree-trunk torsos. "Reese and Ryan, this is Dan Decker. Maybe you remember him from the TV news."

Neither nephew appeared impressed.

Decker cobbled together a dotty grin. "I get it. People your age don't watch much TV news anymore. Marketing polls say they prefer the inter—"

"Did you ask them to leave, Aunt Lee Ann?" asked either Reese or Ryan.

"Mr. Decker and his friend were just saying goodbye," said Lee Ann.

Jess stepped face-first into the chest of one of the nephews.

"It's been nearly fifty years," she said to Lee Ann. "Don't you think it's time this story was told?"

"To what end?" Lee Ann asked. "You have yet to tell me what that would accomplish. Telling this story won't bring them back, will it?"

"Of course not."

"And you can't guarantee it would solve this case, can you?"

"It was stupid for me to suggest that."

"Then tell me what good it would do."

"Closure."

Lee Ann crossed her arms. From yonder telephone line, a bird tittered like laughter at some stupid joke. Unable to find anything funny, Lee Ann froze eye contact with Jess but said to her nephews: "Please escort Mr. Decker and his friend to their car."

Jess ducked out from beneath the grip of one of the burly nephews. "What did I say?" she asked.

The nephew once again took hold of Jess by both her shoulders. Lee Ann waited until she quit struggling against him.

"That's a funny word: *closure*," she said. "It's a word used in novels. TV shows." She eyed Decker. "Poor-quality, so-called investigative pieces. It's a word journalists use to justify sticking their noses somewhere they don't belong, to dig up and rifle through a family's pain and torment." Back to Jess. "Linda is not a *story*, miss. And I am not a character in it. I am a person who lost her sister nearly fifty years ago and is still devastated every single day. This is my life. I have to live it. I have to be reminded every day that she is gone and that the monster who did it lives only thirty minutes away from me in Lake Castor."

Jess wrested herself free from the nephew and came face-to-face with Lee Ann.

"Wait a minute," she said. "You know who did it?"

"Yes, dear. We all know."

"George Berry is still alive?"

A shadow of disappointment darkened Lee Ann's face, and she shook her head. "I've never heard that name before."

The nephew—Reese or Ryan, one—grabbed hold of Jess once again but this time by the torso. He lifted her from the earth and carried her down the sidewalk to the car, where the other nephew held open the driver's side door like a valet for Decker. Jess was tossed into the passenger seat, with the door closed behind her.

She rolled down the window and hollered out to Lee Ann, "Wait a minute . . ."

Lee Ann and her nephews paused their procession. She looked over her shoulder.

"How do you know?" Jess asked.

"I know," said Lee Ann, "because this man calls me every year on the anniversary of the murders to tell me he did it."

CHAPTER EIGHTEEN

James Ballard

1972

Ballard had had his fill of hospitals of late. Would that he could avoid following the detectives to Lake Castor General, but he had to agree the George Berry lead was too interesting to pass up. He laid aside his reservations and joined them for his first interview with the nurses.

There were nine of them. Fresh faced, young, and mighty stricken with grief. Dressed in clean white uniforms, creased and crisp. The news of the previous day registered in their demeanors. Some sat slumped. Others straight backed and defiant. Each dabbed at the corners of her eyes with tissue.

It had caught none of them by surprise.

"By the third night they were missing," said one of them, a blonde, "I knew she would turn up dead. I just knew it in my bones."

Another said, "I feel so horrible, but I'd wished all along they'd hurry up and find her so we could get on with the grieving."

"It's like we've had to grieve for her twice."

"I've never stopped."

Ballard wrote each of their names in his notepad. He'd pleaded earlier with Dorritt and Powers to let him interview them each alone and separately, but they'd rebuffed him.

"These girls have been through so much, Big Jim," Dorritt had protested during the ride to the hospital.

"Even so, you know better than anybody that we'll get better information if we talk to them one at a time."

"We've done that," Powers said. "Several times. We've asked these women everything imaginable, and it's all written up in our notes."

Ballard hadn't liked it, but in the end he'd acquiesced. The battles he had to fight felt endless, and he saw no point in dying on that particular hill. So they'd gathered all the nurses.

"Do you think we're being targeted?" asked a thin brunette. "Like that man did in Chicago?"

The other nurses held their breaths and waited for Dorritt's reply.

"We really don't think so," he said.

"Could one of us be next?"

"Oh my God," exclaimed another. "What about that weird orderly?"

"What weird orderly?" Powers asked.

"The one with the weird eyes?"

"What was his name? Oh my God, I can't remember. Could it be . . . ?"

A small group of three fell into excited murmurs. Speculation flew. The fever infected the others. One by one, their fear took hold of them.

Dorritt did his level best to speak above it. "We've seen no indication that this is anything but an isolated incident. Still, we need to ask a few questions that will help us get an idea about who may have done this. I need you all to think. Did Linda say anything that signaled she—"

"I keep remembering," said one with red hair. "Linda was a very shy girl, and she would have never said anything. But the last couple of days before she went missing . . ."

"Go ahead."

"She . . . well . . . there was definitely something troubling her."

"Did she say what it was?" Powers asked.

The woman shook her head. "But it's like she knew . . ."

"Did she ever say anything about somebody bothering her? A doctor, maybe, harassing her? Maybe an ex-boyfriend?"

"No," said another young nurse. "There was nobody for her but Steven."

"But even someone in love . . ." Ballard wrote as fast as he could in his notebook. "Could there have been another boy? Maybe one you all knew nothing about?"

The energy in the room shifted. Ballard looked up from his notebook to find each of the nurses dipped in disdain.

One nurse in particular had been pushed to the limit. "Are you sure it is the moral character of the victim you want to challenge, Deputy?" She squared her shoulders. "Perhaps you might save some of that skepticism for the character of the murderer."

Ballard stopped writing. He set down his pen.

"Ladies," said Dorritt in a soft voice, "I assure you that Jim didn't—"

"If it's all the same," said another nurse, just as stern, "save your assurances for someone who can use them. These are the same assurances you gave us when you said they had eloped. What good were those *assurances* while they lay rotting in the leaves for two weeks?"

Dorritt opened his mouth, then closed it and tucked his chin into his chest. Ballard also couldn't find his voice and was grateful when the chasm of silence was split by the door bursting open behind them. Into the room charged a red-faced doctor wearing a white lab coat. Behind him trailed a second doctor with less urgency. Upon the entrance of the two men, all nine nurses leaped immediately from their chairs and crossed their hands at their midsections.

"What the hell is going on here?" demanded the first doctor. His chest heaved, and his eyes burned with a terrible conflagration. "This is a hospital, not a sewing circle. Would anyone like to explain why—"

"My name is Lieutenant Dorritt," said the detective. "I'm with the Lake Castor police. This is Sergeant Powers, and we're accompanied by Deeton County deputy Ball—"

"I'm patiently waiting for the part where you tell me why you've got half of my nursing staff in my conference room instead of on the floor, where they can perform their duties."

The second doctor caught sight of Ballard and seemed to take particular interest. The deputy tried to keep his attention on Dorritt's handling of the more explosive physician.

"I'm afraid in the course of our investigation into the murder of one of their colleagues," Dorritt explained, "that we require their attention for a moment. Certainly you've heard about—"

"What I've heard is that for the past two weeks, you have continuously paraded my nurses from their duties. When are you gentlemen going to stop chasing your tails and allow me and the remaining work staff I have to continue their—dear God, look at what you have done."

The doctor motioned a shaky finger toward the nurses, one of whom had collapsed into sobs while two of the others surrounded her and urged her to compose herself. He then threw up his hands, let fly a garbled howl of extreme exasperation, and quit the room in the same bluster with which he had entered. The remaining nurses dissolved into tears.

The second doctor, however, did not join him. Instead, he remained in place, with his attention fixated on Ballard. Ballard struggled for a moment to recognize him—and perhaps he did—but the continuing interrogation of the nurses proved too great a distraction.

"Linda came into my room that night and sat on the bed. She didn't say anything; she just sighed and . . ." The nurse took a moment to allow her breathing to catch up to her. Two other nurses laid hands on her shoulders. "After a minute, Linda got up and left. Something was definitely bothering her, but I didn't ask what it was. We had our exams in three days, and I . . . I wish I had asked her what was wrong."

The doctor didn't budge from his vantage point in the back of the room. He seemed to be reading Ballard's every reaction to the nurses.

"What about this rumor?" Dorritt asked the women. "The one about Linda walking in on someone stealing drugs from the dispensary?"

None of the nurses spoke a word.

"What can you tell us about George Berry?" asked Sergeant Powers. "We know he dates one of the girls who works with you. Is she the one Linda caught stealing drugs?"

At the mention of this, the man in the white coat slipped out of the room.

Ballard didn't like it. Something in the doctor's expression had betrayed him, and he appeared clearly uncomfortable at the sight of the deputy. Ballard closed his notebook, then lurched out of his chair.

"Excuse me," he whispered to the other lawmen, then made tracks for the door, in pursuit of him. No sooner had he pushed through the door and into the corridor than he found the doctor on the other side of it, waiting for him.

"It turns out you've kept quite the secret, Mr. Ballard."

Ballard's stomach turned. The tremor in his right hand kicked up. "You have something you'd like to tell me, Doctor?"

"Perhaps it's you who aren't disclosing everything you should."

Ballard shook his head. "I've never seen you before in my life."

The doctor sighed. "Oh, if only that were true."

Ballard balled his hand into a fist in order to quell the shaking. That attempt failed miserably.

"You should have disclosed that you were a police officer."

"Tell me who the hell you are," he growled at the man, "or I'll haul you down to Deeton and make you tell me."

"My name is Dr. Fenton," said the man. His face reflected all the sadness Ballard thought was possible. "I am the physician who has been treating you for your Alzheimer's."

PART II

CHAPTER NINETEEN

Dan Decker

Present Day

Dan Decker had to hand it to her: Jess Keeler certainly had a lot of spunk. When he parked his SUV in the grass behind her Hyundai, he found her poring over an armful of city maps, aerial photography, and tax records. She compared them to the house that sat to the north side of Gilmore Road. Or perhaps more appropriately, to the carport constructed behind it. She contrasted the position of it with where the trailer park sat at the end of the road, then further consulted her notes.

Decker sighed and climbed out of the car.

"You're a half hour late, Dan," Jess called through the windshield.

"What are you doing, Keeler?"

"These are filled with reference points." She motioned to a black-and-white aerial shot of Gilmore Road. "That there is where Gilmore cuts off Curtain Rod Lane. And over there is the trailer park. Back in 1972, it was named Shady Village, but it recently was changed to . . ." She flipped through the pages to find it.

"You're wasting your time," Decker groused. "Neither the sheriff nor the sister want us to have anything to do with this. It's an uphill battle, and we'll only end up—"

"You don't strike me as the kind of guy who listens when people tell him no." Jess ran her thumb down one of the pages until she found what she was looking for. "I called their main office over in Tucker. I requested a residents list from 1971. Nobody has returned my call, big surprise, but they are about to find out just how persistent I can be. If I haven't heard from them by tomorrow, I'll jog over first thing in the morning and—"

"Seriously," said Decker, "you may want to consider switching to decaf."

Jess returned her attention to the photograph. "I used to think the crime scene was down the road a little, but now I believe it would have been here, and that driveway is where the dead end was. And that house there . . ."

Decker furrowed his brow. Cutting off the driveway was a carport about fifty yards off the road. Beneath it was a minivan on blocks, a workbench, and a boat covered by a tarpaulin.

"That means the rest of the road is on the other side of that carport."

Jess nodded. "As well as our crime scene. Come on."

"Wait, Keeler. What do you think you are doing?"

"Better to ask forgiveness," she said, "than to ask permission."

Decker stayed her with his hand. "No way. Let's be cool about this."

There was no sidewalk—instead a climb up a tight incline to the front porch. Twice, Decker nearly lost his footing, but never his resolve, as he made his way to the door. He knocked. While he waited, he felt the buzzing in his pocket. He thumbed open his phone to read a text.

i miss u

Decker dismissed the text and immediately dropped the phone back into his pocket. He rang the doorbell, then rang it again.

It was on the third ring that the woman threw open the door. Whatever impatience she suffered was miraculously cured upon sight of the man doing the ringing. She flattened her skirt and unpopped her top button. She was maybe fifty, fifty-five, but had obviously spent those years taking good care of herself. She lit up like a sparkler on the Fourth of July and flashed teeth bright enough to blind the whole street.

"Oh," she said. "Oh my Lord . . ."

"We're very sorry to intrude," said Decker.

"Oh my God," she said again. "Is that really . . . is that really *you*?"

"My name is Dan Decker. This is—"

"I know who you are," the woman gushed. She opened the door wider. "Please. Come on in."

Decker could hear Jess's eyes roll. "Actually," he said, "we were wanting to take a look at something on the property. Are you the homeowner?"

"Yes. Me and my . . . well, I own it alone." She bit her lower lip. "I mean, his name is on the deed, but he's moved out long, long ago."

"I'm so sorry to hear—"

"What I'm trying to say," said the woman, "is that I live alone."

"Well," was all Decker could say.

Jess cut in. "We'll get right to it, Mrs. . . ."

"Ms.," she corrected. "And it's Womack." She'd never taken her eyes off Decker. "But please call me Stacy."

"Ms. Womack," said Jess, "we won't take too much of your time, but—"

"Oh, I don't mind at all, Dan."

"Years ago, there was a tragic incident on this property, and we—"

"You mean the murders?" Stacy waved a hand like it was something that happened every day. "Yes, I know all about it. We didn't live here—of course—back then, but you know: full disclosure and material facts, all that. My ex grew tired of all the kids heading back there with Ouija boards, so he built that garage over top of the entrance, but the road is still there. Hey, if you like, maybe I could walk you down there and show you around."

Decker smiled and looked her in the eye. "We'd like that."

Stacy, for the first time, seemed to notice Jess. "Both of you?"

Jess pulled her handheld recorder from her bag and pointed it in Stacy's direction. "If you like, you can tell us your whole life story."

"I suppose . . ." Stacy touched Decker on his forearm, then his bicep. "How about if you let me change into something more . . . give me just a minute, and I'll . . ."

They were halfway to the bottom of the wooded hill behind the divorcée's house before Decker reopened that text message.

i miss u

Again, he dismissed it. However, something in his face must have given him away, for he found Jess squinting at him.

"Is everything okay?"

"Fine," said Decker. He turned to Stacy. "You said you didn't own this property back in '71, when the murders happened. Correct?"

"Me? No, I'm not *that* old, Dan. Me and Carl moved here back in '98. We divorced two years ago."

"That's quite a run," Decker said. "I didn't last half that long with my ex."

"I have a feeling you can last plenty long . . . with the right woman."

Jess asked, "Do you have children, Ms. Womack?"

Stacy locked an arm with Decker's. "What do you think, Dan? Have I had kids?"

Decker sized her up. "Not that I can tell," he said. "What do you do? Yoga? Pilates?"

"You're so bad." Stacy slapped his shoulder. "I've had two kids, but they are out of the house. It's just me up there. You know, all that stuff they said about you on TV . . . it's none of my business, but if you're asking me . . . some women just don't know how to keep their mouths shut."

They reached the bottom of the hill, and a silence passed between them. Years of neglect had cast a shadow across the wooded landscape, but the trees had yet to return to what had once been a road. Instead, there was a thick shroud of fallen leaves and upturned tree trunks. Above them, the clearing had shrunk over time until all that was left was a cicatrix of the clear blue sky.

Jess wrapped herself in her own arms. "Which tree do you think it was?"

Decker shrugged. It could be one of five or none at all. Time had slouched onward with little regard for this slice of God's earth, and the exact location of the killing tree might forever remain a mystery. There was a stillness in the air around them, a complete vacuum of silence, made all the more visible by moments when it was shattered by a calling crow or a scampering squirrel.

This was not, however, at the forefront of Dan Decker's mind. Instead, there roosted that message, that hand reaching out from a past better forgotten. That missive, so seemingly simple, so deceptively innocuous . . .

i miss u

Decker found his hands balling into fists. *The nerve of her . . .* for her, after all this time, to text *i miss u* was nothing, in his opinion, but utter hubris. What exactly, he wondered, did she miss? The ability to creep inside his head and wreck it? What Decker missed dearly was the amount of time and money he had wasted on lawyers and strippers in a vain attempt to forget her after she had demolished his career, his marriage, *his entire life*. That was what *he* missed. How dare she, he wondered, say something so outlandish that—

Jess slapped him hard on his shoulder. "Did you hear that, Dan?"

"Huh?" Decker recalled his surroundings: Bottom of the hill. Crime scene. One of five trees. "Uh . . . what did you say?"

Jess pointed to her grandfather's little green notebook in her hand. She read aloud: "'At the bottom of a crude road cutting through the woods—about three hundred yards—there came a dead end. When turned around and facing out, back toward Gilmore Road, to the right, about thirty yards off the road, were the bodies of Steven Andrew Hicks, white male, twenty years old, and Linda Grace Harris, white female, twenty-one years old. The tree was oak, approximately eight point five inches in diameter, and over fifteen feet tall. It stood between the bodies, which had been untied from it and laid down, then covered with—'"

Jess stopped reading and looked in the direction the notebook had sent her. She passed her sights between each of five sturdy deciduous trunks but could not settle upon any of them.

"It happened here," she murmured reverently. "Can you feel it?"

Decker did not. He felt nothing, save for the festering impatience building within him. All stemming from that text, which he wished he had never read in the first place. He wished he could go back in time and leave his phone in the car. But why, he asked himself, should he stop there? If he had the power to reverse course, he'd take himself back to the very day he'd met Jenna Healey and demand the station not hire her in the first place. In fact, had he his druthers, he would—

"I hate what happened to you."

Decker blinked himself back into the present. Jess had abandoned him to stand among the trees and commune with her grandfather's notebook. Stacy, on the other hand, remained steadfast at his side.

He smiled at her. "What do you mean by that?"

"What those women said about you on the internet." Stacy curled a lock of her hair with a long finger and checked it for split ends. "Any chance of you and your wife getting back together?"

Decker forced a nervous laugh. "I'm afraid that ship has sailed."

"Have you found any new ports to dock in? While you—you know—shelter from the storm?"

Decker enjoyed the attention and felt he could flirt all night. One of the things he missed most was the witty repartee, and he had a feeling Stacy Womack could more than hold her own in that department. However, he didn't seem to have the heart for it.

"To be honest," he said, "I'm not much company these days."

"I see." Stacy turned her attention to Jess, who ran her hands up and down the trunks of each of the questionable trees. "She's cute. A little young, in my opinion, but whatever."

"Her? No. We're partners. We're working together on this—"

"It's no problem." There wasn't a trace of sadness in Stacy's smile. "I like a man who doesn't kiss and tell."

The silence settled between them while they both watched Jess perch cross-legged beneath a tree. She hunched over a yellow pad and scribbled longhand into it.

"I'm a big fan of the true-crime podcasts," Stacy told him. "It's about time someone did a true-crime podcast on this one. It's all my mama would talk about growing up."

"Really? What did your mother know about it?"

"She worked at Lake Castor General for nearly thirty years. Same hospital where that pretty nurse worked before she was, you know, murdered."

"Did they work together?"

"They sure did."

"Is your mother still . . ."

"Heavens, no." There wasn't much distance between them, but Stacy cut it in half. "Mama got cancer back in ninety—"

Jess had appeared alongside them. "Was your mother working there when the murders happened?"

Stacy kept her eyes on Decker. "She did. She knew all about it."

"We've always felt that it was pretty common knowledge in Lake Castor who did it," said Decker. "Certainly if your mother worked there at the time, she must have had an opinion."

"To say the least." Stacy slipped her arms around Decker's waist and squeezed. "Mama always told me it was a doctor who did it."

CHAPTER TWENTY

James Ballard

1972

Ballard couldn't remember.

How long had he been lying in the dark? At what time did he wake, only to stare at the ceiling? The low, fitless rhythms of Cora's slumber only fed his jealousy, as he showed no sign of going back to sleep anytime soon. He was awake. His mind was sharp and racing. This happened every day now, but for how long?

Ballard couldn't remember.

Something tugged at his mind. There was something pressing. There was some reason for him not to pull the quilt over his head and never again leave the bed. Something he was supposed to do. He raced headlong into the many shadows of his memory but could track nothing down. No subtle reminder, no trigger to alert his—

The notebook.

Of course.

He reached for the nightstand, only to find nothing there, save Cora's Bible. Careful, so as not to rouse his wife, he slipped from the bed. His uniform trousers were in the dirty-clothes hamper, but his pockets had been emptied. He checked his jacket, his shirt . . .

Dammit.

Quietly, he stepped out of the bedroom. Dawn's purple light tickled through the window shades. The coffee table, the cabinet near the door: nothing. He peeked into the kitchen. He held, with a firm grasp, an inventory of his every step from the previous night. It had not slipped yet into the fog. He could remember clearly: He'd come home, eaten dinner, watched *McCloud* with Cora. He had sneaked into the kitchen under the guise of scooping ice cream but instead had sucked from the whiskey bottle he'd kept hidden in the—

Aha.

Ballard reached into a spot between the wall and the refrigerator. There, next to an empty bottle of rye, he found his little green notebook. Hoping it might contain some clue as to what had been so all-fired important that afternoon, he flipped through the pages. He stopped upon the arrival at one in particular.

CALL YOUR BROTHER.

What?

When had he written this? More importantly, *why* had he written it? Ballard couldn't remember the last time he had spoken to John, although that didn't mean he hadn't already phoned him ten times since he'd written it. Still . . .

Ballard checked the living room clock. He had no idea what John might be doing at an early hour. The icy dread that accompanied an empty whiskey bottle had slicked his head with sweat. He reached for the receiver and put it to his ear.

John answered on the second ring.

"John, it's me."

"Big Jim?"

Ballard picked up the handset and stretched the cord into the kitchen. He kept his voice low, so as not to wake Cora.

"Jim, is everything okay?"

"I don't remember what I'm supposed to do today."

"I beg your pardon?"

"I'm supposed to—" Ballard licked his rubbery lips. "It doesn't matter. Or maybe it does. I can't . . ."

"Jim, take a breath. Okay?"

The oxygen sparked fires in his brain. His heart rate decelerated. The tremor quit in his right hand.

"Take another one."

Ballard did.

"Now tell me what's wrong."

Where to start?

"John, I can't remember."

"Remember what?"

"How long has it been since you and me talked?"

John whistled low through the line. "I got no idea, Jim. It's been a minute, though."

"That's the problem," said Ballard. "I don't know what all I've told you because I can't remember how long it's been since we've talked. But I need to talk to somebody because I don't think I can hold it together much longer."

"Jesus, Jim. I'm here. Talk to me."

Ballard told him. For the first time since that visit to Dr. Fenton in Lake Castor, Ballard unburdened his soul to another person. There, tucked away in his kitchen, he relayed his every worry to his brother—and then some—over the telephone. When he finished, his only reply was a long, profound silence.

"John?" Ballard asked when he could take it no longer.

"I'm here," answered John.

"You've always known exactly what to do," said Ballard. "I can't count the number of scrapes you got me out of when we was children. And when we played ball, if our team needed three yards, you knew how to get us five. I followed you into Korea and"—something grabbed hold of Ballard's soul, but he shook it loose—"well, you got us both home. But here I am at an absolute loss, and that, I reckon, is why I called you. Maybe I shouldn't have burdened you with it. Maybe that doctor was right and I should say something to Cora or maybe even Red or—"

"No."

Ballard blinked twice. "Do what?"

"You can't tell Cora," said John. "And you most certainly should not tell Red."

Ballard lowered his head into the palm of his hand. John was telling him nothing that he didn't already know.

"If you love her," said John, "then you should not burden her with this. What do you expect her to do? Fuss over you while you dawdle toward the grave? She did not sign up for this. Have you forgotten what it means to be a man?"

"No, but I—"

"A man minds his own responsibilities. He cares for his family. It is your job to tend to your family. How do you plan to see after them when you are gone?"

"When I am . . ."

"You didn't think of that? Jim, this is a fatal disease. This isn't something you overcome; it's a death sentence. And a long one at that. Do you really want Cora to go through that? And Sam? Have you thought of Sam?"

"They are all I have thought about."

John's voice grew more stern. "And the last thing you should do is tell the sheriff. Can you imagine what they might do? They would remove you from duty, and you'd be stripped of your pension. Then what would your family have after you've left? No, you must keep this thing a secret. Take it to your grave. Like a man."

Ballard's chest seized. He realized how close he'd come to making a terrible mistake. He chased his every option to its inevitable outcome over and over and over until he lost all sense of time or place, only to be jarred back to the present by the voice of his wife.

"Are you listening to me, Jim?"

Ballard snapped to. He found himself still in the kitchen, squirreling away the telephone that had long ago disconnected. A full morning sun shone through the shades, and he had no idea how long he'd been there.

"I'm sorry, Cora. What did you say?"

"I asked, What in the good Lord's name are you doing still in your nightclothes?" She pointed up and down at him. "You're not even dressed."

Ballard ignored the heat flaring up in his cheeks. "Dressed for what, dammit? I'm not on duty today."

"Of course not," she said. "We're supposed to go to the funerals with Red."

"What funerals?"

"For those two kids from Lake Castor who got murdered." Cora looked upon him with great disappointment. "How could you have forgotten?"

Ballard rose from the floor. He made no eye contact with her as he returned the telephone to its base, then shuffled down the hall so he might get dressed for the funerals.

"How could you have forgotten?" she had asked him with such disdain.

So easily, dear Cora, he thought but did not say.

Too damn easily.

CHAPTER TWENTY-ONE

Jess Keeler

Present Day

When Jess Keeler initially sat down with her laptop, she promised to spend only twenty minutes researching doctors who reported to Lake Castor General during the early seventies. The possibility that Linda and Steven's killer might have been a doctor had sent an electricity through her. No longer was she despondent over the lack of information; instead she was recharged, *revitalized*, and finding possibilities around every corner.

When Lake Castor General had opened in 1895, it had been the city's first hospital. It had been funded by John P. Hergenrader as a private facility focusing on the care of the employees of the June River Mill and their families. It had become public in 1956 and had become renowned across the region for its quality of care and philanthropy. By 1971, when the murders of Steven Hicks and Linda Harris had happened, there had been over thirty-four physicians employed on a full-time basis, as well as several dozen more with nearby practices who had been contracted.

Jess assembled a document on her laptop that corresponded with each and every physician who had been registered to work at the hospital. She compiled this list by combing through books in the library about the hospital, microfiche at the library, and meticulous phone book searches. She combed records archived by the Virginia Board of Medicine, as well as newspaper obituaries.

Each physician's information was recorded and filed in their own folder, as well as the links to any online articles that might support them. She googled them. She scoured survey sites where patients could rate their doctors for anything of note. She searched social media.

Then she cross-referenced that against the vital information she'd received during her visit with Lee Ann Thompson in Whitfill: that she received annual phone calls from the man claiming to have murdered her sister. If what she was saying was true, then the killer would still be alive. By that rationale, she could cross deceased physicians out of their suspect pool. That narrowed the list down to four doctors, and of those four, there were only—

The jingling of keys in the front-door lock snapped her to attention. By instinct, she jumped from her seat at the kitchen table, only to find her ex-husband, Philip, entering the house.

"Honey," he said, "I've been texting you for an hour."

Jess let fly an exasperated sigh. "I've been busy with stuff for this . . . this . . . this *story*. What are you doing here anyway?"

"I was showing a house in the neighborhood and thought I'd drop by for a quick chat." He removed his jacket, tossed it over the chair, and moved to the refrigerator. "We need to talk about Benjamin."

He had her full attention. "What's going on?"

"He wants to take a break from school."

"What do you mean, *a break*? He was home from school for nearly a year during the pandemic."

"He's talking about a *real* break. Not one full of isolation and online classes. I believe he wants to travel."

Jess's shoulders sagged. She dropped her head into her hands.

"It's not the end of the world, hon." Philip opened the fridge and peered inside. "People take gap years all the time."

"It's only called a *gap year* if they go back."

"And he will."

Jess arched her eyebrows. "I believe we said the same thing when I dropped out of school to give birth to him."

"Jesus, Jess. How long are you going to punish me for that?"

Jess closed her eyes and breathed in, breathed out.

"You've got nothing to eat here," he said, "except for leftover takeout and an orange."

"You don't live here anymore, Philip."

"What about when Ben comes to stay with you?"

"Who do you think the orange is for?" Jess took the refrigerator door from him and closed it. "He's twenty-one years old. He can feed himself just fine."

"Jess, what's gotten into you? I've never seen you like this."

"Like what?"

"So . . . I don't know . . ."

"Focused?"

He shook his head.

"Driven?"

"Obsessed." He placed a hand on each of her shoulders. "Seriously, when was the last time you did something just for you?"

She removed his hands. "What do you think this is, Philip? From the moment we married, everything in life was about you and Benny."

"I never heard you complain."

"That was the problem." She returned to her seat at the kitchen table. She was too worked up but pretended to look over her notes anyway.

Philip didn't give up so easily. He appeared behind her and asked, "What about *him*?"

"Who?"

"Him. *Dan Decker at Six and Eleven*? Is he skipping meals and spending his evening staring at a screen for some blog about a serial killer?"

"I told you: it's a *podcast*, not a *blog*. And he's in charge of going over the list of the residents at the Shady Village Trailer Court and lining up interviews."

"But is he actually doing it? You told me yourself that he was lazy. That he was nothing more than a hollow suit with a seventy-dollar haircut."

"He's different now. Something changed. You should see him, actually. He has a very interesting interview style. It's very casual. I was watching old video clips of his when he was younger—you know, before he was an anchorman. He actually did great work, and I can't help but think if I was able to tap into that drive of his . . ."

Jess saw something uncomfortable register across his face. He seemed to be searching for something to say but was having trouble finding it. She realized then how she must look, defending this other man—ten years her senior—to her ex-husband. She cursed herself for that—but even more when she witnessed Philip's vulnerability.

"Come here." She led him to the living room couch, where she took a seat. "Sit down."

"What?"

"I need you to rub my shoulders."

"You're—"

Jess had written so many blog posts about relationships in all stages. She often posited that there was nothing bigger on a man than his ego, and the only way to appease it was to make him feel useful. And, she told herself, her neck and shoulders had been extremely tight.

"Please? You have the best hands."

He calmed almost immediately after he started his magic.

"Tell me about it," he said.

Jess didn't need to be asked twice. His hands felt so familiar upon her. She needed this. She felt everything surging forward but struggled to keep a fingerhold on the more salient facts.

"According to my grandfather's notebook," she began, "the killer is a man named George Berry. He was very adamant about this and never seriously considered another suspect."

"What was his relationship to the victims?"

"The notebook says that he dated a nurse, Margaret Cornwell, who worked with Linda Harris."

"That sounds interesting."

"It is." Jess let the stress ease out of her shoulders. "However, it conflicts with more-recent information we've obtained. For one, we're hearing rumors that the killer was a doctor. George Berry, from what we've been able to gather, is pretty far from a doctor."

"Time has a way of inflating facts."

"However," she continued, "Dan insists we should look up doctors anyway, even though James Ballard is strongly pointing us in a different direction. That we should cover all our bases. It only makes sense to cross-reference physicians from that time period against any criminal activity. Right?"

Philip's rhythm didn't falter. "Sounds good to me."

"There's a problem, though. While researching area doctors from that time period, we found three other physicians who had been accused of murder. Two of them killed their wives and were still allowed to practice medicine."

"You can't be serious."

"I am. One of them was named Jeffrey MacDonald. He killed his pregnant wife and two kids but practiced medicine up until the day of his guilty verdict."

Philip's hands could have kneaded stone. "I think I saw a movie about that."

"Looking for a killer in a list of doctors," Jess said, "is like looking for a needle in a haystack filled with needles."

"That must be so stressful," he said. She felt his hands creep lower, down the middle of her spine, lower . . . "If anybody can ferret this guy out, it's Jess Keeler."

His hands lower still. Jess allowed it but debated for how much longer.

"We have nothing else to go on," she said. "It's so frustrating. The lead detective on this case was my own goddamned grandfather, and he left nothing but a stupid notebook to lead me. It clearly says the name George Berry over and over with such maddening conviction, but he didn't show his work. All I have is the name. Still, it feels like an absolute betrayal to him to be researching doctors or *anyone* who isn't George Berry. The sheriff, the nurses, Lee Ann Thompson . . . anyone we have spoken to . . . they all deny ever hearing the name George Berry. I swear if I knew how to work a Ouija board, I—hey, will you cut it out?"

He did.

"Would you please go back to working my shoulders? They're really tight." She rolled her neck to offer him more room; a stiffness had truly settled in. "The worst part is that there is one person still living who knew Ballard better than anyone in the world, and she won't talk to me."

Philip let slip the chuckle of a man who knew all too well. "Yes, I'm very familiar with how stubborn your mother can be."

"She still asks about you."

"Oh, I know. Did I tell you she sent me a card last Tuesday?"

"What was last Tuesday?"

"Nothing. But the card said *happy anniversary*."

"Was it our anniversary?"

"No." Philip's hands slowed down. "Wait. You really don't remember when our anniversary was?"

Jess turned to face him. Whatever heat had filled the room had suddenly been sucked away. She looked deep into his eyes and had never felt more horrible.

"Phil, I'm sorry," she said. "I'm an asshole."

"No, you're not." He tried to smile. "We're divorced. It's just another date on the calendar now. Besides, your story . . . it—"

She took his face in both hands. The stubble from his cheeks felt more familiar than anything else on the planet.

"Philip . . ." She could think of nothing more to say. She couldn't remember the last time she had been this close to a man, the last time she had held one in her hands. All she knew was that it had been Philip. How long and how well they had known each other . . .

The devastation of forgetting their anniversary dissipated, but it was quickly replaced by something else. She pressed her lips to his. Her arms coiled around his neck, her hands finding the back of his head, the muscles in his back, the contours of his broad, familiar shoulders.

He kissed her back. The past few months of divorce melted away, but so did the past several years of marriage. The mundane stuff. The quarrels and the dirty socks. The microaggressions and the selfish sex. All twenty years, in fact, dripped away like fat, until she found herself wondering—trying to remember—if this was what they had been like when they were still kids in college. Sneaking out of the dorm to neck or finding a spot where they could be alone. Talking dreams and exploring what pleased each other. The whole world in front of them.

Like Steve Hicks and Linda Harris.

Philip must have felt her sudden hesitation. He pulled back from her and searched her eyes for answers.

"What's wrong?" he asked.

She couldn't shake something from her mind. "Why them?" she asked.

Philip blinked. "Why *who*?"

"Why *them*?" she repeated. "By all accounts, that Creechville cul-de-sac was a popular make-out spot. A lovers' lane, if you will. There would have been several couples parked there, making out. So why did the killer choose *them*?"

Philip recoiled from her. His eyes canvassed her as if he might be seeing her for the first time.

"What?" she asked.

Philip shook his head. He removed her arms from around his neck and stood from the couch.

"What?" she repeated.

"I have to go," he said.

"Philip, what's going on?"

He grabbed his jacket off the back of the chair in the kitchen and made it all the way to the front door before he stopped. His hand on the knob, he did not turn to face her.

"Jess . . . ," he said. If there was more to that thought, he kept it to himself. Instead, he opened the door and disappeared out of it.

Moments later, Jess found herself behind the wheel of her Hyundai. Her hands trembled but steered as if programmed by some macabre god. By the time she realized to where she had been driving, she was nearly halfway there. She killed both the radio and the headlights, then dropped her speed to a crawl as she neared her destination.

The cul-de-sac was much more well lit than it would have been nearly fifty years earlier, before streetlights had been installed. Back then, there had been no homes, only the freshly paved streets, which had marked the promise of the development to come.

Jess parked the car in what she had come to believe was the exact spot where Linda Harris and Steven Hicks had parked his 1969 Ford Maverick that Christmas Eve night, so long ago. She'd referenced an article dated a week after the bodies had been found, which had indicated they'd parked on the right-hand side, facing out. She lined up her car to match that description.

She checked her phone. This would have been the exact time it happened. Many of the bygone reporters had detailed that the couple had left the Christmas Eve party at eleven thirty. Jess imagined they likely would have driven down Halloran Street to Creechville Road, because Steven Hicks's sister lived in the apartment there, and he would be most familiar with that route. Still, Jess had tested each possible approach several times and estimated it never took longer than seven minutes.

How long had Steve and Linda been parked in their car before the assailant approached them? Did he knock on the window and surprise the two lovers? Did he throw open the door and yank them out, or did he lure them of their own accord? Did he have a gun? How on earth could he have subdued a man the size of Steven Hicks?

Now, nearly a half century later, the landscape is dotted with million-dollar homes. Atop the property where Steve and Linda last embraced one another sits a McMansion. The driveway is populated by a tarpaulin-covered boat. The lawn dotted with perfectly planted Japanese maples. The grass is neatly trimmed.

Do they even know what happened here?

The adrenaline buzzed Jess so high that she had half a mind to bang on their front door and tell them—midnight or no midnight—and might have, were it not for the phone buzzing in her hand.

Decker.

u up?

She rolled her eyes. Dialed his number.

"What's your dance card look like tomorrow?" he asked.

"I'm overdue on some deadlines for a couple *Sundial* posts," she said. "I thought tomorrow might be a good day to catch up on—"

"Cancel your plans." Decker cleared his throat. "I found us someone to interview."

"Who are we interviewing?" she asked.

"In all those articles you've collected about these murders," he said, "there's one name that keeps coming up that we've never looked into."

"Impossible," she said. "I've checked into every single person mentioned."

"This name wasn't mentioned in the articles." He paused for dramatic effect. "This name belongs to the person who *wrote* them."

Jess took a breath. "Olivia Crane."

"Bingo."

Jess struggled with so many thoughts at once she feared she might never get them all written down. Chief among them was disappointment in herself for not thinking of this on her own. She had meticulously listed every single name and location but had never thought to research the writer. She balled her hands and searched the dashboard for somewhere to punch.

"She's lived over in Tucker the past forty years, and she apparently *loves* to talk about the glory days," Decker said. "She said she'll meet us if we agree to buy her lunch. She suggested a steak house, but if you have other plans . . ."

"Shut up, Dan."

She could hear his rusty cackle through the line. She had no idea if she wanted to strangle him or—

"What are you doing tonight?" he asked.

She looked out her car window. "I was about to go to bed."

"All by yourself?"

She rolled her eyes again. "Good night, Dan."

"Good night, kid."

"Hey . . ." She held her breath. She wasn't sure what she wanted to say but knew she didn't want to end the call. "Thanks," she said.

"For what?"

"Just . . . *thanks*."

Jess hung up. She paused a moment to take it all in. She glanced back toward the window and saw the stillness of the Creechville subdivision. The wind rolled over the neatly trimmed lawns and precisely pruned hedgerows. In the distance came the thrum of tree frogs, the call of the whip-poor-will. The papery bark of the river birches trembled in the night. Those tucked securely behind the bars and alarms of the McMansions had no idea what went on outside their windows on that night or any others before it.

CHAPTER TWENTY-TWO

RED CARTER

1972

Red Carter believed he had been given a gift. He often told people that it was recompense for a life spent in service of the Lord. This service was committed on the battlefields in Europe, helping save the world from tyranny and hate, then later within the confines of his home county. In an effort to make his job easier, Jesus Christ himself had bestowed the gift of sight upon the sheriff. Red needed no judge or jury to determine if a man was guilty of the crime under which he was being investigated; all Red needed to do was look into his eyes.

There was no set sequence of facial tics or tells that gave away the culprit. Each man was different. Red needed only to lay eyes upon his visage, and he would know, without a doubt, whether the man deserved handcuffs and a stiff jail sentence.

It helped narrow things down, when needed.

For this reason, he relished the opportunity to travel into Tucker and Whitfill, where they were laying the two kids to rest. For he was certain that if it was as personal as strangulation seemed to suggest, the killer would most likely be in attendance at the services. Red felt it deep within his bones that the type of person who had the audacity to drop two bodies inside his county would also be the same type of person to show his face at one or both of the funerals.

However, Red hated the necessity of it. Not because he despised leaving the confines of his own county, where he'd enjoy the power of jurisdiction, and not because he enjoyed a general distaste for the whole of Lake Castor and its environs. He loathed the fact that he'd stretched the limits of all seven of his deputies—and his wife, to boot—but still had little more than a pile of tips, interviews, and rumors, all of which added up to the same thing: diddly-squat.

The boy was buried first. Half of Tucker turned out to watch their football team's captain laid to rest. He was well loved, and the eulogies were legion, which threatened the congregants' ability to egress in time to travel across the county to Whitfill, where they might attend services for the girl. For that reason, many people skipped his interment, so as to avoid traffic.

In Whitfill, the girl's people had been both modest and Episcopalian, but the services were held at the Baptist chapel, which boasted the largest congregation in town. This was due to the expected size of the crowd of mourners. This was not an inaccurate projection. Red arrived early with his wife, Lois, as well as Big Jim and Cora Ballard, and still they were lucky to find a half-empty pew near the back. He took the empty seat next to his wife, then leaned across her to ask Ballard if he'd seen him yet.

"Who?" Ballard asked.

Red replied, "George Berry."

"Who is that?"

Red couldn't believe his ears. Half the reason they'd decided to attend these services was to put eyes on potential suspects, and George Berry had been at the top of Ballard's own list. He fought the urge to reach over and box the big man's ears, to slap him back into focus.

Instead, he settled into his seat as the organist began the processional hymn "Amazing Grace."

Throughout the service, Red's attention was on the other mourners in attendance. The female victim's family consisted only of a mother and surviving twin sister, and their grief could not be more profoundly different. The mother, frail and racked by sorrow, needed the support of two sturdy relatives to remain upright. The daughter had been drained of all emotion. She stood and sat when appropriate but showed not a single spark of life behind her eyes. It was for her that Red felt the most pity.

Behind them sat the nurses who'd worked alongside the female victim. They were a sea of young faces in white gowns, worn in solidarity for their fallen colleague. Red scanned the doctors who sat among them. The classmates from school and folks who had grown up with the girl. Pew after pew of them, each receiving the discerning eye of the Deeton sheriff, all the way down the aisle to the back of the church, where Margaret Cornwell and her boyfriend sat.

George Berry.

What Red knew about George Berry could fit into his hip pocket. The boy was twenty-eight years old. He'd arrived in Lake Castor four months prior to do work as a lineman for Southern Bell. Two months later, he'd taken up with several girls in the area, including Margaret Cornwell, a nurse at Lake Castor General.

Red sized him up, considered him a rough-and-tumble sort. The kind of boy whom good girls lost their hearts over. He fancied the young man had seen his fair share of trouble but had a smile that would get him out of it each and every time.

"Excuse me a minute," Red said to his wife.

"The services have started," Lois told him. "Don't be rude."

Red shook her off. "I need to get a better look."

Mindful of the neighboring mourners, Red lowered his head and crept to the rear of the chapel. Several other late arrivals gathered near the back, and among them, Red found Lake Castor detective Hank Dorritt. He joined Dorritt, standing in the back.

"Fancy meeting you here," Dorritt quipped at the sheriff.

"It ain't a party till the cops show up," Red whispered back. "Where goes your shadow?"

"Jack stayed behind to see Steven Hicks into the ground with the boy's daddy."

Red shook his head. "You're supposed to keep him from getting too attached. You have to keep his focus fresh."

Dorritt nodded toward the back pew. "I saw you eyeballing George Berry. Y'all turn anything else up on him?"

"Now, now . . . you expect me to play nice. But I heard secondhand that you picked up a couple bikers for questioning on my murder case."

"Those boys weren't nothing worth bothering you about," Dorritt said. "If it had been anything more than a jailhouse snitch trying to wrangle a lesser sentence, then I would have called you first thing. Besides, it's not like you've told us jack. We don't hear about any of these people you haul in until you have them kicked."

Red's mood darkened, and he turned his attentions to the female reporter who covered the case for Lake Castor. Olivia Crane sat in the back row and tried unsuccessfully to ignore the two lawmen. He noticed her pen scratching notes into a yellow legal pad in her lap.

"That woman is vile," Red growled. "She can't even take the time off from her job to pay respects to these dead children."

Dorritt hid a grin. "Oh, what names the pot calls the kettle."

"As much resentment as I harbor for that woman journalist," said Red, "it's nothing compared to how much I'd like to get my hands on the son of a bitch who is leaking information to her. Every time I pick up a newspaper, she's writing something ain't nobody supposed to know about. Please, for the love of a shitting god, tell me it ain't one of yours."

"What the hell could we tell her?" Dorritt asked. "You've told us jack-all. Anything we find out about what you all are doing, we read it in the papers, same as everybody else."

Red hoped Dorritt was speaking the truth. Over the past week, there had been all sorts of tips and leads, each of which would prove fruitless and lead them right back to where they'd started. A biker gang, a serial killer down in Georgia, and even Tim Doody's Satanic-cult theory . . . all of them had been pursued until they could be ruled out, yet Red still bristled when he found Olivia Crane somehow had obtained information that he had specifically ordered to be kept secret.

Red stepped away from their huddle and tried to position himself for a better look at Berry. The boy's face was half-hidden in the ear of his girlfriend, Ms. Cornwell, as he whispered something that made her smile.

"Listen, Red," said Dorritt. "How long has this thing been going on between Deeton and Lake Castor? Do you even know?"

Red watched Berry withdraw from his girlfriend's ear and take in his own surroundings. The smile dissolved from his face as he noticed Big Jim Ballard in the pew across the aisle from him. The boy seemed to study the deputy, as if he were aware of something alien to the rest of the room.

"I don't know either," Dorritt continued. "I got no idea when it started or with who. But I tell you what. I know when it could end: right now."

Berry then turned his eyes to the coffin at the front of the room. Inside lay the young woman whom Red had seen, only days earlier, bound in rope and covered with leaves. The spitting image of her sister, who mourned stone faced in the front pew. Berry appeared to consider all this, and his face slackened. His lips parted. His eyes—

"I'm serious, Red," Dorritt was saying. "You and me could end this thing once and for all. We could put aside our differences by simply—"

Then Red caught Berry's face square. The sum split into each of its parts, and finally the sheriff was allowed to take in them all. He could reckon a young George Berry being hauled home to his parents by police for shoplifting. Or later knocking up a girl, then splitting town. He even conjured Berry cheating his taxes well into frailty. But what Red could not see was that young man tying a rope around the throats of two young lovers and pulling it taut.

"He didn't do it."

Dorritt cocked his head. "Do what?"

"It ain't him," said Red. "George Berry is not our man."

Red made to take his leave. Dorritt stopped him by grabbing his arm.

"The hell you say. I heard you could get—"

Red locked eyes with Dorritt. He didn't look away until the detective let him go.

"Hank," said Red, "if you want to waste your time with George Berry, then be my guest. As far as Deeton County is concerned, he is no longer a suspect in those murders."

"So you won't mind us taking a run at him?" Dorritt asked.

"By all means." Red looked over his shoulder toward the front of the chapel. The preacher had offered the pulpit to one of the female victim's teachers, who struggled to deliver a heartfelt eulogy. "But if you turn anything up, I expect you to keep Big Jim apprised of it."

"About that . . ."

Red didn't like Dorritt's tone. He turned to square up on the detective. "What is it?"

"I really hate to ask you this, but . . . I think it's important."

"Spit it out, then."

"Big Jim . . ." Dorritt shifted his weight from one foot to the other. "Is he all right?"

"Ballard?" Red instinctively looked toward the pew he'd shared with Big Jim and their wives. He was caught off guard by the sight of his most trusted deputy. The man who normally seemed so *together*—for lack of a better word—only now seemed *lost.* Red could not identify the look in his old friend's eye but quickly blinked away the image so that he didn't have to. "You could set your watch by Big Jim Ballard. Why do you ask?"

"It's just . . . maybe I should mind my own business, but . . ." Dorritt shrugged. "I don't know; it's just that lately, Big Jim seems a bit . . . *off.* A little shaky, like maybe he's been hitting the sauce too—"

"For once in your miserable life, Hank," said Red, "you may be right."

"You think so? I didn't want to—"

"Yes." Red turned his back to the detective. "You should absolutely mind your own business."

CHAPTER TWENTY-THREE

Jack Powers

1972

Powers stayed late in Tucker in order to see Steven Hicks into the ground. His intentions were to offer comfort to the boy's father, but Jedidiah Hicks no longer found any solace in the Lake Castor sergeant's presence. Since the bodies had been identified and any hope of finding his son alive had been dashed, the elder Hicks could no longer look Powers in the eye or deign to offer him anything but his back. Still, Powers had remained until the coffin had been lowered.

For that reason, he did not arrive to Linda Harris's funeral until the mourners were filing out the front doors of the church. Not to appear rude, Powers smoked a cigarette in the parking lot beside his car. This was where Lieutenant Dorritt found him.

"It's been a long week," said Dorritt. "Let's grab a drink."

"I don't want a drink."

"That's a sure sign that you better have one. Then maybe another after that."

Powers watched the mourners gather around Linda's mother in front of the church. A hearse was backed to the chapel door. That was where he noticed the twin sister, Lee Ann, lighting a cigarette of her own.

"I'll meet you at Tommy's," Powers said to the lieutenant.

"Jack . . ."

Powers nodded toward where Dorritt had parked his car. Dorritt clearly didn't like it, but he stepped off. Powers crossed the parking lot and approached the twin. He pointed toward her cigarettes.

"You mind?"

She shook her head and gave him a cigarette. He lit it with his own lighter.

"I thought that was a real nice service," he said. "Your sister . . . I think she would have been proud."

Lee Ann shrugged with her eyebrows, then sucked another drag off her cigarette.

"I apologize," he said. "I've never been good with condolences."

"I don't want your condolences," she said.

"I know."

"I want justice."

Powers tracked the mourners quitting the front door of the church and milling toward their cars. He had no plans to join them at the graveside. He'd had enough.

"You got to be strong for your mama," he told the girl. "She's going to need you."

"She's lost plenty, I reckon."

The girl was talking about her own daddy, who'd suffered a heart attack four years ago. Her mother had also lost her daddy and a younger brother in the past five years. The short time he'd spent with the Harrises had revealed nothing but heartache and loss.

"It's different when it's your own child," he said to Lee Ann. "You can add up all the funerals in this world and stack them one by one, but none of that will ever match losing someone you gave birth to."

She considered this a minute, then reached for another cigarette. She started to light it off the remnants of the one she was already smoking, but Powers offered her the lighter. After she got it going, she pitched the other one into a flower bed by the doorway.

"The newspapers say you have no leads," she said.

"Not everything gets reported to the papers."

"They seem to suggest that you are not cooperating with the Deeton County Sheriff's Office."

"They do things their way," Powers said, "and we do things ours. Our way is focused on finding out who did it."

"My hope," she said, "is that pride won't stop anyone from doing what's right by my sister."

Powers lost the taste for his own cigarette. He dropped it to the ground and snuffed it with the toe of his shoe.

"I'm new to this job," he told her. "Do you know what that means?"

She didn't answer with words.

"It means that I won't let anything like jurisdictions or state lines get in the way of bringing Linda's killer to justice. It means I couldn't care less if I ever work another investigation. This one is the only one that matters right now."

Lee Ann blew smoke on the end of the cigarette, causing the cherry to blossom. She watched it until it faded to a dull red glow.

"When you catch him," she asked, "will I be able to speak with him?"

"Why do you ask?"

"I have so many questions."

Powers nodded. "We all do, Lee Ann. I'm going to do everything I can to make sure we get to ask them. I promise."

Powers looked again toward the exodus of mourners. His eye caught a flash of someone in the crowd. He turned to Lee Ann and tipped his hat.

"Be strong for your mama," he repeated. He took his leave and headed briskly down the sidewalk to his car. It took only a few steps to catch up with Olivia Crane.

"Ms. Crane," he said. "Leaving so soon?"

"Skip the horseshit, Jack," said Olivia. "You know what that sheriff said to me?"

"I'm sure he's told me worse."

Olivia reached into her handbag for her pack of cigarettes. She fumbled to loosen one from the pack. Powers took them from her and shook one out for her. He lit it. The first drag seemed to calm her considerably.

"This has been one hell of a week," he said.

"The other night," she said, "do you remember what I told you?"

Powers's cheeks burned hot. The investigations and the funerals had managed to help push it out of his mind, but when he stopped for the smallest of moments, he remembered bits and pieces about *the other night*. He and Dorritt had met with Olivia informally at Honey's, the local twenty-four-hour restaurant just off the highway. Everything had been off the record, and the conversation had continued into the parking lot, where they'd swapped belts from Dorritt's flask. Powers hadn't wanted to go home. Jed Hicks no longer waited for him there, and the loneliness could be suffocating. Was that why he'd woken up at Olivia's house the next morning? Was that why he—

"We said a lot of things," Powers said, shamefaced. "That doesn't mean we—"

"I'm not talking about that," she said. "I'm talking about the profiler."

Powers had no idea and could do little to hide it.

"I told you about a psychiatrist who works for the FBI," she said. "He's done work in the past to help identify suspects involved with investigations which had stalled."

"Is he legitimate?"

Olivia nodded. "I wouldn't have mentioned him if he wasn't."

Over near the church, the hearse was backed up to the door, its motor running, ready to go. Powers watched two men in suits assist Linda's bereaved mother into the back of a town car. The surviving twin quit her cigarette and joined them.

"How does it work?" he asked Olivia.

"You show him the case file," she said. "Everything you can get your hands on. He'll take it from there."

"They'll murder me."

Olivia squinted at him. "Who?"

"The other cops. They hear the word *psychic* and they'll—"

"He's not a psychic," she said. "He's a *profiler.* A psychiatrist who uses modern medicine to detect the identity of the murderer."

"And the FBI uses him?"

"To great success. Do you remember that mad bomber in New York City?"

"Not rea—"

"They couldn't catch him, but this psychiatrist studied his crimes, the crime scenes, the way the bombings were carried out." Olivia had grown excited and needed to catch her breath. "He predicted what part of town their suspect would live in, that he would live with his mother, and what he would be wearing when arrested. It all matched. The investigators claimed his profile was crucial to identifying him."

Powers could imagine Dorritt's reaction. Worse, he could imagine the reaction of Captain Jessup and Sheriff Carter. All of that paled in comparison to his memory of the conversation he'd had with Lee Ann only moments earlier.

"I'm going to do everything I can," he had told her. *"I promise."*

"I'll call him tomorrow."

Olivia cut the distance between them. She took his hand. "Jack . . ."

The warmth from her threatened to break the wall he was using to keep his emotions in check. The funerals, the investigations . . . the frustration of it all. He averted his eyes from her.

"Jack . . ." Olivia took him in her arms. "This has been so hard on you."

She wrapped her arms around him. Put her head into his chest.

"Olive," he said, but he didn't know what else to say.

"You should come home with me again tonight," she told him. "You shouldn't be alone."

That sounded like a good enough idea. He'd come to hate being alone at night. He took her face in his hands and brought his mouth to hers.

When they pulled out of the kiss, he heard a familiar voice behind him.

"Well, well, well." The sick, spreading smile on Red Carter's face was anything but welcoming. "I guess I finally figured out who was in bed with the press."

CHAPTER TWENTY-FOUR

Jess Keeler

Present Day

Olivia Crane refused any comments beyond small talk until she had eaten her meal. That meal was a large rib eye, a baked potato, and broccoli, which she packed into her tiny frame alongside two buttered biscuits. All this was delivered to the table by a fleet of fawning waitresses who fussed over the former newspaperwoman as if she were some type of obscure celebrity.

"Would you care for another glass of sweet tea, Ms. Crane?" asked one waitress.

Another asked, "Can I ask Ron to save you a slice of that bourbon-pecan pie you love?"

Jess had seen Olivia in old photographs dated nearly a half century earlier but would still have been able to pick her out of a lineup. Decades had dulled some of that fire by which she'd become known during her days on the Lake Castor crime desk, but it took only the promise of discussing the Christmas Eve murders for those embers in her eyes to fan back to life.

Throughout lunch, she regaled them with stories of days gone by, of journalistic derring-do. She told a thrilling story of the time she'd stared down the Ku Klux Klan and another of how she'd defied threats from the local motorcycle club. By her recounting, she'd thrown elbows with the good-old-boy network in local media and come out with fewer bruises than they had.

"It was a different day back then." She winked to Jess. "I can't tell yet if your generation of women has it easier or harder than we did."

"One thing's for sure," offered Decker. "There's certainly a lot more of them these days."

Olivia cast him a sour glance. "And there's still no shortage of men like you, from what I can gather."

Olivia continued as such, reliving her glory days until she'd finished every morsel on her plate, dabbed her mouth with the napkin, and then allowed the waitresses to serve her coffee. She took her first sip, then returned the cup to its saucer.

"Okay," she said. "Let's get started."

Jess cleared the table settings in front of her and replaced them with her recording equipment. As she inserted memory cards, batteries, and audio cables, Decker prepared their subject.

"After my colleague gets set up," he told Olivia, "I'm going to ask you a few questions."

"I know how an interview works," Olivia answered.

"Of course you do," Decker said offhandedly. "A few of these questions, however, I may ask again in a slightly different way. That's because this is a podcast, which uses audio, so we will need to—"

"Is he always like this?" Olivia asked Jess.

"The mansplaining?" Jess shrugged. "It's gotten so I tune it out."

Decker launched into it. He did not start with the events of that night but rather probed into biographical material, then the events of her early career. He let her guide them from her days writing home-decor articles for the Sunday edition of her hometown paper in Whitfill all the way to the crime desk for the *Lake Castor Herald*. Jess nearly twisted her stomach to fidgets because Decker barely referred to the notes and questions she had typed up for him, especially since it took nearly an hour of softball questions to warm her up before he finally approached the evening she had met Sergeant Jack Powers.

"It was the night after Christmas," Olivia said. "They had been missing for two days. It was nearly ten o'clock, and I was at the crime desk. There was no one else there, just me, when Hank and Jack showed up and told me they had two missing kids."

"Was it normal to be the only reporter at the desk that late?" Decker asked.

"It was for me. I was the only female writer on staff, and my copy had to be cleaner than everyone else's or else . . . well, you know. What was truly unusual was for the detectives to go to the press that early after two kids missed curfew. But given the good nature of these two kids, it had become more and more unlikely that they had eloped. It was obvious that something bad had happened."

"What was your relationship like with the police?"

"I got on well with Lake Castor," she said. "Especially Jack. And Hank. Even during the early days—those two weeks—when the whole city was looking for them. Probably even more so, after . . ." She took a breath. "After they were found."

"How did that relationship change?" he asked.

"I think Jack recognized how the media could effectively be used to help their investigation. More so than Hank or anyone else at Lake Castor and certainly more than other law enforcement agencies."

"Like Deeton County?"

Olivia rolled her eyes. "Don't get me started."

"Can you give an example of that tension?"

"Did you read my articles about—oh, what was his name—the serial killer?"

Decker's jaw dropped. "Wait. What serial killer?"

"Wendell Lee Peddicord," said Jess. "Captured in Georgia. Tied women to trees."

Decker was flabbergasted. "You knew about this?"

"It's written in my notes." Jess pointed to her Trapper Keeper and the yellow notepad he'd disregarded earlier.

Decker flipped like mad through the pages in the yellow notepad. While he did, Olivia cast a new eye over Jess.

"You've done your research," she said.

"I've read every one of the articles you've written about these murders," Jess said. "In fact, I think I've read every article ever written. Which is easy because there weren't many. That surprised me because it's a good story."

Olivia held her gaze. Dozens of thoughts seemed to crash behind her eyes. None of them would be verbalized because Decker slapped the table and pointed to a page in Jess's notes.

"Here it is," said Decker. "Wendell Lee 'Junior' Peddicord. Serial killer. Caught after tying women to trees and raping them. I thought you said Linda Harris wasn't sexually assaulted."

"She wasn't," Olivia said. "Peddicord would go on to confess to killing those women in Georgia and South Carolina but claim he had nothing to do with what happened to Steve and Linda. His attorneys proved he had a rock-solid alibi for Christmas Eve, but I think the courts in Georgia were happy enough that they got him for their own murders."

"So he was definitively ruled out?" Jess asked.

"He was. Just another one of a great many frustrating red herrings which popped up throughout this investigation."

Jess scribbled notes furiously into her notepad. Olivia watched her for a moment.

"You remind me of us," Olivia told her. "Jack and I would sit up all night and talk about this case. It just consumed us."

Jess cocked an eyebrow. "It sounds like you had developed a good relationship with Sergeant Powers."

"Well, for one," said Olivia, "I married him."

"What?"

Decker arched an eyebrow at Jess. "You didn't already know that? Interesting."

Olivia ignored him. "I did marry him, yes. But it didn't last long."

"Where is he now?" Jess asked her. "I've looked everywhere, and I can't find him."

"We haven't spoken since he remarried—oh, what was that—twenty years ago or so."

Jess nudged her with an elbow. "You don't expect me to believe that you don't know how I can find him, do you?"

"If I looked, I bet I might could dig up an address or a phone number."

Jess turned to Decker and winked. To Olivia, she asked, "What happened to the two of you?"

Olivia stared into her coffee cup as if she might find the answers to the questions asked by the past half century. "This case . . . it's one of those. I'm warning you now. For some people, like Jack, it gets inside of them, and it ruins them for anything else. I've seen it firsthand."

Decker leaned forward. "Is that what happened to Deputy James Ballard?"

Olivia fell silent.

"He was a deputy for Deeton County," he said.

Olivia met his gaze. "I know who Big Jim was."

"Did this case ruin him as well?"

Olivia returned her attention to her coffee cup. "I'm afraid," she said, "his story is not mine to tell."

Jess let out a breath she was unaware she had been holding. She released her grip on the pen and let loose some of the tension in her shoulders.

"Aside from the serial killer," Decker said, "Sergeant Powers must have had other theories. Can you share any of them?"

"I really couldn't remember any names . . ."

Jess leaned forward, elbows on the table. "What about George Berry?"

"Ahh." Olivia turned her head to the ceiling. "I haven't heard that name in a long, long time. Where did you get that? To my knowledge, that name was never released to the press."

Jess covered her grandfather's little green notebook with her hand. "Like you said: I've done my research."

The twinkle in Olivia's eyes indicated that she appreciated the challenge. "I always thought Mr. Berry shouldn't have been ruled out as quickly as they did."

"They ruled him out?" Decker asked. "How?"

"That's just it. They didn't."

"What do you mean?"

Olivia motioned for her coffee cup to be refilled. "Once Red Carter got his sweaty hands on Sean Gray, he wasn't willing to look at any of the other suspects. Me, personally, I never thought—"

"Wait." It was Jess's turn to rifle through her notes. "Who is Sean Gray?"

"I don't remember all the details," Olivia apologized. "I heard it third- or fourth-hand. It was some young man who worked at the hospital and somehow or another popped himself onto Sheriff Carter's radar. I know Deeton County liked him more and more for it but weren't willing to share information with Jack and Hank. Since they still had eyes for George What's-His-Name . . ."

Decker leaned forward in his seat. "Gray was a doctor?"

"No, not a doctor," she said. "He was an orderly or a janitor. Something like that. I'm sorry; my memory these days . . ."

"It's okay." Jess put her hand on Olivia's. "This is great. It really is."

"I wish I could help more," Olivia said. "It's just . . . I did everything I could to put it out of my mind. You'll see . . . this case . . . it's one of those . . ."

"Really," said Jess. "It's okay. It's just . . . we've been hearing talk about a doctor."

"Yes," Olivia said. "So did I. But Sean Gray wasn't a doctor. I don't remember every little detail as well as I used to, but I remember specifically that he did not fit the profile."

Jess cocked her head. "What profile?"

Olivia's eyes went dark. She stared at the coffee cup, which she turned round and round in its saucer.

"Olivia . . . ?"

"So much time has passed . . ." Regret, or something like it, flooded Olivia's face. "For such a long time, there wasn't a day that went by where I didn't think I might have done something. That I could have . . ."

Olivia reached a shaking hand into her purse.

"What do you mean?" Jess asked. "What could you have done?"

Olivia's hand came out with an aged sheet of paper. Jess could see it had been typed with a typewriter. Possibly mimeographed. Jess reached for it to take a better look, but Decker was much quicker.

"What is it?" she asked.

"Jack had reached the end of his rope," Olivia told them. "This was his first case, and I think he was starting to realize that it might never get solved. He would have done anything. I told him about a psychiatrist who specialized in the analysis of murder cases and crime scenes, who could—"

"A *profiler*," said Jess.

"Yes. It wasn't as common back then. In fact—"

"Oh my God . . ." Decker could not peel his eyes away from the sheet of paper.

Jess thought her heart might beat out of her chest. "Dan, what is it?"

Olivia continued: "Jack knew it would never get approved, so he paid for it out of his own pocket. He thought it might give him the edge in narrowing down a suspect. They'd liked to have set him on fire when they found out about it, but he didn't care. He just wanted to catch the guy who did it. He told me to run it in the paper so that everyone would see it and maybe someone might come forward, but I knew that meant they'd come for his badge. So I didn't. They came for it anyway, and I've regretted not publishing it ever since."

Jess could stand the suspense no longer. She snatched the paper from Decker's hand and swallowed the words whole. She couldn't believe her eyes. There, in front of her, was an actual document once held by Sergeant Jack Powers, which detailed the inner workings of the man who'd killed Steve and Linda. Her head spun, and she seemed to be capable of taking it in only piecemeal . . .

The killer will be an athletic man, between 25 and 40 years old. He will be a loner. Neat and precise, with an average or above-average education. He will be clean shaven and have no criminal record. He will not wear flashy clothes.

This killer would have acted alone, would have taken no unnecessary risks, and would have known the neighborhood of the slayings well.

He will have suffered from childhood rejection by his mother and consider himself above other persons capable of judging him. He will be arrogant. He finds people to be an imposition to him and their only purpose is to benefit him. He will be paranoid, "out to cleanse the world." His positioning of the bodies is a way of displaying his cleverness, as if to say, "Look at me. Look at what I have done."

Jess realized after reading it the third time that she had forgotten to breathe. She looked up with what felt like brand-new eyesight and realized Decker and Olivia were still speaking.

"Did Jack have a suspect who he felt fit that profile?" Decker asked.

"He did," she said slowly.

"Can you tell us about him?"

"No," was all she said.

Decker tried it a different way. "Can you tell us what Hank and Jack thought about this unnamed doctor that we keep hearing about?"

"No. I can't."

"Why not?" Jess demanded.

"He never turned up in their investigation," she said. "Not in those early days, anyway. Not before Jack and I had gone our separate ways."

"Why is that?"

"He wouldn't become a suspect. Not until after . . ."

"After what?"

The corners of Olivia's mouth wilted like dying daisies. "Not until after Jack had been kicked off the force."

Jess readied her pen. "Why was he—what happened?"

The waitresses arrived before Olivia could answer. They set steaming slices of bourbon-pecan pie—cooled only by healthy dollops of brown butter ice cream—before each of them, and Olivia's expression shifted from tortured contemplation to sheer, utter joy.

"Oh my . . ." Olivia clapped both hands to her bosom. "Please tell Ron I said thank you, thank you, thank you."

Before she could dig in, Jess stopped her. "Wait," she said. "Tell me what happened to Jack Powers. Why was he kicked off the force? Who took over the investigation when—"

Olivia held up a hand. "Now is not the time."

"It's precisely the time," Jess insisted. "You are the only person who has even acknowledged George Berry to us. Can't you tell us why they stopped investigating him? Can't you tell us wh—"

"No, dear." Olivia motioned to the pie with her eyes. "Not until we've had our pie."

Jess looked to Decker, who had already taken a bite and angled for a second.

"I enjoy things now," said Olivia. She dipped a nutty forkful of unctuous sweets into her softening ice cream, then stabbed it into her mouth. Her eyes closed, and she was transported elsewhere. When the moment passed, she opened her eyes and focused them on Jess. "Back then, when I was your age, I was so hungry. Too hungry, even. But I wasn't smart enough to slow down, or taste food, or enjoy . . . love."

Jess turned her attention to the floor. She felt her cheeks flush hot.

Olivia continued: "It's taken ahold of you. Just like it did with Jack and me. Just like it did with Big Jim. Just like it does with everyone. It's not going to let you go. I watched this case destroy so many people. Lee Ann would kill me for saying this, but I swear Steve and Linda got off easy."

Olivia waited for either of them to comment. When they didn't, she took another bite. She and Decker chewed their pie in silence until eventually, Jess joined them.

"This story isn't done yet," Olivia said to them finally. "Not by a long shot."

CHAPTER TWENTY-FIVE

Jack Powers

1972

"Tell me," Powers asked the young man, "where you were on the night before Christmas."

George Berry rolled his eyes. "Man, I done told y'all twenty times already."

"Tell me again."

"I was with Ellroy Fickle."

"And we told you that Fickle said you weren't." Powers leaned back in his chair and kept both eyes on his suspect. "In fact, Fickle said you told him to back you up. He said you told him no matter how bad we threatened him, he was to stick to the story that you gave him."

"If y'all leaned on him the same way you're trying to lean on me," Berry sneered, "then I bet he'd tell you he wears his grandma's underwear."

"Nobody's leaning on anybody," Powers said. "We play nice up here in Lake Castor. It's nothing compared to what might happen if we sent you down to Deeton, though. Am I right, Big Jim?"

Ballard removed his sport coat and draped it over the back of the empty chair at the table. Despair flooded Berry's eyes at the sight of the big man's imposing frame.

"Why did you kill them?" Ballard asked.

"I told you I didn't kill nobody."

"Was it because she was pretty?" Ballard unbuttoned the cuffs of his sleeves.

"Brother," said Berry, "you better get back from me."

"Was it because she told you no?"

"I swear," Berry pleaded to Powers. "You better get him back."

Ballard slowly stepped closer to him. "Or what, George?"

"Get him back!"

"What are you going to do, George? Tie me to a tree?"

Powers wasn't sure how much of this was an act. He also wasn't sure if he would be able to pull the deputy off the suspect, should things go haywire.

"Jim . . . ," he said.

Ballard ignored him. "I'm afraid I might be a bit more of a handful than a couple of twenty-year-olds might be. But I don't see any reason we shouldn't try."

"Get him away from me!"

"Jim," said Powers, "I got this."

They had gone hard at Berry for the past two hours. Earlier that afternoon, they had snatched Berry from a work crew stringing line off FM 809. Berry had come easily but bucked the moment he'd heard why he'd been rousted. The reaction had seemed genuine. Powers no longer liked him for it, but Ballard had insisted.

"We got nothing concrete to go on," Powers had argued.

Ballard, on the other hand, had motioned with his little green notepad. "I got all I need right here."

Still, as the clock ticked closer to dinnertime, Powers had seen little reason for Ballard's conviction. In order to cool the deputy off, Powers offered a change of pace.

"We all want the same thing here, Mr. Berry," he said.

Berry pointed at Ballard with a shaking finger. "Tell that guy he better stay the hell away from me."

"Jim?" Powers showed his teeth. "He's calm. You're calm, aren't you, Jim?"

Ballard answered with silence and two angry eyes.

"See?" said Powers. "We're all calm, Mr. Berry . . . hey, may I call you George? I'd like it if you called me Jack."

"Whatever."

"Great. George, you like to party, don't you?"

"What?"

"To party. You know, expand your horizons, like."

Berry laughed. "Whatever, man."

"No, I'm serious." Powers kept his tone light and easy. "Lake Castor isn't that big of a town. It's even smaller up at that hospital. Trust me; word gets around."

"Is that right? What kind of *word*?"

"That you and your girlfriend, Margaret Cornwell, know a thing or two about having a good time."

Berry shrugged. "Nurses, man. What can I say? They get bored and like to chatter."

"Oh, come on." Powers scooted the chair closer to the table and leaned forward on his elbows. He used a familiar tone, like maybe they were having a beer in a backyard as opposed to a Q&A in a police station. "Who doesn't like to party? Me? Shoot. I get off work on Friday, and this badge comes off. I ain't a cop again until Monday at seven a.m."

"I bet."

"Cops work hard, but they play even harder. Am I right, Big Jim?"

Ballard still said nothing.

"Case in point." Powers tugged at his necktie like it had grown too tight. "What I'm saying is that nobody's hauling you in for having a good time."

Berry gave in. "So I like to get high. It's 1972, man. That don't mean I killed anybody."

"Of course not. We're not interested in any of that. We don't even care where you get it."

Berry shifted nervously in his seat.

"But while we're on the subject," Powers added, "where did you get it?"

"Fuck off."

"Seriously, George. We're curious."

Berry crossed both his arms.

Ballard stepped closer to the table. "Want me to ask him?"

"I didn't kill that nurse," said Berry.

"We're not talking about her," said Powers. "We're talking ab—"

"I said I didn't kill that fucking nurse!"

Ballard moved in. "What about her boyfriend?"

"Wha—"

"You keep on about how you didn't kill the nurse," Ballard growled, "but what about her boyfriend? Did you have somebody helping you?"

"The fu—man, I didn't kill *nobody*."

Powers felt all the air leaving the room. Berry was miles from where they needed him, and Ballard was chasing him there. "Jim . . . ," he said. "Mr. Ber—*George*, we're not talking about that right now. We're talking ab—"

"Tell him to sit down, man." Berry had shrunk down in his seat. "I got rights. Y'all can't do this. He needs to sit down."

"Jim, please . . ."

The door opened. A cop in uniform filled the doorframe.

"Sergeant Powers," he said.

"Not now," said Powers. "I'm in the mid—"

"You said this was urgent." The cop held up a manila envelope. "You said you wanted to know the minute it arrived."

"Yeah, but—" Powers realized what it was. He was out of his seat in a flash. Before he hit the door, he turned to Ballard. "You cool?"

Ballard didn't take his eyes off the suspect. "Oh," he said, "I'm cool."

Berry's pleas and protests were cut short when Powers slammed the door behind him. He snatched the envelope from the cop's hands and carried it with him into the observation room, where Lieutenant Dorritt watched Berry's interrogation through the one-way mirror.

"I told you that drug angle was getting us nowhere." Dorritt took his feet off the table and killed the intercom's volume. Ballard's questioning in the adjoining room continued without sound. "There's not even a record of any missing drugs from the dispensary. No one has reported anything stolen."

"Just because there's no record . . ."

But Powers's attention was on the file folder inside the manila envelope. He opened it and scanned the pages. His eyes moved so quickly through the material that he caught only every third word, but all his mind kept repeating was *Bingo.*

"I hate to admit it," Dorritt said, "but it's probably nothing more than silly workplace gossip."

Powers continued skimming the pages. He flipped through them, catching bits and pieces, until he found what he was looking for.

The killer will be an athletic man, between 25 and 40 years old. He will be a loner. Neat and precise, with an average or above-average education. He will be clean shaven and have no criminal record. He will not wear flashy clothes.

Powers showed it to Dorritt.

"What the hell is this?" asked the lieutenant.

Powers flipped shut the folder and let Dorritt read the front. "It's a psychological profile of the killer."

"It's a *what*?"

"The FBI uses psychiatrists to analyze the evidence," Powers said. "They look at the case file, then use—"

"I know what the hell an FBI psych profile is, goddammit. What I don't know is why you have one."

"Because I commissioned it."

Dorritt looked like he might explode. "Dammit, Jack . . . I told you specifically *not* to do that."

"I paid for it myself."

"That's not the—" Dorritt stopped. He started again. "Jack, if Captain Jessup finds out about this . . ."

"Why does he have to know?" Powers pointed to the file. "We can't use it in court anyway. All we need is a little guidance. Something that points us in a direction we may or may not be thinking of. And if it points us somewhere and it turns out to be something, we'll run it down. We'll find evidence."

Dorritt still didn't like it.

"We've tried everything else," said Powers. "What can it hurt?"

Powers knew Dorritt was at his wit's end with this case. Over the past week, more-recent investigations had landed on their desks. Someone was shooting Blacks down in the Back Back. A girl had reported a rape out near Barton Wood. Crime in Lake Castor had yet to slow. There had been less movement on this case, and Ballard's insistence on George Berry had given the case its only signs of life.

Still, Dorritt wanted the guy.

"That doesn't sound anything like the guy we have in there," Dorritt said, pointing through the one-way glass at Ballard and Berry.

"Not at all."

"What does this mean?"

The words tasted like filth in Powers's mouth. "It means we're right back where we started."

They watched Ballard pace half moons like a jaguar behind Berry's back. He said things to him that neither detective could hear through the glass.

After a moment, Dorritt said, "Maybe we're not."

Powers waited to hear more.

"What if the reason there is no record of missing drugs," Dorritt said, "is because the records were covered up?"

Dorritt gave Powers plenty of time to add up the math in his head.

"Wait a minute . . ."

Powers was still putting together the pieces, everything clicking suddenly into place, when there came a loud crash from the interrogation room. His focus cleared in time to look through the glass and see something that sent both detectives scrambling.

Ballard had finally snapped his chain.

CHAPTER TWENTY-SIX

James Ballard

1972

Ballard had more than one way to convince a suspect that their best course of action was to confess. He liked Jack Powers but understood as well as anyone that the detective was too early in his career to recognize opportunity. Ballard knew they had Berry on the edge. He also knew there might be no second chances.

GEORGE BERRY IS GUILTY.

NEED PROOF.

GUILTY GUILTY GUILTY.

Underlined, and in his own hand. Ballard could not remember when or why he had written those words, but he could also no longer remember his own birthday. The last time he'd seen his mama. Where she was buried. Ballard racked his brain trying to drum up something that might remind him why he was so convinced of Berry's guilt, but he kept coming up dry. Instead, he told himself if he had bothered to write it down . . .

Then it must be true.

To assume otherwise . . .

Ballard decided to get moving.

"Sergeant Powers is a nice guy," Ballard said.

Berry shifted in his seat. His eyes cut nervously between the mirror on the wall and the door over Ballard's shoulder.

"Despite all that, he's still a good cop. But nice guys don't always get things done." Ballard placed both his palms flat on the table and leaned closer to Berry. "Me? I happen to get things done."

"You're greasing the wrong pole, man." Berry's face lost all color. "I told you over and over that I had nothing to do with what happened to that nurse. *Or* her boyfriend."

"You went to the funeral."

"*Everybody* went to that funeral," Berry insisted. "How many of them did you yank in here?"

"You knew the area well. You knew how easy it would be to get someone down there and how much time you'd have to do with them what you wanted."

"You know how many people know about that little dirt road? Hell, some Friday nights, it's got more cars than a drive-in picture show. You ain't got shit except a hard-on for me, and you know it."

GEORGE BERRY IS GUILTY.

"People saw you down there that night."

"People is lying."

"I say it's *you* who are lying."

Berry threw up his hands. "Eat shit, cop. I ain't lying. Hook me up again to that lie detector thing, and you'll see that I—"

"You already failed it twice, George."

"I didn't fail. Y'all said it was . . . it was—"

"Inconclusive is the same thing as failing, in my book. Those machines can't get to the bottom of all the shit you're trying to hide." Ballard cracked his knuckles. "But I can."

Berry kicked the table. "I ain't trying to hide nothing."

Something tugged at Ballard. He reached for the thought but couldn't grab onto it in time. Before he could chase too far after it, Berry pounded both his fists on the table.

"For real, man. All y'all can go straight to hell. When you pigs ain't got shit on somebody, you try and pin it on them. I read about what y'all did to those kids down in the Back Back. I see the news. And now y'all are trying to put these two murders on me. This shit ain't fair."

That flash again, but this time it was colored red. A switch flipped in Ballard's head. He reached out across the table and grabbed Berry by the head. He pulled that head down with all his might until it slammed on top of the table. Berry cried out, but that served only to further Ballard's anger. He lifted Berry's head and brought it down again.

The doors behind him flew open. Before Ballard could deliver further harm to the suspect, Powers and Dorritt were yanking him free.

"Dammit, Jim!" Dorritt gripped him from beneath his shoulders. It took everything the Lake Castor detective had, and then some, but he finally was wrenched free from Berry. "Jim, what the hell has gotten into you?"

"This son of a bitch killed those two kids," Ballard said through clenched teeth.

"This guy is crazy!" Berry shouted. "He ain't right in the head."

Which only fanned Ballard's flames. He charged the suspect again, but this time Dorritt was ready for him.

"Get him out of here," Powers demanded.

Ballard didn't give up so easy. "Tell me why you did it!"

"Hank, get him the hell out of here!"

Dorritt wrestled the deputy out of the room and into the hallway. Once they were alone, Dorritt pinned him to the wall.

"Take a deep breath, Jim."

Ballard did.

"Now take another."

Ballard did. The world eased back into focus. The fight did not leave him entirely, but it left him enough to quit the weight from his shoulders. The tension in his neck. He found no further use for struggle.

Dorritt let him go. He took a step back and looked up the police station hallway and back down it. "Tell me," he said, "that all was an act for the benefit of our guest."

Ballard said nothing of the sort.

"Come on." Dorritt led him toward the door of the observation room. "Let's put our feet up and watch the kid work."

The observation room pitched them into darkness, save for the light coming through the one-way glass looking into the next room. Dorritt took a seat and motioned for Ballard to do the same. They had a front-row seat and watched as Powers approached Berry easily.

"You good?" Powers asked the young man.

"Am I good?" Berry touched his hand to his forehead and came away with blood. "Did you see what that son of a bitch did? I'm going to hire a lawyer. I'm taking you all to court, man."

Powers handed him a kerchief. "Big Jim comes from the old school, George. You know how those old-timers can get? They're like a dog with a bone sometimes. Me? I can change my mind about a suspect when I get new information."

"What kind of information?"

Powers sat on the table, his leg perched on the edge. "Entertain me: You've been dating Ms. Cornwell a good while, right?"

"Margie?" Berry blinked a couple of times. "Yeah. Whatever."

"And we've already determined that the two of you were known to party."

Berry rolled his eyes and blotted the cut on his head with the kerchief.

Powers continued. "There's always been a rumor floating around the hospital that Linda caught someone stealing drugs. We know that."

"And I told y'all a million times now that we never took no—"

"Maybe you didn't," Powers said. "But maybe you know who did."

"Maybe I *what*?"

"It's a rumor we've heard in a handful of places. So if you and Margaret Cornwell weren't the ones stealing drugs, then who was it?"

Berry shifted his eyes from Powers to the one-way mirror, behind which Ballard leaned forward in his chair.

"Let me help you out," said Powers. "Maybe you've heard tell of some doctor who got his hand caught in the cookie jar."

"A *doctor*?"

It was Ballard's turn for skepticism. He turned to Dorritt.

"Hank," he said, "what the hell is he doing?"

"Shh," said Dorritt.

On the other side of the glass, Powers leaned closer to Berry. "Think, George," he said. "You hang out with a lot of pretty nurses. Those girls spin enough yarn to knit a sweater, don't they? Surely one of them told you something we might like."

Berry's mouth opened half as wide as his eyes.

"Look, son," said Powers. "We know you didn't have anything to do with killing Steve or Linda."

Ballard couldn't stand it. "Hank, what's going on?"

"Just a minute."

"No."

Something in Ballard's expression must have registered with Dorritt, because he muted the sound from the interrogation room. He reached for a file folder left on top of the table and slid it toward Ballard.

"Read it."

"What is it?" Ballard wanted to know.

"Just read it."

Ballard flipped it open to the first page. He flipped to the second. He didn't like anything he read. Something welled up in him so bad it awakened the tremor in his hand. He fought to keep his emotions—

The killer will be an athletic man, between 25 and 40 years old. He will be a loner. Neat and precise, with an average or above-average education. He will be clean shaven and have no criminal record. He will not wear flashy clothes.

—in check, but there was nothing he could do. The words on the paper in front of him ran together, and Ballard could not ascertain whether that was because his eyes had gone screwy or if it was yet another symptom of his cursed diagnosis. Either way, he squinted until he couldn't possibly twist his face any tighter and—

This killer would have acted alone, would have taken no unnecessary risks, and would have known the neighborhood of the slayings well.

He will have suffered from childhood rejection by his mother and consider himself above other persons capable of judging him. He will be arrogant. He finds people to be an imposition to him and their only purpose is to benefit him. He will be paranoid, "out to cleanse the world." His positioning of the bodies is a way of displaying his cleverness, as if to say, "Look at me. Look at what I have done."

—made little progress in stemming the tide of his fury.

"Is this what y'all call police work up here in Lake Castor, Hank?"

"It's a new day, Jim." Dorritt didn't appear to like it much, but they were the cards he had been dealt. "It calls for new methods."

"The old ones ain't let me down yet."

Dorritt retrieved his files before Ballard had a chance to wad them into a ball. "If you got anything else, now is your time to speak. If you have a single thing that tells us Berry is for sure the man, then I'll jump ship and leave my own partner with his silly new-age theories. All we got right now is Berry telling us the same answers to the same questions, and the polygraph does us no favors. If you got something, I'd love to hear it, Jim. Anything."

Ballard did. It was written in large block letters and underlined in his notebook, but he had no idea why he had written it.

"There has to be more done to eliminate him," growled Ballard, "than a look into his eyes or the opinions of a headshrinker. I need to be *satisfied*."

Dorritt shrugged his shoulders. Before he could add anything, Powers opened the door and entered the room. He flipped on the light.

"We've gone up and down every avenue," Powers said. "If we keep him any longer, he's going to want a lawyer. We can't hold him unless we charge him."

"So charge him," said Ballard.

"With what?" Dorritt asked. "Being an asshole? That's still not a crime in Lake Castor, Jim."

Ballard dropped into his chair. To keep still his shaking hand, he crossed both arms over his chest.

Dorritt leaned out the door and told someone, "Find Mr. Berry a ride home, will you please? Thank you." He closed the door and asked his partner, "So what do you propose we do now?"

"We grab a list of every doctor and physician who worked at Lake Castor General," Powers said. "There's something there. I don't know what it is, but we'll find it."

"I don't like it," said Dorritt. "Captain Jessup told us to go easy over at that hospital. He won't like it if he hears we're looking into doctors."

"Why's that?"

"Because doctors have lawyers. *Big* ones."

"If I cared what the captain liked," said Powers, "then I wouldn't have commissioned that psych profile."

Dorritt sighed. He looked to Ballard, whose expression offered him no help.

"What do you say, Jim?" asked Dorritt. "You want to go look into some big shot doctors?"

Ballard wanted nothing more to do with them. He wanted nothing more to do with any of it. He wanted to climb into his truck and drive home so fast he might outrun that damned disease in his head and, in the few moments he had before it caught up to him, hold his wife in his arms one last time. Then he would collect his firearm and a single bullet, walk out into the woods behind his—

"Jim?"

Ballard shook his head. "Knock yourself out, boys," he said. "I think I need some time to collect my thoughts."

For a while after the two detectives left him there in the observation room, Ballard watched Berry through the one-way glass. He focused on that smug expression of his, those pretty-boy eyes. That rugged cynicism that Ballard had seen on the faces of one too many derelict pieces of trash running up and down Red's county roads and finding their way into a world of trouble. Ballard was quickly losing faith in himself, but he was resolute in his convictions. He knew he would never have written those words if he didn't mean them to be true. There was not a single drop of ink spent in those pages on words that had not been thoroughly vetted. The first page—

YOUR NAME IS DEPUTY JAMES W. BALLARD.

—as well as the last.

GEORGE BERRY = GUILTY.

And Ballard knew he should stop at nothing to prove it.

Ballard entered the interrogation room and grabbed his sport coat from the back of the chair. He motioned for Berry to rise.

"Come on, son."

Berry narrowed his eyes. "Where are we going?"

"I'm going to take you for a little ride." Ballard slipped into his sport coat. "I'm going to give you one last opportunity to clear a few things up."

CHAPTER TWENTY-SEVEN

Jess Keeler

Present Day

Jess Keeler was overwhelmed. Two weeks had passed since she and Decker had interviewed Olivia Crane and received the FBI psychiatric profile of the killer, and they had yet to uncover any additional information. Not because it didn't exist but because she'd barely had time to investigate.

Life kept getting in the way.

School had let out for the summer, and Benjamin had suggested he move home until the fall semester. He'd grabbed a job waiting tables at a Lake Castor restaurant, and Jess had fought an uphill battle every day to keep him interested in returning to school. Each afternoon as he woke up and plopped himself down in front of a video game, she felt like a worse and worse parent. To add to the misery, he'd taken up talking to a couple of girls he knew from high school who had never left town or attempted to discover anything of themselves.

Another item on the back burner as of late: her blog. Even during the divorce, she had never gone more than two days without uploading some sort of content to the *Sundial*, even if it was an inspirational meme she'd cribbed off another website. As it stood, her last post had been a recipe for gluten-free, vegan macaroni and "cheese" that she'd uploaded over three weeks prior. Even her Instagram had gone dry.

The dishes stacked up, the laundry was left unfolded, and she had no idea how long it had been since she'd carried the trash to the curb. Still, when she found a spare moment when she didn't have a dozen places to rush to, she dove into her notes from that interview with Olivia Crane. Something she had said nagged at Jess, and she would not be able to let it go until she had researched it exhaustively.

"Once Red Carter got his sweaty hands on Sean Gray, he wasn't willing to look at any of the other suspects . . ."

Jess flipped open her laptop and got to work. She could find no social media presence for a Sean Gray who would have been alive at the time of the murders. A Google search turned up nothing. Her collection of online newspaper archives turned up one article about a man named Sean Gray who had been arrested for stealing a motorcycle outside Raleigh in April of 1972, as well as another one three years later about a man with the same name who had escaped prison. Her search ended when she found that man's 2004 obituary.

"If he died nearly twenty years ago," Jess said to her empty living room, "then there's no way he could have made those phone calls to Lee Ann Thompson."

Furthermore, she had to admit the motorcycle thief in the articles—if he was the same person Olivia claimed was at the top of Sheriff Carter's suspect pool—did not appear to match the FBI psychiatric profile of the killer.

Neither, for that matter, did George Berry.

Certain passages from that profile did seem to favor another possible suspect in their pool: doctors. If the profiler believed the killer to have an "average or above-average education," to display arrogance, and to consider himself "above other persons capable of judging him," then

Jess deduced it would more likely fit the description of a physician than a motorcycle thief or a lineman for the phone company.

With that in mind, she opened the files on her laptop that she had compiled on the doctors working at Lake Castor General in 1971. There were four physicians still living. One of them was a neurosurgeon who had been retired for over a decade. Another surgeon had left medicine for academia, and an obstetrician had been in palliative care following a severe bout with cancer. The last one, an internist named Dr. Christian Alexander Dean, was still seeing patients at an office in Lake Castor, not far from the hospital. He didn't have a website, but his phone number was listed. Jess dialed, and her heart nearly leaped into her throat when someone picked up.

"Dr. Dean's office," said a woman through the line. "How may I—"

"Mom?"

Jess snapped shut her phone. She turned around to find her son, Benjamin, standing in the kitchen doorway. The look on his face . . .

"What is it, Benny?"

He held out his own phone. "It's Grandma," he said. "I think something is wrong."

Midafternoon found Jess Keeler sitting with Benjamin in a waiting room at Lake Castor General, where she'd been stationed for nearly an hour and a half. All she'd been told was that her mother had become disoriented while working her volunteer job at the church and that she was stable. Still, Jess might have twisted herself to fits waiting to hear what was wrong, so she and her son kept themselves busy. While Benjamin scrolled listlessly through games on his phone, Jess walked the halls and tried to imagine how different they must have looked fifty years earlier.

She didn't have to imagine for long. Down one corridor, she stumbled upon a series of framed portraits that detailed the evolution of the hospital throughout the years. Each year was chronicled with a photograph of the staff of physicians and nurses posing at the front of the hospital. Jess walked the hallway until she came upon 1971. There she could clearly see Linda Harris standing among her coworkers.

She could also see the doctors.

Jess consulted the files she'd compiled on her laptop. She'd included whatever available photographs she could find of the four living doctors. She compared those against the portrait on the wall. It didn't take long for her to identify them all, including Christian Dean, the doctor she had attempted to call earlier that day.

Something about him tugged at her mind.

The killer will be an athletic man, between 25 and 40 years old . . .

Jess stepped closer to the photograph. She leaned in to better see his eyes.

Neat and precise . . . he will be clean shaven . . .

Jess pulled her phone from her pocket and dialed. Decker answered on the fourth ring.

"Dan," she said, "I need you to help me get the hospital to release personnel records on four doctors."

"They're not likely to do that, toots."

"You're Dan Decker," she reminded him. "You don't take no for an answer."

"I'll make some phone calls, but no promises."

"Thank you."

"Since when are you interested in a doctor? I thought you were all-in on George Berry."

Jess's shoulders slumped. "I'm starting to think George Berry may be a ghost. But if there's any truth to the rumors that the killer may have been a doctor, then it wouldn't be a bad idea to try and get them on tape. There's one named Christian Dean who is still practicing, and he—"

"Wait a minute," Decker said. "Where do I know that name?"

"He's one of the four doctors who are still alive from—"

"No . . . I've heard that name before."

A physician's assistant in purple scrubs appeared at her side. He placed a gentle hand on Jess's shoulder.

"Ms. Keeler," he said.

"Yes? I'm Jess Keeler."

The PA smiled warmly. "The doctor would like to have a word with you about your mother."

Jess disengaged the call without a goodbye to Decker. She returned to the lobby and instructed Benjamin to stay in his seat, then hurried after the nurse to the examination room where they'd kept her mother. As she neared the door, she realized she couldn't imagine living without her. Suddenly, every argument and cross word they'd suffered since she was a child—Jess abandoning the cheerleading squad for journalism classes, Jess dropping out of school to have a child and marry Philip, her mother's inability to communicate—felt so inconsequential. She wanted to rush headlong into her mother's arms and apologize for all of it and pray against all hope that it wasn't too late.

"Mom," Jess said as she entered the examination room. "Are you okay?"

Samantha Bowen had recently dressed but still sat upright and rigid on the exam table. She smiled as perfunctorily as she could.

"I'm fine, sweetie," she said. "It's nothing."

"They said they found you panicked at the church. They said you didn't know where you were. They said you—"

"It's okay." Samantha took her daughter into her arms. "I've just been a bit overworked. I haven't been getting the rest I usually get."

Jess pulled free of her mother's embrace and inspected her. "Did you call Kirk?" she asked.

"Who?"

"Your husband, Mom."

Samantha shook it off. "I'm not married."

"Your *ex*-husband. Did you call him?"

"No. And I'm not going to. This is none of his business."

"None of his—" Jess turned her eyes to the ceiling and bit down on her tongue. "What about Dad? Did you call Dad?"

"Jessica," said her mother, "I'm fine."

The door opened, and the doctor entered. He was a fussy man who obviously had other things on his agenda that afternoon. Still, he pulled up a chair and faced the two women.

"We've got the test results back," he said. "There are obviously a few things that concern us."

"What kind of things?" Jess asked.

"I'd like to run some more tests before we commit to anything."

"That's not going to work, Doctor." Jess stood firm. "My mother was found disoriented. She's never been like that in her life."

The doctor arched his eyebrows and cut a glance toward Samantha. Jess had no idea what that look meant until she heard her mother say sheepishly behind her: "Actually . . ."

Jess spun to face her. "Mom?"

Samantha held eye contact. "It comes and goes," she said. "It's not like it's anything permanent. Looking back, it started as something small. I'd walk into a room, then forget what I was going in there for. Once I started a pot for some pasta, then forgot about it until the water boiled out and blackened up the bottom of my pan. Another time . . ." Her voice trailed away.

"What are you telling me, Mom?" Jess turned to the doctor. "What is she telling me?"

"Like I said." The doctor shielded himself with the clipboard. "I'd like to do some more testing."

"Testing for what?" Jess felt like she might jump through her own skin. "You've got some kind of idea what's going on here, Doctor. What is it? Cancer? Something worse?" Jess couldn't breathe. "Oh my God, what's worse than cancer?"

"I'd like to test her for Alzheimer's."

The air was sucked out of the room. Jess looked around her for a seat and, not finding one, supported herself by leaning against the wall. She looked at her mother and swore she'd never seen her before.

"Alzheimer's?"

The doctor met her gaze. "I won't know anything without some more cognitive testing, but an early indicator would be genealogical."

"What does that mean?"

"It means that oftentimes, it's hereditary." The doctor turned to Samantha. "Did either of your parents suffer from dementia, to your knowledge?"

Samantha reacted like she'd grabbed a live wire. "No," she said. "My mother was fit as a fiddle until she died a couple of years ago."

"And your father?"

"My father was a—" Her face darkened. "He was a drunk."

Jess's jaw dropped. "He was?"

"Yes," said Samantha. "A horrible one."

"In his later years," the doctor said very carefully, "when he was your age . . . did you happen to notice any—"

"He didn't live to my age." Samantha searched like mad for something to do with her hands. She glanced nervously toward her daughter, then back at the doctor. "He died very young."

Jess felt an electricity pass through her. She had never, in all her life, heard her mother say as much about her grandfather. She despised the circumstances but still reveled in the opportunity. She thought also about the notebook, which threatened to burn a hole in the pocket of her blue jeans.

"How did he die?" asked the doctor.

"He was a policeman," said Samantha in a near whisper. "He was killed in the line of duty."

◆ ◆ ◆

Jess felt like the weight of the entire world had settled upon her shoulders as she walked her mother out of the clinic. Benjamin trailed behind, his eyes still pasted to the screen of his phone. No one said a word until they reached the car, and Jess held open the door for her son.

Jess paused. "Mom . . ."

"Not now," said her mother.

"Mom . . ."

Samantha hushed her daughter and cut eyes toward Benjamin, as if to warn her about touchy subjects in front of her own son.

Jess, on the other hand, wasn't having it. Gently, at first, she urged Benjamin toward the back seat. Less gently when he initially resisted. Once he was inside the car and she'd closed the door behind him, she blocked her mother's access to the passenger seat.

"Right now," Jess told her mother. "We need to talk."

"Can't this wait, Jessica? I've had a hell of a day."

"We've waited my entire life. I want you to finally tell me about my gra—your *father*."

"I told you time and again to leave that story alone."

"It's not just the story." Jess steeled herself. "And I'm not going to, Mother. So you might as well tell me."

"No. It's not your business, and it's not the business of whatever audience you're selling yourself to. It's *mine*."

"I'm going to find out anyway. Wouldn't you rather be the one to tell me?"

Samantha gave in. As she exhaled, her entire body slouched, as if whatever had been holding her up for so long had finally given out. She shielded her eyes with her hand, not so much from the sun but perhaps from her daughter.

"My father . . ." Samantha weighed each word carefully before she spoke it. "He was such a good man. He cared so much for my mother and me. And then . . ."

"What?"

"When they found those two kids in Deeton . . . he changed. That case . . . it destroyed him. I don't know if it was inside him that entire time and it didn't come out until . . . I don't know anything except he grew bitter and angry, and the only way he could deal with his rage was to drink and drink and—Jessica, what the hell are you doing?"

Almost as if by instinct, Jess had reached inside her purse for her recorder. Immediate shame coursed through her veins, leaving her numb and unable to speak or move, save for her eyes, which turned instantly upward in time to see the disappointment in her mother's face.

"Dammit, Jessica . . ."

Jess dropped the recorder back into her bag. "Mom . . . please. I need you to—"

"I can't stop you from writing about those damn murders." Samantha's voice took on an edge that could have cut glass. "I will, however, insist that you not write about my father."

"Mom, he was the lead investigator on the case. I can't just—"

"I'm *begging* you."

Jess threw up her hands. "Why, Mom? What are you afraid of me uncovering if I start digging into James Ballard?"

Samantha recoiled, as if she'd been struck. She drew a hand to her mouth, then seemed to think better of it. Instead, she dropped both hands to her sides and steadied herself.

"I need you to promise me," she said.

Jess squared her shoulders. "Promise you what?"

"That you won't write about my father."

Jess shook her head. "I can't do that, Mom. I've committed to this story. I've committed myself to seeing it through."

Samantha turned her head to look into the back window at Benjamin. She smiled tightly and waved. She turned back to Jess, and there wasn't the slightest trace of that smile.

"If those doctors are right," she said, "I don't know how many memories I am going to have left."

"Mom. I don't think that—"

Samantha waved her off. "I don't want the last ones I have with you to be of more disappointment."

CHAPTER TWENTY-EIGHT

Dan Decker

Present Day

Dan Decker racked his brain for a good half hour, wondering where he remembered that name from.

Christian Dean . . . Christian Dean . . . Christian Dean . . . Dr. Christ—

When it came, it hit him like a Buick. He raced into his kitchen, to the counter where—beneath an old pizza box and several moldering Chinese-food containers—he found the notes he'd compiled on the Lake Castor Christmas Eve Murders. Past the Google image searches of the crime scene, beyond the photocopies of James Ballard's notebooks lit up by Jess's scribbled notes in the margins. Rifling through them all until he came to the list of tenants at the Shady Village Trailer Court in 1971.

Down the list.

Beeler.

Byrum.

Clarksdale.

Dean.

There it was.

Dean, Christian. Unit 114.

Decker cross-referenced that with a couple of quick taps on his laptop to find that Dean formerly owned property in a subdivision bordering the cul-de-sac off Creechville where the two victims had been abducted on Christmas Eve, 1971.

His first thought was that property cost a pretty penny. His second was to wonder why someone with such an expensive home would also be renting a trailer off Gilmore Road. His third was that this little piece of information gave Dr. Dean access and provided proximity to both crime scenes.

Decker licked his lips.

Next, he made a phone call.

No sooner had Decker ordered drinks than he saw Fletcher Stallings had entered the room. For years, the rival network chief had tried to lure Decker away from Channel 10. Decker had never once considered it.

Times had changed.

Fletcher was already shaking his head long before he arrived at their table. "I'm sorry, Dan," he said, "but I can't stay. Between the new ballpark and that shooting over in Tuck—"

"Sit down and eat, Fletch." Decker pulled out a chair. "This joint makes a mean poke bowl. Those pork meatballs get great rev—"

"No time, Dan."

"How about a drink? One drink?"

"I can't. I only agreed to this meeting bec—"

The drinks arrived.

"Rye Manhattan with two cherries." Decker grinned. "Like old times."

"Fine." Fletcher took his seat. He didn't remove his jacket. "One drink."

Decker asked the waitress to give them a minute. He watched after her a moment before shaking his head.

"Back in the day," he said, "you and I would have worn her like a suit."

Fletcher closed his eyes. "Dammit, Dan. Will you never learn?"

"I've learned plenty. Hell, I've had all the time in the world to learn. It's all I do anymore: look inward and *learn*."

"Is that right? What have you learned?"

"That I belong on television."

Fletcher killed half his cocktail in a single swallow. "Dan . . ."

"Hear me out," Decker said quickly. "I've got this story . . ."

A text buzzed his phone. Decker could see clearly it was from Jess. It read, Dan can you call me? I need to talk. He turned over the phone on the table.

"This story," Decker said, "it's real juicy. It's a cold case, and it happened right here in Lake Castor. Fifty years ago. They called it the Lake Castor Christmas Eve Murders, and it was all anyone ever talked about. It's virgin territory, Fletch."

"A cold case, Dan?" Fletcher's face balanced amusement and disappointment. "You can't be serious."

Decker fought the urge to drain his drink and took it instead in sips. "I'm more than serious," he said. "This is it. You remember how we've always talked about landing that big one? How we always said we wished we had our own *In Cold Blood* but for the new age?"

"Sure, but—"

"I've found it."

"Oh? For whom?"

"That's the beautiful thing, Fletch. I'm not working for anyone. This one is all me."

"You're working alone?"

"All alone." Decker swallowed. "I'm doing this for us."

"For us?"

"Yes sir. For your network. You always said if you had someone like me, we would outscore every other news net—"

Decker's phone rang. Before he could turn off the ringer, he saw it was Jess calling. He silenced the phone and set it back on the table.

"Dan, I'd love to help," said Fletcher. "And who knows—maybe one day I can. But right now the entire world has signaled a change in culture, and while no one's virtues are lily white, the public expects their institutions to be—"

"I haven't told you the best part."

Fletcher held his glass to his lips but did not drink.

"The lead suspect," Decker said, "is a doctor."

Fletcher's expression didn't change. He drained his drink and set the empty glass on the table. He reached into his pocket for his wallet.

"A *doctor*, Fletch," said Decker. "That's a pretty big fish. From what I'm to understand, it was pretty common knowledge that he was involved, and it appears the medical community might be covering for—"

"Lake Castor General?"

"That's right."

"You know they are an advertising partner, don't you?"

"Yeah, but Fletch—"

Fletcher sighed. "Dan, I'm going to do you a favor. Cold cases aren't our bailiwick. That's fuel for monthly-subscription streaming services, not major news networks. What's a big story these days is institutional corruption. What I wouldn't give for a dirty cop or some homegrown racism right now, because that's where the market share is at. Not digging up dirt on a couple of kids where the only remarkable thing about them is their death and the fact that nobody cared enough to solve it fifty years ago."

"You want institutional corruption?" Decker talked fast. "That's the tip of the iceberg with this thing. There's something going on with the lead detective back in '72. The sheriff back then was some Buford Pusser type who threatened reporters, and I'd bet everything I own that—"

Again, his phone buzzed. Decker snatched it and slipped it into his pocket.

"Do you need to get that?" Fletch asked.

"No sir. That's actually my partner on this story. I can—"

"Your *partner*?"

"More like an intern."

Fletcher rolled his eyes. "What's her name?"

"Ha ha. It's not like that, Fletch. She's actually—"

"Let me guess: Brunette? Legs? How much younger is she, Dan?"

"She's actually not all that young. This is more of a—"

"Dammit, Dan." Fletch rose from his seat. He motioned for the hostess to summon the valet. "You used to have it all. Do you realize that? You were beautiful. You had the wife, the career, the trust of a three-point-five-million market share . . . you pissed it all away, and for what? A piece of tail."

"Fletch, if it's a problem, I can take her off the story. I don't need her—"

"Maybe you're right and there is hope for a comeback, but let me tell you, Dan: Maybe you ought to stay out of the public eye for a while. Lay low. Take a sabbatical. Hell, teach a class. Get your shit together."

Fletcher took his leave. Decker stayed behind and ordered another drink. While he waited for it, he slumped in his chair and thought about how many more opportunities he might have in life.

He reached for his phone.

Jess had left several texts, two missed calls, and a voice mail. Rather than fuss with any of it, he dialed her number.

"Hey, kid," he said after she answered. "Sorry I missed your calls, but I was in the middle of a very important meeting about our story. I've had a thought and you—"

"Dan . . ." She sounded like she had been crying. "I need to talk to someone, and I don't think I have anyone else."

"What is it, kid?"

"It's my mother . . ." She choked back a sob. "Dan . . ."

Decker sighed. He glanced at the door, the direction in which Fletcher had disappeared. He'd be long gone, Decker thought. So would everyone else.

"I'm here, kid," he said into the phone. "How about I pick you up and you tell me all about it over coffee?"

CHAPTER TWENTY-NINE

Jack Powers

1972

By mid-April, Sergeant Jack Powers had yet to give up. Despite taking additional cases that came his way through Lake Castor's Crimes Against Persons division, he still ate, drank, and slept with his mind on the double homicide of Linda Harris and Steven Hicks. He still took the phone calls from Jed Hicks, even though they came less frequently. He still devoted every minute of his ever-dwindling free time to running down every single doctor who'd ever worked at Lake Castor General during Linda Harris's time there and systematically eliminating them from his list.

It took time.

He thanked the stars that he didn't have to do it alone.

While Lieutenant Dorritt's interest in the case had waned considerably, Powers had found the perfect confidant in Olivia Crane, the crime beat reporter for the *Lake Castor Herald*. The two of them took solace by meeting after their shifts had ended at Powers's apartment or in booths tucked away at coffee shops and diners or, as they did that night, at the offices at the *Herald*.

They had met there many times and enjoyed the silence left behind after the other journalists had quit for the day. Cigarette smoke still lingered in the air, and both Powers and Olivia added to it with their own, chain-smoked and washed down with a bottle and a million different ideas about how next to proceed. Their movements had become routine: first they picked a doctor's name from the list, then they would research that name in the many databases provided by the newspaper, and then the name would be crossed off.

There were many more names to go.

They were in the middle of one such investigation—

"I've got a Culton Yarborough here, says he was a gynecologist at the time of the murders. What have we got on him?"

"I've got an article that mentions he was detained for driving while intoxicated, but I can find no record of it with the department."

"Those doctors, man . . . they got reach. They can cover up anything."

—when they were snapped out of it by Dorritt's sudden appearance. He knocked before entering the office, then entered slowly.

"I had a feeling if I couldn't find you at the Metro Diner," said Dorritt, "that I'd likely find you here. You got any cigarettes left, or did you smoke them all?"

Powers offered him the pack, then lit one for him. "You ever heard anything on a doctor at LCG named Yarborough? Says he was a gyne—"

"I just got off the horn with Captain Jessup," Dorritt said. "He wants to know where we're at with that shooting down in the Back Back."

"It's a shooting," said Powers. "It happened down in the Back Back. There's been a dozen of them this year. It's what happens down in the Back Back. It's hardly news."

"That's right," Dorritt said through clenched teeth. "It's not *news*. It's our *job*. If you spent half the time on that shooting or the one that came before it or, hell, even the ones yet to come as you do on these two dead kids—"

"It's my personal time. I'm off the clock."

"My point exactly."

Powers relaxed his shoulders. "Listen, Hank—"

"I don't want to listen," snapped Dorritt. "I want *you* to listen."

"No, Hank . . . hear me out."

Dorritt closed his eyes. "You have ten seconds."

"Olivia has the phone number for this guy. He *intuits* things."

"Intuits? You mean a psychic?"

"Not a psychic," Olivia said. "He's a *medium*—"

Dorritt still wasn't buying it. "A fucking *psychic*?"

"It's a medium, Hank," said Powers. "Investigators in plenty of other jurisdictions use them all the time when they hit dead ends."

"Where did you hear that? The funny pages?" Dorritt had had enough. "Okay, that's it. It's over."

"Hank, I—"

Dorritt didn't listen. He grabbed his hat and started for the door. "No," he said, "it's over. All of it. I'm pulling the plug."

"Hank—"

"I'm going to Jessup and telling him to shelve it. It's been four months. It's gone cold."

Powers squeezed between Dorritt and the door, blocking his exit. "Hank, listen," Powers pleaded. "I'm close. I can feel it. Two more weeks."

"No."

"Two more *days*, then."

Dorritt tried and failed to sidestep the sergeant.

"What are we supposed to tell his daddy, Hank? What do we tell Elizabeth Harris? What about Linda's sister?"

"You don't tell them anything." Dorritt jabbed another cigarette into his mouth and lit it. He blew smoke over Powers's shoulder. "I told you, goddammit, not to make that promise. *Never make that promise.* Right now, you and me have cases backed up. My wife hasn't seen me for longer than fifteen minutes since those two went missing. My kids . . ." Dorritt took another drag. "It's not healthy, Jack. You can't make every case personal. You have to learn to let them go."

"I'm not like you, Hank. I'll never be—"

"Let it *go*."

Dorritt turned to Olivia. "And you should be ashamed letting him get like this. You say you love him?"

Olivia didn't blink. "I do love him."

"Then you should know better."

This time, when Dorritt made for the door, Powers stepped out of his way. The lieutenant had been gone all of fifteen seconds when Powers snatched a stapler off a desk and launched it at the door.

"Don't you talk to her like that!" he hollered in the direction of Dorritt's departure.

Olivia inched toward him. She put her hands on his shoulders. "Jack . . ."

"He knows better than to talk to you like that."

"Jack . . ." Olivia turned him to face her. "Jack, he's right."

"I'm not going to stop."

"Jack . . . Jack . . ." She gently stroked his hair. "Shh."

"I'm not going to quit."

Olivia kissed him. Soft at first. "Jack . . . shh."

"I won't be like them," Powers said. "I won't turn so . . ." She kissed him again. "So . . . *cynical*."

She kissed him again but this time refused to let him stop her. She kissed him harder. Desire flooded into him, and he found his hands rising from the desk to take her by her hips. His mouth covered hers. The taste of her threatened a frenzy. He pulled her tighter by the hips, then let his hands reach higher up her back. The back of her neck. She was soft in his arms and had completely given herself over to him. *How nice,* he thought, *it must be to want nothing more than another human to love. To be able to think of nothing else but what you can do for each other.*

Did Steve and Linda find that?

Powers shook off the thought as he pressed himself closer to Olivia. He turned her around so he could better position her on the desk. He wanted her. He parted her legs and pressed himself between them. His mouth drew away from hers, then hungrily canvassed her neck, his tongue tracing the contours of her throat while his fingers danced along the buttons of her blouse.

What kind of man would strangle a woman?

Powers tried to drown it out by pulling back her collar to better access her body, but it would not go away.

What kind of man would—

"That's it," he said.

Olivia tried to catch her breath. "What?"

"The psych profile."

Olivia blinked once. She blinked again.

"What?"

Powers pulled away from her. "We need to release it to the public."

"Jack . . ."

Powers turned his back on her and rifled through the pages on her desk. After a brief shuffling, Powers found the folder containing the psychological profile of their killer. He turned and held it high for Olivia to see.

"Someone out there knows this man." He tapped the folder with his finger. "Someone knows him, and we aren't going to be able to find them. We need them to come and find *us*."

Olivia reached for the pint bottle of whiskey they had been sharing and drained it in a single swallow.

"What do you say, Olive?" he asked her. "Can you run it tomorrow?"

"Not on your life, Jack."

His face blanched. "What do you mean? Olive, this would mean a hot headline."

"It would mean your badge." Olivia crossed her arms. "I'm not doing it."

"If I don't pull every damned string to catch this guy," Powers growled, "then what the hell is the point of that stupid badge?"

Powers pocketed his cigarettes. He grabbed his car keys.

"Jack, where are you going?"

He ignored her. He stepped out of the office and didn't stop until he was outside the *Herald* building. It was nearly midnight, and the hum of the Lake Castor streets had dimmed to nothing. Overhead, the tall buildings rose. On the horizon loomed the silhouette of the mill building. Beyond that, the hospital.

Jack knew if he was going to bring this home, he would have to do it alone.

"I promise," he said to the night, "that I will stop at nothing."

CHAPTER THIRTY

Jess Keeler

Present Day

It didn't take long for Decker to lull the woman into a false sense of security. Barbara McCullough had worked as a nurse throughout the COVID-19 pandemic and was used to reporters and journalists asking about her experiences. She was skeptical, but Decker's killer charm kicked the door wide open. After a half-dozen phone calls from both him and Jess, the former nurse finally relented and agreed to meet them at the All-Niter.

Barbara's life became an open book. Decker asked her about growing up in the Appalachian hills and what it meant to be the first person from her family to attend college. She discussed her rigorous training in nursing school and some of the things she had done with her classmates to blow off steam. She brought up experiences with COVID-19 and some of the more well-known luminaries in the medical community whom she had met.

Decker rested his chin in the palms of his hands. "Do you mind if I ask you about some more of your coworkers from when you started working at Lake Castor General in 1971?"

"I don't see why not," she said.

"Do you remember an orderly named Sean Gray?"

She furrowed her brow and seemed to think on it a minute. "The name doesn't sound familiar . . ."

Jess dug through her notes in her Trapper Keeper until she found a photograph from a newspaper article that covered Gray's motorcycle-theft arrest. "This was a picture of him back when y'all worked together."

Barbara studied it. A small light went off behind her eyes. "Oh yes," she said. "I vaguely recall him. If I remember correctly, he was fired."

"Can you remember why?" Decker asked.

"I think he made a few of the nurses uncomfortable. He had a way about him. It could . . ." Her memory trailed off a moment; then she blinked it away. "I can't imagine why you'd be interested in an orderly, however."

"We're interested in several different people," Decker said, with a smile. "For instance, there was a doctor here during your first few years. His name was Dr. Christian Dean. Did you ever have the opportunity to work with him?"

Jess noted that the name triggered an immediate reaction. Barbara was *startled*.

"Of course," Barbara said. "Dr. Dean is a . . . he's one of the foremost . . ." Her eyes danced across every surface in the coffee shop but could not settle on a single thing. "He's kind of a . . . he has sort of a—I'm sorry, but what does Dr. Dean have to do with your story?"

Her reaction was similar to those of the other medical professionals they had wrangled for interviews over the past several weeks. Doctors, nurses, physician's assistants, administrators . . . all of them had reluctantly agreed to interview with them, but their demeanors had darkened when the topic had turned to Dr. Christian Dean. The emotions exhibited by their interview subjects ranged from anger to resentment to outright *fear*.

Since they had narrowed their focus on Dean, Jess and Decker had gone hard on investigating him. There was not a wealth of information about him, but mountains were available in comparison to Sean Gray and George Berry. He had attended medical school at the University of North Carolina. He was discharged from the army after serving three years as a doctor, although sealed records prevented them from finding out why. He'd joined the staff at LCG in the late sixties and did not seem to be well regarded by anyone who'd worked alongside him.

In fact, everyone who had been interviewed tended to shut down the conversation whenever his name was brought up. Including Ms. Barbara McCullough.

"This is a very small community," Barbara apologized. "You don't understand what it's like."

Decker's voice was soft. "Why don't you tell us?"

"Doctors . . . in many people's minds, they are one rung below God. Some of them think they can get away with anything. Oftentimes, they do."

"Like what?"

Barbara looked over both her shoulders, as if someone else might be listening. "Dr. Dean, he . . . he's kind of . . ." She collected herself. "Let's just say he has a bit of a temper."

"How so?"

She sighed, as if unsure how to proceed. "Surely you've heard about that little incident in the parking garage?"

Jess leaned across the table. "No," she said. "What happened in the parking garage?"

"I really don't think I should . . ."

"It's okay." Decker's boyish grin took over. "We don't have to talk about anything you don't want to talk about. But tell us what happened in the parking garage."

Barbara bit her lower lip. "It's not like it's not common knowledge around here anyway. But there was a woman . . . what was her name?

Anyway, she pulled into a parking spot, and Dr. Dean said it belonged to him. I don't know all the ins and outs, but I know he grew angry about the whole thing and . . . well, there's no other way to say it, but he attacked her."

Jess raised her eyebrows. "He *attacked* her? Like, physically?"

"There's all kinds of disagreement on what actually happened," Barbara said, "but I am the one who treated her in the ED after. I'll tell you, she had been battered. She told me . . ." Again, Barbara checked to make sure no one else in the All-Niter was paying attention. "She said Dr. Dean knocked her to the ground, removed his shoe, and struck her several times in the face with it."

Jess didn't know what to say. Her chest constricted, and she found it difficult to breathe. She could tell by the expression on Decker's face that he was equally as confounded.

"We've researched Christian Dean," Decker said, "but never found anything about this incident. Why wouldn't this have been reported in the local news?"

"The hospital . . ." Again, Barbara appeared uncomfortable. "They like to handle things in house, if they can."

"You're saying that hospital administration covered up an assault by one of their own physicians?"

Barbara's eyes hit the floor. Her face blanched. "I'm afraid I may have said too much . . . I appreciate you taking an interest in my work, but . . ."

Jess could hold back no longer. "Ms. McCullough," she said, "are you familiar with the 1971 murders of a nurse named Linda Harris who worked at Lake Castor and her boyfriend, Steven Hicks?"

"I really shouldn't be talking to you."

"We have reason to believe that—"

"I have nothing more to add."

◆ ◆ ◆

After the nurse had left, Jess could hardly contain herself. "Did you see the way she reacted when you mentioned his name?" She drained the last of her cold coffee from the cup. "Or how about what she said about the hospital covering for Dean?"

Decker appeared lost in thought. He stared out the window in the direction in which the nurse had departed.

Jess kept at it. "We've got to find a way to get ahold of his disciplinary record. Every time I've tried to crack that egg, I keep getting shut down. Same as his military records. There's something there, and we're getting close. I can *feel* it."

"We need more than a feeling, kid."

"What we need is information on that assault in the parking garage." Jess glanced around the room for the waitress. "First thing we need to do is find out the name of the victim. If we could get her to tell her story on tape, the audio would be damning."

Decker shrugged. "It's no surprise that hospital administrations cover for the bad behavior of doctors. It's still a far cry from murder."

"Sure. But every time we scratch a little bit of the surface, there's more and more that makes Dean look like a fitting suspect. The fact that he's still alive to call Lee Ann Thompson on the anniversary of the murders, combined with the insight from the FBI profile, as well as the way he is regarded by his colleagues and anyone who knew him. Your revelation that he'd rented a trailer near the crime scene back in the sev—"

"None of this proves he killed two kids."

"But it paints a clearer picture of a reasonable suspect. A better one, at least, than we have with Sean Gray, who's not alive to make any phone calls, or George Berry, who doesn't seem to exist outside of my grandfather's notebook."

Decker had yet to look away from the window.

"So I'm left with two big questions." Jess held up a finger. "One, if Dean is our guy, then why is it George Berry's name all over the pages of that notebook and not the doctor's? Why has he never been hauled in for questioning? Why was he not a suspect?"

"And the second question?"

"What if my grandfather was wrong?"

Decker perked up. His eyes came alive, as if he were suddenly rejuvenated. "Go on . . ."

"I mean, the only thing I've gotten my mother to say about him was that he was a drunk, and she only told me that very recently."

Decker leaned back in the booth and watched her. His gaze softened. "Are you okay?" he asked.

"What do you mean?"

"It's a lot," he said softly. "This thing with your mother. I can't imagine . . ."

Jess forced herself to take a breath. "I suppose I've been digging harder into the story in order to distract me. We've scheduled a mess of tests; then it seems like the waiting will begin. Of course, I'm worried about her, but I'm ten times more worried about Ben. He loves his grandmother and . . ."

Decker reached over the table and placed a hand on Jess's wrist. Her first instinct was to yank it away. She was not used to seeing this side of him. His edges seemed to have softened since she'd told him the news of her mother. She appreciated his kindness, but she also resented it.

"Truth be told," Jess said, "when we were in that doctor's office and she answered those questions about her father, it was the most I had ever heard her talk about James Ballard."

"Maybe I should sit down with her," Decker offered.

"Why?"

"You could turn on the recorder. I'd warm her up. Get her talking."

"What good would that do?"

"Two birds, one stone." Decker shrugged and went for another bite of Jess's pie. "We'd finally have audio of someone who knew the lead detective, and you'd get your mother to open up about your grandfather."

"No."

Decker threw up his hands. "Why not?"

"She'd never go for it, especially now. Even before the diagnosis, she wasn't exactly excited that I was digging into this story. It took forever for me to convince her that the story was about the murders and not her father."

"He's the lead investigator, Jess. To claim he is off limits is naive at best. The information we have—however scant and dubious it may be—is because of him and your involvement. And this information that he was a raging alcoholic certainly shines a light on a lot of the mysteries in that notebook of his."

Jess scratched her scalp with the end of her pen. "I don't know, Dan. I think we have a lot more to investigate right now without digging into my family. What do you say we see what else we can find on this angry doctor?"

Before Decker could reply, he was interrupted by the arrival of the waitress and her coffeepot. She leaned over their notes as she filled their cups.

"I don't know how y'all spend so much time on something y'all ain't getting paid for," she said.

Decker draped his arms over the back of the booth, opening up his chest. "It's called *passion*, sweetheart. I'm chock full of it."

"You're chock full of something." The waitress turned from him to Jess. "I've been talking to a couple of the regulars about your story. Some of them remember it very well. You ought to talk to them."

"That's a good idea." Jess didn't mean it. She was up to her eyeballs with people who had heard about the murders and just wanted to talk about it. To tell their half-baked theories to someone. What she needed was one person of actual substance who might shed a little—

"One fella who comes in every morning is retired Lake Castor police," the waitress said. "He didn't work that case specifically, but he was on the job when it happened."

Jess nearly broke her fingers reaching for her pen. "And he'll talk to us?"

"He would be excited to." The waitress refilled Jess's cup. "He always felt like this was one that got away. He left me his phone number to give to you."

Jess answered with a grin. "Thank you very much."

The waitress left, and Jess turned to Decker. However, he looked far from pleased.

"What's wrong with you?" she asked.

Decker shook it off. He reached into his pocket and produced a few crumpled bills, then tossed them onto the table.

"Have you ever wondered," he said, "if maybe the police weren't exactly the good guys?"

CHAPTER THIRTY-ONE

James Ballard

1972

Ballard's hand shook like nobody's business. He'd found he could go entire days without thinking about the momentum with which his mind was rotting. He'd only lately begun accepting the truths of his age. An old knee injury that had formerly nagged only before a thunderstorm might suddenly rouse him in the middle of the night. His vision blurred after dark. He no longer felt like a sum but instead felt like a system of quickly deteriorating parts.

The worst, however, was not the creak in his bones or the cobwebs in his head. What he hated most was the dissolution of his aptitude. Over the years, people had come to depend on him. Ballard took pride in what he meant to people—and not just his family, either—and how his mere presence tended to put folks at ease. In fact, he couldn't remember the last time that—

Of course he couldn't.

He still held out hope that the memory loss was something that might pass or something he might manage. The doctor in Lake Castor was always talking about *outliers*; perhaps Ballard might be one of them.

There was no way, he believed, that a god could create him only to deliver him to—

No, he told himself, there was still a chance this might be a mistake. A passing phase, even, that arrived with age and not the dire forecast predicted by Dr. Fenton. In fact, just the previous evening, while Ballard had been on the phone with his brother, he'd felt *lucid.* So lucid that he ev—

"Jim? What's going on?"

Ballard snapped to. Everything folded into view. He found himself in the middle of his living room. Cora stood in the doorway with her hand rested on the light switch.

"Why are you standing in the dark?" she asked him.

"I was . . ." Ballad had no idea. "I . . . did you need something?"

"No." Cora's face twisted, and she pointed to something over Ballard's head. "Do you?"

Ballard realized only then that his own hand was raised to the sky, as if he were waiting in grade school to ask the teacher a question.

Shame racked his body. He snatched his hand out of the air and thrust it into the pocket of his bathrobe. He found himself resenting her. More than that, he resented *himself.*

"If I could have one goddamn private moment," he spat at her. "I swear to God, Cora . . . it's like I'm not even allowed to *think.*"

Cora's jaw popped open. She covered it with her fist. She took two steps backward from the doorway.

The shock of it surprised Ballard as well. He'd heard the words and recognized them as his own but still could not determine from whence they came. He would never shout at his wife.

Or would he?

He'd never raised a hand to her, never in all his life, yet he found himself in that very position. She cowered against the far wall, with her hands shielding her head. Ballard stood over her, his hand reared back.

He took a breath, recovered, and then threw his arms around her. He drew her into his chest. Beneath him, she trembled.

"Do you really think I'd hurt you?" he asked her. He was stunned she would take so long to answer. "Cora, sweetheart . . . I love you so much."

"I love you too, Jim."

But she said it in a way that made Ballard feel cold.

◆ ◆ ◆

"Are you listening to me, Jim?"

Ballard snapped to. The ticking of the clock on the far wall had grown so loud it had distracted him from the voice on the other end of the telephone. "I'm sorry . . . what were you saying?"

"I was asking what the guy told you today."

"What guy?"

"Your meeting this morning. With your union representative."

"Oh." Ballard didn't remember ever mentioning this to his brother, but that didn't mean it hadn't happened. Why wouldn't he? His big brother, John, had always been a rock, a solid foundation. Ballard would have told him anything.

"How bad was it?"

"For one"—Ballard flipped open his notepad to the last page he'd written and read aloud—"he said my benefits package clearly dictated that I would get my pension if I retired next February. Seventy percent if I fulfill my obligations to the holidays. Half if I can make it to September."

John whistled low. The line was silent for a moment.

"What about sick days?" asked his brother. "You should have plenty of those stacked up by now. Right?"

"Apparently I used them all."

"You did? When?"

Ballard couldn't remember, nor could he concentrate on a satisfactory answer. Not with that clock ticking maddeningly louder.

Tick tock tick tock tick.

"Jim?"

"Yeah, I'm here."

"Buck up, little man," said his brother. "How is the case coming?"

"I don't . . ." Ballard squeezed his eyes shut as tight as he could. When he opened them, he found himself still in his office. Still holding his notepad. He rifled through a couple of pages. "I have one suspect."

GEORGE BERRY IS GUILTY.

"Great!" cheered John. "When are you going to slap cuffs on him?"

"I can't . . . I . . ." Ballard closed his eyes again, but it didn't stop the images. He saw himself loading George Berry into his county car. He saw the drive down FM 809. He saw the moonlight; then everything else was shrouded in shadow. Everything, that was, except for . . .

"No," he said. "That wasn't me."

"Do what, Jim?"

"I think I might have . . ." The spit in Ballard's mouth dried to sand. "I'm afraid I might have hurt that boy."

John was quiet a moment. Then he said, "What you need to do, Jim, is forget about it. You hear me? Forget all about it. That's what you're good at."

Ballard wanted to throw the phone against his office wall. Anything to shut up that damned clock.

Tick tock tick tock tick.

"Keep your head down, Jim," said his brother. "This is just like Korea. Get in, do your time, put up with Red's mood swings another ten months, and get the hell—"

"I'm not going to make it another ten months." Ballard couldn't believe the words were leaving his mouth, and he could do nothing to stop them. "Sometimes I don't think I'll make it another ten minutes. Right now, they all think this is from the drinking. But soon I won't be able to hide it any longer."

"Jim, I—"

"I just need to make it long enough to earn out. I need to leave something for Cora and Sam." His words became brittle. "It's not their fault. They shouldn't have to . . ."

He could hear John breathing through the line. "There is one way, little brother, that might allow you to shave off some time."

"Spill it."

"I reckon you could die in the line."

Tock tick tock tick tock tick tock.

Ballard let that thought spin round and round in his head. He'd always considered John to be the voice of reason. They had enlisted together to fight in Korea, then after the war . . .

Ballard closed his eyes and stabbed his palms into them.

He couldn't remember a thing about John's life after Korea. Was he married? Did he have any children? Ballard racked his brain left and right, wondering when he had told John about his diagnosis, how often they talked on the phone. Where did John even live these days? How could someone so important as his own damned brother have been extracted from the files of his memory—and he had only just now discovered it? Was it too late? Could he get the memory of John back? Who else would disappear from—

TICK TOCK TICK TOCK TICK TOCK.

The thoughts flew at Ballard with such ferocity that he hardly noticed when someone else had joined him in the room. He was jarred into consciousness by Tim Doody and another deputy—*Christ, what was his name?*—who stood in the doorway of the briefing room, looking at him like he had grown nine more heads.

"You making a call, Big Jim?" asked Tim Doody.

Ballard looked at the phone receiver hanging useless from his hand. The call had gone dead; there was no one on the line. He hung it up and wondered what he was supposed to do next.

"Hey, Big Jim," said the second deputy, "we've been looking everywhere for your boy George Berry. We talked to the guys up at Honey's, to the nurses . . . everywhere we've looked, and nobody's seen him. Not since January."

"He's out there," said Ballard.

"Maybe so," said Tim Doody, "but do we think the best use of our time and resources is looking for him?"

"He ain't *nowhere*," Ballard insisted. "A man don't just disappear."

Tim Doody sat on the edge of Ballard's desk and leaned in close. "You know as well as me that sometimes they do. We've seen it happen. Hell, we've even *made* it happen."

A bitter taste formed on Ballard's tongue. He wanted to lash out. Not necessarily at Tim Doody and his colleague but for lack of anyone else . . .

"Listen," said the other deputy, "LCPD says you were the last to see him. They said you drove him home after they questioned him."

"What are you saying?"

"I'm not saying anything, except maybe we shouldn't be looking so hard at George Berry." The deputy took a breath. "Maybe we ought to let him stay gone."

Ballard threw a finger in the face of the second deputy. "I don't even know who the hell you are."

Tim Doody backed off the desk. He tapped his colleague on the shoulder, and—

TOCK TICK TOCK TICK TOCK TICK.

—they both retreated from the briefing room. Ballard sat alone in his stew of resentment until he found himself joined by Deputy Ennis What's-His-Name, the one the other boys called *Mr. Tibbs.*

"This thing just came in, Deputy Ballard," said the deputy. "I thought maybe you might want to look at it."

"Why the hell would I want to look at it?"

What's-His-Name didn't blink. "A young couple out parking last night in a Lake Castor lovers' lane claim a man approached their car with a thirty-eight."

"Yeah. So?"

"This man, he tells the couple that he's a cop," he said. "Says he needs to commandeer their vehicle and orders them both into the passenger seat. He keeps the gun on them until he drives over the state line, into Deeton, where he tells the guy to get into the trunk. Guy refuses, and a struggle ensues. He and the girl manage to get away and—"

"What the hell does this have to do with me?"

The deputy squinted at his superior. "I reckon this case has a lot of similarities to the one you're working, sir."

"Speak up, boy. I can't hear you over that damned . . ." Ballard hitched a thumb at the clock on the wall.

"I thought the double homicide you're working might—"

"Were these two kids found tied to a tree?"

"No sir."

"Then there aren't any similarities."

Worthy's jaw hung, and Ballard never thought he'd seen a man struck more dumb.

"Fine!" Ballard shouted. He stood from his chair and ripped the top drawer out of his desk. Papers flew to the floor like ticker tape. Ballard reached for the second drawer. "Look through my files, goddammit. You want me to do every goddamn thing for you. You want me to solve them all?"

Worthy backed up. "Sir, I apologize. I was just—"

"You were just telling me how much better a deputy you are?" Ballard kicked at the papers but nearly slipped on a file folder. This touched him off even more, so he kicked a hole in the side of his desk.

He aimed to do a lot more than that but thanked what remained of his senses to get out of there. He stormed out the door of the briefing room and stalked the hallway to . . . to . . . he had no idea where he was going. He passed the bathroom and thought once or twice about hiding out in a stall until he could regulate his breathing, but he needed to walk it off. He needed the exercise. His brain was going ninety miles per minute. He discovered the answers before he could ask the questions. Nothing was making sense. He turned down one hallway, then another, before backtracking and passing the bathroom again, then . . . he looked left. He looked right.

He was lost.

Ballard's chest grew tight.

He clutched at it. Ripped open the top button of his shirt, then the one below that. The badge on his uniform grew heavy, heavy . . . he put his back to the wall and turned his head to the ceiling. Air couldn't get in fast enough, not through his clenched teeth. Was this it? Would Cora ever forgive him? Was there really anyone up there?

Ballard had, for so long, been inundated by the sound of that horrible ticking clock that he could not put a finger on the moment that it had fallen silent.

He slid down the wall until he was seated on the floor. He tucked his head into his knees and felt a fire in his cheeks.

Please . . .

CHAPTER THIRTY-TWO

Jess Keeler

Present Day

[END MUSIC CUE]

DECKER: You may be asking yourself, at this point, why we have failed to introduce you to any of the original investigators. We have spoken about them at length throughout this podcast. We have described for you, to the best of our ability, what they have done, as well as what they have failed to do. We introduced you to Jack Powers's ex-wife, the journalist who covered the investigation from the start. But we have yet to produce a single person wearing a badge.

JESS: There are several reasons for this. First and foremost, many of them are no longer alive. Deputy James Ballard passed away nearly fifty years ago. Sheriff Red Carter followed him soon after. Henry Dorritt, of the Lake Castor Police Department, died in 1987.

DECKER: The only surviving member of Red Carter's infamous seven deputies is Ennis Worthy, who now serves Deeton County as its sheriff. He, however, refuses to discuss an ongoing investigation with journalists and therefore will not participate in our story.

JESS: In fact, that represents the attitude of nearly every law enforcement officer we've encountered. When we asked for records pertaining to the case, we were denied. When we approached any current investigators to speak with us about operating procedures, they turned us down. There seemed to be some truth to the fabled "thin blue line," as we could locate no willing participants to lend their voice to our story.

DECKER: Until now . . .

LT. DICKSON: My name is Lieutenant Charlie Dickson. I'm retired now, but I worked in the Crimes Against Persons squad for the Lake Castor Police Department.

DECKER: And you were working there in 1972?

LT. DICKSON: I was. Yes sir.

DECKER: Do you remember the murders of Linda Harris and Steven Hicks?

LT. DICKSON: Of course I do. Now, I didn't work it, but I was there. I believe I was working—oh, what was it . . . it's been so long—I was on a shooting downtown on Clay Street. Some old boy stuck up a liquor store and killed the cashier. If you give me a minute, I might remember the name of the boy who—

DECKER: Can you describe for us what it was like back then? Lake Castor was going through some difficult changes, so I imagine it must have been exciting to work crime.

LT. DICKSON: Oh, it was. Sure. Every day there was something. But that deal with those two kids they found down off Gilmore Road . . . there wasn't never nothing like that. Not before and certainly not after.

DECKER: What can you tell us about the lead investigators on that case, Henry Dorritt and Jack Powers?

LT. DICKSON: Hank, he was a good old boy. He saw things through to the end, usually. Smart cop. Good cop. There was a lot of trouble with Deeton County and their sheriff, but Hank had a way of talking to old Red. I believe Hank ran into some trouble at the end of his career, but it wasn't his fault.

DECKER: And Powers?

LT. DICKSON: Jack . . . now Jack never could let that thing go. It was his first case, I believe, and he didn't know how to turn it off. You hated watching him get so caught up like he did. I think he just had too big a heart to be a good investigator. He got obsessed. He would stop at nothing to slap cuffs on the guy who did it. Even now, it's never long before the conversation turns to that damn case and what he could have done or should have do—

JESS: Wait a minute. Based on what you just said . . . it sounds like you are still in contact with Jack Powers.

LT. DICKSON: Well, sure I am. We call each other every year on our birthdays.

◆ ◆ ◆

"I'll only be gone for two days," Jess promised her son. "Mr. Decker and I will be driving down to the coast to interview a former investigator named Jack Powers. I'll have my ringer on, and this here is Mr. Decker's personal cell phone, just in case you can't hit me on mine. He knows to keep an eye out for your call, so you don't hesitate."

Benjamin groaned. "Mom, you've been over this list a hundred times."

Jess sighed and realized he raised an excellent point. Perhaps she was overworrying. Maybe she was blowing things out of proportion.

But all she had to do was take one look at her own mother, Samantha Bowen, sitting on the divan in her Lake Castor house to know that everything was not going to be *all right*.

Things were never going to be the same ever again.

Her mother had always been a stubborn woman. While she was not a big woman in size, her demeanor and resolve could always back her up. Jess had watched both those qualities being winnowed away over the past couple of months. Her mother wandered lately between passing fogs of confusion and bouts of furious anger.

She'd spent the past hour sitting on the divan in a slack-jawed stupor.

The drugs, Jess told herself. *That's only because of the drugs.*

"Humor me, Benjamin," Jess said. "This is my mother we are talking about."

Benjamin sighed. Jess reached out and tousled his mop of dirty-blond hair. He'd finished his second-to-last semester at school with his best grades yet and agreed to spend the rest of his summer helping her with his grandmother. She would never command the vocabulary to state how proud she was of her boy, but she knew summer would soon be gone.

Soon, Jess would have no one to help her.

"She's not to drive anywhere," Jess said. "Don't let her car keys out of your sight."

"I know, Mom."

"In fact, maybe you better let me take them."

"It's not necessary, Mom. I got this."

Jess felt awful for needling the boy, but she felt ten times worse for what she might have bequeathed him.

"There is evidence that this disease may be hereditary," the doctor had told them. *"It would be a good idea to have yourself tested."*

It wasn't herself that Jess was worried about.

She kissed her son on the forehead, harder than necessary. She hugged him tight.

"Don't worry about a thing, Ma."

Easier said than done, kid.

Jess walked to her mother and knelt to eye level. "When I get back," she said softly, "we're going to talk again about you coming to live with me."

Samantha rolled her eyes.

"I'm serious, Mother."

"That's not going to happen, Jessica."

"You can't live by yourself anymore, and we're not putting you into a nursing home."

"I'm fine."

Jess took a tone she'd never expected to take with her mother. "The police brought you home last week because you were shopping at Karstein's in your bathrobe, Ma. That's not *fine*."

"I don't know why you keep bringing that up," said Samantha. "I told you I took an Ambien. You got brought home twice by the police when you were younger, and I never mentioned it once."

Benjamin perked up. "Is that true, Mom?"

"Shut up, Benny." Jess turned back to her mother. "I keep mentioning it in case you've forgotten."

"Enough with the *forgetting*." Samantha's voice raised an octave. "Has it ever occurred to you that I only forget the things that don't matter? When you get as old as I am, you have to focus only on the memories that are worth keeping."

"You better remember that Benjamin is in charge," Jess warned. "You better do exactly as he says."

Jess pretended not to see them wink at each other, but it made her feel better. She hated the thought of either of them looking back on this time together as *punishment*. The both of them had always gotten along better with each other than either of them had with her.

She gathered her things and quietly left her mother's Lake Castor house.

CHAPTER THIRTY-THREE

Red Carter

1972

Spring arrived—and with it: a break in the case.

Things happened fast. It all started when Bobby McCoy heard tell from Cherry Winston down at Shady Village about a boy named Sean Gray. She and Gray enjoyed an on-again, off-again thing, and he had been with her the night after the bodies had been found just up Gilmore Road from her trailer. According to Ms. Winston, Gray had stayed glued to the television set, flipping through any channels that might feature the news story. After that, he had grown "sullen and weird." Two days later, he'd sold his car. The following day, he was gone.

Bobby McCoy and Tim Doody further investigated Mr. Gray. It turned out he'd already done time as a juvenile for a stolen car. Upon release, he'd married a woman and sired two children. To support his family, he'd accepted a job as a janitor at a hospital, where he had been fired for harassing comments he had made to some of the nurses.

That hospital: Lake Castor General.

Red ordered Sean Gray to be located and delivered to his office toot sweet. Days went by, then weeks. The longer Red waited for the young man's appearance, the more he slavered at the opportunity. The hope had become all but unbearable when finally they caught word that a highway patrolman had arrested Sean Gray for wrecking a stolen motorcycle down near Raleigh, almost two hours away.

He immediately dispatched two deputies to fetch him.

After spending most of the morning and afternoon pacing his office and demanding accountability, he received word that Gray had been delivered to "the Box," which was a small ten-by-ten room in the basement that they used to interview suspects in private. He grabbed his jacket and a fresh Lovera and was halfway out the door of his office when Lois stopped him.

"You have a call on two, Red."

"Not now, dammit." He pushed his way around her. "I've been waiting a long time for—"

"Redmond Allen Carter, you get your butt back here right now."

Something in her voice spun Red around to face his wife. There were times throughout their marriage when Lois might give in, but she also knew very well when to stand her ground.

"Honey," he said, changing his tone, "you know how important it is that I get a look at this boy. There's a fresh goddamned chance that he's the one who—"

"This case has waited since Christmas to get itself solved, and I reckon it can wait another ten minutes for you to take this phone call." She crossed both her arms and declared that she would not be moved. "Those two kids won't be any less dead."

Red saw no point in further protest. "Fine," he sighed. "Just who in Sam Hill is on the phone that it's so all-fired important? Spiro T. Agnew?"

"Cora Ballard."

Red froze in his tracks. He could think up a long list of people he'd rather talk to than Big Jim's wife. He knew, without being told, what it was she wanted to talk about, and it wasn't a topic he enjoyed breaching.

"Lois, I don't have time for—"

"You don't have time for anything else," she insisted. "Cora and Jim are our friends, and when one of them says they have an emergency, you take the damned call."

Red realized he could put it off no longer. He rounded his desk again and picked up the phone. "Cora," he said, "I need to ask you to keep this quick. I have a—"

"I'm worried, Red." Her voice was thin and shaking. "I'm worried to death about Jim."

Red knew any chance of this being a quick telephone call had been scattered to the wind.

"There's something wrong with him," she said. "I don't know what it is."

Red waved Lois out of his office, then sat behind his desk. "It's this case, Cora," he said into the phone. "It's a head-scratcher. I reckon it's probably eaten Big Jim up that it's gone this long without any type of resolution, but I swear we're about to break it op—"

"It's not the investigation," she said. "It's something else."

Red's gut told him that she was right. He could smell the booze on the big man's breath. The first time or two, he had cut his deputy some slack. Lately, all he'd been cutting him were dirty looks. It had gotten so bad that Red couldn't stand the sight of him. He'd dispatched him to jobs that called him across the county so that he often wouldn't have to be in the same room with him. First, the insolence, then the drinking . . . furthermore there was the unresolved matter of what Red feared had happened to George Berry.

Red felt he had let things slide with Big Jim for so long that it only made him complicit. He swore over and over that after what had happened with Cappy Jenkins, he would not let another of his deputies stray that far from the good and proper. But who, he wondered, was he kidding? They stepped so often over that line in the name of doing good police work that Red or anyone else could never stuff that genie back in the bottle.

However, Cora's phone call meant Red could look away and pretend no longer.

"He never used to drink," said Cora. "He never used to . . ." The tone in her voice turned darker. "He never used to do a lot of things. But now . . ."

"You know as well as I do that it takes an awful big heart to pump blood through a man Jim's size." Red slipped the Lovera in his mouth and faked a laugh. "Big Jim just wants to see this thing solved. And I tell you what, Cora, that day is coming sooner than later. If you'll let me—"

"Can't you put someone else on it? Hasn't Jim done his time? Isn't there somewhere else he might—"

"Cora, I don't have to tell you of all people how Big Jim would react if I pulled him off this thing when we're this deep into the game. Sweetie, that would rankle him to no end."

"Still—"

Red tried another tactic. "I know this is a lot for you to deal with, but you're not dealing with it alone. Neither of you are. You have me and Lois, of course, and every last one of my six deputies. And Jim's brother can—"

"Who?"

Red shifted the Lovera to the opposite side of his mouth. "His brother. What's his name, John?"

"John?"

"Yes ma'am. He was talking on the phone with him the other day for nearly an hour. I'd have liked to have a coronary because we were in the middle of—"

"Red," she said, her tone flat and deliberate, "Jim's brother is dead."

Red nearly bit his cigar. "Do what?"

"John Ballard didn't come home from Korea," said Cora. "He died in battle."

How had Red not known that? He felt his stomach turn and thought he might lose his breakfast. He wanted to lash out at everything, to smash the lamp on his desk, to throw the cupful of ballpoint pens. He wished to draw his weapon and fire holes into the awards and accolades that festooned his office walls.

Instead, he said very calmly, "Cora, I'd love to catch up. Honest I would, but now is not a very good time. I believe we are this close to finally putting this thing to bed, but I still got a couple of t's that need to be crossed. How about we catch up real soon?"

"But Red—"

"Nobody's got a closer eye on your husband than me and Lois right now. I'll be on him like stink on shit; you have my word. I'll talk to you directly."

Before she could say anything else, Red hung up the phone. He stared at it for a good long while and calculated a mess of things in his head. None of them came to anything worth a damn, so he leaned back in his chair and hollered out the office door for his wife.

"How is she?" Lois asked, pointing at the phone.

Red ignored that. He asked instead, "Lois, I need you to get Big Jim in here. Toot sweet, you hear me?"

"He's busy, Red. He went down to—"

"Goddammit, Lois." It was all he could do to keep from flipping over his desk. "I didn't ask if he was busy; I asked you to get him in here."

Lois met his anger with a good bit of her own. The two of them stared at each other long enough to melt snow. After Red finally relented, Lois straightened her blouse.

"I can't run fetch him for you, Red," she said, "because he's downstairs with your suspect."

"Do what?"

"Yes," Lois told him. "He went down there to meet Sean Gray as soon as we hauled him in."

Red sprang from his desk so fast he didn't realize he'd dropped his Lovera until he was halfway to the stairwell. He didn't turn around for it; instead, the only thought racing through his head was that he hoped he could get there in time to stop Ballard from doing something stupid.

CHAPTER THIRTY-FOUR

James Ballard

1972

Ballard had learned long ago that rage, when used properly, could be his most useful tool in law enforcement. He came custom built with all his own biases, prejudices, and triggers, but there was no reason they needed to serve as a weakness. Red had taught him from the beginning that if he used every single thing at his disposal in the pursuit of bettering the lives of Deeton County residents, then they would be forgiven in the eyes of the Lord.

"Our one true mandate," Red had told him, "is to protect the citizens of Deeton."

"It's not to uphold the law?" Ballard had challenged.

Red had laughed that off. "No, son," he had said. "In order to keep our people safe, we will have to break many laws."

Over time, Ballard had learned to manage his anger. That same frenzy in him that had delivered him home safe from war was less acceptable amid polite American society. Red had shown him a use for it. He'd found a release. Ballard had developed a safety valve. By applying pressure in the proper locations, he and Red and Cappy Jenkins and

Ernie Bass and Tim Doody and the select few others had kept Deeton reasonably quiet.

But lately, as Ballard's faculties had deteriorated, so too had his restraint and self-control. He would see it transpiring before his eyes as if it were happening not to him but to an actor in a picture show or on the television. He would look with horror at the smashed plates or bloodied fists. The holes in the wall. The looks on their faces or the echo of his own hollers.

He knew it was all about to come crashing down around him. That self-control was slipping through his fingers. Reason was in short supply. His every thought had become consumed with how bad luck separated him from every other person on earth and how little time he had left. All he had left was rage.

For that reason, he wasted no time in arriving to the sheriff's office. He'd heard they'd finally captured the suspect who had eluded them. Ballard wanted a crack at him. He *needed* a crack at him.

He wanted one final victory before the whole shithouse went up in flames.

Ballard took the stairs two at a time, then threw open the basement doors. Just beyond several shelves used to store evidence, he arrived at the small ten-by-ten cage, where Tim Doody and Bobby McCoy waited with their suspect.

The Box.

Ballard himself had built the Box with his own two hands, dispatched to that duty by Red during the thirteenth year of his tenure. Together with Cappy Jenkins and Ernie Bass, he'd spent the summer of 1965 fastening the steel bars to joists and ensuring the room was soundproof. While there were suitable interview rooms upstairs and a brand-new jail across the street, the Box had been built for an entirely different purpose. It had been created to get results.

"Is that him?" Ballard asked, nodding toward a young man in chains sitting in a metal folding chair.

Tim Doody nodded in the affirmative. "AD Porter called it in. Said they picked him up down in Wilson after he wrecked a motorcycle he stole. He heard we were looking for him, so he gave Red a call."

Ballard studied the man. He wore faded bell-bottoms and a handlebar mustache. He lacked for a haircut and a shave. The handcuffs had been slapped tight, which meant he'd offered some trouble upon arrest. The dark bruise beneath his eyes meant that trouble had been denied.

The suspect took one look at Ballard and had plenty of reason to grow nervous. Talking shit to highway patrol was one thing; throwing sass in the basement of a Carolina sheriff's office to a deputy the size of Ballard was something different altogether.

"Hey, man," he said, "I think I better talk to a lawyer."

Ballard unclasped his wristwatch. He loosened his tie. "We'll be sure to call you one. But I'm going to ask you a couple of questions first."

Which made the young man even more apoplectic. He turned to the other two deputies with pleading eyes. "Y'all can't do this," he said. "I said I want to talk to my lawyer, so you have to let me talk to him. I know how this works."

"Is that right?" asked Tim Doody. "You read the rule book?"

"I know my rights."

"He's got a point," said McCoy. "He asked for a lawyer, so it's up to us to get ahold of one. What do you say you and me run upstairs and see if we can get one on the horn? We'll leave Big Jim down here to find out what he needs to know."

The young man's eyes went wild. "No! Don't leave me down here with him!"

"What is it?" McCoy asked. "You want a lawyer, or you want us all to stay down here? You can't have it both ways."

In the meantime, Ballard removed his jacket. He unbuttoned the cuffs of his shirt and rolled his sleeves up to his elbows. He unholstered his weapon and placed it on the table near the door.

"I didn't steal that motorbike," the young man insisted. "I know it was due back to the rental company on Friday, but I lost track of time. I was on my way to return it when I ran out of gas. I swear I would nev—"

Ballard hitched his pants, then stepped into the cage they called "the Box." He loomed over the suspect like a bad debt.

"Boys," he said to the two deputies, "why don't you two run on along and see about his lawyer."

Despite the suspect's pleas, Doody and McCoy took their leave. Once alone with the suspect, Ballard got to work.

"You know we've been looking all over for you."

Perspiration beaded the young man's head. "How the hell was I supposed to know that?"

"Why'd you run?"

"Run?" The young man made to move his hands, but the handcuffs kept him tight to the chair. "Man, I didn't *run*. I got tired of sticking around this lousy town. I was locked up, you know. Some bullshit about a stolen car, which, by the way, I didn't steal. Because of that, I don't like being in the same place for too long. Looking at the same faces. Dating the same girls."

"Lee's awful pretty," Ballard said. "She must not have liked you running off like that."

The boy cocked his head. "Who?"

"Don't play dumb with me," Ballard growled. "This goes off a lot easier for both of us if you play it straight."

The young man opened his mouth to say something but thought better of it.

"You and me," said Ballard, "we got a little catching up to do. It seems like our last visit ended abruptly."

"Last visit?" The young man looked around the room. He eyeballed the door. "Man, I don't know what you're talking about. I ain't never seen you before in my life."

Ballard's vision flooded red, but he kept the rage at bay. It would be there if he needed it later. Instead, he focused on the fact that he had all the time in the world with his suspect. If he wanted, he could pluck him apart, limb by limb, and not worry about him lighting into the bushes or escaping into the darkness. He thought of this punk wrapping that rope around the necks of those two kids and pulling it taut. He thought of that smug face and how that must have been the last thing they had seen.

But he also thought about the toll this case had taken on his own life. This punk and his actions on that cold Christmas Eve would later serve to derail much of what had once been a celebrated and storied career in law enforcement. It wasn't fair. To have been forced to focus on him and his disappearance when perhaps he should have been spending more time with his own wife and daughter . . .

Ballard was going to take his time. He was going to enjoy this. And if he didn't get what he wanted, then he was going to take it.

"You say you have alibis coming out your ears," Ballard said, "but we've managed to poke holes in every single one of them. You couldn't pass the polygraph, and now you expect me to believe this story about a motorcycle?"

"Polygraph?" The man twisted in his seat. "Man, I think you got the wrong—"

"We got you, buddy. My only regret in life right now is that I have to turn you over to the district attorney in one piece."

"If you got me, then please go ahead and charge me. Because this whole thing is making me—"

Ballard heard the door open behind him. He turned and watched Red slip quietly inside. The boy stretched his chains and leaned forward in his chair. "Hey, man," he hollered to Red, "y'all keep pinning things on me that I ain't done!"

"You claim you were with Ellroy Fickle," Ballard said, "but Fickle says that was a lie. You said you—"

"I don't know any Ellroy Fickle!" said the kid.

"You said the same thing about Margaret Cornwell, but we have it on good authority that they had to turn the hose on the two of you, it got so hot and heavy sometimes."

"Who the hell are you—"

"Jim . . ."

Ballard could hear Red behind him, but he ignored him. He had been in enough interrogations to know that he had the suspect on the ropes. He was bound to crack. Enough pressure, and he would—

"Man, you're crazy," said the kid. "You got a screw loose or something because you ain't—"

"What did you say?"

Ballard had to keep control. They weren't out in the woods. They weren't under the cover of darkness. Sure, they were in *the Box*, and Red could take care of anything, but the mess . . . Ballard had to keep it in check.

"Jim . . ."

Ballard waved off the sheriff. He grabbed the young man by the collar and yanked him so hard that the chair left the ground. Ballard pulled him so close they touched noses.

"You got away from me once," he growled, "but you ain't walking out of this cage until you confess it to me. We can place you at the scene. We got you with motive. You and your little girlfriend got caught stealing drugs. You had mud all over your truck that matched the—"

"I don't drive a truck, man!"

Ballard threw him, chair and all, against the bars of the cage. He didn't wait for him to land before he pounced atop him and reared back, would have hit him, had Red not launched into him with everything he had. The two lawmen tumbled to the ground and rolled across the floor to the corner of the cage. Ballard scrambled, but Red held him firm.

"Jim, what the hell are you doing?" gasped the old man.

Ballard bucked against the sheriff but still could not wrest himself free. "I've got him, Red. He got away from me once. But we've got him now and—"

"You got who, Jim?"

"Berry. George Berry."

Red blinked twice. "That's not Berry, son. It's . . ."

That was when it all melted away for Ballard. It was no longer George Berry, chained to a tree, but some punk kid in bell-bottoms handcuffed to a chair in the Box.

His hand shook.

He turned to find Red staring at him.

"Jim," said the sheriff, "what did you do?"

"I think . . ." Ballard's mouth filled with sand. His stomach pitched forward, and nausea flooded him. "I think I may have done something terribly wrong."

Over Ballard's shoulder, he could hear the kid whimpering. Ballard covered his eyes with his hands, but it did not shield him from the images in his mind. Of all the things to never forget . . .

Red was firm. "You need to talk to Cora, son."

"I . . . I can't . . ."

"You need to talk to somebody."

"My . . . John. I talk to John."

"Who?"

"My . . . my brother. I talk to my brother, John."

Red twisted his face into a scowl. "Jim . . ."

Then Ballard knew. He knew what was going to come out of Red's mouth before he even opened it.

"Jim, your brother is dead. He died over twenty years ago."

CHAPTER THIRTY-FIVE

Red Carter

1972

Red charged onto the ground level of his sheriff's office like an angry bull. He threw open the door to the stairwell and pounded his feet against the tiled floor.

"Lois, dammit," he hollered, "get me Nick Brandon on the telephone."

His wife's face fell upon the sight of him. "Dear Lord, Red. What happened?"

Red pushed his way past her and headed for the squad room.

"Red, sweetheart, you're bleeding."

"You hear me, woman? Get the DA on the damn phone, and do it toot sweet."

Red burst through the squad room door. He caught three of his deputies off guard. The only one doing anything worth half a shit was Ennis Worthy, so he took him by the arm.

"That kid down there," Red said, pointing toward the basement, "I want him transferred to one of the cells upstairs."

Tim Doody and Bobby McCoy dropped what they were doing and stepped closer. "Sean Gray?" McCoy asked. "What happened, Red?"

"If I need to find somebody else who can do what they are told, then let me know." Red turned his back on them and headed out of the squad room. "Otherwise, get it done."

Red slammed shut his office door and fell into the chair behind his desk. He plucked a fresh Lovera out of his desk drawer but couldn't bring himself to put it in his mouth. Instead, he fiddled with it and waited for the phone to ring.

What had happened? How long had it been happening? Was it something that he could have stopped? Red dropped his head into his hands. He closed his eyes tight, hoping it might stop—even for just a fleeting moment—all the questions that ricocheted around in his brain.

The phone rang.

"Red?" It was Lois. "I got the DA on hold."

"What are you waiting for, woman?"

The only sound through the line was a click, followed by Nick Brandon's voice. "What's going on, Red?"

"I'm shutting her down, Nick."

Brandon's confusion was audible over the phone. "What the hell, Red?"

"We've been on this thing for months now," Red said. "We're no closer to solving it than we have been."

"We can't leave this unsolved."

Red let the air play within the silence before finally he said, "Maybe we don't have to."

Despite the hell that Big Jim Ballard was giving him, the last thing he wanted was for one of his deputies to get in trouble. To cast a bad light on Big Jim would chase shadows from his entire office, and Red couldn't have that. He'd effectively shut down any questions from the days of Cappy Jenkins, and he'd rather cut off his right hand than play Whac-A-Mole with moody cops under his authority.

He also didn't want further investigation into whatever had happened with George Berry.

For that reason, he needed to offer up a sacrificial lamb.

"You mean the boy you hauled in on that motorcycle charge?" Brandon asked.

"I think he's going to have to do."

Red could tell Brandon didn't like it at all. "You got anything you can make stick on him? At least tell me that. Tell me you got something more than *a good look at him*."

Red wished he could. He had looked deep into Gray's eyes. Eyes that were flooded with fear and pain after the thrashing he'd taken from Big Jim and his half-crazed mind. He'd looked, but all he could see was darkness.

"We got him for a stolen motorcycle," said Red.

Brandon sighed heavily. "Red . . . I need something more. I can't ring him up for a double murder when all we got is a stolen motorcycle."

"I'll sleep at night on this one, Nick. I think he knows more than he's letting on, but I don't think he's guilty all by himself."

"Since when does that matter?"

"What in good hell is that supposed to mean?"

Brandon chose his words carefully. "You've got a great track record of making people confess to things when you want them to."

Red found himself slowly disassembling the Lovera. He'd unwrapped the paper and spilled the tobacco across his desk. He began tearing it into smaller and smaller pieces.

"I got one term left in me, Nick," he said. "There's already things I've done that are going to follow me to the grave. Lord knows they may even keep me from my reward. I'm thinking the best I might be able to do is change things for the next guy who comes along."

"You've picked an awfully convenient time to find Jesus, you sanctimonious son of a—" Brandon's words jumbled into something Red swore belonged to a foreign tongue. Once the DA caught his composure, he spoke in a tight, controlled whisper. "We promised, Red. We promised to close this case before the election."

"It looks like we lied, Nick."

Brandon started to say several things but abandoned them all. When finally he realized he was arguing with a brick wall, he said through clenched teeth: "You're going to burn in hell, Red."

Red nodded, then said, before hanging up the phone, "At least I won't be there alone."

Red stepped out of his office and beelined for the front door. Once outside, he fumbled through his pockets until he found a book of matches. He tugged one loose, then used it to light the Lovera between his lips. Instead of doing the math on how long it had been since he'd lit one up, he watched the leaves fall from the fiery dogwoods, which had been planted three years prior. The air was once again turning cooler.

Another day would soon pass. Then weeks. Red had no idea what the future held, but he was certain of one thing.

He would never again in his lifetime hear the names of Steven Hicks and Linda Harris.

CHAPTER THIRTY-SIX

Jess Keeler

Present Day

Jess and Decker were greeted at the front door by Charlotte Powers, a heavyset woman in her seventies. She'd told them on the phone the previous night that she had been taking care of her husband, Jack, since he had been released by the Cherry Acres Retirement Community shortly after a COVID-19 outbreak had rampaged through their care facility. He'd spent the past two years living in their suburban Beaufort, North Carolina, home.

"You must be the journalists." She opened the door wide but blocked their entrance. "Jack doesn't get many visitors. Heck, he doesn't get *any*, except for my brother. He's . . ." Her words trailed away.

"We look forward to speaking with him," said Jess. "He was a major player in this investigation from 1972, as I explained over the ph—"

"I'm very familiar with it." Mrs. Powers's voice grew heavy. "He's spoken of it often. Sometimes even in his sleep."

Jess smiled, for lack of anything else to say.

"There is one concern," Mrs. Powers added. "His memory . . . Jack is not well. He's suffered two strokes, and he's . . ." She put on a brighter face, then tried again. "Sometimes he is very present. But other times . . ."

"We'll go easy on him," Decker promised.

"I think a quick chat might do him good. Perhaps thirty minutes."

Jess got the message. They would have to work quick—and under the supervision of Mrs. Powers. She clicked on her recorder to ensure she missed nothing. It was a trick Decker had taught her from earlier interviews.

"Most subjects can't wait to talk," he had told her. "While you're busy setting up your equipment, they're dropping valuable audio about first impressions and memories and what have you, and if you don't have it on, then you will plain miss it."

She followed his advice there at the Powerses' kitchen table. All audio was rolling as Jack Powers was brought into the room in a wheelchair.

By all accounts, Jack Powers had been a "big man." Some reports had him at six and a half feet tall. The man who sat before them in the wheelchair was but a shadow of that image. He had grown frail, although he was still big through the shoulders. He sat stooped in his chair, and his head was remarkably free of any hair. His eyes flitted in quick, furtive movements, and his hands trembled when they weren't fiddling with a piece of torn-up paper towel on the tray that accompanied his wheelchair.

Decker didn't blink as he offered his hand. "Mr. Powers," he said, "my name is Dan Decker, and this is my colleague, Jess Keeler. We're here to talk to you about the murders of Linda Harris and Steven Hicks."

"Oh goodness," said Powers, as if it might have been a surprise. "Oh goodness."

Jess clicked on her second recorder and pointed the boom mic toward the older man. Over his shoulder, Mrs. Powers watched her with both curiosity and determination.

"I haven't thought about that case in a long time."

Jess could tell by his wife's reaction that was a lie.

Decker pretended not to notice. He started off the interview easy, with some warm-up questions about Jack Powers's early life—where he had grown up and gone to school, if he'd always wanted to be a cop—before starting in on his professional career.

"What can you tell us about when you first joined the Lake Castor Police Department?"

Powers looked lost a moment, as if he were working a difficult calculus problem. When finally he looked up, he said, "I can't quite remember."

"Not a problem," said Decker. "How about when you were promoted to sergeant and joined the Crimes Against Persons division?"

"Hmm." Still, Powers appeared dumbstruck. "I'm afraid I can't . . . you don't understand; it's been so long. I can't . . ."

Decker leaned back in his chair. "Certainly you remember the Lake Castor Christmas Eve Murders. You were assigned the case as a missing persons. You remember that?"

Powers passed a hand over his eyes. "I was so young. That was several lifetimes ago. You see, I had a stroke . . ."

"What do you remember, Sergeant Powers?"

Powers sat up as straight as his crooked back would let him. "I remember one thing clear as day," he said, "and that's the name of the man who killed those two kids: Christian Alexander Dean."

Jess nearly dropped her pen. She swore the air pressure changed inside the room. She checked—then double-checked—that all her recorders were operating.

"Can you tell us what makes you so sure?" Decker asked.

As if a switch had been flipped, Jack Powers became very lucid. "After I had been removed from the case, I began haunting the hallways of the hospital where Linda had worked," he said. "I showed that FBI profile to nearly anyone who would have a word with me. That number, by the way, grew shorter each passing day. But while I was there, I observed some very strange behavior from the good doctor. He is a man who is very quick to anger."

"We heard about an incident in the parking garage," Decker said. "Allegedly he beat a woman."

"There's nothing *alleged* about it." Powers gripped the armrests of his wheelchair. "He beat her within an inch of her life, and nobody did anything about it. The hospital covered it up, and she received a settlement along with a nondisclosure agreement."

Jess sucked in cold air. "I find that very hard to believe."

"I don't care if you believe it or not," said Powers. "It happened. Just like a little hit-and-run down in South Carolina. He killed a pedestrian in the middle of the night and didn't so much as spend a night in jail for it. You can look up a long list of incidents he's had regarding his anger, but they've been covered up."

"Do you care to speculate why?" Decker asked.

"Because he's a doctor. Our society deifies doctors. Especially rich ones."

"Even in the case of murder?"

Powers shrugged. "Nobody ever had the balls to accuse him of it."

"Why not?"

"I asked that very question every damned day until I was kicked out of the department."

Decker crossed his legs. "Did you ever have occasion to speak with the doctor?"

"I did."

"And how did that go?"

"About as well as you might expect. The doctor never confessed to anything, but he made a glib statement about the murders that I will never forget."

"What was that?"

"That it was a damned shame, what happened." Powers grew solemn. "He said it was a shame because it caused him and his staff so many interruptions. He said it like the murders of Steven and Linda were nothing but an inconvenience to him. He said—and I won't ever forget this—that I would never prove he had anything to do with it because there had been no proof left that would tie him to it."

Decker whistled low, then asked, "What initially drew you to him?"

"Beg pardon?"

"Dr. Dean blipped onto your radar but no one else's. There must have been a reason."

Powers thought about it for a long moment. When finally he spoke, he said, "It wasn't just me. Big Jim liked him for it as well."

"What?" Jess could not hide her surprise. "Do you mean Deputy Ballard?"

Powers nodded.

Decker leaned forward in his seat. "What gave you that impression?"

"Because he questioned him too."

Jess nearly broke her arm snatching her notes from her bag. The Trapper Keeper. The little green notebook. She flipped through every scrap of paper in her possession but found nothing.

"It doesn't mention Dean's name anywhere in his notes," she said.

Powers cocked his head. "You have his case notes?"

"Some of them." Decker nodded.

"Let me guess," Powers offered, with a wry grin. "He was hell bent on Berry."

"I take it you never agreed?"

Powers shrugged. "Maybe for a day or two, early in the investigation. Berry was an idiot. He was a thug. But he wasn't a killer."

"Why would you say Ballard was so convinced Berry was guilty?"

Powers opened his mouth but seemed to think better of anything he might say.

Decker folded his hands together in front of him, with his fingers forming a temple. "We've heard some say that Ballard was a drunkard."

Jess covered the microphone with her hand. "Dan!"

Decker raised a finger to silence her, then returned his attention to Powers.

"He had his demons," Powers said. "I'm afraid they caught up with him in the end."

Jess shifted the subject. "What about the phone calls?"

Powers's face fell flat. "I'm sorry. What phone calls?"

"Lee Ann Thompson received several phone calls from a man who claimed to be the killer," she said. "What are your thoughts on those?"

Powers's jawline tightened.

Jess tried it from a different angle. "Lee Ann Thompson was Linda Harris's sister. They were twi—"

"I know Lee Ann. I know her very well."

"Then you must know about the phone calls."

"I . . ." Powers struggled to compose himself. "I don't . . . I can't . . ."

Decker leaned back in his chair and studied the former investigator. "You're telling me that as close as you claim to have remained with the victim's sister, she's never told you anything about those late-night phone calls?"

"What are you trying to insinuate?"

Jess acted quickly. "Nothing, Sergeant," she said. "He's not trying to insinuate anything. We just want to be very clear about everything so that we get it right. There is so much that remains a mystery to us. Like some of the other suspects in the case. How seriously did you ever take any of them?"

Powers arched an eyebrow. "Like who?"

"Like Sean Gray?"

Powers's chuckle turned into a dry cough. His wife appeared with a glass of water with a straw, which he sucked at until he could regain his composure.

"Gray was a punk," he said. "He had nothing at all to do with it."

"But he worked at the hospital," said Jess. "He must have known Linda."

"That's about the extent of the connection. Oh, I think he might have been in or around that trailer park or something else, but it was reaching at best. Still, Red Carter wasn't going to take a loss in that column and needed to save face. So he pinned it on that stupid motorcycle thief with the worst luck, and the rest is history."

Decker rested his elbows on his thighs. "You're telling us that Gray was framed?"

"He wasn't ever charged," Powers said, "but most everyone over in Deeton could pat themselves on the back and tell themselves *job well done*."

"Tell me more about Red," said Decker.

Powers's expression turned sour. "I hate to speak ill of the dead . . ."

"Don't let me stop you."

"Red Carter was an old-school sheriff," Powers said. "He expected the sun to rise and set in his county on his command. If he thought you were guilty of something, you had two choices: confess to it or get the hell out of town as quick as you could."

"That sounds a bit extreme."

"You don't know the half of it." Powers licked his lips. "If he couldn't pin something on somebody, they sometimes had a tendency to go missing."

Jess felt ice blanketing her skin. Her head went dizzy. "You don't mean . . ." She searched for the words but couldn't find them. "Sergeant Powers, you're not saying . . ."

"Sergeant Powers," Decker said, picking up her slack, "you're not insinuating that Red Carter would have people *disappeared*, are you?"

Powers sipped again from his straw.

"Let me ask you again but in a different way." Decker collected himself. "George Berry seems to have absolutely vanished. His trail ends in 1972. Any newspapers, phone books, internet searches . . . any trace of him seems to have dried up, as if he disappeared from the face of the earth."

Jess grew sick to her stomach. She wanted more than anything to shut off the recorders, but her arms were too weak to lift them. She listened in horror, unable to stop the interview from continuing.

"Harnett," Powers whispered.

Decker's brow furrowed. "I beg your pardon?"

"Harnett George Berry," said Powers. "He sometimes goes by HG. Mostly goes by Harnett. But never George. Not since he left Lake Castor."

Jess's reflexes caught fire. She whipped out her phone and was already typing.

"You'll find a total of four Harnett Berrys," Powers told her, "but Harnett *George* Berry lives in Sumter, South Carolina. That's where he's resided since 1973."

"I found him." Jess could not look up from her screen. "Holy shit, Dan. I've *found* him."

For the first time in what felt like an eternity, Powers looked away from Decker. He massaged the bridge of his nose with a shaking thumb and forefinger.

"Why did he move?" Jess asked.

"You'll have to ask him. It's his story to tell, but boy, is it a doozy."

"How about *your* story?" Decker asked.

"I'm afraid I don't have one."

"Oh, come on, Sergeant. I've told and heard a million lies, so I sure as hell know what they smell like. Don't nothing stink like you telling me you don't have a story."

"My story," Powers said, growing visibly irritated, "is that I don't know why you are asking me all these questions about Sean Gray and Harnett Berry when everyone knows who the killer is."

"You're certain that it is Dr. Dean?"

"Hell yes!" Powers slammed his hand on the armrest of his wheelchair. "He says it himself on the damned phone every year."

Decker smiled like a dog who'd just shit the carpet. "I thought you said you didn't know anything about the phone calls, Sergeant."

Powers's first instinct was to drop his jaw. He quickly recovered and twisted his face into unrelenting anger. He gripped both armrests until his knuckles whitened.

Mrs. Powers cleared her throat, then moved uneasily between Decker and her husband.

"Dear . . . ," was all she said.

Jess felt everything going off the rails. She had spent months searching for Jack Powers, and after only ten minutes or so, the interview was ending.

"Tell me," she said quickly, "what do you mean that Big Jim had already interviewed Dr. Dean? This is the first I've heard of it."

Powers, yet to compose himself, looked to his wife and nodded.

Mrs. Powers gripped her husband's wheelchair with both hands. "I'm afraid Jack has grown very tired," she said. "I think that's enough questions for today."

"But wait—"

"I said that's enough."

Mrs. Powers backed her husband out of the room and away from both Jess and Decker.

The interview was finished.

CHAPTER THIRTY-SEVEN

James Ballard

1972

Ballard feared another bolt of whiskey might dull his perception, but he took one anyway. He needed to use every bit of the skills he'd honed over the past couple of decades to suss out any clues. He waited for the liquor to settle the upset in both his belly and his mind, then set out to analyze his surroundings.

Boxed macaroni.

Boxed spaghetti noodles.

Jarred spaghetti sauces.

Canned tomatoes.

Red. Blue. White. Blue. Red. Red . . .

So many colors.

Ballard jammed fists into his eyes and rubbed them until they were near raw. He tugged the flask again from his pocket and had gone only so far as to unscrew it before he was jostled from behind.

"Pardon me, Big Jim."

Trucker hat.

Plaid shirt.

Long face.

Beard.

All of which added up to nothing in the recesses of Ballard's memory. He grasped and reached for hope in the darkness of his recollection but withdrew only fistfuls of cobweb and despair.

"Hi-dee," Ballard managed through trembling lips.

The man registered the confusion upon the deputy's face, then arched an eyebrow after catching a glimpse of the small flask in his hand.

"Hell, I don't blame you none," said the man. "I get stressed enough when Marge sends me out for groceries, and I'm not trying to solve any murders. How's that thing going, anyway? Y'all turn anything up yet?"

Groceries . . . Ballard felt a shift in gravity. This time, when he gathered his surroundings, they began to take form. The blurs in his vision retreated to the peripheries.

"I'm . . ." He fought to steady his voice. "I'm *shopping*."

"As am I," said the fellow. "Marge said it's tuna casserole tonight, so maybe you ought to hand me some of that."

Ballard remembered the flask in his hand and quickly stuffed it back into his pocket. His breathing quickened. His body temperature rocketed; then the bottom fell out of it. Fearing he might keel to the side, he steadied himself by grabbing hold of the pasta shelf.

"Are you okay, Big Jim?" asked the man. "You ain't looking so good."

"I'm fine," he snapped. He wished the man away—and, with him, perhaps the entire world. Everyone served some greater purpose, it seemed, and that purpose could be nothing other than to confound him. He despised them all. He fought for a moment to recall someone he didn't think the universe better without but could not be bothered with it, for there were more-pressing matters on his mind than that or the pestering fellow in the trucker hat.

For instance: What had he come to the grocery store to buy?

How far back could he remember? Not parking the car. Not driving to the store. Certainly not—there . . . he caught hold of a fleeting memory by its toe. At home, in his garage: standing over his workbench when Cora came out to ask him if he would run to the store and fetch a . . . fetch a . . . it waited for him there, at the tip of his own tongue, where he might never catch up to it. Ballard could remember the smell of sawdust in that garage, the sheen of his freshly waxed pickup truck, and even the scent of roses in Cora's perfume but not at all what she had asked him to run to the store and buy.

And what had he been doing when she'd stepped in?

Ballard closed his eyes.

He had been staring at his own service weapon. He'd been thinking up loopholes in his insurance policy. He'd been thinking of every way imaginable to spare his sweet Cora and Samantha from the anguish that was no doubt headed their way when—

"Is that Big Jim?" hollered a woman's voice from down the aisle. "Where is that lovely wife of yours?"

Ballard felt the collapsing of his soul as an older woman shuffled toward him with a cart. Her name . . . *her name* . . . and he grew eternally grateful for the idiot next to him when he said: "Ida Crabtree. How is it we only ever run into each other when we're shopping?"

Ida Crabtree, thought Ballard. *Married to Bill Crabtree.*

"Where else am I going to see you?" She raised an eyebrow in mock condescension. "You quit going to church. Not like Big Jim here, who makes it a point to show out for every service. Never once does he miss a Sun—"

The Crabtrees live at 105 Buchanon. Their children are named Priscilla and . . . Priscilla and . . .

"Just picking up a few things for dinner. How about y'all?"

Priscilla and Aaron. Aaron is Samantha's age. Last year, he hit three home runs in a game against Roxboro.

"Not much. I was just asking Big Jim about those two kids from Lake Castor."

"Oh yes," said Ida. "I haven't read anything about that in the papers for a while, but I heard from Mike Howard's wife that y'all picked up a boy for that. Some kid from Lake Castor who stole a car or something like that."

We are at Grundy's Food Mart, which is located on Beaver Dam Road. I am here shopping for . . . for . . .

"Did you now?" asked the man. "Do y'all really think he done it?"

"I . . ." Ballard wiped perspiration from his brow. "I . . . I . . ."

"I understand if you can't talk about it," said the man, "but if y'all got somebody up at the jail that you think done it, can't you at least let us know about it?"

Ballard honestly had no idea. He could neither remember nor care. There seemed to be a swelling queue in his head of things competing for what remaining capacity for memory he had left, and he could barely remember if what went on at work was near the top of it.

Instead, he thought of Cora.

Cora and Samantha.

He thought of the time he and Cora had taken Samantha to the beach when she was nine or ten. The memory of how he'd kept her close, even though she had been on the precipice of growing away from him. Still, he'd let her venture just a bit farther than she should, and before he could grab hold of her, they both had been swept away in a rip current. Then, like now, Ballard had struggled to find his feet beneath him. He'd swum with the shore, away from the shore . . . both right and left. He'd gone under to fight it, but his own survival had not been the battle he'd waged. Rather, he had lashed against that silent, deadly current to save his daughter. He had not cared if he swallowed every drop of water thrown at him by that ocean; he had not cared if his limbs were drained of any will to live. He had fought until he had hold of his daughter and would have sunk to the bottom of the sea had he not found—just as suddenly as he had lost it—his footing.

That memory pressed harder into his mind's eye, harder than any other one—namely the murdered kids from Lake Castor or what the name of the man in the trucker hat was or, least of all, what he'd come to Grundy's to buy. That memory of what it felt like to give it all up, only to have that ephemeral god grant him mercy—and grant it also to his daughter. To his wife, who remained hysterical at the water's edge.

I need more time with them.

This time there would be no rescue at the hand of God. There would be no respite in the sand. His sentence was certain. So, as he thought of his wife and child, was theirs. He could hide it from them for only so much longer. Soon, his deterioration would register in their minds. Soon, they would begin to suspect, and it would not be long before—

"Big Jim?" Ida placed a hand on his arm. "Is everything okay?"

"Uh . . ." Ballard's chest grew tighter. "I . . . I . . . I can't remember."

The shadows quit Ida Crabtree's expression. "Oh, bless your heart," she said. "That happens to me all the time."

"Does it?"

"Absolutely. Do you want to know what I do?"

Ballard did, more than anything.

"Just walk around the store until it all comes back to you."

She made it sound so easy that Ballard half expected it to work. As if it were all he needed to do and he should rush headlong back to the doctor to report this great triumph. He barreled down the cereal aisle, through the produce department, and then all the way back to the meat market. He tugged the little green notepad from his shirt pocket and flipped through pages upon pages of notes.

YOUR NAME IS DEPUTY JAMES W. BALLARD.

YOUR WIFE'S NAME IS CORA.

YOUR DAUGHTER'S NAME IS SAMANTHA.

YOU LIVE AT 809 WAYNEL—

Nothing about why he'd stopped at the grocery store, nothing about what he was to do for his wife and child, nothing of a single matter of importance. All around him, he heard voices, as if everyone were talking at once but talking through a fog and in a language unknown to him. They spoke in some sort of indecipherable code, or perhaps instead it wasn't words but laughter. Was it him at whom they were laughing? Had he become some sort of cosmic punch line?

The first to approach him was a stock boy, young and pimple faced. He inspected Ballard with eyes as wide as hubcaps, as if afraid to speak properly to the big man, which explained his mumbles and murmurs.

"Speak up, boy," Ballard snapped. "What in Sam Hill are you saying?"

"Talk to me a moment about your alcohol consumption. Has it increased in the past couple of months?"

"I beg your—"

Ballard blinked, and away went the stock boy, the meat market, and all the rest of Deeton. In its place was Dr. Fenton and his office, smack dab in the middle of downtown Lake Castor. Ballard dropped his head into his hands so that he no longer had to look the doctor in the eye. His jaw shook loose the words from his throat.

"More often, it seems."

Dr. Fenton nodded. "This is not unusual. My first inclination might be to write a prescription for the episodes, but drinking alcohol will only—"

"I'll get it under control, Doctor."

"I'm serious. It's—"

"I said I'll have it under control."

Fenton squinted as if to add further scrutiny. In the end, he shook his head, as if he had decided against something he had yet to discuss aloud. "All the prescriptions in the world won't matter for long," he said. "You will eventually find it impossible to face this alone. The longer you delay speaking to your family—"

"Not right now."

Fenton must have registered the edge in Ballard's voice, for he wrote the prescription and did so in silence. Once finished, he ripped it from his pad of paper and handed it to the deputy. He watched as Ballard folded it and tucked it into his shirt pocket, next to the little green notebook. He seemed to measure whether to speak again.

"I have something else I'd like to talk with you about," Fenton said finally.

"If it's about bringing in my wife, then you can—"

"It's not." Fenton put down his pen, as if to signal a change in gears. "It's in . . . it's in a different capacity altogether."

Ballard nodded and folded together his hands.

Fenton pointed to the uniform's breast pocket. "You may want to get your notebook."

Ballard blinked twice, then retrieved his notepad. He opened it to the first clean page.

"There's been a detective hanging around the hospital." Fenton's voice took on a new quality. "He's been showing everyone an FBI profile . . ."

"Yes." Ballard sighed. "We had nothing to do with that. Lake Castor police are nothing but a handful of thumbs. I'm told the detective who released it was—"

"I didn't contact Lake Castor," Fenton interrupted, "because I think this is of a more sensitive nature. I trust there is a level of confidence between you and me. Am I right, Deputy?"

Ballard got the picture. He nodded.

"Go on," he said.

Fenton took a breath. "Some of the traits mentioned in that profile—above-average education, athletic, between twenty-five and forty years old . . . I hardly think of those as exclusive qualities."

"Beg pardon?"

"I mean, I'm sure you've received tips from well-meaning people . . ."

"You have no idea."

Fenton leaned forward in his chair. "But there are other qualities mentioned in the article which gave me pause."

"Dr. Fenton—"

"Hear me out." He awaited Ballard's attention. "The article also suggested he was a loner. A neat and precise man. That he most likely would have acted alone."

"Yes, I read that, but—"

"It also suggested the killer would be subject to moments of terrible temper."

Ballard massaged the bridge of his nose with his thumb and forefinger. "Sure," he said. "That describes a lot of people."

"We have a doctor here." Fenton looked over both his shoulders, as if to ensure their privacy. "I believe you've already encountered the wrath of Dr. Christian Dean. Remember when you and your colleagues arrived to interview the nurses?"

"Ah yes," said Ballard. "I remember him."

Fenton opened a drawer and produced a copy of the profile. It was in such a pristine condition that Ballard hesitated to handle it.

"It describes the killer as someone who considers himself to be above other persons and capable of judging them. I cannot think of a better description of my colleague. He is an incredibly brilliant man, but lately his impatience has surpassed his acumen. He's been . . . *lashing out*. I thought it might be routine stresses from the medical field, but after I read the article, certain things began to fall into place."

"All due respect, Dr. Fenton," said Ballard, "but I don't see how—"

"The article claims the killer would have been 'out to cleanse the world.'"

Fenton tapped his finger on the last paragraph of the article.

"There is something in Dr. Dean's voice," Fenton said. "There is something behind his eyes. When he gets angry . . . I mean, everyone gets angry. Everyone loses their temper. But Dr. Dean . . . it's like he loses *himself* to the temper."

"I don't understand what you expect me to do. This is not my—"

"Perhaps you might have a word with him."

"I hardly think that would be appropriate. For one thing—"

"Just sit across from him. Examine him, much as he might examine you, were you his patient. You are far more experienced than I when it comes to detecting the evils of man. All I ask is that you sit with him, and if you feel he is not—"

"Dr. Fenton, if I do this . . ."

"Talk to me for a moment about your alcohol consumption. Has it increased the past couple of months?"

The heat inside Ballard sparked a conflagration. "You already asked me that!" The edge took hold of his voice. Tears stung in his chest. He blinked fury from his eyes and, once he had fingered away the sting, took new consideration of his surroundings.

It was no longer Fenton sitting before him at the desk but rather a different doctor. Ballard recognized him immediately. Dr. Dean, the red-faced physician from before, when they had last interviewed the nurses.

He reached again into the fog but did not know if it had been moments that had passed or rather hours or even years.

Ballard consulted the little green notebook.

CHRISTIAN DEAN.

DOCTOR.

TEMPER.

DID HE KNOW VICTIMS???

He looked up at the doctor, who seemed not only to register Ballard's confusion but also to revel in it. It wasn't simply satisfaction behind those eyes but also considerable degrees of contempt.

It was that contempt that braced Ballard like cold water to the face. He was awake. He was alive. More so than he had been in—

"I assure you," said the doctor, "that you have told me nothing of the sort. It's none of my business how much you drink, but if you're not prepared to be honest with me, there is so little I can do for you. I only agreed to this meeting—without an appointment, mind you—because Dr. Fenton alleged it was urgent, but if you are going to insist upon wasting my time . . ."

"We're not here to talk about me, Dr. Dean." Ballard again checked his notebook. "I'm trying to establish whether or not you knew Linda Harris or Steven Hicks."

"And as I told you," said the doctor, "I don't recall encountering either of them. I am a very busy man and haven't inclinations to fraternize with nurses or students."

Something in the doctor's demeanor unsettled Ballard. He could have been a photographic image of the FBI's profile. The doctor was clean shaven, wore no flashy clothes, and—aside from the reported bursts of temper—avoided attracting any attention to himself.

Ballard settled in.

"What about the cul-de-sac where they were taken from," he said. "How well did you know that neighborhood?"

"This is the second time you've asked me that," said Dr. Dean. "I'm tired of repeating myself."

"Could you please answer the question?"

"I already have."

Ballard did not think he in fact had, but . . .

"Humor me, Doctor."

Dr. Dean sighed. "I don't blame you for not remembering. In your condition, I'm certain you often—"

"The neighborhood, Doctor. How well did you know it?"

"Well, for one, I live near there. But that's no secret. Several people do, in fact. Surely you're not going to tell me that everyone who lives there is a suspect. If so, then I—"

"That neighborhood is located between the hospital where you work and the street where you live. Have you ever taken a shortcut home from work?"

"If I said yes, that still doesn't make me a killer."

"When you've taken these shortcuts, have you ever seen anyone parking?"

"Parking?"

"Making out. Necking. Couples sitting in parked cars."

Dr. Dean made a sour face. "I don't have time to pay attention to other people's activities."

"Answer the question."

"I'm more likely to see the trash they leave behind."

"Beg pardon?"

"Cigarette butts. Beer bottles. Used prophylactics." Dr. Dean showed his teeth. "Thank God they're used; I'd hate to think of their kind proliferating beneath our . . ."

"Please, Doctor. Go on."

Dr. Dean crinkled his nose.

Ballard continued. "You were telling me about *their kind*. What kind is that?"

Dean's blue eyes flashed like icicles in a pair of headlights. The contempt behind them deepened.

"I'll answer that question," he said, "if you answer one of mine."

"Okay, Doctor. Shoot."

"Talk to me a moment about your alcohol consumption. Has it increased the past coup—"

Ballard's hand shot out like a gun crack. It made contact with a framed photograph on the doctor's desk and sent it against the far wall. Its shattering gave the deputy no satisfaction, so he did so again with a second picture frame. He followed that with the doctor's desk calendar. He would have cleared Dean's desk of all its belongings and adornments, had he not caught sight of the smug satisfaction on Dean's face.

Ballard cursed himself for the rash reaction, which only furthered his anger. He fought like hell to regain control of his breathing, of his heartbeat, of his—

"Where were you the night they were killed?" he asked.

"When who were killed?" asked the doctor.

"Steven and—" Ballard took a deep breath and let it out slowly. "Where were you?"

"I don't even know what night that was."

"It was Christmas Eve, Doctor. It's called the Christmas Eve mur—"

"I already answered this. If you insist on my repeating everything, then—"

"You haven't told me shit. You think I don't know what you're doing? Answer the goddamned question."

"I will if you sit down."

"I *am* sitt—"

But he wasn't. Ballard found himself standing by the door. Had the lights dimmed? Surely it had been brighter when he'd first stepped into the office, and it wasn't just his imagination. Perhaps the doctor had somehow—

Dean spoke slowly. "I'm afraid your condition is only going to further deteriorate. This impairment of judgment is irreversible. It's most evident with these sudden explosions of anger or in your manner of—"

"This is irrelevant to my investigation." Ballard felt like every breath was a struggle. "If you'd only answer—"

"Is it, in fact, *irrelevant*?" Dean rose from his desk and walked to the file cabinet. He opened the top drawer. Ballard considered—only for a moment—that he should draw his sidearm and stop Dean, should he produce his own weapon. He shelved that instinct; better, perhaps, for Dean to take him in the line of duty than for Cora and Samantha to have to deal with a fraction of Ballard's despair. "Surely your sheriff is aware of your affliction. Have you disclosed ev—"

Ballard collapsed against the wall. He would strike out, if he could, but found his limbs to be useless. All the fight had quit him. He thought once again of that rip current. Had he only let it slip him away . . .

"If there are no further questions, Deputy . . ."

"Only one." Ballard struggled to right himself. "Did you kill Steven Hicks and Linda Harris?"

Dean ticked an eyebrow. "Have you anything you can prove?"

"Not yet. But if I take what I know to my sheriff . . ."

"And by that rationale," said the doctor, "what should happen if I take him everything that *I* know?"

Ballard's knees buckled. The glimmer he saw in Dean's eye added up to one thought: *checkmate.*

"If there's nothing else"—the doctor smiled—"I'll have to ask you to leave."

Dean held open his office door.

"We'll meet again, Doctor."

"When we do," said Dean, "please be sure that my attorney is present. All future questions should be directed to him."

Ballard did not wait for Dean to escort him through the door, nor for it to close behind him. He plunged himself headlong from the office, down the corridor, and into the men's room, where he collapsed over top of the commode. There, he ripped the latest pages from his notebook, those that mentioned Christian Dean. After, he sicked up everything he'd ever eaten in his life, all the air he'd ever breathed, and all the love he'd ever felt.

CHAPTER THIRTY-EIGHT

Jack Powers

1972

Sergeant Jack Powers could not believe his eyes. He had shown up at Lake Castor General in hopes of something—*something*—that might break the logjam. After visits with several nurses resulted in their exhausted refusals to speak further with him (*"What good will it do to keep talking about it, Sergeant? Nobody seems to care anymore."*) and doctors no longer took the time to answer questions, Powers had begun to ponder the futility of it all. Perhaps the nurses were right. His own police department had refused to invest further resources into the matter.

To go even further, Powers had been suspended from duty. His commission of the FBI psychiatric profile of the killer had been a step too far. Chief of Police Grantham Jessup had put Powers on four weeks' leave, without pay.

That would not derail Powers, however, as he continued to investigate every lead he could muster on his own time. However, as the days turned into weeks, those leads had all but dried up, sending him right back to where he'd started: the hospital.

Which was where he saw Deputy James Ballard staggering from a doctor's office to the men's room. The big man was in such a state of shock and disarray that Powers felt compelled to follow him.

He entered the bathroom and found Ballard leaning his full weight against the sink, splashing water onto his pallid face.

"Funny to find you here, Big Jim."

Ballard spun to face the detective, and Powers feared he might need to defend himself. The deputy seemed not to recognize him, those dark eyes tight pools of forever black and tinged with fury. Powers took two steps backward and turned up his hands.

"Whoa, whoa, Jim . . ." Powers faked a grin. "It's me, buddy. It's Jack. Lake Castor police. We're on the same team."

"Not now, Sergeant."

"Actually . . ." Powers was taken aback by the condition of the big man. He remembered Ballard to be nearly forty pounds heavier, recalled nothing of the gray in his skin, the hollows in the eyes. "I'm not here as a cop. I'm here on my own. Lake Castor's not even on the case anymore. They pulled us off, and I . . ." Powers swallowed thickly at the memory of it. "It turns out I can be a cop in Lake Castor or I can give a shit about catching the son of a bitch who killed those two kids. The brass made it real clear there's no way to do both."

"Bully for you, Jack. Now, if you don't mind . . ."

Ballard muscled past Powers for the hand towel to dry himself. Powers caught him by the arm.

"Thing is I *do* mind." Powers was surprised at how light Ballard felt in his grip. "I came here to interview a couple of nurses on my own, but I saw you come out of that doctor's office like maybe you'd seen a ghost. What's going on in there? What have you got?"

"Nothing." Ballard blinked several times, as if he were trying to purge something from his mind. "I'm not here on official capacity. I'm here—I'm . . . it's actually none of your business what I'm doing here."

Powers did not relinquish his grip. "I've sacrificed too much to back down now," he said. "I don't care about any grief from Deeton and Lake Castor. I don't care about any of it. I'm not a cop today; I'm a man who wants to solve a double homicide."

Ballard used all his force to push Powers off him. He struck out at the first thing his fist could find, which turned out to be the bathroom mirror. That mirror shattered into a thousand shiny pieces.

"I don't give a flying fuck about your homicide," growled the deputy.

Powers opened his mouth, but something in Ballard's voice gave him second thoughts about uttering a single word. The two men locked eyes and contemplated the coming fires of hell inside of each other until Ballard, spent of all his hate and hopes, unclenched Powers from his grasp, then staggered out of the bathroom.

Powers remained inside to offer a wider berth to the deputy. That interaction was a lot for him to unpack, but he retraced his thoughts to their roots, which delivered him from the men's room to the door from which he'd first seen Ballard leaving.

DR. C. A. DEAN

Powers knocked. A voice told him to enter.

"May I help you?" asked the man behind a large desk.

An athletic man, between 25 and 40 years old . . . Neat and precise . . .

"Are you Dr. Dean?" Powers asked.

"I am. To whom am I speaking?"

"My name is Sergeant Jack Powers, and I'm a detective with the Lake Castor Police Department."

Dr. Dean showed no emotion. "I have to warn you, Sergeant Powers: I am quite busy this afternoon. I might recommend you to my assistant if you would like to make an appoint—"

"I'm not here for medical help, Doctor."

"Oh?"

He will be a loner. He will be clean shaven.

"A colleague of mine . . ." Powers hitched a thumb over his shoulder. "He just left your office. His name is Deputy Jim Ballard. He's with Dee—"

"Yes."

Powers left space for Dean to fill, but the doctor didn't take the bait. He glanced over the framed accolades and accommodations adorning the walls.

He will have no criminal record and would retain an excellent work record.

"May I ask why it was that you were meeting Deputy Ballard?"

"You may ask," Dean said, "but I'm afraid I cannot answer. As I'm sure you know, doctors are not obliged to confide any information delivered by their patients."

"So Ballard is your patient?"

Dean met him with a flat stare.

He considers himself above other persons capable of judging him.

"Did you know a nurse who worked here by the name of Linda Harris?"

Dean checked his watch. "Sergeant, there are so many nurses who work here that I can't poss—"

"This one was murdered. She was strangled with her boyfriend and tied to a tree. Surely you remember that one."

"That murder to which you refer," said the doctor, "happened over nine months ago. In another nine months, no one will even remember it."

Powers felt everything inside of him turn to ice.

His positioning of the bodies is a way of displaying his cleverness, as if to say, "Look at me. Look at what I have done."

"What did you say?"

Dean had already gone about the business of gathering papers and stacking them inside a briefcase.

"I'm quite busy, Sergeant," he said. "If you have any further questions . . ." He motioned Powers toward the door.

Powers ran every stop sign and red light making his way back to the station. Once inside, he beelined for the records room in such a bluster that he frightened the girl behind the desk half to death.

"Jack," she started, "what are you doing here? I thought you were supposed to be—"

"I don't have any time to explain," Powers said, "because I'm pretty sure Hank and the chief will be looking for me by now. But I need you to do me a big favor."

"Sure, Jack. What is it?"

Powers ducked his head out the door and looked up and down the hall. He imagined he would have mere moments before anyone arrived to shut him down. Time was of the essence.

"I need you to get me everything you can on someone down at Lake Castor General." He wrote the name clearly on a sheet of paper. "His name is Dean, Christian Alexander. He's a doctor."

CHAPTER THIRTY-NINE

Jess Keeler

Present Day

Jess punched the details into her car's GPS. Without waiting for Decker to buckle his seat belt, she threw the car into gear and left the small cul-de-sac where Jack Powers lived. Soon, she was on the highway and headed west.

"According to my phone," she said, "it will take us four and a half hours to get there."

"To get where?" Decker asked.

"Sumter."

"What the hell is in Sumter?"

"Harnett George Berry."

Decker slapped the dashboard. "We're not going to South Carolina."

Jess kept her eyes on the road and the needle at seventy-five miles per hour.

"Okay," Decker said. "*I* am not going to South Carolina."

"It will be mighty expensive to Uber back to Lake Castor, Dan."

Decker cleared his throat. He twisted in his seat. "Keeler, we're hardly prepared to interview George Berry. We only found—"

"Harnett," she said.

"Fine. *Harnett* Berry. We only found out literally fifteen minutes ago that he was even alive and not a figment of your grandfather's extremely active imagination. Hell, we only found out a *lot* of things thirty minutes ago."

"And we could have found out more if you hadn't rattled Jack Powers's cage so bad. Seriously, Dan. If you're going to behave that way with Harnett Berry, maybe it's best if you wait in the car. He was in the middle of telling us all kinds of information about Dean's anger-management issues, and you interrupted him with all these questions about my grandfather's drinking and Red Car—"

"How are we not talking about all the other crazy accusations he dropped?"

Jess increased her speed.

Decker continued, "Or how he straight up lied to us about not knowing about those phone calls?"

"We don't know that he lied."

"First he said he didn't know; then he said that the killer identified himself on the phone calls."

Jess shrugged. "He had a stroke, so maybe . . ."

"I think there's a lot more going on than a deteriorating brain."

Something tugged at Jess. A thought—a fleeting one—tickled her mind, and before she could grab hold of it and work it out, it was gone.

"There's something fishy going on," Decker said. "Jack Powers definitely knows a lot more than he's letting on."

"I agree," she said, "but you're never going to get it out of him, or any other law enforcement officer, by being combative and accusatory. You shut him down, and he stopped answering questions at that point. What's the point of interviewing these people if you can't get us good audio?"

"We got good audio. In fact, we got *great* audio."

"We got audio of you pissing him off."

"Which is damned good audio. Wait until I write it up, and I'll show you."

Jess raised her eyebrows. "Great. We've got four hours. I'd love to see that."

"Four hours?" Decker squinted to better see a road sign. "Jesus. I'll do it after I nap."

"No way." Jess slapped his thigh until he sat up straight. "Slam an energy drink or something. You've got copy to write."

"Fine." Decker grimaced. "Can I borrow a pen?"

◆ ◆ ◆

[END MUSIC CUE]

DECKER: It is often argued that we should not judge the police of yesterday by today's standards. Crime scenes in current times are processed differently than they were fifty years ago. So was evidence. No investigator working homicides in 1972 would understand the significance of DNA for another twenty years; therefore it would be unfair to criticize them for failing to preserve evidence.

However, upon taking a closer look at the investigation into the murders of Steven Hicks and Linda Harris, we find there may still be plenty to criticize. How much time would investigators spend chasing false leads or, worse, leads conjured out of thin air in order to further their own biases? Thanks to the actions of a handful of overzealous law enforcement officials, we may never know the truth about what happened on Christmas Eve, 1971. Jurisdiction issues, the inability to communicate, all the egos and departmental dick swinging . . . how much of it contributed to allowing a killer to walk the streets of Lake Castor undetected?

Instead of asking ourselves these questions, we thought we'd ask former Lake Castor police sergeant Jack Powers.

JESS KEELER: Lee Ann Thompson received several phone calls from a man who claimed to be the killer. What are your thoughts on those?

SGT. POWERS: (silence)

JESS KEELER: Lee Ann Thompson was Linda Harris's sister. They were twi—

SGT. POWERS: I know Lee Ann. I know her very well.

JESS KEELER: Then you must know about the phone calls.

SGT. POWERS: (silence)

DECKER: You're telling me that as close as you claim to have remained with the victim's sister, she's never told you anything about those late-night phone calls?

SGT. POWERS: What are you trying to insinuate?

[MUSIC CUE]

DECKER: Jack Powers was not an easy man to interview. He'd recently suffered a stroke, so it took some effort to get him warmed up. But among many revelations he offered—and we'll get to those—there was this little exchange near the end of the interview. It may seem inconsequential, but it has led us to ask ourselves if it might indeed be the investigators who need to be investigated.

SGT. POWERS: I don't know why you are asking me all these questions about Sean Gray and Harnett Berry when everyone knows who the killer is.

DECKER: You're certain that it is Dr. Dean?

SGT. POWERS: Hell yes! He says it himself on the damned phone every year!

DECKER: I thought you said you didn't know anything about the phone calls, Sergeant.

SGT. POWERS: (silence)

[MUSIC CUE]

DECKER: If Jack Powers was willing to lie to us about knowing about the phone calls, what other evidence or information might he be willing to lie about? And we're not only concerned with Powers. Why was Deputy James Ballard so intent on Berry's guilt, when all fingers seem to point in the direction of Dr. Dean? Some might argue that Ballard's fascination with Berry bordered on obsession. Others have claimed it might be the result of judgment clouded by alcoholism. Could Ballard's weakness for liquor have—

"Dan, what the hell are you doing?"

Decker took his eyes off the road long enough to glance at Jess in the passenger seat. She held his handwritten pages in her hand.

"It's copy," he said.

"It's . . ." She searched like mad for the words. "You can't do that, Dan."

"Hey, kid," he said softly, "it's where the story is leading us."

"It sounds more like where *you* are leading the story." She folded Decker's pages, then stuffed them inside her Trapper Keeper. "Tell me what you think Sergeant Powers stands to gain by lying about the phone calls."

Decker squinted into the horizon. "I don't know yet, kid. I just know he's lying. And I also know that those phone calls were the main clue that led us to his number one suspect, Dr. Dean."

The sun was already heading for the hills. The GPS claimed only thirteen minutes left for the drive. Jess imagined they would likely catch Berry as he sat down for dinner. Or perhaps poured his first cocktail of the night. Jess's stomach fluttered with anticipation as she wondered what revelations Berry might open for them, all the questions that ached within her that might be answered once he materialized into something more than a name scratched into her grandfather's notebook.

"Let me ask you a question, Keeler," Decker said. "Why are you doing this?"

Jess answered immediately. "You know why."

"I know you originally told me it was to avenge the journalism career you abandoned in college when you got pregnant." Decker measured his words carefully. "Lately, however, your approach has smacked of somebody writing a love letter to her grandfather and a handful of dirty cops."

Bile burned in Jess's throat. "That's not fair, Dan, and you know it."

"Then why, Jess? If you're not willing to follow the story *all the way*, no matter what, no matter what it uncovers, then why are you even invested in it?"

Jess let the air settle between them as he exited the highway. "Our job," she said very slowly, "is to speak for Steve and Linda. They have no voice of their own anymore because someone took it from them. Our job is to find out who that was. Not to vilify a group of men who were only doing their jobs to the best of their ab—"

"Our job is to sell an interesting story," Decker said.

"Don't you mean *tell*?"

Decker's gaze colored with condescension. "Sweetheart, we are under no obligation to anyone except our audience. They deserve the best story we can tell. Right now, dirty cops are the cause célèbre. There's blood in the water, kid, and the people have developed a taste for it. You give the audience a story of organizational failure, toxic masculinity, and cover-your-ass politics, and today's generation will eat it up. But your basic cut-and-paste unsolved homicide has hit an expiration date."

"I'm concerned by this newfound criticism you're showing towards law enforcement," she said. "It smacks of bias. I never would have teamed up and worked this long with you if I thought for one minute that we were writing a hit piece."

"It's not a—" Decker double-checked the GPS, then turned onto a country lane that bisected two tobacco fields. They drove farther and farther from civilization. "Look, we're under no obligation to anyone but our audience. Our audience deserves the best story we can tell. They deserve a through line."

"We have one. The murders."

"Au contraire." Decker waggled his eyebrows toward the floorboard, where her knapsack sat. "Our through line is in that bag."

"My grandfather's notebook?"

"You said yourself that something was wrong. Something was wrong with Deputy James Ballard and wouldn't nobody talk about it.

Not even your mother. How Sheriff Worthy's guard went up as soon as we brought up your grandfather. How that notebook carries on at the end there, and how maybe that—"

"I said that back when his notebook was our only lead. We have so much more to go on now. Why does Dr. Dean lash out at women? What was his connection to Linda Harris? Was he in love with her, and did she spurn his advances? What was his alibi for Christmas Eve? We have so much more now without needing that old notebook."

Decker frowned. "To what lengths would Deeton County have gone to frame a suspect? Was Sean Gray unnecessarily targeted? Did Red Carter and his most trusted deputy really make suspects disappear when they couldn't—"

"We're not writing about my grandfather."

"You're saying we're not writing about the *lead investigator* on the case?"

"We're not writing about my family."

"Give me one reason."

Jess felt a fire stoking in her cheeks. "Because . . . I promised my mother."

Decker said nothing. She turned her head away from him so that he wouldn't see her lose it. However, her eyes caught something that immediately changed the vibe.

"What the actual . . ."

Decker saw it too. "Oh my . . ."

Neither of them could believe their eyes. The last country lane had curled into so many switchbacks that neither of them had realized they had not seen another house for miles. However, the first one they came upon was not one to be missed.

In front of the home was a flagpole, which hoisted the largest Confederate flag either of them had ever seen. It was protected by several feet of barbed wire and electric fencing. About five hundred yards behind it, there rested a house, which had been added onto and then added onto again for years beyond that. It sat beneath the fickle shade of several other flags, most of which commanded **DON'T TREAD ON ME** or **MAKE AMERICA GREAT AGAIN**. The grounds had been kept meticulously, and the back half of the land was blocked by privacy barriers.

"Holy shit." Decker whistled low. "If ever there were a place to fight a last battle for a lost cause . . ."

As if to answer them, the automated GPS said, "You have arrived at your destination."

Decker parked. He didn't kill the engine.

"Still want me to wait in the car?"

CHAPTER FORTY

Dan Decker

Present Day

The man's face was pockmarked, worn by decades of hard living, and pressed into the space between the door and the jamb. He did not remove the chain. He appeared to have just woken up, despite the late hour in the afternoon.

"Can I help you?" he asked.

Decker opened his mouth to answer, but he was momentarily distracted by the **Trump 2024** flag whipping violently in the wind over the porch. Luckily for him, Jess stepped in.

"Mr. Berry," she said, "my name is Jess Keeler. This is my colleague, Dan Decker. We're both journalists from Lake Castor, and we're here to talk to you about—"

"Lake Castor?" The elderly man's rugged face twisted into confusion. "The only good thing ever come out of Lake Castor is a toilet brush my ex-wife bought twenty years ago. I'm still using it. You want to see it?"

"We apologize for the intrusion," said Jess. "It's very important that we talk to you."

"Well, it's not important that I talk to you. I got no time for fake-news media."

"If you'd just allow us two minutes to explain why we need to speak with you, then you'd—"

"I think I know why, and even if I'm wrong, you can kindly step the hell off my property."

Jess stepped closer to the door. "Two minutes," she said. "It will all make sense, Mr. Berry. Just give us two—"

"So far, I've asked nice. I'm more than happy to ask you the other way."

"In 1971, two young lovers were murdered. They were strangled and found—"

"Lady, if you think I know the first thing about—"

"The killer has never been identified. We know you were considered a suspect but—"

"Then y'all should know I ain't the type to call the police," Berry said. Neither of his hands were in plain view. "I prefer to handle things my own self."

"Is this because of what happened in—"

"Keeler." Decker put a hand on her arm and attempted to steer her away from the porch. "He asked us to leave."

"Mr. Berry, please. Just give us—"

"Jess."

Decker didn't like the feeling he had about the place. Maybe it was the sun-bleached rebel flag fluttering overhead or the half-dozen rusted junk heaps dotting the front lawn. Maybe it was the pit bull stretching the chain that hadn't stopped barking since they'd first stepped foot on the property. It could be any number of things; Decker didn't like it.

He led Jess away from the man's porch. Twice, she stopped, as if to turn around and give it one final go. However, Decker kept a firm hold on her. They were halfway across the lawn and back to her Hyundai when they heard Berry unhook the chain.

"Put yourself in my shoes," he hollered from behind them. "I was only a kid. I didn't know my rights, and I got these cops climbing up my ass for some shit I had nothing to do with."

Jess broke free from Decker's grip and walked halfway back to the patio. "That's what we want, Mr. Berry," she said. "We want to understand."

Berry looked her up and down. "Back then, I would have told you I was invincible. But that cop, man . . . he wouldn't let it *go*."

Decker caught up with Jess just as she reached for her recorder and flipped it on.

"What cop?" Decker asked.

Jess spoke over them both. "How well do you remember when you were first named as a suspect for the murders of Steven Hicks and Linda Harris?"

"I remember I didn't have nothing to do with that," he spat.

"Of course," said Decker. "Tell us more about that cop, though. I want to hear it."

The look Jess cut him could have fried eggs. "We have a lot of things we'd like to discuss with you, Mr. Berry. We're not cops. We're not newspaper writers. We're just two people trying to find out the truth of what happened."

Berry looked up the road, then back down it. "I don't know . . . it was so long ago . . ."

"Give us ten minutes," Decker said.

Berry seemed to think it over some, then shrugged. "Okay," he grunted. "Ten minutes. But at the very least, can we take this inside? I don't want my neighbors to . . ." He didn't finish the sentence, and no one bothered to remark on the absence of any neighbors.

Jess stepped forward before Decker could stop her. "We don't mind at all."

Berry led them back to the porch, where his front door remained open. Decker watched the man's loping gait. Berry was tall. Spindly. A touch upset and frazzled but suddenly calm, as if someone had flipped a switch. He held open the door and allowed Jess inside, then waited for Decker, who had hesitated.

"Come on in," said Berry. "I don't want to air-condition the whole neighborhood."

Decker did. He tried hard to ignore how dark it was inside the house. The entry hallway was long, and there was nothing on the walls. It opened into a living area, which was lit by candles. As Decker walked toward it, he noticed two things. One: there was a ten-foot cage in the center of the room.

The other was the sound of the door locking behind him.

A million thoughts hit Decker at once. Had they told anyone exactly where they were going? How long would he be trapped in that cage with Jess before Sheriff Worthy or someone put it together that they had gone to interview George Berry? *Would* they put it together?

If they didn't, would there be anyone to mourn him? Would Cassandra come to his funeral? Would Jenna?

Would there even be a funeral?

All those thoughts and more flooded his brain as he contemplated the ten-foot-tall steel cage in the center of George Berry's living room.

From behind him, Berry slowly drawled, "Come on in and have a seat on the sofa. I'd offer you some coffee or a beer, but . . ."

If Jess was bothered by the cage, she didn't let on. Instead, she plopped down on the sofa as she unpacked the folders and notepads from her bag, then laid them across Berry's coffee table.

"Mr. Berry, we're here to talk about your involvement in the murders of Linda Harris and Steven Hicks."

Berry did not sit. Instead, he leaned against the wall and crossed his arms over his chest. "Who said I had any involvement?"

"Weren't you questioned by the po—"

"Uh, hang on." Berry pointed to the recorder Jess had placed alongside her notes. "I said I would talk to you, but you ain't putting me on tape. That's a deal breaker. You're going to have to turn that off."

"Absolutely not," she said. "It says in the case file that you were listed as a suspect in the murders. It says you were hauled into Lake Castor and questioned."

"I . . ." Again, Berry's eyeballs cut to the recorder. "I can't," he said. "And you can't make me, neither. I know my rights."

"Jess," said Decker. "Cut it off."

"But we need—"

"Kill it."

She did. Decker caught resentment in the shadows of her face, but he pressed on. To Berry, he said, "Let's back up a minute. You weren't from the Lake Castor/Deeton area, were you?"

"No, I—"

Jess butted in. "According to my notes, he's from Greenwood, South Carol—"

"Mr. Berry," said Decker.

Berry's eyes flitted from Decker to Jess before finally settling on Decker. "She's right. I'm from up Greenwood way."

"You go to school up there?"

"Yeah."

"They got football, right? What were they? The Fighting Lions?"

"That's right. Lions." Berry got into it. "You from down yonder?"

"No sir, but I'm a football guy. I moved around a lot when I first started doing the news. Everywhere I went, I caught a local game." Decker had a pen but used it only for clicking open and closed. "You play any?"

"Oh yeah, sure. Back in my day, you either played football or wore a dress. I played defense. I was an end."

"I would have taken you for a linebacker."

Berry rubbed his left bicep. "I could have, but back then one of the top exports out of South Carolina was corn-fed cowboys. Believe it or not, I was one of the smaller guys on the team."

"Wow. Y'all go deep?"

"Second round my sophomore year." Berry seemed wistful. "Our star quarterback went down in the second game of my junior year. We were lucky to finish with two wins. I didn't play my senior year."

"Why's that?"

"Life, I reckon."

Decker tilted his head, as if to urge Berry to keep talking.

"My pop died," said the old man. "I had to find work."

"I'm sorry to hear that."

"I got a job stringing line for Southern Bell. It paid good enough. And it let me travel some. Send money back home."

Decker checked to make sure Jess was writing everything down. In that moment, he became distracted by the cage in the center of the room. He blinked until he could cast out the image and return focus to the interview.

"Is that what brought you to Lake Castor in '71?"

Berry nodded. "Yeah. It was a big deal. Previous to that, I had never been outside of town, except for away games."

"You must have been excited. Tell me about that."

Berry went on a bit about Lake Castor. The guys on his crew. Working for the phone company. He grew comfortable. Relaxed. He began to open up. Decker maintained eye contact—but easy eye contact, like he'd learned in his early days of interviewing. It was all coming back to him. It was like riding a bicycle.

Just so long as he kept his mind off that damned cage . . .

"About then was when I guess I hooked up with Margie."

Decker furrowed his brow. "Margie?"

"Margaret Cornwell," said Jess. "She was a nurse at the hospital where Linda worked."

"Yeah." Berry must have forgotten that she was in the room. "That's right."

"What was she like?" asked Decker.

"Who?"

"Marga—uh . . . *Margie*."

"Oh. She . . . uh, she was cool. She had blonde hair, I guess. She liked to party."

"Party?"

"Yeah. It was the seventies, man. Hippies weren't the ones having all the fun."

Decker laughed. "I read about all that in the history books."

"Let me tell you . . ." Berry wiped his nose with his sleeve. "Like I said, I'd never been further than a county or two from my house, growing up. Lake Castor was a whole other world. You could get anything you wanted."

"Especially if you were dating a nurse?"

Berry didn't like the way that sounded. He eyed Decker suspiciously for a moment, then let it all melt away.

"It wasn't like that," he said. "I made friends with some old boys who rode bikes. I kept it easy with the colored crowd. I had me a girl here or there."

"Nurses?"

Berry nodded. "I mixed with all walks of life."

"Did you know Linda Harris?"

"The girl that got killed?" Berry shook his head. "I'd seen her a couple of times. Never really socially. They said we were at that same party on Christmas Eve, but I really don't remember that, man. I only think about it because that cop kept telling me I was there."

Decker watched Jess sit straight in her chair. "What cop?" she asked.

"We'll get to that in a minute," Decker said quickly. "First, I'd like to hear what you knew about her."

"I didn't know shit, really." Berry pretended to pick lint off his blue jeans. "She was quiet. Real nice, I guess. Really into that guy she was seeing. I don't think I ever saw them apart."

"Was she hot?"

Berry looked up, then over to Jess. He seemed to wonder if the question was a trap.

"Come on, George," said Decker. "You had to have had an opinion. Football guy like you."

"Yeah, she was good looking. But she didn't party. I wasn't much into following a chick to church, if you get what I'm saying."

"I do," Decker said. "Why do you think the cops were interested in you?"

Berry showed teeth. "They had to have a hard-on for somebody. I guess I fit the part."

"Tell me about that."

Berry did. He talked about how Lake Castor police had brought him in for questioning. One of the cops had gotten tough, but Berry had had nothing to hide. They'd even hooked him up to a polygraph, which he'd passed.

"But that one cop," said Berry, "he couldn't handle it. He kept saying I only passed the lie detector because I *manipulated* it. The other detectives set me loose, but not this guy. He couldn't let it go."

Again, Jess spoke up. "Which guy?"

"I don't . . ." Berry suddenly didn't seem so confident. "Man, it was so long ago . . ."

Decker clicked his pen again. "This cop . . . why do you think he had such a hard-on for you?"

"Because he didn't have nobody else." A dark shadow crossed Berry's face. "Man, that dude came at me rough. Came at my friends too. I used to run with this old boy named Fickle, and he'd have liked to beat the shit out of him just because Fickle claimed to be with me the night those two went missing. That cop kept showing up at my job, giving my foreman hell . . ."

"Do you have any proof of this?" Jess wanted to know.

"Proof? Lady, do you have any id—" He took a breath, then turned to Decker. "I had to move, man. Just up and leave everything I had."

Decker sat back and crossed one leg over the other. "Why did you move?"

Berry shrugged.

"Geo—er, *Harnett*," said Decker, "please tell me. I wasn't there."

Berry still said nothing. He stared at the floor and let his anger mount.

"We just want to know what happened," Decker said. "If it means anything to you, Ballard is long gone. Almost all of them are. No one can hassle you now." Decker waited a beat. "And besides, we don't consider you a suspect at all."

"You don't?"

"No," said Decker. "We believe somebody else did it. A doctor."

"A doctor?" asked Berry.

"Yeah. You ever hear anything about a doctor killing them two?"

Berry looked to Jess, then back to Decker.

"Or anything," Decker continued. "Harassing nurses? Stealing drugs from the dispensary?"

Something clicked behind Berry's eyes. "The only time I heard that," he said, "was when that one cop kept asking me that."

"Ballard?"

"No. The other one."

Decker made a motion for Jess to write that down. She didn't.

"They was working me over for, like, *hours*, man; then all of a sudden that other one walks in with a file and starts asking about a doctor. Same as you're doing right now. Next thing I know, they're saying I can go."

"Just like that?"

Berry answered slowly. "Yeah. I thought it was a trick. Who knows? Maybe it was."

Jess doubled down. "That's the last record of you in the case file. Shortly after, according to these notes, you fled."

"Fled?" Berry scoffed. "Man, I didn't *flee*."

"You quit your job," Jess said. "You changed your name, and you left in the dead of night. What kind of person does that if they don't want to appear guilty?"

Berry laughed out loud. "You think I ran because I was *guilty*?"

Decker asked, "Then why, Harnett? Tell us."

"Because I *wasn't* guilty!"

Jess opened her mouth, but Decker shushed her with his hand. They gave Berry room to breathe, then waited.

"I didn't flee," Berry said, spitefully. "That big cop—Bullet, Billings . . . whatever—he drove me home from the interview in Lake Castor. Or at least, that's what he told those cops he was going to do. Instead, he drives me out to the country. He don't take the cuffs off me. I asked him where we're going, and he decks me in the jaw."

Berry lifted his lip and showed a spot near the back of his mouth that was missing a tooth.

"You're saying Ballard hit you?" Jess said.

"Lady, he did a lot more than *hit* me."

Jess wasn't having it. She began stuffing her paperwork back into her knapsack.

"What are you doing?" Decker demanded.

"Are you going to sit here and listen to this?" she spat. "From a guy who probably still thinks the news is *fake* and wanted to overturn an election? No thank you."

"Sit down, Keeler."

"No. I—"

"Sit down."

She did but took her sweet time doing so. She did not take out her pen or her notepads.

"Mr. Berry," said Decker, "I want you to tell us in your own words what happened to you when Deputy Ballard drove you out to the country."

"I don't know, man . . ."

"Mr. Berry, this is real important." Decker had forgotten what it felt like to *close*. It all came back to him in a rush, and his head was swimming. "There is a murderer still walking free after fifty years. Those two kids have never seen justice, thanks to how the case was investigated. You were a major figure in this case, and what happened to you on that little drive into the country with Deputy Ballard needs to be told."

Berry sighed, but not half as loud as Jess did.

"You have a very compelling story," Decker continued. "If what you are telling us is true—and we have no reason to believe it isn't—then you will be a very important voice to the narrative we're assembling about this murder and why it was never solved."

Jess cleared her throat, but Decker kept going.

"We need you to tell that story of what happened," said Decker, "but I want you to do it on tape."

"I don't know, man . . ."

"Ballard is gone. He died a long, long time ago. So has the sheriff and nearly anybody else who had anything to do with that investigation."

"Still . . . I got kids. *Grandkids.* I live around here, man." Berry shifted uncomfortably on the sofa cushion. "I put all that behind me."

"The world needs to hear your story, Mr. Berry." Decker's accent shifted to the one he used on television. Those honey-soaked pipes just needed a little greasing. He laid it on thick. "Although it doesn't sound important to you, your story could help us catch a murderer who has eluded authorities for nearly fifty years."

Berry's jaw dropped. "Really?"

"Absolutely. I want you to tell us everything all over again, from the beginning. But this time, I want to turn on our recorders."

Berry rolled the thought around in his head. "All right, then," he said. "Let's do this shit."

CHAPTER FORTY-ONE

James Ballard

1972

Ballard couldn't find it.

He'd removed all the dishes from the cupboard. He'd pulled all the items from every drawer. All these things he'd stacked like cordwood atop the kitchen counters. Knives, plates, coffee mugs. Forks, spoons, soup bowls. All the detritus that made up a family's life piled and shoved to every flat surface.

Still, he could not find it.

Ballard did not stop there. He understood what had been happening to his mind. For a lesser man, one without the deductive instincts instilled by twenty-some-odd years of detective work, this would be devastating. When a fraction of their synapses had decided to up and quit, what then could they rely upon? Ballard, on the other hand, knew his brain could no longer be trusted. For that reason, he understood he must have placed it somewhere unlikely.

For that reason, he emptied the refrigerator as well. The oven. The china cabinet filled with items that he no longer recognized. In fact, as he took another look around the kitchen, he realized he no longer recognized any of it. Not the wood paneling, nor the Formica countertops. Not one item from the pile of cutlery and plates he had stacked throughout the kitchen.

Not one inch.

Still, he would not be deterred. He continued to forage through unfamiliar terrain. However, it was not his inability to find it that shook him most to his core but instead the fact that he had so much trouble remembering what *it* was. Why had he torn up this room? For what was he searching?

Ballard could not remember.

His only thought was that he would, of course, realize what it was once he found it. Once he set eyes upon whatever item he had lost, only then would he—

"Jim?"

The light had switched on. How long had he been standing in the dark? He blinked furiously, then turned to the—

"Jim? Dear Jesus, what the hell have you . . ."

The face in the doorway near the light switch was unfamiliar to him. Instinct drove his hand to his holster, where he found nothing but disappointment.

"What the hell are you doing in my house?" Ballard demanded of the man.

"*Your* house?" The man could not take his eyes off the destruction Ballard had wreaked upon the countertops. "Jim, this is my goddamn kitchen. What are you doing?"

Ballard surveyed the room once more. He realized suddenly why nothing had looked familiar to him. He clutched his stomach with both hands, as if that might possibly keep its contents in place.

"I'm looking for my . . ." Once again, he could not remember. "I can't find my . . ."

"Where's Cora, Jim?" The man stepped carefully into the kitchen, his eyes covering every inch except for the lawman standing in the center of it. "Is Cora okay?"

"She's . . ."

Something softened behind the man's eyes. The confusion was still there, but it was replaced by something else, something that offered Ballard's soul no quarter.

"Come on, Jim," said the man. "Let me walk you home. I'm sure Cora is—"

"I don't need your help." Ballard swatted away the man's advances. "Keep your fucking hands off me."

"Fine, Jim. Fine."

Rather than endure another second of that man's pity, Ballard shoved his way past him. No sooner was he beyond the fluorescent pale than he heard the man call him from the kitchen.

"Jim? Is this what you were looking for?"

Ballard found the man reaching into the trash can. When he rose from it, he was holding the lawman's badge.

CHAPTER FORTY-TWO

Jess Keeler

Present Day

[END MUSIC CUE]

DECKER: To hear George Berry relay his truth was exceptionally heartbreaking. Previous to our encounter in South Carolina, the only picture we had been offered of him had been provided to us via the notes of Deputy James Ballard of the Deeton County Sheriff's Office. That image is one of a scofflaw, a rebellious youth constantly thumbing his nose at authority. With a glaring lack of credible leads, he was immediately cast as the primary suspect.

But how far would law enforcement go to prove his guilt? We, in the twenty-first century, find instances of police overreach and zeal to be commonplace, but would it still shock us to discover that investigators had gone to great lengths to close this case?

Here's what happened.

On the evening of January 24, 1972, George Berry was released from Lake Castor police custody after being held for several hours. However, his release that afternoon is the last time anyone would ever report seeing Berry again. After that, he disappeared.

So where did he go?

To answer that question, we located George Berry. It wasn't easy. Berry had every reason to disappear.

GEORGE BERRY AUDIO: I quit going by George after I left Lake Castor. I reckoned when I moved back down here, I could start fresh, and maybe nobody could find me. It worked. Or, at least, it worked until you two found me.

DECKER: According to Berry, Deputy James Ballard offered to escort Berry to his home in Deeton. But where they ended up was a whole other story.

GEORGE BERRY AUDIO: That old boy was driving the highway into town; then he cut off and took a road into the woods. I asked him where we was going, and he told me to shut up. Said it just like that: "Shut up."

DECKER AUDIO: Then what happened?

GEORGE BERRY AUDIO: We followed one back road, then another. I'll tell you I weren't no stranger to Deeton County backwoods, but it weren't long before I was lost. I wanted to say something, but what could I say? That old boy was big, and he had a gun and a badge, and me . . . well, I didn't have nothing except the wherewithal to keep my damn mouth shut.

DECKER AUDIO: What was going through your mind?

GEORGE BERRY AUDIO: What do you think was going through my mind? I was scared shitless.

DECKER: According to Berry, Ballard drove him deep into the Deeton woods, then pulled over.

GEORGE BERRY AUDIO: He told me to get out of the car. I told him I didn't want to. He pulled his pistol and told me he didn't give a good goddamn what I wanted—I was getting out of the car. So I done it.

He got out and shoved me against the car. Told me he knew I killed those two kids, and even if he couldn't prove it, he wasn't going to let me get away with it. Told me if I confessed to it, he would go easy on me. I told him I couldn't confess because I didn't do it. That's when he broke my finger.

DECKER AUDIO: He what?

GEORGE BERRY AUDIO: He broke my finger. This one here. Snapped it right in two. I was on the ground howling, but I could hear him plain and simple tell me he'd break the other nine if he felt like it. Told me to get up and follow him into the woods.

DECKER: At this point, Ballard led Berry at gunpoint into the woods. They walked for what Berry said "felt like forever," then arrived at a tree big enough for Berry to just fit his arms around.

GEORGE BERRY AUDIO: That's where he cuffed me. He slapped those bracelets on me and stuck me to that tree and asked me if that was how I done it to them two kids. Asked me how it felt, now that the shoe was on the other foot.

DECKER: Whether this is true or not is unknown. Berry is the only man alive from that encounter. But his description of it is harrowing.

GEORGE BERRY AUDIO: He told me that if I wasn't going to admit to killing those two kids, then I'd spend the rest of my short life cuffed to that there tree. He took his gun out of his belt and stuck the barrel of it right here. To my forehead. He thumbed back the damn hammer and said he had no problem splattering my brains across that forest.

DECKER: At this point, it would be natural for a modern audience to foretell doom. However, Berry is alive to tell the tale.

So what went wrong?

GEORGE BERRY AUDIO: All of a sudden, that big dude started wandering around like he was lost. He got to talking to folks that wasn't there. He dropped to his knees and collapsed into tears. I ain't never seen nothing like it, but I wasn't about to wait around for him to get his shit together. Instead, I'd been working on the cuff on my left hand, and as soon as I got that son-bitch off, I ran like a maniac toward the woods and didn't never look back. I didn't even go back to my trailer to pick up my things. I just ran and didn't stop running until I got home to South Carolina. And all those years later, here I am.

DECKER: Yes. All these years later. As the only man alive to tell this story, Berry paints a vivid picture of exactly why the murders of Linda

Harris and Steven Hicks have gone unsolved. The actions of these investigators created an environment where the perpetrator of such a sensational crime could slip the binds of justice. Red Carter, the corrupt sheriff of a rural county; Jack Powers, the overzealous and inexperienced investigator; and James Ballard, the vengeful alcoholic with a pen—

"Dammit, Decker." Jess ripped off her headphones and fought the urge to throw them against the wall. "Why can't you read the copy that's on the page?"

Decker pinned back his shoulders. He shifted the earphones off his ears and positioned them on top of his head. "I did a little rewriting."

Jess jerked the script from the stand in front of her, which sent a bulldog clip clattering to the floor of the small sound studio they had rented. She rifled through the pages so hard she nearly tore them. She saw nothing that resembled what she had written. After she'd seen enough, she waved the pages in Decker's face.

"I spent three weeks on that script," she insisted.

"But you had yet to segue into his account of what happened the night Ballard took him home. My rewrites provided the perfect opportunity to do that."

"No, they didn't," she said, "because we can't use any of what he said."

Decker's eyes bugged. "And why the hell not?"

"We don't even know if anything he said is true! You saw his house. You saw those flags. Those people are capable of anything."

Decker threw up his hands. "You have the nerve to preach to *me* about smacking of bias, but do you hear yourself right now?"

"What happened to double confirmation? Without it, what you are writing is called *manipulation*."

"What the hell do you think journalism is these days? I hate to break it to you, but things have changed since your 101 classes. It's one thing to read Joan Didion and watch *All the President's Men*, but we aren't exactly the Martha Gellhorn and Bob Woodward of our generation. We're two assholes working our asses off to entertain an audience."

The sound engineer's voice filled the studio. "Do the two of you need to take a moment?"

Jess waved up at the sound booth. She had found the engineer, Buffy, through an internet search and had been able to negotiate friendlier rates. Buffy watched them from above and listened through a set of headphones.

"Everything is fine, Buffy," Jess called. "We're just . . . rewriting."

"I'm going to take five," she announced. "I have a full day booked, Jess. When I get back with my coffee, I'm going to insist everyone be ready to record. Am I clear?"

Jess lowered her head and counted to ten. When she finished, she looked up to find Decker going over notes in the margins of his script.

"If I didn't know better," Jess said, glowering, "I would accuse you of trying to sandbag this entire thing. Half the time, I have to fight tooth and nail to get you to show up for any meetings or do any research. You refused to write *any* copy, and when finally you do, it's this . . . this *garbage*. It's only been the last week or so that I haven't had to drag you off your couch or some barstool to take any interest in our work."

"That's because we've finally found the lede, kid." Decker waved the script like a madman. "Doesn't it get you juiced? Man, I haven't felt this *alive* since . . . I can't tell you the last time a story like this has fallen into my lap. A handful of corrupt investigators each narrowed their focus on a different suspect—Ballard liked Berry, Carter fingered Sean Gray, and Powers was all-in on Dean—and in the meantime, the real killer got away with it."

Jess struggled to maintain her composure. Decker no longer appeared recognizable to her, and she wondered if he had become this person overnight or if perhaps she had miscalculated and he had been this person all along. She hoped against all hope there was still a chance to bring him back around.

"It feels like we are writing two different stories right now, Dan," she said as slowly as she could. "The story we should be working on is how two kids were murdered fifty years ago and their killer is on the loose."

"The killer is unidentified because of across-the-board police corruption. Systemic abuses of power. Overzealous—and quite possibly incompetent—investigators. These very subjects right now are topics in the national conversation. A run-of-the-mill cold case is *not*."

"Systemic corruption?" Jess laughed out loud. "You're reaching."

"Am I? Let's take a look at it." He ticked off his fingertips. "George Berry was bullied and perhaps nearly killed by an unscrupulous investigator. The investigators hung the blame on an unwitting motorcycle thief named Sean Gray, who subsequently died in prison. And all the while, another suspect—the prominent citizen Dr. Dean—practices medicine with nary a mention. Why, Jess? And most importantly, why aren't you asking yourself these questions?"

"Because I'm not interested in a *cause du jour*. I'm interested in who killed Steve and Linda. I thought you were, too, but lately it seems that—"

She was interrupted by the buzzing of her phone in her pocket. She drew it out and saw Sheriff Worthy was returning her call. She motioned for Decker to wait.

"Hello, Sheriff," she said into the phone.

"You left quite an intriguing message, Ms. Keeler," said Worthy. "You said you found George Berry?"

"We did," she said. "We had a nice long chat with him and recorded every word of it. I think you might find it interesting."

"I'm certain that I might."

"Just as we might find any information you might have about the case to be interesting."

Jess could hear a wry chuckle through the line. "Ms. Keeler," he said, "what would you say to lunch tomorrow? How do you feel about barbecue?"

When Jess finished the call, all she could offer Decker was indignation and a smug grin. "This is why," she said, "we have to scrap the Berry audio."

Decker blinked slowly. "Give me one good reason. *Besides* wanting to protect your grandfather."

"I'll give you two," said Jess through clenched teeth. "One, we're not going to give a platform to someone making wild accusations, like George Berry, who may or may not have taken part in an insurrection on our government on January sixth. And two, we finally scored an interview with Sheriff Ennis Worthy based on our acquisition of this information." She took a deep breath and let it out. "I think we stand a very good chance of leveraging it—along with other things we might uncover—to earn a peek at the case file. That would earn us access to more information on Dr. Dean's behavior or, at the very least, talk Worthy into going on record."

"We can ask him to go on record about Berry's accusation."

"If you do, you'll run the risk that he'll never speak to us again."

"Then his silence will speak louder than anything he might say."

Jess wanted to pull out her own hair. "Dammit, the story is *Dean*. It's *Dean* who killed Steve and Linda. How can you not get this through your head?"

"All we've got on Dean are a bunch of theories floated by a dirty cop."

"How can you say that?" Jess's voice rose to an impossible octave. "Dean fits the FBI profile. For another, he's shown an incredible penchant for violence. And most importantly, he's the only physician still alive to make those phone calls."

"Fine, he's an asshole," said Decker, "but that doesn't make him a killer. Forgive me if I don't believe a man's reputation should be ruined because of a handful of minor mistakes."

"Are you sure we're still talking about *Dean*?"

Decker's eyes narrowed. "You promised me a shot at redemption, kid."

"And I promised my mother I wouldn't go after her father."

Decker stalked across the studio to where Jess kept her notes. He fished through her Trapper Keeper until he found a picture of Steven Hicks and Linda Harris. The two victims were dressed to the nines, smiling at the camera, before one of their last dates with one another.

"You don't owe your mother a damned thing." Decker pointed to the photograph. "You owe *them*."

Jess felt it all slipping away from her. Everything she had worked so hard for to this point seemed to hinge on Decker's shifting priorities. She racked her brain, trying to think of some last-ditch attempt to reason with him, to get him to see things her way before one of them said something irreparable.

"What if I asked you to leave my grandfather out of your story?" She was briefly reminded of the first night they'd met. "As a favor?"

There was something unsettled behind Decker's tight grin. He appeared to contemplate something—maybe *two* somethings—then allowed the smile to fade away. He began to gather his things.

"What do you think you are doing?" Jess demanded.

"No hard feelings, kid," he said as he slipped into his sport coat. "I wish you the best of luck."

"Where the hell are you going?"

Decker made it to the door to the studio, then paused with his hand on the knob. "It appears you are right: you and me *are* working on two different stories."

Jess stood tall and squared her shoulders. "I'm working on the murders of Steve and Linda."

"Maybe so," Decker said, "but my story is about the *truth*."

Nothing Jess could think of to say felt like it could possibly hurt him enough, so she kept her mouth shut as he left the room. Long after he had gone, she wondered if that had been the right decision.

When Buffy finally returned to her booth, she spoke into her speaker. "Where is Mr. Decker?" she asked.

"He left to work on a different story," Jess answered.

"Does this mean you're ending the project?"

"He'll be back," said Jess. She realized she had yet to take her eyes off the door by which he had exited. "This is all he has."

CHAPTER FORTY-THREE

Jess Keeler

Present Day

Jess took the booth in the rear of a barbecue restaurant off a Deeton County back road. The lunch rush had ended an hour ago, so the only movement in the place was a tired old Black woman who filled the squeeze bottles with vinegar sauce and wiped tables with a dirty rag. Occasionally, she cut eyes toward Jess to see if her party had joined her or if she needed a refill of her sweet tea.

It wasn't until after what felt like an hour that the cowbell over the front door jingled, and in walked Sheriff Ennis Worthy. The older man nodded toward the waitress, then took his seat across from Jess in the booth. He removed his hat and tossed it on the bench next to him.

"Thank you for meeting me, Sheriff," she said. "I promise not to take up too much of your time."

"I can save you plenty," he said. "You can record me telling you I won't comment on an active investigation several times with different affectations, or we can do it just the once, and you can replay it. Either way is fine, but it's all you're liable to get out of me."

Jess produced her recorder and set it on the table between them. "So long as you say it clearly so the audience gets it."

The waitress appeared before them. "Your usual, Sheriff?"

"That sounds nice, Mindy. How's Thomas doing?"

"Better now," she said. "He'll appreciate you asking after him."

"Y'all got the butter beans today?"

The waitress smiled. "You know that's right."

After the waitress left, Worthy turned to Jess and said, "I hear tell y'all spoke with Jack Powers."

Jess's focus remained on setting up her equipment. "We also talked to George Berry."

"Those must have been very interesting conversations."

"Decker would have called it *juicy audio*." She held her breath a moment. "Nowhere near as juicy, I'd imagine, as the conversation I'd like to have with Dr. Christian Dean."

Worthy blinked. "Who?"

"I thought you'd be a better poker player than that, sir. Dr. Dean has been on police radar for some time in both Deeton and Lawles Counties. At least, according to my notes, he is. I wouldn't know otherwise because I've yet to find anyone who will talk on the record about him."

A smile crinkled the lower half of Worthy's face.

"I can tell by your expression," she said, "that I'm on the right track."

Rather than comment, Worthy drank from a mason jar filled with sweet tea.

"Can you at least tell me if you still have the rope that was used in the murder?"

Worthy set down his glass and raised a single eyebrow. "We do," he said.

"Have you tested it for DNA?"

"Whose DNA?"

Jess shrugged. "The doctor's? Anyone's?"

Worthy nodded toward the recorder. "Is that thing on?"

"It can be."

"Make sure it ain't."

She did.

"You don't have enough," Worthy said. "Not to go after Dr. Dean, you don't."

"What about you? Do you have his DNA?"

"I won't comment on an active investigation."

"Let me help you out," she insisted. "Let me see the case file."

"No way."

"If it would help the case," Jess reasoned, "then what could it possibly hurt?"

Worthy wiped his mouth and chin with his weathered and cracked hand. "Miss," he said, "you've done a real good job. I half expected you to fold up and quit a long time ago. You've gone and uncovered things ain't no other reporter been able to and, hell, maybe even more than some of the investigators who have worked on it. But you're a hair away from getting in over your head. I won't be party to escorting you any deeper. Now, I understand you've got a story to tell and you'd like to record my voice in order to tell it. I'll let you tape me telling you I won't comment on an active investigation, and that should about do it. Correct?"

"But it *is* the doctor, right?"

"I won't comment on an active invest—"

The food arrived. The waitress set a barbecue sandwich in front of each of them. Jess's was accompanied by an unctuous bowl of macaroni and cheese, while the sheriff received a bright and colorful bowl of succotash. There was a moment after the teas were refilled when silence settled between them. After Worthy finished whispering his prayers, he dove into his lunch.

"I have another question," said Jess.

"If it's about these murders . . ."

"No. Not these murders. A different one."

Worthy took another bite.

"I'd like to hear about how my grandfather was killed."

Worthy stopped chewing.

Jess reached again into her Trapper Keeper and produced a photocopied newspaper article from the *Roxboro Courier*. There hadn't been a lot going on that day in 1972, but the item was still pushed to a corner column.

DEETON DEPUTY SLAIN

Jess's hands trembled as she pushed the newspaper closer to Worthy. The sheriff did not look at it.

"It says here," Jess said, "that Ballard was killed by an unknown assailant. The only quote is from Sheriff Carter, who promised to 'employ every resource,' but then there's nothing. Not in the next day's paper, or the next, or any of the ones after that. What happened?"

Worthy thought for a long moment before he spoke. "What do you know already?" he asked.

"I heard it was a shooting. That he died on the job. Was it while working this case?"

"No. It had nothing to do with those murders." Worthy seemed to measure his words with thimbles. "You see, Red ran this whole county with only seven deputies, so those murders would never have been the only thing Big Jim—or anyone, for that matter—would be working on. We all pulled our weight in different departments for Red."

"Of course."

"Big Jim was killed during a routine traffic stop."

Jess fought the surge of a million questions that suddenly bubbled to the forefront. She struggled to keep her breathing in check. *What would Dan do?* she asked herself. *He would let them talk.* She lifted her recorder from the table and turned it on, then placed it between her and the sheriff. She steadied her hand on her notepad and spoke as slowly as she could.

"Please," she said, "tell me about that."

Worthy sighed. More than once, he cut his eyes toward the recorder, although he never indicated that he'd like it shut off. He sat back in his seat and turned his head toward the ceiling, as if finding the memory somewhere up beyond the rafters of that restaurant.

"I was one of the first on the scene," he said finally.

"On the scene when he was killed?"

Worthy nodded.

Jess said, "That had to have been difficult."

Worthy's smile was tight. "I wasn't *the* first, however. That would have been Red. He put out the call. *Ten thirty-three.* The code no deputy wants to ever hear."

"What does it mean?"

"Man down; officer needs assistance." Worthy licked his lips. "We'd already dropped what we were doing and were en route when Red hollered over the radio that it was Jim . . . 'It's Jim, dammit.' I got there first, but it was already too late. I found Red sitting with him, holding Jim's hand."

"He was dead?"

Worthy shook his head slowly. "He wasn't gone yet, but he was on his way out the door. I stepped to him, but Red . . . Red asked me what was I waiting for, to get my Black ass processing the scene."

"The scene? What happened?"

"Somebody shot him. Big Jim had pulled them over, same as he'd done probably a thousand times before. This time, though, somebody must have got the drop on him and got away."

"Must have? They were never caught?"

Worthy sighed. "Never were."

Jess realized she'd gripped her pen too tightly to write but had no idea what she'd write anyway. This was more than she'd ever been told by her mother or anyone. She held her breath and offered Worthy enough silence to continue.

"I remember," he said, "all the others came tearing up behind me. Every last one of his deputies. Red let go of Jim's hand and started barking his marching orders. Preserve this section over here; process that thing over there. Ordering folks around, and all the while, his friend lay bleeding out. I couldn't take my eyes off Big Jim. He was dying."

Worthy's cadence slowed. He spoke like his words tracked through molasses. "All the while," he said, "Big Jim had on this . . . this *smile*. Like maybe he knew something the rest of us didn't. Like he'd been let in on some secret. I tell you what—I've spent about a half century in law enforcement, and I've been present when a great many persons have quit this mortal coil. But I ain't never seen them go like that."

Jess tore her eyes away from the sheriff for the briefest instant to make sure that her recorder was still operating.

Worthy said, "I'll never, in all my days, forget what Red said to me."

Jess didn't dare speak.

"He said, 'He's not viable.'"

"What?"

"He ordered me to process the scene. He said our immediate imperative was to preserve any evidence which might assist in a conviction of the son of a bitch who killed Big Jim. I asked him, What about Jim? I said he was still alive. Red said—and I can't never forget it—that I was to forget about Jim. *He's not viable.*"

Jess drew a shaky breath. She became suddenly aware of how loud the din of the empty restaurant was.

Worthy's lips curled into a wry, reflective smile. "That's a hell of a thing to say, don't you think? I mean, a man is bleeding out in front of you . . . *he's not viable.*"

Jess couldn't think of a single thing worth saying.

"I mean, these two men knew each other," Worthy said. "Red and Big Jim were thick as thieves. They had dinner at each other's houses. Their wives did things together. They'd come up about the same time, but there at the end . . ."

"That's so . . ." Jess searched for the words but came up empty. "That's just . . . I've heard stories, but I . . . Red Carter must have been one cold son of a . . ."

"He retired the next day."

Jess squinted, as if that might possibly help her hear better.

"Some folks say Red would never be half as successful without Big Jim by his side." The booth creaked as he leaned forward and placed both his tired arms across the table. "Some say Jim's murder plain broke his heart."

"What do you say?"

Worthy thought on it some. "I say he could never live with the guilt."

"Guilt? For what?"

"For putting Big Jim out on that road to begin with. Especially when he—"

"You said Red was first on the scene."

Worthy blinked, as if he suddenly remembered where he was and whom he was speaking to. "He was," he said.

"How did he arrive?"

"By car, of course."

"No," Jess said, a bit too quickly. "How did he arrive on the scene? If he was the one to alert the other deputies, then who was it that alerted him?"

"I don't know." Worthy shrugged. "A witness called it in, maybe. Red never said."

That didn't sit well with Jess Keeler. Something inside her got rankled and stayed rankled. She shifted in the booth.

"Sheriff, don't you find that a little unusual?"

"Why?"

She rustled through the pages on her clipboard but couldn't find anything pertinent. "Let me try this a different way. Was there conflict between Ballard and the sheriff?"

Worthy narrowed his eyes. "What kind of conflict?"

"It's documented that Ballard was adamant that Berry was the guilty party. We've had several interviews with people who say that Red Carter disagreed with him. And honestly, some allegations that were made by Sergeant Powers have me concerned."

All expression quit Worthy's face. He crossed his arms.

Jess kept at it. "So you show up at a crime scene where one cop lays dead, and the only other person on site is the other cop who had a disagreement with him. You tell me there were never any arrests or positive iden—"

"Turn that thing off."

It took a moment for Jess to realize she had not been slapped. She fumbled with the buttons of the recorder until it had been turned off.

"Sheriff Worthy," she said, "I only ask because—"

"That's the problem with media these days," he said. "Y'all feel like you ain't done your job unless you've taken down a good cop. Right now, you're going after *two* good cops. And why? For a story that will better sell?"

Jess felt heat coursing through her cheeks. "Sheriff," she said, "I wasn't—"

"You want to uncover a real shit stain of a human being? Then why don't you focus your efforts on the damn doctor? Why don't you talk about the evil he's done? Instead, since you can't dig up enough dirt on him, you go after two dead cops."

"Sheriff, the last thing I want to do is go after cops. Believe me. What I want, more than anything, is to *understand.* I will never meet or talk to these men, so someone will need to speak for them. Someone needs to tell me what everyone seems to want to keep hidden."

"Cops are human," said Worthy. "They have flaws. And whenever the media can't get a story that's juicy enough, they capitalize on the mistakes made by law enforcement. They act like we're supposed to be superheroes, but we're not. We're not *characters* in some *story*. We're not foils to help catch a killer or help him go free. We're human beings with wives and children. We had childhoods of our own and things we wanted to stand for when we grew up. Same as you, same as everybody. And nine times out of ten, we want to catch the people who do wrong by our citizens. Like the man who killed Steve Hicks and Linda Harris, as well as the man who killed Big Jim Ballard."

Worthy flattened both his palms against the table like he might stand up, but he remained in his seat. After a handful of blinks, he managed to shroud himself in his usual cloak of country cool.

"What you need to know," he said, "is that Red Carter himself died a couple months after Jim."

Jess didn't need to use words to ask her next question.

"Some say he couldn't live with Jim's death on his conscience," said Worthy. "Not because he pulled the trigger but because he believed he could have stopped it. Others say it was because his life had no purpose outside of law enforcement. All I know is that Red Carter sat on his front porch until his demons whittled him away to nothing, and then he fell over and died."

Jess readied her pen at the paper but again could think of nothing worth the ink.

"I won't be party to you dragging law enforcement through the mud," said Worthy. "If you're going to do that, then you will do it without the assistance of my office."

Although she dropped the subject with Ennis Worthy and Deeton County, it was far from dropped in her own mind. If Decker really planned to write a story about Ballard, Jess felt it was her duty to find out what he might uncover.

She drove out to where Deputy James Ballard had drawn his last breaths. It was a long country highway that connected Virginia to South Carolina, but the stretch of it that cut through Deeton had seen little improvement. She passed three handmade crosses that commemorated other folks who had died along that road but found nothing at the spot where newspapers and remaining documentation claimed Ballard had bled out. On one side was a cattle pasture. On the other was infinite forest.

After a moment of silent reflection at the roadside, she produced a photocopy of one of the newspaper articles from her folder. She read it for what had to be the sixteenth time.

Storied Deeton County Lawman Slain in Traffic Fatality

Deputies located a firearm they believe to have belonged to the assailant.

"While no arrests have been made," said Sheriff Red Carter, "we will not give up our pursuit of the person, or persons, who committed this horrible crime against the people of Deeton County."

Jess held up the article so as to match the photograph of the crime scene to the landscape that lay before her. Time had hardly touched this part of the world. Everything in black and white looked familiar. The fence posts, the trees . . . even a grainy shot of a young, skinny Deputy Ennis Worthy standing at attention.

Yet nothing seemed to add up.

Jess had no intention of letting Worthy off so easy. She resisted the urge to text Decker and say that perhaps he was right. That there was a distinct possibility that there was more to the story than a fifty-year-old unsolved murder. That maybe they should look further into each of these investigators—even if it meant exposing her own grandfather.

But in the meantime, the days on the calendar ticked ever closer to Christmas Eve.

Soon another anniversary would pass.

Soon it would be fifty-one years since Steve and Linda had left a holiday party for some private time with each other, then suffered a horrible fate at the hands of an unnamed killer.

Even without the necessary information about her own grandfather, Jess had a job to do.

CHAPTER FORTY-FOUR

JAMES BALLARD

1972

Ballard awoke. He lay with his eyes open and allowed the cobwebs to clear from his mind, for his eyes to adjust to the darkness. He took in his surroundings slowly, allowing each detail to settle into the others, before he realized he was in his own living room. He had fallen asleep on the couch. The only other clues he could find were a watered-down cocktail on the end table and the broken lamp lying shattered next to it.

He rose to his feet. Across the room, he could make out the shape of the grandfather clock left to them by Cora's great-aunt. He rubbed his eyes but still could not read it. The smaller hand rested on the four, while the larger one was positioned between the eight and the nine.

Is it the smaller hand that reads the hour, or is it the—oh, fuck it.

He drained the dregs of his cocktail, but it left his head no less muddy. With a blossoming resignation, he staggered into the kitchen.

Yes, he confirmed to himself: it was most certainly his kitchen. Still shamefaced from the incident at his neighbor's house the previous month, he'd vowed never to make that same mistake. He took comfort by acquainting himself with the color of his own wallpaper, the family photo behind magnets on the fridge. Cora's recipe book on the countertop.

And of course, the large table he'd hewed by hand from a fallen chestnut after Hurricane Donna. It came back to him in a rush: how he'd treated the wood for two years before taking the saw to it. How he'd disliked the imperfections on the backside of it, which was why he'd turned it to the wall. How he'd forever discussed crafting matching chairs, but time had gotten the best of him.

Time . . .

He had been younger then. So had Cora. Their lives in those earlier years had been powered by so much love. Love for each other. Love for their prospects. Love that had surrounded them and created their child, Samantha. Love that had protected them for so long, until . . .

Until what?

What had happened to it?

Had it gone and left them?

Did it still burn somewhere?

It did. It had to.

To say otherwise . . .

Ballard understood that he had forgotten so much, but if he forgot about the love he had for his family, then his end had certainly arrived. He squeezed his eyes shut and balled his hands into angry fists. He fought with every ounce of energy to keep that memory inside of him, to never let it escape, to hold fast to it until it was tattooed to his consciousness, was certain to be his very last thought.

He reached and grasped for more evidence of this love. Such as the memory of the day Samantha had been born. How Lois Carter had sent two deputies to fetch him, to tell him to drive directly to the hospital.

Toot sweet!

How they'd flipped alive the cherry lights and ignored all three county stop signs until he'd arrived at the hospital, hat in hand, just in time to watch his wife deliver his beautiful baby girl.

Samantha.

Red had been there to pass out cigars and slap him on the back. Same as Red had been at his side when Cora had lost the second one. How fast Ballard had driven her to the hospital and feared upon all fears that she might not make it. That she might abandon him and Samantha alone in this world. How he hadn't been ready yet to let her go.

Not now . . . please . . .

He'd kept one hand fast to the wheel and the other in hers. He had thought of nothing but the road before them and the violent pounding of his heart. He'd prayed and prayed and prayed—

Please . . . give me more time . . .

And in the end, she had pulled through. They'd lost the baby, but Ballard had cared about nothing else in all the world but Cora and Samantha. His family. He'd shielded her from certain death that afternoon. She would heal, but never again would Ballard ask her to—

Ballard steadied himself against the kitchen counter. His lips parted to better take in air.

For he could *remember.*

He remembered *everything.*

Just the memory of that joyous day invited all other memories to come and play. The time when he was a boy and had found a box turtle in the creek, then brought it home to raise as a pet. How he'd been caught by his father for shoplifting a candy bar and had his hide tanned with a hickory switch. Or the day he'd met Cora.

Suddenly, all muddy waters ran clear.

Could it be?

Could he be . . . ?

Yes. Ballard had been cured. To make certain of it, he tested himself. He walked throughout the kitchen and placed his hand on the knife block. The cutting board. The cookie jar. He recalled how the family had acquired each item. The toaster oven had been a birthday present.

The blue-edged china had been a wedding gift. He remembered where each item had been purchased. The arguments they each had witnessed.

He remembered last year. He remembered last month. He remembered last week, when he'd carried George Berry into the woods and—

No. Not that.

A shadow fell across his mind. From behind its darkness, there flickered a light. One that, only moments earlier, had shone so, so bright. However, it was not yet ready to dim. That light . . .

That light . . .

Love.

Love. Love. Love.

Love is that light.

Think only of that love.

It would cure them. Ballard was certain of it. He needed to tell it to Cora. He should wake her and tell her all about it. Tell her how much of a fool he had been to be afraid. He needed to tell her that fear would ruin them and that all the cure they'd ever need in this world was—

"Is everything okay?"

And as if summoned, there she stood. So beautiful. Cora. His wife. Only no longer was she the woman who had suffered over him but instead her younger self. Free from the torments of time, free from worry. She had returned to the woman she had always been: Cora when they'd married. Cora when they had fallen in love. Cora when they had first met.

Cora.

He went to her.

"I love you, honey."

"I love you too."

"No . . . listen." He pressed his head to her bosom. "Do you hear that?"

"It's nearly five o'clock in the—"

"Your heart . . ."

"You're scaring me."

"Don't ever be afraid again. You don't need to."

"Come to bed."

"Yes. Yes, dear." He took her in his arms. "That is precisely what we must do."

She writhed beneath his fingers. So much smaller now that her vibrancy seemed to shoot hot bolts from her. Much like the day he'd known he would marry her. They'd stood beneath an arbor, and the sunlight had blossomed the flesh of her cheeks. Her pale-blue eyes had glistened pink from the peonies. The air had been scented with jasmine and magnolia.

He *remembered.*

He remembered it all.

"It's been such a difficult year." He pressed his face tighter into her. "But your love . . . that is what has delivered me from it. The love I have for you, and the love you have for me."

"I've been so frightened."

"Don't be." He took her face in his hands. Again, he was taken aback by how young they had become, as if suddenly released from an evil spell. How fast the blood now coursed through them and how electric their bodies had become. "Never fear anything again. We are in control of it all."

He put his lips upon hers. First lightly, as old lovers might while trying to reacquaint. She resisted, but he held her more firm. He enjoyed the heat passing between them, enough battery to fire the last of his silent synapses. He could throw away notebooks, could discard the crossword puzzles. All he'd ever need was right there in his arms. He kissed her harder. With more deliberate force. No longer as if they were old lovers, but now like newlyweds. Hands grabbing, pushing her against the—

"What are you doing?"

"It's our secret," Ballard whispered. "Just you and I know."

"Don't—"

"We won't ever tell anyone."

His tongue entered her mouth. He pressed his erection—the first he'd had in months—against her midsection. She knew all of a sudden that he was *alive*. He took hold of her shirt by the buttons and ripped it open.

"Stop . . ."

She slapped at his chest, but he forced her back.

"It's not what you think," he told her. "We're so young again. We will forever be this young."

And she was. He cast her shirt to their feet and covered her nakedness with his hands. Her skin around her neck, her shoulders, her breasts. He cupped her and covered her with his mouth. All synapses fired. *He had been cured!* He had to show her. He had to make her see.

"I will show you," he said to her. "You will see it."

The love, the love, the *love*. It filled him. It fueled him. It fired into his—

"Daddy, please stop!"

Ballard blinked open his eyes. His hands still moved with detached abandon, but he pulled his face from hers to better see his wife.

Only it was not his wife.

No. Standing naked in his arms was—

Samantha.

"No . . . I . . ."

"Daddy," she wailed in a whisper. "Please . . ."

"I . . ." He gathered himself best he could. "Where is your mother?"

"No, Daddy."

"Where is she?"

Samantha covered her mouth. "I won't tell her."

The horror of it shook Ballard. He fixed his hands behind his back, as far as humanly possible from his daughter. His eyes wide but nowhere near as wide as hers. How had they betrayed him? When had this happened? What had he done—oh, what had he done?

"Baby . . . it's not—"

She recoiled from him. She collected her shirt from the floor and used it to cover her breasts. She could not wrest her eyes from him, as if trying to make some sick sense of what she had seen.

"Honey," he said. "It's not . . . I'm not . . ."

But the words failed him. They were gone. Gone, too, were the memories. He'd held the secret only a moment earlier, but that moment—as well as the other revelations that had come before it—had quit him. All that remained in that moment was the image of his daughter . . .

Heartbroken.

"Daddy . . ."

Ballard sank to his knees.

"I just wanted to tell you," he said. "I just wanted you to know."

"Stop it, Daddy."

Ballard tried again. "I knew the secret. I knew it, but . . ."

"Daddy." She could barely say the words. "You're scaring me."

Ballard could not rise to his feet. He held his hands out before him, searching them for the answers to all the questions, but namely, *What have you done?* He would have continued staring dumbstruck at them, were he not distracted by the sound of his daughter racing wildly up the stairs, latching her door, and then dragging her dresser across the floor to place in front of it.

Once upon a time, Ballard thought to himself, he had known the answer.

He remembered that much. But he agonizingly searched like mad for what had been the question.

He had no options left.

Except for one.

CHAPTER FORTY-FIVE

Dan Decker

Present Day

If the snow had been forecast to accumulate, there would be no one driving those southern roads. Since it wasn't, the Bojangles parking lot was crammed full of cars, and the line at the drive-through snaked clear out to Pleasant Ridge Road.

Decker shook off the snowflakes dusting the front of his jacket and pressed it dry with his right hand. With his left, he held open the door to the restaurant for Christina McNeal, the young lady accompanying him.

The only other customer in the building occupied a booth near the soda fountain. He wore a beige overcoat and collected biscuit crumbs in his mustache and beard. Decker escorted Christina to the booth and slid into the seats across from him.

"Who's the girl?" asked the man.

"She's cool," Decker said. "Christina, I'd like you to meet—"

"I don't need nobody knowing my name," said the man. "I could get fired for even *talking* to you, Decker."

"My bad." Decker showed both his palms, then rested them on the table. "Still, you don't have to worry about her. She's my new partner."

"Really?"

"No . . . not like that. She's my partner on the *story*."

"Whatever." The man reached under the table. He came up holding a thick manila file folder. He held it just out of Decker's reach. "You didn't get these from me. You hear?"

"Yeah, yeah." Decker retrieved the folder. "It's all in here?"

"Everything you asked for." The man wiped grease from his fingers, one by one, then tossed the napkin onto the table. "This makes us even, Dan."

Decker nodded, but his eyes were fixed on the contents inside the files. His eyes swallowed them whole, page by page, until finally Christina shook him by the shoulder.

"What is it, Danny?" she asked. "Is it what you were looking for?"

"All that and more." Decker laid the file open upon the table. He sifted through the papers like they were ancient treasure. "Remember how I told you that Lee Ann Thompson, the surviving twin sister of the female victim, received phone calls for years from the man claiming to be her killer?"

Christina nodded. "Yes. And for some reason you were skeptical."

"This here confirms my skepticism." He slapped the papers with the palm of his hand. "That guy right there is an old contact of mine with the—well, it doesn't matter who he's with. What matters is that he was able to run down some info on those phone calls. You see, it would only make sense that if Lee Ann were really receiving these phone calls, she would have notified authorities. And if she did, they would put a trace on the calls. And that if there were a trace on those calls, there would be a record of them."

"And there were?"

"There *absolutely were*. Every year, same time. From 1992 to 2004, those phone calls came from a phone booth in east Lake Castor."

"What happened after 2004?"

Decker sipped from his steaming Styrofoam cup of coffee and allowed the tension to build. He was a master showman, and this was his milieu. *It's great to be back.*

"In 2004, the calls started coming from a small town on the coast. Beaufort."

Christina took a moment to process, then said: "Wait . . . isn't that where—"

"It's exactly where Jack Powers has lived for the past several years." He leaned back in the booth. "But there's more."

Decker saw it: *that spark*. It lit her eyes like tinsel. When she'd answered Decker's ad for a research assistant only weeks earlier, he'd made himself a promise to *keep it professional* this time. However, his cockles had warmed, and he fought an urge to reach a hand to her cheek, to cup the back of her head, to draw her ever closer to his lips. To celebrate this discovery together. Instead, he retrieved a page from the file.

"Every year, no matter where the call came from," Decker said, "the calls came at midnight. Pretty much on the dot. Look."

He ran his finger down a list, each entry reading 12:00, 11:59, 12:01, and so on. Until 2012.

"That year," he said, "the call came twenty-three minutes late."

"What was so special about that year?"

"That was the year they installed cameras in the Beaufort strip mall where the calls had been coming from."

Christina's jaw hung on a hinge. Her eyes flitted directly to the file folder, anticipating what was coming next.

"You have video of Jack Powers making the call?"

"Not exactly." Decker slipped a black-and-white glossy from the file and showed it to her. The time stamp was damning, and the grainy image captured Jack Powers, aged and wheelchair bound, staring up at the surveillance camera over top of a pay phone booth. His wife, no doubt assisting him, was completely oblivious.

But not you, Jack . . .

"After this photograph," Decker said, "the complicit couple made their way back to the car and drove to the nearest pay phone which had no security cameras. Apparently that took . . ." Decker consulted the spreadsheet again. "Twenty-three minutes."

"Oh my God," said Christina. "So you were right? The cops were trying to frame the doctor?"

"Nowhere in our investigation," Decker began, "did anything truly implicate Dr. Dean. All we had was a rented trailer, a shady FBI profile, and these phone calls. Those late-night interruptions seemingly named and implicated him in two murders, but nowhere else was there a single scintilla of evidence which ever brought his name into question."

"Why do you think Jack Powers wanted to implicate him?"

"Perhaps for the same reason James Ballard was convinced the killer was George Berry and Sheriff Carter liked Sean Gray: because they had no one else they could rightfully accuse."

Christina leaned back in the booth. "Can you imagine how that doctor must feel? To be railroaded and have his entire life upended because of a couple accusations?"

Decker thought that over. "Believe it or not, kid," he said, "I can. But how about we take it one step further than *imagination*? Let's you and me go have a word ourselves with the good doctor."

The building was nondescript and tucked away beneath taller, newer buildings that seemed to swallow it whole. It didn't look like it had been updated since the late eighties, which gave it a timeworn quality, one that made Decker take note.

Etched onto the front door: **DR. CHRISTIAN DEAN. INTERNAL MEDICINE.**

The receptionist behind the desk was an older, severe woman who seemed to require great effort to smile.

"Welcome to Dr. Dean's office," she said flatly. "May I help you?"

"I'd like to see Dr. Dean," Decker told her.

"Do you have an appointment?"

"No, but I'm not here for medical help." He stepped aside to let Christina in behind him. She remained in the background as she fumbled through her bag for the sound equipment. "We're writing a story that Dr. Dean will be interested to hear about."

"A story? What kind of story?"

Christina stepped forward. "Don't you recognize him?" she asked. She pointed to Decker. "This here is Dan Decker, as in *Dan Decker at Six and Eleven*."

"No." The receptionist looked lost. "I . . . I'm afraid I don't . . ."

Decker granted her a reprieve. "May we please speak to the doctor?"

"I'm afraid he'll be quite busy."

Decker looked over his shoulder at the empty waiting room, then out the front door at the empty parking lot. The snow fell at a faster clip, and traffic on the roads had completely disappeared.

He turned back to her and smiled his trademark grin.

"What's your name, sweetheart?"

"Phyllis."

"We will take only a minute of his time, Phyllis."

Phyllis did not return the smile. Instead, she disappeared through a doorway in the back of the office to fetch Dean.

Christina's eyes were wide. She showed Decker her hand and how it trembled. He smiled and put both hands on her shoulders.

"Ain't this a kick?" he asked her.

"I've always wanted to go on assignment," she said. "Is it always this exciting?"

"It is when you have the right partner."

Her lips parted, but any electricity between them would have to wait. The door from the examining rooms opened, and Dr. Christian Dean entered the waiting room. He didn't look like any eighty-year-old Decker had ever come to imagine. Instead of personifying the frailty of old age, Dean appeared to be a bastion of health and virility. He was an extremely fit man with thick arms and strong hands. Short but barrel chested. His hair had shocked completely white, but he had a full head of it. His eyes were sharp, blue, and alert.

"May I help you?" he asked them both.

Decker jumped to action. He stuck out his hand. "Dr. Dean," he said, "thank you for your time. I know you are a busy man, and the last thing we want to do is—"

"Phyllis said something about a *story*?"

"That's right, sir. My colleague and I have been—"

"A story about *what*, if you don't mind?"

"Yes, well . . ." Decker looked behind him at the chairs and magazines on the coffee table. He then looked in front of him at Phyllis, the receptionist, who had yet to quit the room. "Perhaps it might be better if we spoke in private."

Dean turned to Phyllis but also considered the front door and the clock on the wall.

"I'll give you five minutes," he said. "Phyllis, will you please direct our guests back to Examination Room B?"

"Yes, Dr. Dean," she said. She held open the door that led them beyond the waiting room and deep into the bowels of Dean's medical practice.

Decker felt a strange but familiar feeling in the pit of his stomach. It overtook him, and he realized that he'd learned very little since coming face-to-face with the steel cage in George Berry's living room. They had told no one that they would be interviewing the doctor. No one, save for Phyllis, had any idea where they were.

Phyllis led them to a small examination room and closed the door behind her. Decker's eyes canvassed the room. The exam table, the instruments, the hand sink.

"Why did the two of you never interview the doctor?" Christina asked.

"Who?"

"You and your previous partner?"

"She had a different agenda," Decker said. "It's another one of my rules, kid: When you begin to truly investigate a story, sometimes it takes you in new directions that you weren't expecting. You can't hold on to presupposed biases in order to tell the story you *want*. You have to process new information and adjust. We're not *reporters*; we're *journ—*"

The door to the exam room opened, and Dean entered. He'd removed his lab coat, beneath which he wore only a clean white undershirt. The fabric stretched taut over his chest and abdomen and strained at the biceps. Once again, Decker's attention drifted from the old man's regimen to his brusque, impatient demeanor.

"Now can you tell me what this is all about?" asked the doctor.

"Dr. Dean," Decker began, "my partner and I are writing a story about Lake Castor in the 1970s, and we could greatly benefit from your expertise. May I ask: Have you always wanted to be a doctor?"

Dean appeared annoyed. He checked his wristwatch. "I'm afraid I'm very short on time. If you'd like to schedule an appointment with Phyllis, perhaps we can set something up where—"

"We're here to talk to you about the murders of Steven Hicks and Linda Harris." When Dean showed no reaction, Decker added, "They were the victims in what became known as the Lake Castor Christmas Eve Murders of 1971."

Dr. Dean didn't blink, but he let it all sink in. His lips curled into a dry sneer. "That happened fifty years ago." He took a seat on the stool next to the examination table. "In another fifty years, no one is even going to care."

Decker narrowed his eyes. "What did you just say?"

In the meantime, Christina reached into her bag in order to retrieve her recording equipment. She had recently purchased a handheld recorder, as well as a shotgun microphone. She laid them each out across the examination table while she dug through her bag for the connecting cables.

Dean paid her no mind. "I'm afraid there's not much I can tell you about that," he said, "because there's not much that I know about it."

"Didn't you work at the same hospital as Linda Harris?" Decker asked.

"I worked at Lake Castor General, same as a lot of people did. How many of them have you questioned?"

"I'm afraid there aren't many people left from those days, but everyone we've spoken to has told us you were at the top of your field. I reckoned it wise to have a word with you."

Dean pursed his lips and contemplated his near-perfect fingernails.

"Did you know her?" Decker asked.

Dean shook his head. "I didn't know her at all."

"Can you tell me why police considered you their number one suspect in the murders?"

"No. They never told me. You'd have to ask them."

"So you admit, then, that you were a suspect?"

The doctor winced and straightened his posture. "I understand that some rogue former investigator had a wild hair or two. Obviously nothing ever came of it because I've been right here in Lake Castor practicing medicine for nearly a half century. I don't think that would happen if anyone had serious proof for these allegations."

Decker caught a glimpse of Christina, who held fast to the microphone. Her focus was tight.

"This *rogue investigator*," said Decker. "Can you remember his name?"

"No. I'm far too busy to bother with rumor and conjecture. I'm a doctor, not a gossip columnist."

"Fair enough." Decker smiled. "Does the name Jack Powers sound familiar to you?"

If it did, Dean wouldn't dare let on. Instead, he shook his head. "No," he said. "I . . . listen. A detective—large man, no badge—came by the office one day a long, long time ago on what felt like something of a fishing expedition. He brought up an indiscretion from my past—a motor vehicle accident—then accused me of having something to do with what happened to that nurse and her boyfriend. His reasoning seemed to be that if I could be found guilty of one thing, then I could possibly be found guilty of the other. Obviously—despite parking outside my home and practice—he could do neither. One day he cornered me as I was leaving dinner in town—oh, where was it again . . . it doesn't really matter—and I told him he couldn't possibly have any proof because there wasn't any. He must have seen the error of his ways, because afterward I was left to continue the business of saving lives . . . until now, that is."

Decker tried to get a read on Dean. Something didn't seem to be adding up. He pushed that thought aside and kept at him.

"Dr. Dean," Decker said slowly, "are you aware that the Deeton County Sheriff's Office has been meeting with a blogger who plans to name you as a person of interest in a podcast about the murders?"

Dean twitched his head as if he were shaking off a fly. "I don't even know what a podcast is or what it might possibly have to do with me."

"This blogger has been gathering evidence. *Information* is more like it."

Dean's face remained flat, nonplussed.

Decker continued: "Information about you, Dr. Dean. She has been using this information to name you as the person authorities believe to be responsible for those murders, as well as other crimes."

Dean cast a look over Decker's shoulder at Christina and her recording gear. Something flashed in his eye. It was gone by the time he turned back to Decker.

"She can gather all the information in the world," Dean told him. "That still won't matter to me or anyone else because it would be a far cry from proof that I ever did anything."

"Could we get you to go on record saying just that?"

"I don't see what would be the point."

"This blogger is tenacious," said Decker. "Unfortunately, bloggers and podcasters don't operate by the same standards and rules that journalists do. They have a tendency to get their hands on information that they otherwise should not have and then manipulate it to their will once they've obtained it. It's a shameful practice."

Dean's cheeks flushed. "I don't know what kind of information about me could possibly interest her. There's nothing out there that could possibly prove I had anything to do with the death of those two kids."

"Of course not," Decker said, "but her allegiance, I'm afraid, has been placed somewhere else. Not with the truth. She's dug into your records with the medical board—"

"Doctors are called before the medical board all the time." Dean's tone grew a sharp edge. He rose from the stool and steadied himself with a hand on his examination table. "If those records told both sides of the story, then it would paint a completely different picture."

"I can relate to that more than you know, Dr. Dean." Decker winked. "However, she's also shown an intense interest in your criminal record."

"She'll find nothing there either," Dean snapped. "Anything that could remotely be construed as criminal was expunged. Nondisclosure and confidentiality agreements will tie her up in court."

Decker felt a tickle at the bottom of his belly. He was reminded of poker games with men of lesser skill. He reached for another card.

"She's also discovered that you were discharged from the army," he said.

The blood ran out of Dean's face until he turned whiter than the snow falling outside. He drew up a hand to his chest, as if he might suffer a stroke. His breathing grew irregular.

"My army records are supposed to be sealed," he said.

"They are." Again, Decker debated the benefits of remaining silent. He opted against his better intuitions. "That is the issue with the blogger at hand: she's a pit bull. Trust me; I know what it's like to be unjustly accused of something. You are going to want your voice to be heard. My colleague and I are in a position to facilitate that for you. What we propose—"

"What you propose is to stick your nose in my business?" Dean opened and closed the hand he'd tucked just below his chin, as if to better circulate the blood flow. His eyes turned hawkish and gray.

"No, Dr. Dean," said Decker. "What I offer is *vindication*. It's an opportunity that doesn't come around often. I know I would have jumped at the chance, and I didn't have a former investigator and a podcaster slandering my name the way you do. What I had was—"

"There's nothing in my army records that should interest you or anyone else."

"It's difficult to say," said Decker, "because they are sealed. Perhaps you might like to tell us in your own words how it makes you feel that someone is accessing your personal information in order to—"

"If they are sealed," Dean growled, "then what benefit might I have in commenting?"

"Things have a way of coming unsealed," Decker said wryly. "We have a way of getting ahold of things these days. Whistleblowers and whatnot. But I am a firm believer that where there's smoke, there's not always a fire. If you work with me and perhaps take control of the conversation, I can help allay people's fears."

"I can do better than that." Dean was clearly out of breath. "I'll goddamn show them to you."

Decker arched an eyebrow. "You have them?"

"You bet your ass I do."

Decker exchanged glances with Christina, who pushed the microphone closer into the space between him and the doctor.

"Yes." Decker swallowed. "That would be great."

"It will only take a moment to find them. Please, wait right here."

Dean let the door slam.

"Did you hear that?" Christina whispered. "He's going to give us the army records."

Decker watched the closed door like he was trying to decipher glyphs etched into it. Something nagged at him, and he didn't know what.

"That was *amazing*." Christina slapped his shoulder. "I've never seen anything like that. You had him eating out of the palm of your hand. I can't believe you're going to get him to hand ov—"

"Something doesn't feel right," said Decker. "I think we may have made a mistake."

Christina looked at him like he might have ten heads. "Do what?"

"Seriously," he said. "I think we better leave."

"Why?"

"Dean is . . . there's something—I can't quite put my finger on it, but—"

"You're being ridiculous, Danny. You need to keep your eye on the ball. Jess Keeler is trying to set him up for a murder he didn't commit, and you are going to be the one who—"

The door behind them opened, and Dean entered the room. He glanced briefly at Christina, then at Decker. His lips formed a tight smile; then he brought up his right hand, which held something shiny. Before Decker could bring his eyes around to it, the shiny thing exploded, and so did Decker's shoulder.

Decker fell over the top of the examination table and brought it down with him as he hit the floor hard. His world skewed to a dutch angle, and from that vantage he watched Dean's arm rise to Christina. The second explosion rocked her from view.

"Wait!" Decker shouted from the floor. "Don't . . . wait!"

His protests were lost to the thunder of a third explosion, this one on the other side of the toppled table. The pain in Decker's shoulder spread its long fingers across his chest and dug in hard. The door to the exam room flew open, and in charged Phyllis.

Phyllis . . .

Decker reached out a hand to warn her, but Phyllis could see nothing but Dr. Dean.

"What the hell are you doing?" she wanted to know.

"Look what you made me do!" Dean shouted into the corner of the room. "Goddammit, look what you made me do!"

"I told you I could handle them," Phyllis hollered at him. "You should have listened to me."

Phyllis . . .

Decker put his good hand to his shattered shoulder. When he drew it back, it was covered in hot, red oil.

Not oil . . .

"This wasn't my fault," Dean screamed at Phyllis. "They came in here accusing me. They said they knew about my army records. If they hadn't—"

"We'll handle it," Phyllis said. She said it again for good measure. "But this one . . ." She motioned to Decker. "Oh dear. He's still alive. What do you want to do?"

Dean ripped away the examination table with one hand and threw it against the far wall. Decker tried to turn his head to look for Christina—but for the pain.

The pain . . .

Instead all he could see was that shiny in Dean's hand, that oh so shiny, and how he brought it back up but this time to Decker's face, and all he heard—

"Look what you made me do."

—was the horrible sound of thunder, thunder so loud it shook the building, shook them all, shook all the earth until . . .

PART III

CHAPTER FORTY-SIX

Jess Keeler

Present Day

Late spring came—and with it, an angry sun. As the mercury climbed ever higher in those final weeks of May, there were few places in South Carolina's low country to offer respite. One of them was a beer distributor's warehouse, which was cooled to near-winter levels. That air filled with the sounds of its industry: the beeps of forklifts, the sliding up and down of roll-up doors, the engines of large trucks.

These sounds punctuated the background while Dustin Gray told his story to Jess Keeler during his lunch break.

"The last time I saw my daddy," he said, "was about forty years ago. I was seven, and he was in a Florida penitentiary. Mom drove us all night to get there so he could sign the divorce papers. I remember crying all the way back to Virginia because I knew, even back then, that I would never see him again."

Sean Gray had left his family in Lake Castor on January 10, 1972, which was shortly after the bodies of Linda Harris and Steven Hicks had been discovered in that wooded hollow just over the North Carolina state line. Just months later, he would be arrested on a stolen-motorcycle charge. Strange peculiarities would then fuel suspicions of his involvement in those murders. Gray would spend the rest of his life in and out of the penal system until finally dying from cancer shortly after earning a compassionate release.

Jess had tracked Gray's only son through meticulous internet searches, then arranged to meet with him during his lunch break. She'd brought with her the Trapper Keeper filled with the data she had collected on Sean Gray during the past several months of digging. While there were still numerous gaps in her research, what she held in her folder was legion compared to what Dustin Gray knew about his father. She had agreed to share it with him, so long as he committed to sharing his story on tape.

She checked the levels on her recorder, then tucked the microphone closer toward him.

"How did it feel," she asked, "when I revealed to you that your father had died?"

Dustin ran a hand through his sandy-blond hair, then turned his head to the ceiling of the employees' break room. He sighed.

"Disappointed, I guess. In a sense: relieved. I'm pretty sure that must sound weird to you."

"Not at all."

"It's just . . . I spent so much time and money trying to find out more about my father. He'd always been a sort of mystery to me, especially when he up and left—" Dustin dabbed at the corner of his eye with the sleeve of his uniform. "Well, at least now I guess I can quit searching."

Jess squeezed his wrist. "Thank you," she said, "for sharing your story."

"And thank *you*." He nodded. "For all you've done for me."

Jess reached for her bag. "And now, about that other business."

"Yes. Of course."

Jess produced the manila envelope that Sheriff Worthy had given her, then laid its contents on the break table between them. Plastic gloves, two cotton swabs, a bottle of distilled water, and another, smaller paper envelope.

"It's amazing," said Dustin, "that you're doing this all by yourself."

"I'm not alone." She dropped the distilled water onto the cotton swabs, just like Worthy had shown her. "I have a sound engineer who helps edit the footage. The assistance from law enforcement has been invaluable. And in the early days, I had a research assistant, but he—" Rather than explain Dan Decker's departure from the project, then subsequent disappearance several months earlier, she changed the subject. "If you'll open wide, I'm just going to lightly swab the inside of your cheeks. You'll hardly feel a thing."

"If my father was innocent of those murders, then I'll do what I can to prove it." Dustin allowed her to rub the inside of his cheek with the cotton swab. She repeated the motion with a second one. "However, if I end up proving he was guilty, then at least maybe I can provide some closure for the victims' families."

Jess could hardly wait as she walked back to her car to call Sheriff Worthy and tell him the good news. When she reached for her phone, she noticed she'd already missed a dozen calls and even more text messages. Before she could read a single one of them, her phone buzzed again with a call from the sheriff.

"I was about to call you," she chirped into the receiver. "I just left an interview with Sean Gray's son. I managed not only to record a fascinating, heartfelt narrative about one of our three suspects, but I also obtained two cheek swabs. You can test Gray's familial DNA against the rope from the 197—"

"Ms. Keeler," said the sheriff, "are you driving right now?"

"Not yet." She climbed behind the wheel and immediately cranked the engine so she could start the air-conditioning. "But I'm headed back to Lake Castor today. My plan is to swing by Deeton and drop off the DNA at your office. What time will you—"

"Ms. Keeler, I have something to tell you, and I'm afraid it's not going to be good news."

She took her hands off the steering wheel. "Is it my mother?"

"No. Your mother is fine."

"What is it?"

"It's Mr. Decker."

"Oh, thank God." She pushed out all her air and laughed. "I thought for a second it was something serious. Tell me—what's that old bastard gotten himself into now? Where's he been the last five months? Holed up in some shitty motel room with an eighteen-year-old?"

"No, Jess," he said. Jess realized this was the first time Worthy had ever used her first name. "I'm afraid what I have to tell you is much worse than that."

Sheriff Worthy gave it to her straight. Back at his office, he disclosed to her the ME reports, crime scene photos, and notes taken by the investigators assigned to the case. However, that didn't stop Jess from obsessing over the plague of theories that had infected the internet.

Word had leaked almost immediately that Decker's remains had been found alongside Christina McNeal's. One gossip column reported that they had been found naked, which suggested scores of rumors regarding sexual misadventure. Another hinted at a jealous rage sparked by one or the other, which had led to a murder-suicide. The theory most floated was one regarding a jealous ex-lover who'd discovered the pair in flagrante, then dispatched them both in a hail of gunfire.

Each and every tweet, article, and vlogger capitalized on the more sensational aspects of the case. How both Decker and Christina had been shot twice. How their bodies had been thrown into the woods, then covered with leaves. How they'd been located just over the state line, on the edge of Deeton County.

"It's hard to tell because we've had an exceptionally cold winter," Sheriff Worthy explained to her. "However, we have reason to believe their bodies have been in those woods for at least ninety days, which corresponds with the last of their reported activities."

"What activities?" Jess asked.

"They pinged a cell tower in downtown Lake Castor." The sheriff opened a manila file folder and spread its contents across his desk. "Ms. McNeal's last post on Instagram placed her at a Bojangles at the onset of that December snowstorm. She also had a location tracker on her phone's Snapchat app. We traced it to an intersection in Lake Castor."

"Let me guess." Jess felt her stomach somersault. "That intersection is Arris and James."

Worthy didn't answer. He didn't have to.

Jess clenched her teeth. "The same goddamn intersection as Dr. Dean's medical practice."

"We questioned Dr. Dean."

"And?"

"He says he didn't do it."

Jess wanted to flip the desk. "Of course he did. Did you hook him up to a lie detector?"

"No ma'am."

"Did you get his DNA?"

"We asked for it."

"And?"

Worthy said, with a flat expression, "He told us to talk to his lawyer."

"Did you?"

"His lawyer is a son of a bitch, like most of them. In fact, he's a cut above most of them."

"So get a warrant."

"For what?"

"Check his office for blood."

"It's a doctor's office," said Worthy. "They will have cleaned it top to bottom with solvents you and I have never heard of. And even if we did find blood . . . it's a *doctor's* office."

Jess looked down at her hands and found she'd balled them into fists. She searched every which way for something to lash out against but found nothing near satisfying to destroy.

"You know he did it," she growled. "You know that bastard killed Dan."

"Law enforcement is bound by a rigid set of rules." Worthy interlaced his fingers atop his desk. "This isn't a *Dirty Harry* movie where we can exact any kind of justice we want. We don't necessarily do things the way they used to when your grandfather was active. We believe in due process."

"I read the news," Jess snarled. "I see what kind of due process that cops dish out. I've seen the cell phone videos. Is the only reason Dr. Dean is still walking the streets because he's not an unarmed Black kid?"

Worthy sat back in his seat and let her words echo into the room.

"I'm sorry." Jess rubbed her eyes with her fists. "That wasn't fair. I didn't mean that. It's just . . . I'm just . . ."

"You think I don't understand how you feel?" Worthy crossed his arms over his chest. "I met with the Lawles County sheriff, and he and I interviewed that son of a bitch—before Dean lawyered up. You should have seen the look on his face. Smug. Like he had one over on us. I tell you what—I've been in the same room with over a dozen people like him in my lifetime. My eye has been trained and my ear tuned to it. Whether it's some punk kid stealing a tractor or a man killing his wife . . . I got a nose for that bullshit." Worthy wiped his mouth. "Pardon my French."

"So what can we do?"

"Lorne has men on him. It's not pretty, and it's not immediate, but if he messes up, Lorne will be on him like a skunk on a june bug. Mark my words."

"And what if he doesn't mess up?"

"Guys like that . . ." Worthy no longer seemed to see the point. "He's eighty years old." He shrugged. "He's bound to face judgment. Either in a court of law or a court much higher. I know that much to be certain."

That would most certainly not do for Jess Keeler. She punctuated her periods of furious anger with moments of reflective grief. She found precious few moments when something did not remind her of Dan Decker. She fought tears in her beer at the Lake Castor bar where they had first met and could hardly touch her coffee when visiting the diner where they had often sifted through their notes. Or the dive bars where they had celebrated discovering new information. Or the stoplight where he had once tried to—

She had to stop.

To catch her breath.

If anything served to douse momentary lapses of warm nostalgia, it was the relentless media coverage. Within twenty-four hours of the identification of Decker's body came the various news angles. *Slate* asked if it was appropriate to mourn such a troubled public figure, while the *Guardian* questioned his dubious legacy with women. *People* ran a thousand words on his ex-wife, Cassandra, while two networks teased an in-depth interview with her.

None of these explorations, Jess felt, would ever come close to nicking the surface of the man whom she had come to know over the past year as a good friend and colleague. Could anyone on Twitter describe his rakish sense of humor and devilish charm? Would any of the interviewers ever properly pay tribute to the inspiration he'd sparked when he'd fleshed out a story or sat down for an interview? Would it forever be lost to time that he had been working diligently to get back his groove and find himself? So often, she believed, these stories never got to the bottom of the victims, and she wished—

Wait . . .

Jess had been watching a retrospective of Decker's career—a mash-up video assembled of all his highlights as a reporter, anchorman, and subsequent news story—when a thought struck her. She closed her laptop to get a better hold of it.

Over the past several months, she had learned to respect the victims of such violent crimes as more than set pieces to a murder mystery. They were human beings with hopes, dreams, and motivations. Something had sparked them during their lives, and something had given them meaning. She had learned to treat them as more than just *characters*.

She realized she should be doing the exact same for their killer.

◆ ◆ ◆

No one could stop her.

Not even Sheriff Worthy, although he tried.

In fact, Jess respected that he more or less pulled out all the stops.

The first of the reinforcements he enlisted was neighboring Lawles County sheriff Lorne Axel. Axel, a square-jawed, broad-chested lawman in his fifties, joined them at the Lake Castor studio where Jess Keeler recorded audio with her engineer, Buffy.

Axel pointed to a small microphone. "Is that it?"

Buffy nodded. "It's the smallest one I have."

"Where are you planning to hide it?"

Buffy lifted Keeler's lapel. "I was thinking under here. I can stick the wire through her shirt, where it will reach around back of her and plug into this mic pack."

Axel arched his eyebrow. "And you don't think the doctor will see it there? What about if you hid it in her bag? That way, in case he—"

"What the hell are you doing?" Worthy wanted to know. "When I asked you to come help, I didn't mean for you to help her do it. I want you to talk her out of it."

"It's a free country, Ennis." Axel didn't bother to look up from the tableful of Buffy's equipment. "She can do whatever she wants."

"What if what she wants will get her killed?"

"Then you'll have it all on tape." Jess stared straight ahead as Buffy affixed the microphone to her lapel, then moved it to the inside of her jacket. "Maybe that will be enough evidence for one of y'all to get off your ass and arrest the bastard."

"What makes you think you are going to get him to say something that Lorne and I couldn't?"

"You said yourself that law enforcement is bound by a certain set of standards and rules," she said. "I am not law enforcement. I'm a blogger. We have no standards."

Worthy threw up his hands and marched to the opposite side of the room so he might have space to collect himself. Jess raised her arms so that Buffy and Axel might find the best spot for hiding the microphone.

"I've studied this man more than I've studied anything my entire life," Jess told them all. "Dr. Christian Dean is a narcissist. He's also a misogynist. He's prone to fits of rage and, if my theory is correct, mad sexual frenzies. I know more about his buttons than he does, and I'm ready, willing, and able to push the hell out of them. So yes, I think I can get him to say something that you couldn't."

"What if," Worthy angled, "instead of going through with this tomfool plan, we head back to my office and spend the day going through the case file?"

Jess didn't blink. "I'd love to take you up on the offer to look at the case file I've asked to see for nearly a year. We can do it as soon as I finish my interview with the doctor."

Before Worthy could comment further, his phone buzzed. He checked the screen, then licked his lips.

"If I can't convince you how stupid this idea is," he said, "then perhaps someone else can."

He opened the front door, and the frame immediately filled with two large corn-fed Virginia boys in overalls. They entered the small studio, checked it out, and then motioned behind them for their aunt Lee Ann Thompson.

When Linda Harris's surviving twin sister stepped inside the door, her attention split between the two sheriffs but settled on Jess. They locked gazes, and some sort of acknowledgment seemed to pass between them.

"I'm sorry to hear about your friend," said Lee Ann.

"I'd say I hoped you didn't drive all this way for condolences, Lee Ann," said Jess, "but something tells me that's not why you came."

"I called her," said Sheriff Worthy. He turned to Lee Ann. "Ms. Keeler here is planning to go by herself and interview the doctor."

Lee Ann's face showed no emotion. "What do you expect me to do about that?"

"Talk some sense into her."

Lee Ann considered that, then did the same with every inch of Jess Keeler's frame. She looked her up and down, then finally stepped away, back to the safety of her two country nephews.

"There's no need," she said. "This young woman has more sense than anyone else who's ever worked this case."

CHAPTER FORTY-SEVEN

Dr. Christian Dean

Present Day

Some people might never learn.

That was what Dr. Christian Dean thought as he looked into the incredibly stupid face of his patient, a slack-jawed, heavy-lidded man named Mr. Hampton. His every feature contributed to the landscape of a person with stunted mental abilities: his cartoonishly large ears, his lack of definition at the chin. He'd wager Mr. Hampton the type to text while driving or drink the local water.

Yet even worse were the idiocies fleeing from Mr. Hampton's mouth.

"My mama smoked every day of her life," Mr. Hampton told the doctor, "and she lived to be ninety-eight years old."

Dean sighed. "That may be," he said. "But did your mother have a BP of a hundred and seventy over a hundred and five? That's stage-three hypertension. I'm fine to continue treating you and taking your money, but I'm afraid you're wasting everyone's time if you insist—"

"I'm working on it, Doc." Mr. Hampton wiped his nose with the back of his wrist. "Now's just not a good time."

"I have medical evidence and a lifetime of practice which indicates the opposite."

Mr. Hampton laughed and leaned back in his chair. "Save the lecture, bro. I've heard it a million times." He pointed at the pen on Dr. Dean's desk in front of him. "I'm just here to get my prescription filled."

Dr. Dean saw little point in arguing with Mr. Hampton's type. His fifty-plus years in the medical profession had taught him not to care. They would all kill themselves off slowly, but not until they'd squandered their every last penny they could earn to whoever was smart enough to wrest it from their grease-pocked fingers. Tobacco, Budweiser, Big Pharma . . . the medical complex. All of it was a game, and Dr. Dean knew exactly which team he played for.

He pulled out his prescription pad and placed it on the desk before him.

"Very well," he said. "At least tell me you've read the book."

Mr. Hampton looked lost for a moment, then shook his head. "Ah, no. I mean, I read parts of it. It was a bit too technical for me. But my buddy Clay is into that stuff. He doesn't smoke as much as me, but I kicked it over to him."

Dr. Dean put down his pen. "You gave my book away to someone?"

"I guess so." Mr. Hampton laughed nervously.

"*My* book?"

"I mean, you gave it to me, so . . ."

"No. I loaned it to you."

"Whatever." Mr. Hampton glanced over both his shoulders at the shelves of books behind him. "I'm sure you have a million of them, right?"

"That was a *loan*."

Mr. Hampton threw up his hands. "Okay, fine. I'm sorry. I'll go on Amazon right now and order you another one. It will be here tomorrow. Now will you please fill out my—"

Dr. Dean rose from his seat. His chair clattered to the floor behind him.

"No, I won't," he said, "but you can get the hell out of my office."

Dr. Dean bustled around his desk to the door.

"Hold on, man," said Mr. Hampton. "It's just a *book*."

Dr. Dean jerked open the door. "I should have my head examined for thinking you could even *read*."

It was Mr. Hampton's turn to stand.

"Hey, man," he said. "You can't talk to me that way. I'm the customer, and the customer is always right."

"No, you are the *patient*." He grabbed Mr. Hampton by both shoulders and yanked him with a mighty ease out of his office. "The *patient* is a lot of things, but only rarely is he *right*."

Dr. Dean shoved the man into the waiting room and might have followed him out the front door to beat out what remained of the patient's stupid, feeble brain, if it weren't for Phyllis. She squeezed herself between the two men and hurried Mr. Hampton out the door before Dean could do further damage. When she returned inside, she closed the door and spun the sign on it from **OPEN** to **CLOSED**.

"You have got to stop doing this," she said.

"It's not my fault," Dean told her. "He disrespected my property."

Phyllis took him by the hand. He jerked it away. She tried a softer approach.

"You're too trusting of them," she said. "They will let you down every time. You know that."

"He tricked me into thinking he might be different."

Phyllis took him into her arms. "That's because you have a good heart." They held each other a moment, until his erection grew between them. A smile crept upon her lips. "Apparently, you have a very *good* heart."

Dean took her on the examination-room table. When they finished, he collected his clothes and sat on the stool to re-dress himself.

"You can't let them get to you like that," said Phyllis.

"It wasn't my fault." He pressed out his slacks with the back of his hand, then slipped into them.

Phyllis took a look around her at the examination room. "I was hoping that incident with the reporters might have cautioned you about your temper."

"That wasn't my fault either."

Dean knew Phyllis would push it no further. They had each said their piece. Instead, she cleaned up the exam table and readied it for the next patient.

"This last month has been so stressful for you," she said. "Retirement is never easy, especially when someone is still fit enough to practice. On top of that, selling the house and moving to Florida . . . this is a major life change. It's *several* major life changes."

"I could practice another thirty years," said Dean. "I feel like I'm in the prime of my life."

"You've earned the right to relax," she said. "If anybody in this world deserves to rest"—she snaked one arm around him and lowered the other to his thigh—"it's you."

If he were truly in his prime, he fancied he might have another go at Phyllis, who, at fifty-six, was still a quarter century younger than him. But he had been distracted as of late. Besides the retirement, besides the selling of the house that he had built himself, besides leaving the only life he had known for over a half century . . . there was the matter with the *police*.

That damned sheriff had a way of showing up when Dean least expected it. He'd stopped for breakfast at the All-Niter, same as he'd done every Wednesday since 1984, and there had been Sheriff Lorne Axel, hawking him like a biscuit sandwich. Same as he had two days later when Dean had ordered barbecue from Mac's. He'd seen him parked in his county car at the end of Dean's dead-end street when the doctor had finally lost any decorum and stamped the asphalt between them.

"I have a mind to call my lawyer on you," Dean had hollered into the sheriff's window.

Sheriff Axel climbed out of his cruiser and leaned against the driver's side door. He chewed calmly on a toothpick and kept both hands by his side.

"What for?" he asked.

"Harassment."

"I'm not harassing anybody," said Axel. "I'm standing smack dab in the middle of my territorial jurisdiction, as I have been mandated by the citizens of Lawles County to do for the past twenty-some-odd years."

"I've seen you following me."

Axel smiled sideways. "You have something of a temper, don't you?"

This only served to further anger Dean. He searched Axel's hearty exterior for the best place to land a blow.

"How often do you lose that temper, Doctor?"

Dean could not control his hands balling into fists.

"Did you lose it when Dan Decker and his colleague got to asking you a few prickly questions about your past?"

Dean planted both his feet.

"I bet you'd like to try a swing at me right now, wouldn't you?"

Dean took a step back. He could take the sheriff. He could take ten men just like him.

"If you're feeling froggy," said the sheriff, "then why don't you jump?"

But Christian Dean was smarter than that sheriff. He had known the old man was simply working to lure him into a fix that he couldn't get away from. Dean wasn't stupid. He was not the type to make a stupid mistake.

Not anymore . . .

Dean shoved away that memory, as well as the memory of the sheriff at his doorstep, and even shoved away poor Phyllis, who'd insisted that he relax.

"Not now, Phyllis," he said. "I've got too much on my mind."

"You have no other patients for the rest of the day," she told him. "If you won't let me help ease your tension, maybe you should find another outlet."

"Like what?"

"Like, I don't know." She brushed the front of his lab coat and offered it to him. "What did you enjoy doing in your younger days? How did you use to relax?"

Dean gave it some thought, then gently agreed with her. Early the next morning, he gathered up his things, then took a drive into town.

It had been years—maybe even decades—since he'd visited the Frog Hollow Racquet Club, yet he could still find his way with his eyes closed. Outside, the fitness center had changed very little. The award-winning rosebushes still lined the redbrick facade, and the wrought iron trellis still bracketed the members' entrance.

Dean took that entrance and found himself in front of the receptionist's desk, which was manned by a woman who had clearly lost her shape.

"There seems to be a problem with your account, sir." She tapped her keyboard again. "It's not showing—"

"It's been some time since I've darkened these doors," he said, "but I enjoy a lifetime membership, as was promised to all the club's initial investors. You know, there were twelve of us originally. All men who saw Lake Castor had a need for a fitness center that catered to the—"

"I don't see anything here when I—"

"I *built* this place, goddammit." Dean banged both his fists on the desk. "I don't have time to be lectured by someone who can't even bother to make herself presentable. What the hell are you wearing? *Sweatpants?*"

"Perhaps I should call my manager." She picked up the phone.

"That's right," said Dean. "Get Jerry up here. He's going to get an earful. Maybe times have changed, but standards haven't."

The man who greeted them wore no suit jacket, which rankled Dean even further.

"Where the hell is Jerry?" he asked.

"Gerald Rombauer retired six years ago," said the man without a suit jacket. "And the reason we can't access your membership, Dr. Dean, is that you were banned from the premises back in 2002."

"Banned?" Dean had a mind to box the bastard's ears. "What in Sam Hill for?"

"Apparently you have an issue with anger."

Dean was inches away from showing the man how little he actually knew about *anger* when two security guards arrived at his elbow.

"If you don't mind," said the manager, "we'd prefer you not make a spectacle like you did the last time."

Dean decided not to test his own acumen against the security guards but instead relieved himself outside the front door atop one of those prize-winning rosebushes. He told two passing tennis players where they might stuff their rackets.

The following afternoon, Dean decided to drive a bit more after lunch before heading back to the office. He knew every road as if he had paved them himself. He had spent a lot of time driving them. Years of canvassing the town—this way and that—to and from work, then the hours after work. Those long hours after, when he'd often find himself on roads like Creechville.

When he had first started at Lake Castor General, Creechville had been a network of dead ends and cul-de-sacs cutting through an empty field on the edge of a golf course. Fast-forward fifty years, and there sat some of the nicer, more expensive homes in Lake Castor. The homes were populated by doctors and lawyers . . . and their wives.

He drove slowly so as to better see one of those wives bent over her hydrangeas near the mailbox. So as to better see the young mother walking a baby in its stroller. The two women in sports bras and yoga pants jogging along the rough outside the ninth hole.

He kept his distance behind them while taking in his surroundings. It was still midafternoon, when most husbands would be at work. The air was alive with leaf blowers and tree trimmers but on streets beyond the periphery—not this one. Perhaps a mailman might coast by, or perhaps he already had.

Dr. Dean reached across the seat and popped open his glove compartment. Inside, he found his .38 revolver, a fake patrolman's badge, and a pair of handcuffs. He parked and silently opened his car door. He had barely lowered his foot to the pavement when along came a police cruiser. Dean grumbled curses beneath his breath, then closed the door and drove out of the subdivision.

He found himself again driving absently. He cruised one neighborhood, then another. He took the familiar roads that skirted the deep forests of Lawles County. It felt as if the car steered itself. Before long, he found himself parked and standing outside the hulking frame of what had once been one of his first private medical offices. Once upon a time, it had been a state-of-the-art facility featuring elite medical care. As his eyes took in the boarded-up windows and crumbling architecture, he felt a sadness that had, to that point, been alien to him.

"She's got good bones."

Dean spun at the sound of the woman's voice but softened when he put eyes on her. She had put herself together well. Her clothes fit, except in the places where they didn't. She had a tight jawbone and a healthy color to her skin. He was particularly drawn to her lips and how full they were.

"I used to call this place home. Many, many years ago." He took her in once more. She was young. "Long before you were even born, I reckon."

Her bra strap had slipped off her shoulder. She straightened it, then pushed a lock of hair behind her ear.

"I've studied all these old Lake Castor buildings," she said.

"That's a peculiar hobby."

"It's hardly a hobby," she said with a tight smile. "Researching the past is my passion." She looked over the building once again. "I've heard they slated this building for demolition next spring."

Dean nodded and again felt a strange pang in his chest.

"That's a shame," said the woman. "I bet if those old walls could talk, they might tell a pretty fascinating story."

"I'm afraid that story would only be fascinating to those with an interest in the medical arts."

"I have an interest in times gone by," she said. "Especially the golden days of Lake Castor. A lot of history passed through that hospital."

"That much is true."

"Most of the doctors who worked here have passed on, I'm afraid."

"There are very few of us left."

Again, she fussed with her bra strap. Dean fought the urge to recommend she try a size more appropriate to her body.

"How do you think future generations will regard old landmarks such as this?"

Dean's face darkened and twisted into a scowl. "I'd find myself surprised if future generations remembered how to speak proper English."

The woman laughed. Dean thought it strange that he couldn't remember the last time he'd made a young woman laugh. He felt an electricity charge up his spine. He thought more than once about adjusting her pesky bra strap but instead put his hand to her elbow. The feel of her flesh fired hot bolts through him.

"Is everything okay?" she asked him.

"If you are interested," he said, "I can tell you more stories about what it was like back in Lake Castor's heyday."

"I would love it," she said, "but it's a touch chilly for my taste. Is there somewhere we might go to warm up and talk?"

"Yes," he said. "So long as you don't mind taking a ride from a stranger."

She smiled. "What's your name?"

"My name is Dr. Christian Dean."

She stuck out her hand. "So you're no longer a stranger."

Dean liked this. He smiled as well.

"And what, pretty lady," he asked, "is your name?"

"Jess," she answered. "My name is Jess Keeler."

CHAPTER FORTY-EIGHT

Jess Keeler

Present Day

Dr. Dean offered to drive them back to his office, where they might sit, chat, and hopefully get to know each other a little better. He promised to share with Jess Keeler all the "war stories" from Lake Castor's bygone "golden era," when the June River Mill had been up and running and the town had been able to sustain a healthy medical profession.

Jess accepted.

The entire ride into town, Jess kept an eye out for Buffy's orange Honda, which carried their equipment, as well as both sheriffs. Dean, on the other hand, kept an eye on her legs.

"This town has changed so much," Dean said as they neared his office. "I watched these buildings get built, then their windows get boarded up. Now I watch them turn into something else entirely."

"How does that make you feel?" Jess turned her body to face him so that her microphone might better pick up his answers.

Dean kept his comments behind his clenched teeth and jaw.

Aside from the microphone hidden behind the lapel of her sleeveless blouse, Jess had two others, as well as a tiny GoPro camera attached to her notebook.

"As long as you keep this pointed at him," Buffy had instructed her earlier, "then we should have a visual on him as we follow behind in my Element."

"Will we be able to hear everything?" Sheriff Worthy wanted to know.

"Only the GoPro will transmit." Buffy made sure all the microphones were securely fastened behind her belt buckle. Or beneath her blouse. Or in her handbag. "The rest of these will only record."

"And we'll get that footage as soon as Ms. Keeler returns, right?" asked Sheriff Axel.

"You'll get *copies*," said Buffy. "The originals will remain with us."

"Unedited, of course."

Buffy took a moment to think that over. "Fine," she said. "But so long as you realize these tapes are our property to do with as we see fit for broadcast purposes."

Sheriff Axel also mulled it over some. "Agreed. But you will hopefully do the right thing when this goes to court, as we'll see fit for *conviction* purposes."

"What happens if we lose the feed from the GoPro?" Sheriff Worthy wanted to know.

Buffy and Jess exchanged glances. Her expression was pregnant with foreboding.

"Let's hope that doesn't happen," was all Buffy said.

Worthy turned to Jess. "I can't talk you out of this?"

Jess answered him by not answering him.

"Then please," the old lawman had said, "be careful."

Those words reverberated in Jess Keeler's mind as she walked the parking lot from Dr. Dean's car to the front door of his doctor's office. She felt a gentle breeze cut through the early-summer air and could not resist a shiver. She took in her surroundings. The front of the building was shaded by a giant pin oak. Overhead, white wisps of cirrus punctuated a clear blue sky. She wondered how Dan Decker had viewed this very vista on the last day of his life, then let that shiver harden to hatred as she followed the doctor into his office.

His receptionist rose from her desk at the sight of them.

"Dr. Dean," she said, "I had no idea you would—"

"I don't have any more patients for the rest of the day, do I, Phyllis?"

She didn't need to refer to his calendar to answer. "No. I . . . no."

"Why don't you take an early lunch?" he offered. "In fact, take the rest of the day."

Phyllis inspected Jess and puckered her mouth with displeasure. "I'm afraid," she said, "that I don't think this is a very good id—"

"That will be all, Phyllis."

Phyllis recoiled from the tone in his voice. She recovered from it—as Jess imagined she must often do—then gathered together her things.

"If you need me," she muttered, "then you know how to get ahold of me."

After Phyllis had left the building, Dr. Dean motioned to a small couch on the far wall of the waiting room. "Why don't you make yourself comfortable?"

Jess did, as best as she could. She took a seat on the sofa—but in the middle, which would force the doctor to either play his hand by choosing to squeeze in beside her or take a chair on the opposite side of the room. Her gamble paid off, and he took a seat across from her.

"Did you grow up in Lake Castor, Dr. Dean?" she asked.

"No," he answered. "I was born up in Ohio, but my parents moved me down to the Carolinas when I was two years old. I went to high school in Lumberton, and I attended medical school at UNC."

"Wow," said Jess. "What year did you graduate?"

"1966."

"You don't look old enough to have graduated college in 1966."

Dr. Dean arched an eyebrow. "I credit my father for that. He raised me to value physical fitness, as well as instilled me with his superior genes."

"He sounds like an interesting man."

"He was. He died in 1971."

"I'm sorry. How did he pass?"

"Leukemia." Dr. Dean folded his hands in his lap. "But we're not here to talk about my father, are we?"

"No sir. We're here to talk about you." Jess reached into her handbag and—careful not to disturb any of the recording equipment—retrieved her yellow notepad and pen. "How long after you graduated before you came to Lake Castor?"

Dr. Dean opened his mouth to answer, but a better thought crossed his mind. "If you like," he said, "I can give you a copy of my curriculum vitae."

"Ooh." Jess smiled. "Do you make that offer to all the girls who come to your office?"

She watched his eyes cut to her neckline. To her lips, which she pursed as cutely as she could. Then, finally, back to her eyes.

"I graduated cum laude from State." He puffed out his chest, as if he might have feathers to preen. "After that, I could go anywhere I wanted. I chose to practice here in Lake Castor."

"Can you imagine how many people consider their lives infinitely changed because of that decision?" Jess crossed her legs. "You must have affected so many families over the years."

"You can say that." Dean squared his shoulders and opened himself up to her. "I remarked the other day about how I came to realize it was time to retire because I seem to have outlived a great number of my patients."

"You're too young to retire."

Dean blinked. Jess immediately realized she had laid it on too thick. The doctor no longer seemed to study her as if she were a lavish dinner—but instead the bill.

This rattled her. She collected both her purse and notebook.

"Would you mind too horribly if I used your ladies' room?" she asked as she stood.

Dean rose from his seat and pointed toward the door that led from the waiting room. "Of course," he said. "It's just inside the corridor." He opened the door for her. "Please pay no attention to my personal effects. As my practice winds down, we have far fewer patients. For that reason, I've taken to freshening up in the bathroom whenever possible."

She barely squeezed a *thanks* around the sob forming in her throat. She quickly pushed into the bathroom and locked the door behind her. She collapsed atop the sink, ran the tap, and then splashed her face with water.

"Keep your head on straight, Jess," she whispered to her reflection. "Don't get too eager."

While Dean's sudden scrutiny unsettled her plenty, it was another thought that gave her the most concern: What if Dr. Christian Dean was innocent? After all, he'd never wavered from his innocence in the matter. What if, she wondered, she was picking on a poor, defenseless old man?

She nearly slapped her own face.

She bore down her stare into her reflection.

Get yourself together, girl.

Dean did it.

He killed those two kids.

He killed Dan.

Jess let her breathing regulate, then looked around the room for something to defend herself with. There wasn't much. The plunger tucked behind the toilet would be too unwieldy. The toothbrush on the counter too impotent. She doubted that she would necessarily need anything, *but still* . . .

She took one final look in the mirror.

This is it.

◆ ◆ ◆

Jess returned from the restroom with a recharged focus. She took her seat and immediately rearranged her belongings so as to get the best audio/visual. Dr. Dean opened his mouth to address her, but Jess did not wait to volley fire across his bow.

"One particular incident which took place after you arrived in Lake Castor," she said, "was the 1971 murders of Linda Harris and Steven Hicks."

Dr. Dean's face fell.

Jess kept up. "Linda Harris was a nurse at Lake Castor General at about the same time you worked there. Did you—"

"I didn't have occasion to know her," said Dean, perhaps a bit too quickly. "Nor would she have stuck out in my memory over the thousands of nurses I've known throughout my career. It seems to me the only remarkable thing about her was that she was killed—and on a holiday of some sort. That is, if I remember correctly."

Jess felt the tips of her fingers and toes turn cold. "That's odd," she said, "because every nurse and doctor who I've spoken with seems to have this story at the forefront of their memories. This seemed to be a defining experience for so many of them. So the fact that you don't seem to remember anything about it—"

"That's a shame, if you ask me."

"What?"

"That the sum total of their experiences at Lake Castor General would be informed by something such as that."

Jess had to hand it to him. He gave the impression of a man who didn't have a single nerve in his body. However, since she'd studied his every move through newspapers and accounts of his neighbors and those who'd crossed his path in the past fifty years, she knew the truth to be quite the opposite.

She knew exactly where his nerves were and how to get to them.

"Let's try this a different way," she said. "You lived in the small Huckleberry Hollow subdivision, am I right?"

Dr. Dean nodded. "I did."

"And that was just across the street from the Creechville subdivision, from where Linda and Steven were abducted."

"If you say so."

"In fact," she said, "it's smack between the sites where they were abducted and where their bodies were found."

Dean's cheeks flushed near the bridge of his nose. He slowly raised his left hand to just below his chin.

"I may have heard something like that," he said. "Since I don't know all the details, I can't—"

"I also have some questions about a trailer you rented down in North Carolina, across the road from where the bodies were found."

Dean clenched and unclenched his hand, at about chest level.

"Do you remember that trailer, Doctor?" Jess asked him. "It was rented under your name, but apparently at the same time, you were living in your home with your wife and children. So tell me: You had two residences at the same time. Why did you rent it? What did you need it for?"

Dean continued to clench and unclench his fist. His eyes fixed on a far corner in the room.

"You won't believe it," Jess said, "but it was actually my colleague who linked you to that trailer. That little detail had gone ignored by detectives for decades, and even myself. But that lazy bastard stumbled upon it and found a credible link from you to the crime scene."

Dean appeared to vibrate in his seat, his hand still clenching and unclenching.

"My colleague's name," she said, "was Dan Decker."

Dean's face twisted into a scowl of contempt. He pursed his lips like he might spit fire.

"We seem to have gotten off topic." He pressed his shaking forearms against the chair to help him rise from it. "How about I see about finding you that copy of my résumé?"

"Very well, Doctor."

"I'll be right back."

Dean quit the room, and Jess could still hear him struggling to regulate his breathing on the other side of the door. She said in a low voice into the recorder at her lapel: "Score one for our team."

Jess threw a cursory glance at her notes and mentally prepared for the next set of questions with which she planned to pepper the doctor. She adjusted herself, then sat straight backed in her seat. She felt like she'd drunk confidence from concentrate and could take on whatever Christian Dean threw at her. Her first order of business, she reckoned, would be to—

What was that?

Jess felt a breeze cross her that set the hairs on her neck ablaze. Her arms were blanketed in gooseflesh. She scanned the room for any sign of something that might be amiss but could find nothing. She heard nothing, smelled nothing . . . the only thing she had was a *feeling*, and it was one too strong for her to ignore.

"Guys," she whispered into the recorder at her lapel, "I don't know if you can hear me, but something feels . . ."

She had no idea how to finish that sentence. Feels *what*? She could not describe what she felt, other than that something horrible had happened there. A shudder raced the length of her spine.

"I think I may be in trouble."

As if to reinforce that thought, she felt something urging her toward the door. Something more than a compulsion. Something . . . *familiar*? She stood but didn't move.

She kept her eyes on the waiting room door, where she expected the doctor to emerge any moment with his CV.

Or . . .

Jess couldn't explain it. She would never be able to put words to it. On the other hand, she didn't feel like she needed to.

Instead of trying, she got the hell out of there.

◆ ◆ ◆

The All-Niter diner.

Sheriffs Axel and Worthy hunched over a laptop in the back booth. Their excited whispers were drowned out by the postlunch hubbub. Lee Ann Thompson stood behind them. The waitress kept their coffees filled, which was no easy task, considering Jess drained her mug before it had time to cool.

"I should have never let you go in there alone," Worthy grumbled to himself.

Buffy ignored everyone around her as she uploaded the sound files to four different zip drives. One for each of the sheriffs, one for herself, and a backup. While waiting for each, she removed Jess's hidden microphones.

"I don't know what we were expecting," said Sheriff Axel. "We knew he wasn't going to up and confess to her."

"This was reckless, irresponsible, and unnecessary," Worthy said. "We needlessly endangered this woman."

Lee Ann's eyes burned like lasers into the screen on the laptop, which showed the familiar image of Dr. Dean's waiting room, as well as the doctor himself in the chair across from the couch where Jess had sat only moments earlier. She was flanked on either side of her by the hulking frames of her two nephews.

Worthy wouldn't let it go. "If anything had happened to you . . ."

Jess placed a hand on his shoulder. "I never felt like I was in any danger."

Worthy squinted. Even he would know that to be a lie. When Jess had rushed headlong from the doctor's office, she could do little to hide the fear flushing her face. She could not explain what had shaken her so or if any of it was unfounded. That ominous feeling had come suddenly and lasted only a moment, but it had been enough to fetch her out of the seat and rush her from the building.

What was that?

"He was never going to tell us what we wanted to know," said Axel, "but you did a great job anyway. He was opening up."

"But he closed down fast," said Buffy. "You heard him. Jess really rattled his cage. It's more evident without the video. You could hear it in his voice. That man was angry."

Worthy put his face in his hands. "I'm glad you got out of there when you did. There's no telling what might have happened when he came back into the room. He's been known to carry a gun. He could have—"

Jess's eyes had never left Lee Ann. "Are you okay?" she asked. The older woman's face remained passive as she watched the video of Dr. Dean, but her eyes betrayed her true emotions.

So did her trembling hands.

"He was so smug," said Lee Ann.

Both sheriffs quit their bickering. Buffy stopped packing away her cables and wires.

"That smile." Lee Ann's voice dropped to a whisper. "He's so . . . *cocky*. It's like he knows he's going to get away with it."

Worthy stepped forward. "Lee Ann, I—"

"I'm right, aren't I?" Lee Ann's eyes bugged wide. "He's going to get away with it."

Nobody seemed to know what to say.

Worthy took a stab at it. "I promise you we're not letting up on him. We've got him on the ropes. Time has proved that when the doctor is under pressure, he acts out."

"And we'll keep up that pressure," added Axel. "I'll assign a deputy to him, and that man's sole reason for living will be to make sure Dean knows he's priority number one for Lawles County. If . . . I mean *when* he steps out of line, we'll be on him."

Lee Ann was nonplussed. "But he'll get away with it," she said.

Neither lawman spoke. To Jess, it seemed no one did. A hush had fallen over the entire diner. Forks stopped scraping plates; dishes quit their clamor. Even the jukebox had fallen silent.

Unable to abide the stillness for a second longer, Jess reached into her handbag and produced the toothbrush she had found in Dr. Dean's office bathroom. She held it up for them all to see but especially for Lee Ann.

"He's not going to get away with it," Jess said. "Not if I have anything to do with it."

CHAPTER FORTY-NINE

James Ballard

1972

The skinny one's name was Billy. Folks called his brother Cootie. Together, the Brown brothers helped facilitate the acquisition of whatever folks across Deeton County might require, so long as it wasn't peace and stability. Rather, they trafficked in marijuana. Heroin. Even guns, from time to time.

Neither of them was incredibly bright. Their mother was a sort of local pincushion. Their father could be any number of men. They came from a long line of shiftless sorts, which was why Ballard had chosen them from the start. In fact, he found them to be the delicious combination of *stupid* and *known to be armed*, so he waited for them to be alone, driving out of downtown Deeton to a backcountry highway.

Ballard flipped on his siren.

When approaching a roadside vehicle, Deeton deputies had been trained to touch the driver's side rear taillight with their fingertips so that their fingerprints might identify a car used in the shooting of an officer. Ballard did not bother with that; either because he forgot or because he had ulterior motives.

He was no longer cognizant of his actions.

"Let me see your hands," he called at the two boys.

Out on that roadside, the Brown brothers must have known full well what Big Jim Ballard would be capable of. He held his service revolver in his shaky right hand while he threw open the driver's side door with his left.

"Cootie, you get out of that car and drop to your knees," he said. "Keep both hands on your head or I'll shoot Billy in the face."

"I don't want to kneel in the road," said Cootie. "It's hot, and I don't have any—"

"I ain't going to ask you again, Cootie."

The younger Brown brother did as he was told. Billy, in the meantime, stared hate-fire at the deputy from the passenger seat.

"We ain't done nothing wrong, Big Jim," said Billy Brown. "You got no right to pull us over, and you damn sure ain't got no right to treat us this way."

"What am I going to find when I ask you to turn out your pockets?"

"You ain't going to find shit, Big Jim."

Something in Billy Brown's smile said he thought he might be smarter than the deputy. It was precisely what Ballard had been hoping for.

"You don't think we saw you following us?" Billy asked. "We spotted you, oh, back about Tyrelle Street and clocked you in the rearview the entire way out of town. If we had anything to begin with—and that's a mighty big *if*—then we would have gotten rid of it long before you flipped on your lights."

"Yeah," said Cootie, still on his knees. "We would have gotten rid of it."

"We'll see about that," said Ballard. "Turn out your . . ." He forgot the word he was looking for, which only fanned the flames within him. Rather than fuss further with it, he pointed the gun to the back of Cootie's head. "Turn them out!"

They did as they were told. Cootie produced a crumpled pack of matches and a couple of loose cigarettes. Billy tossed out a pocketknife from the car.

"See?" Billy grinned. "We ain't got nothing."

"What about the gun?" asked Ballard.

Billy's face fell. "What gun?"

"That one."

Ballard reached behind him and produced a small .44 from his waistband. He tossed it to the driver's seat, next to Billy.

"That ain't . . . you can't . . ."

"Pick it up."

Billy pressed his back against the passenger-side door, scooting as far in the seat as he could away from the weapon. "That ain't mine," he insisted. "I ain't never seen that gun before in my life."

"I told you to pick it up."

"You must think I'm pretty goddamn stupid. I ain't going to—"

Ballard shut him up by slapping his brother upside the head with the butt of his own revolver. Cootie fell to the mud and brought his hands to his face to stanch the flow of blood.

"Hey!"

"If you want to find out what I'm going to do to him next," Ballard hollered, "then leave that gun where it is. If not, then I suggest you fucking pick it up."

Billy kept eyes on it but didn't dare move a muscle.

"Fine then," said Ballard. In one swift move, he smashed his gun against the side of Cootie's head. Something broke, but it was unclear if it was the weapon's stock or the younger Brown's orbital bone. Whatever it was did not stop Ballard from striking him again, and again, and again.

In fact, his beating of Cootie Brown's head reached such a merciless rhythm that he didn't hear Billy behind him, screaming for Ballard to stop, until the deputy had nearly pulped the boy into hamburger.

"I said stop it now—or I swear to God!"

Billy had the gun on him. Ballard turned to face him but stayed on his knees, atop the boy's brother.

"Do it, Billy. Do it now."

The gun shook in both of Billy's hands.

"Shoot me in the goddamn head, or I swear I will beat your brother until he stops moving."

"Get off him," said Billy.

"I'm not going to. The only way is for you to shoot me off him."

Tears ran down the older boy's face. He started to lower the weapon.

"You better not just shoot me once either," said Ballard. "There's six bullets in that chamber, and you best put all six into me. Do you hear me, boy? Because if I climb off your brother and have to take that gun away from you, the two of you are going to have matching faces."

"Please . . ." Billy's voice cracked. Ballard could see his knees weakening.

"Do it now!"

Billy straightened his aim once again, but his face cracked, and the boy collapsed to the mud in a fit of sobs. He covered his head with both hands.

A rage overtook Ballard. In a fiery fit, he leaped from atop the younger Brown to attack his brother. He lifted him by the shoulders and slammed Billy's head hard into the pavement.

"Kill me, you little shit!" Ballard demanded of him. He slammed him again to the asphalt. "I order you to kill me!"

But Billy would not. Ballard lifted him again, this time with every intention of beating the older brother into submission. However, something within him gave out. He wasn't sure if it was his body or his hatred or perhaps even his will to go on, but whatever it was had quit on him before he could deliver either boy to glory, and he was not sure if he was grateful for it.

Leaving the boys writhing and moaning in the roadway, he staggered back to his county car. His mind was exhausted of all reason. Above him, the clouds raced across the firmament as if searching for some respite they might never find—Ballard, down below, finding it only in the understanding that he need not worry about remembering what he had done on that roadside. Nor what he had done anywhere else in all the time he had been granted in this world.

He reached his hand, pulped with gore, for what he hoped was the answer.

"Red," he whispered into his two-way radio, "I need your help."

CHAPTER FIFTY

Dr. Christian Dean

Present Day

Dr. Dean leaned forward in the driver's seat to better see the woman. She parked her car beneath the carport, then stepped briskly to the mailbox. The temperature had leveled out the past couple of days, but the heat still gave her cause to wear shorts, as well as an undershirt that would have dampened from sweat, adding a glistening sheen to her—

The woman spun around and cut eyes at him. She squinted for a better view, then twisted her mouth like she'd tasted a lemon. Dean slipped the car into gear, then silently crept his car forward, toward her. However, it was too late; once she recognized him, she sliced a direct path up her front lawn to the door, which she promptly disappeared behind.

It was hardly a minute before her husband appeared on the porch.

Dean killed the engine and climbed out of the car. He stepped around the front of the vehicle but didn't dare step foot onto the man's property.

"I thought I told you to stay away," called the man on the porch.

Dean called back, "I wanted to see the boys."

"They're grown and don't live here anymore. Besides, you were told not to bother them."

Dean toed the property line. "I'm selling the house," he said. "I'm closing down my practice and finally retiring. Looks like I'll be moving away for good."

The man sighed. He stepped off the porch but didn't venture more than a couple of yards into the lawn.

"When?" he asked.

"Soon."

"I'd like a date, Dad."

Dean breached the property line, then shrugged. "I have a few offers but no one under contract."

Dean made to cut the distance more, but the younger man stayed him with the raised palm of his hand.

"Stay back, Dad. Keep clear of my house, and don't come near my family."

"Aren't you curious at all where I'm moving, Luke?"

"Not even—" Luke rolled his eyes. "Sure. Where?"

"Florida."

"I suppose that's far enough away."

"I don't know why you're still so hateful," said Dean. "Your mother was no angel herself. If she hadn't—"

"Don't, Dad."

"She was never—"

"Don't."

The air hung between them like clothes on a line. Kids a couple of streets over hollered back and forth at one another. Traffic could be heard from a distant highway. Overhead, summer clouds tracked at a languid pace.

Luke said, "There's been a reporter coming around asking questions."

Dean couldn't help the narrowing of his eyes. "Is that right?"

"She was asking about you."

Dean struggled to keep his hand from rising to his chest. He felt the blood pumping into his each and every extremity. He tamped down his rancor best he could, which he feared would not be near enough.

"I don't know why anyone would be interested in me."

"I didn't talk to her," said Luke. "I told her we wouldn't be participating in her story."

"That's a good boy."

Luke continued: "I told her that my family had nothing at all to do with you and we haven't for many years. That, as far as we were concerned, you were dead. You died years ago."

Dean recognized the spiteful tone in his son's voice. Both men were cut from the very same DNA. Dean thought more than once about reaching deep into his son's throat and ripping out his every chromosome.

Instead, he stood there with both arms at his sides in idiot fashion. For the first time in his own memory, he felt rendered impotent by time.

His son said, "Maybe it's a good thing you're moving away."

Sometimes Dean could remain silent for days. As his practice had dwindled over the last year, he had seen fewer and fewer patients, and it had passed—often without notice—that he couldn't remember the exact moment he had last spoken a word. During that time, he could delve deep into quiet reflection—not so much into his own character but into the character of others and how he might best teach them the error of their ways.

Not that he often indulged. As time had worn on, he had become more and more content to let people make their own beds and dig their own graves. He had become less concerned with the instruction of politesse and intelligence and could not help but hide his terrible authority as he watched the world burn.

Perhaps they have it coming.

He wished to spare his children and grandchildren from that fate and would have—but for his wife's cursed genetics. Her influence upon his offspring had damned them from the beginning. He had learned from her that she could be molded into the woman she should be but that she would always fall short of—

He stopped the car at the entrance of his cul-de-sac and leaned forward in the seat for a better view. He rubbed his eyes with his fists to make sure they weren't mistaken. They were not.

A car was parked in front of his house. Two people—a young man and woman—stood on his lawn with their cell phones, pointing them in the direction of his house. He nearly ripped the steering wheel from its column as he pulled the car into the drive, then leaped from the driver's seat to demand what the good hell they were doing on his lawn.

"My name is Julie Parkman," said the young woman. She was dressed smart, and her hair was clean and straight. "I'm a Realtor with Jobman-Williams. We had a showing today at two. I spoke with your assistant, who assured me—"

"Have you never heard of a sidewalk?" he demanded of them.

The agent opened her mouth to speak but was given no opportunity to do so.

"Are you aware of the damage you wreak upon my lawn when you march your dirty shoes across it?" Dean swung his arm wide over the expanse of his front yard. "Are you causing this so that my property values might further drop?"

"Sir, I assure you, we—"

"You and I both know I'm sacrificing tens of thousands of dollars by selling before the market has hit its peak," he bellowed. "How much more do you plan to gouge me?"

The man changed his mind almost immediately about Dean's property. He waved off both the doctor and the Realtor and, much to Dean's despair, walked the lawn back to his car.

"Mr. Hetherton!" The real estate agent tracked after him. "Wait, Mr. Hetherton! I've got another listing in this neighborhood which—"

"Stay off my lawn!" Dean hollered after them. He did not wait to watch them vacate his property. Instead, he stormed inside his home and inspected it immediately for damage.

Dean blamed the reporter. She had him on edge. Lately, it seemed to him that everyone was lying in wait for him, ready to spring a question about some innocuous moment or acquaintance from his past. Moments that might otherwise be pushed to the back of his mind, such as what had happened with that newsman and his assistant on that cold, snowy day.

In fact, Dean hadn't thought about him until that bitch reporter had lured him back to his office and coaxed the memories from him. Hearing the name had struck a nerve, one that since had kept him on his toes. He vowed not to be fooled again. Not after those first two, then the girl. He mistrusted *everyone*. Everywhere lurked potential dangers. The waitress at the barbecue restaurant might be secretly wired for audio. The cashier at the pharmacy could be a plant from the local paper. Or later that afternoon, the two people at the gas pump next to him who kept pointing their cell phones in his direction.

"May I help you?" Dean called over to them.

The two women whispered to one another; then one pointed her phone again at him.

"Did you just take my photograph?" he asked her.

One of the women giggled and pointed at him.

"I gave you no permission to photograph me."

The women tittered their way back to their car. They climbed inside.

Dean blustered toward them. "Get out of the car. Give me your phones."

Each woman yanked her door closed. The passenger rolled up her window.

"Who the hell are you?" Dean demanded. "Who the hell do you think you are?"

He continued to holler it as the car sped out of the gas station lot. He considered giving chase but decided against it. He realized he might be on edge. Everywhere he looked, it seemed that people were talking about him. As if they were sneaking glances or perhaps sifting through his garbage.

For what?

Dean thought he might find the answer as he pulled into his office parking lot and, once again, found the lid to his trash can had been removed and tossed aside. He threw the car out of gear and stormed his way to the receptacle. Sure enough, the bags had been torn open and rifled through. Some even appeared to be missing.

What are they looking for?

What might they have found?

When he thought his rage could not possibly blossom further . . .

"Dr. Dean? Dr. Christian Dean?"

Dean spun to find a man standing before him in a suit. He held a microphone in one hand, and a local TV news-station logo was emblazoned upon his lapel. Behind him, a man in a polo shirt hoisted a camera on his shoulder, then steadied his focus on the doctor.

"Was it the two of you molesting my trash cans?" Dean demanded. "Can no one respect another's privacy?"

"Dr. Dean," said the man in the suit, "my name is Joe Aguilar from WLCX News Eleven. Can we talk a moment about *Something Bad Wrong*?"

"I haven't the slightest idea what that is," said Dean, "nor am I the least bit cur—"

The reporter tucked the microphone farther into Dean's face. The blood vessels in his cheeks popped like fireworks. "It's the true-crime podcast by Jess Keeler and the late Dan Decker," he said. "It details Lake Castor's Christmas Eve Murders from 19—"

"I don't know anything about that," Dean grumped. "I'm afraid I was far too—"

"The podcast names you as the primary suspect for the murders," Aguilar said. "It lays out a pretty strong case for—"

"I don't even know what a podcast is!"

"It's an audio documentary, and this one presents a rather compelling case for your involvement. Do you have a comment?"

"I would if I had any idea what any of this means. Since I wasn't aware of this . . . this *documentary* until right now, I couldn't possibly have—"

"Do you deny that you were a suspect in the murders?"

Dean balled both his hands into fists. "The only thing I am, I'm afraid, is a doctor—and a busy one at that. I don't have time for radio documentaries or fake-news gossip."

"Ms. Keeler makes several allegations, all of which she backs up with—"

"I'm afraid I have no time for any of this," stammered Dean. "If you have any further questions, I suggest you take it up with my lawyer. Now, if you don't mind . . ."

Dean pushed his way past the reporter and threw open his door to his practice. Once inside, he pulled down the shades and turned the sign from **Open** to **Closed**.

"Phyllis!" he called into the waiting room. He lifted one of the blinds with a finger and peeked out at the reporter, who conferred with his cameraman. "Phyllis!" he called again. When still she did not materialize, he shouted even louder, "Phyllis, where the bleeding hell are you?"

She rushed into the room, flustered. “Dr. Dean,” she said. “I’m sorry, but I—”

“Did you hear tell about some *podcast*?” he wanted to know.

“It’s nothing. It’s a little radio show. They do them all the time about stories all over the country. It will be forgotten in a week.”

“So you heard about it?”

She nodded tersely. “I’ll handle it.”

“I trusted you,” he said.

“Dr. Dean, I promise you that I’ll—”

Dean interrupted her with a sharp cross from his right hand to her jaw. She fell back two steps but remained upright. She gingerly rose a trembling hand to her lip, then inspected her fingers for blood.

“You’re right,” she whispered. “You’re absolutely right. I should have told you about it right away. I thought I could—”

Dean hushed her with a jab to her throat. She dropped to her knees and held her neck with both hands while gargling desperately for air. This gave Dean an opening to her right cheek, which he checked with his left fist.

“Look what you made me do, Phyllis.” He drove a foot into her ribs. Then another. “This is all your goddamned fault.”

She shielded her body with her hands, which brought Dean’s feet to her face. When she rushed to cover her head, he took aim at her torso. Phyllis parried the blows as best she could but still could find no respite.

“I trusted you, Phyllis,” Dean shouted above the melee. “I thought you were different. But you are not. You are just like the rest of them.”

“Please . . . ,” she whimpered, “I’m sorry, Doctor. I’m so—”

Dean landed a kick to the side of her head. She dropped her guard. For the briefest of moments, she opened herself up to him.

It was all the time he would need.

CHAPTER FIFTY-ONE

JESS KEELER

Present Day

The rope used to kill Steven Hicks and Linda Harris had been a sisal rope, originally fifty feet in length. It was common and sold at nearly every hardware store in the early seventies. Although they had tried diligently, no one had ever been able to determine for certain where the rope had originally been purchased. There were claims that Sean Gray had stolen a similar rope from a neighbor just days before Christmas Eve, but it was impossible to prove and, with the original claimant deceased, even harder to mention in Jess Keeler's podcast.

Sisal rope was known for its strength and ability to hold knots, as Ennis Worthy had discovered when he'd had to cut away the rope from the bodies of the two young lovers. He had then stored the pieces—knots intact—in manila bags with clear, concise descriptions of where they had been taken from. *MALE VICTIM—HANDS* and *FEMALE VICTIM—FEET* as well as *BOTH VICTIMS—THROAT* were scrawled in his handwriting, along with the dates they had been taken and a comprehensive record of each time since that the bags had been opened.

Fifty-one years later, Ennis Worthy held those very same bags. Jess Keeler tucked the recorder closer to his lips and asked how that felt.

"We didn't know anything about DNA when we collected these ropes." Worthy sadly turned those envelopes over and over in his hands, as if he imagined every possible contaminant sneaking into it over the past half century. "Of course, we do things a lot different now. My only hope is that we were able to preserve this rope enough to extract evidence."

Jess turned the recorder toward the young technician who now had possession of the rope.

"Can you explain what happens next?" Jess asked.

The young technician smiled and said, "You observed as we soaked the rope with fluid. We now run that fluid through the M-Vac machine, and it will extract the DNA from it. We will then analyze the DNA, then test it against what was extracted from the toothbrush and the swabs you submitted."

"How long will that take?" asked Jess.

"Forty-five days," was the answer.

Jess followed Worthy outside to his car. Clouds loomed on the horizon, but the air had yet to succumb to autumn. Worthy watched the faraway lightning a moment before climbing into his county car.

Jess joined him in the passenger seat. She had yet to turn off her recorder.

"Do you think it will work?" she asked him.

Everything about Worthy was slow and deliberate, including the way he turned his eyes to the coming storm. "It has to," he said.

Worthy's phone buzzed. He checked the number, then thumbed alive the call.

"Just dropped it off," he said. Then: "She's right here with me."

Worthy switched it to speaker. The voice of Sheriff Lorne Axel filled the car.

"I got some news for the both of you," he said.

"Did you find it?" asked Worthy.

"I did."

Jess cocked her head. "Find *what*?"

"We need to talk," said Axel. "Why don't you leave your recorder in the car?"

She did. They met at the All-Niter, back in Lake Castor. Lately, the waitress had quit asking what they wanted. Instead, she'd drop them each cups of coffee and lots of cream, then make herself scarce.

"Since your little podcast hit the air," Axel told them both, "we've been flooded with tips from citizens."

"So have I," Jess said.

It was true. Since the previous week, when episode six had revealed Dr. Christian Dean as the primary suspect, the emails had flooded her inbox. Several had turned out to be crackpot, while others had been determined to be more useful. One woman from Nebraska had found an old story about how Dr. Dean, as a young medical student, had been arrested for flashing a pair of coeds. This record had been quashed and unavailable to the twenty-first-century lawmen, but it still existed in an old bygone newspaper article. Still, others called with time-wasting rumors of Dean's behavior and known associates.

"However," Axel told them both, "one particular rumor put a bug in my ear. I kept hearing about a story about two lovers who were abducted by a gunman claiming to be a cop. I'd looked high and low for it, but there never seemed to be anything officially recorded anywhere."

"When did this happen?" Jess asked.

"A couple of months after the Harris-Hicks homicides," said Axel. "Same MO. The couple was taken from a lovers' lane in Lake Castor, then transported to just over the state line, into Deeton. Except this time, the male victim fought off his attacker, and the two kids escaped to safety."

Jess leaned forward in her booth. She had yet to touch her coffee. Her eyes bored into Worthy. "Please tell me you investigated this."

Worthy shook his head. "I vaguely remember this. It's my recollection that I turned it over to Deputy Ballard. I'm ashamed to admit that I never followed up on—"

"This is ridiculous." Jess threw up her hands. "I can't believe my—"

"I was a rookie," said Worthy. "Back then, I was lucky to do what I was told. There was so much going on . . . not that it's any excuse."

Jess wanted to fire further shots across his bow but could determine from the pained expression on his face that she could cause no more shame than he already felt. She let it go.

"Do we have any information on this assault?" she asked the old man.

Axel nodded and pushed a manila folder closer to her. "We have the original case file."

"What? How . . . ?"

Worthy said, "We had them in storage over in Deeton. It wasn't easy, and it took two of my men to find it."

Jess snatched it up. Her habit was to skim, then give a second, more thorough read. She forced herself to wait for a third examination before she brought out her paper and pen to take notes. It didn't take that long to get the gist.

In the spring of 1972, two young lovers had been out parking when they had been approached by a man with a .38 revolver. He'd ordered them into the back seat, then driven them at gunpoint across the state line. Once there, he had found a secluded dirt road and parked. He'd ordered both of them out of the car, then instructed the young man to lock himself in the trunk. The young man had refused. A struggle had ensued, which resulted in the weapon being knocked into the bushes and the young couple escaping.

Jess pointed to their names in the file. "Has anyone spoken to these two?"

"We've yet to find them," said Axel. "It's unknown if they're even still—"

"I got this." Jess pulled her laptop computer onto the table. She tapped her keyboard, scrolled, and then clicked. "Here we are," she said. "The woman lives in Richmond. And he"—she tapped, scrolled, and then clicked some more—"lives in Winston-Salem."

An uneven smile crossed Worthy's lips. Axel leaned back in his seat and winked at Jess.

"Well?" he asked them both. "What are we waiting for?"

That first couple of weeks after the release of her podcast, *Something Bad Wrong*, Jess tried not to pay attention to the media. A lot of it focused on the more sensational aspects of the murder, while others communicated the horror of a suspect at large or the tangle of jurisdiction that had prevented a quick conclusion to the case. A great many contemplated the role of the citizen journalist as an investigator working with law enforcement.

However, the most painful discussions were those that dealt with "The Troubled Legacy of Dan Decker." Of course, Jess had been no stranger to her late partner's past indiscretions in the workplace, but she bristled when writers celebrated a takedown of a fellow journalist.

"Dan Decker's last act was a noble one," declared one blogger for *Slate*, "but it does little to atone for the degradation and harm he did to dozens of women and their careers."

"While we laud him for his relentless and selfless pursuit for justice in a small-town slaying," argued a post in the *Guardian*, "he must not be absolved for his thoughtless actions in the workplace."

Even worse was a tweet from a leading feminist: "The fires of Hell can't roast #DanDecker hot enough."

At first, Jess had been quite liberal about the interviews she had given. The podcast itself provided enough fodder for journalists to probe for an angle. Still, she found it inevitable that the conversation would soon turn to the working relationship she had shared with Decker.

"Did Dan Decker keep the relationship professional?" asked one local news reporter.

"How could you justify working with him," asked another, "given his past indiscretions and behavior towards women?"

"Were you shocked that he was found dead with Christina McNeal, a much younger woman who fit the profile of several others he had groomed and seduced?"

Jess had taught herself not to bristle when she heard those particular accusations. She had practiced her smile in the mirror and delivered the only statement she ever planned to offer when discussing her late partner.

"I'm afraid I can't comment on my relationship with Dan Decker. He was a fine journalist and an even better friend. I miss him dearly."

Still, when articles accused her of benefiting from his death, she could not help but chuckle at the delicious irony.

She had a feeling Dan would have laughed even harder.

He would also have found humor in the newfound celebrity she enjoyed. Not only was she stopped at the supermarket or the post office or the local bar by listeners of her podcast begging for a spoiler to the episodes yet to drop, but she also experienced easier access to new interview subjects, like the female survivor of the 1972 assault.

Her name was Carrie Frederick, and she agreed to meet Jess and both sheriffs at a church in Richmond where she ministered.

"I normally would never discuss this publicly," Reverend Frederick told them as Jess activated her recorder. "However, after I heard your podcast, I knew this was Jesus calling on me to help those poor families in any way I could."

In fact, Reverend Frederick had only ever told her story three times. Once, in 1972, when she had told then-deputy Worthy and two uniformed cops from Lake Castor. The second time was to her ministry, when she had offered a sermon about the ever-present love of Christ.

The third time was in the rectory of her church to Jess, Worthy, and Axel.

"I remember it like it happened yesterday," she said. "At the time, I was a student at Virginia State, and I visited my boyfriend, Donald Riker, for his birthday. We had dinner, then went for a drive. We'd only entered those roads leading through the forest when he suggested we pull over and park down a little dirt road."

"This was in Lake Castor?" Jess asked.

The reverend nodded. "We climbed into the back seat and weren't there for longer than ten minutes before we heard someone knock on the window. Don was over the seat and behind the wheel in a flash, but the car stalled out, and before you know it, there was a gun in his face."

Reverend Frederick's face darkened, and she turned toward the image of a crucified Christ on the wall opposite them.

"What happened then?" asked Sheriff Axel.

"The man ordered Don into the passenger seat. He had a gun on him. He told us he was a police detective and we fit a description of somebody they were looking for. He showed us a badge, but all I could see was his gun."

"What kind of gun?" asked Worthy.

"I don't know guns very well, Sheriff."

"Was it black?" he asked her. "Or was it chrome?"

"Not black."

"So chrome. Was it a revolver, or did it have—"

"It was a revolver."

"Did you get a look at his face?"

"No." She rubbed her eyes with her hand. "I didn't want to. I didn't want him to think there was any reason to . . . I didn't want to see him."

"Of course," said Jess. "Then what happened?"

"He started the car. He drove further into the forest. I watched out the window so I could hopefully find our way home, if it came to that. When I saw us cross the state line, I started to worry."

Jess fought the urge to reach across the table and take the woman's hand. Instead, she nudged the recorder closer.

"That must have been awful."

Reverend Frederick nodded. "You have no idea. Or maybe you do. All I know is that my concern ratcheted when he pulled the car down another dirt road and ordered us both out of the car."

The room fell completely silent. Neither lawman nor Jess dared say anything to break the woman's concentration.

She considered each word before she spoke it. "Don got out. The man with the gun opened the trunk and told him to climb in. Don agreed but said only if I went in there with him. The man refused and said, 'No, she stays out here with me.'"

"That bastard," Axel whispered.

"The man didn't like that. He hit Don in the head. I think with the gun, but I don't know. Don fought back. He fought real hard."

"How long did they fight?" Worthy asked.

"It felt like forever." Reverend Frederick folded her hands together, as if she were praying. "I tried to see out the window, but it was too dark. Instead, I could hear them. Don sounded like he was in trouble, but I didn't think I could be any help. I covered my head with my hands and prayed like I'd never prayed before. Then, when it felt like I was at my absolute worst, I heard a voice so loud shout, 'Carol, *run*!' So I ran."

Reverend Frederick's story was backed up by the man who had been with her that night. Donald Riker had tried his level best to put that night behind him. However, he'd sustained a gruesome injury on the wrist he'd used to deflect blows from their attacker's gun. More than fifty years later, that wrist still nagged at him, especially during cold weather.

That would be far from his only scar.

"I wasn't going to let him lay a hand on Carrie," he told them. Jess and the two sheriffs had met him at his home in Winston-Salem, where he'd invited them all in for coffee. "That's when he hit me. He kept hitting me too. I blocked a couple of them, which is where I got this nasty little scar here. But I gave back as hard as I got it—let me tell you."

"You got a good look at him?" asked Worthy.

"Of course I did." Riker hunched his shoulders, as if suddenly aware he might have to again defend himself. "My number one concern was protecting Carrie at all costs. As soon as I saw she'd left the car and run for the woods, I realized I wanted to make this guy pay. So I got a couple licks in. Knocked his gun out of his hands. At that point, I thought maybe I ought to make a run for it myself."

Jess smiled at his bravado. "Carrie said you saved her life by telling her to run."

"We argued about that a lot back then," said Riker. "That wasn't me who told her to run. I never in my life called her *Carol*."

"So who was it?"

Riker smiled. "We both have our theories. Her faith and my lack of one is eventually what drove us to our separate ways."

Jess felt a familiar shiver take hold of her. It reminded her of that afternoon in Dean's doctor's office. She tried to shake it off, but—

"At any rate," said Riker, "we got away."

"Yes, you did," said Axel.

"You saved Carrie Frederick," Jess said, "but maybe there's still a chance for you to be a hero."

"Point me in the direction, and I'll be happy to."

Axel licked his lips. "You said you got a good look at him."

"I did."

"Would you recognize him if you ever saw him again?"

Riker's eyes narrowed. "I'll never forget his face so long as I live."

Jess had been hoping for such an answer. While Dr. Christian Dean infamously avoided photography, she had obtained Dean's yearbook from the year he'd graduated medical school. Operating from strict instructions provided by the district attorney, Worthy had ordered Jess to cull seven photographs of men similar to Dean from the same yearbook, as well as his own. Each photograph had been recorded, then slipped into individual envelopes. Dean's yearbook photo could not be opened first or last, so she'd placed it third in the stack.

When Riker opened the first envelope, his face predictably fell.

"It's not him." He sighed.

"Replace it back in its envelope," Worthy instructed, "then move on to the next one."

Riker did. The second photograph offered him more interest.

"The jawline . . . maybe." Riker turned the photograph this way and that. "Not the eyes, though. This guy's eyes were more . . ."

Jess felt her arm hairs stand at attention when he reached for the third envelope. She tried her best to maintain a poker face but could not deny the electricity humming between her and the two lawmen. That current crackled and popped when Riker's eyebrows arched and his eyes bugged.

"This . . ." Riker struggled for composure. "Y'all, this . . ."

Jess leaned forward. "Yes?"

Riker straightened his shoulders. He took another look at the photograph. He squinted and held it closer, then farther, from his face.

"This is him," he said. "This is the man who attacked us."

Jess leaned over the table to make certain he held the photograph of Dr. Dean.

"On a scale of one to ten," Axel said very carefully, "how certain are you that—"

"Without a doubt," Riker said, "I'm an eleven."

CHAPTER FIFTY-TWO

Red Carter

1972

Red recognized the gun.

It was an old .44 used to kill Dane McGraw back in '66. He and Jim Ballard had taken it off Bertie Matthews, who they knew had done it. Bertie had told them as much. But since he had confessed after a bit of roughing up and done so without the recent requirement of a Miranda warning, Matthews had been allowed to walk free.

Red had sworn on a Bible to uphold justice for the people of Deeton County, and Dane McGraw, although deceased, had been one of those people. Therefore, Red had seen it as his God-given right to see that justice served, and it had been when Bertie Matthews had been thrown in the back seat of a car occupied by Red, Cappy Jenkins, and Big Jim. Matthews had never been seen again, Dane McGraw had been avenged, and the scales of justice in Deeton County had once again been balanced.

That gun, however, had had a tendency to pop up ever since. It had once been used when a couple of boys had driven down from Baltimore to test the waters of an expanding narcotics enterprise. The ballistics had matched the weapon used in a handful of other unsolved murders, usually involving unsavory elements crossing into or out of Red's county. Had anybody bothered to look further, they might have suspected a vigilante or, worse, one of those *series killers*.

But no one had ever bothered.

Because Red had not commanded it.

Red knew the gun well and identified it on sight, lying there in the middle of the lonely highway, not two feet from the hand of one battered Billy Brown. Billy sat upright, leaning against his car and holding his jaw. His left eye was swollen shut, but he was in much better shape than his brother, Cootie, who lay sprawled and bleeding across the asphalt.

Red picked up the gun. It felt too familiar in his hand. He inspected the cylinder and found no rounds had been fired. The barrel did not smell of gunpowder. He eyeballed the two boys.

"Stay here," he commanded. "Neither of you boys move."

Beyond them, parked on the side of the highway, was Big Jim's county car. As Red approached, he could make out the hulking figure of his deputy in the driver's seat. Any concern he had for his right-hand man slowly gave to rage with each footfall. He sidled up alongside the driver's side window and looked inside.

He didn't like what he saw.

Big Jim Ballard looked a good fifteen years older. He appeared to have dropped twenty pounds since Red had seen him last. His face seemed gaunt, the skin pale, and dark circles ringed his eyes. Red turned his eyes away—from either embarrassment or shame—and instead studied the landscape, as if to imagine what might have possibly occurred there.

"This is bad news, Jim," he said after a moment. "This one is going to be hell to clean up."

His voice creaked, "Red . . ."

"No," Red said, "you listen to me. I banished you to traffic detail for a reason, boy. It's because I couldn't handle you shoving your stink under my nose the way you have been. I'd kept it to myself, what with your drinking and general ineptitude, but I'm afraid it's done boiled over with this here. You know what this is going to cost me? I'm going to have to call Tim Doody and have him haul both these boys out to the woods in order to keep this one quiet. I actually have half a mind to have him haul you out there instead. I'm serious, Jim. We've put the fear of God into a great many people to help them get their minds right, and maybe now it's time we put it into you."

"Red . . ."

Red hushed him. "I want you out of my sight. Not just out of my sight, son, but out of my damned county."

"Red, please."

"I've never in all my days fired a deputy from my seven because I reckoned it would only cast doubt upon my judgment. But I fear keeping you anywhere near me and mine will only serve to damage me tenfold. What the hell happened to you, son?"

Ballard's jaw trembled. He struggled to remain upright, and his bloody fists gripped the steering wheel in front of him.

Red ignored him. "There was a time when I would have bent over backwards for you. But hear me, buster: them days are gone."

"Red."

That time, the sheriff heard something in Ballard's voice. Hell, he'd heard it all along, but his anger had spoken louder. Red stopped and, for the first time in months, looked his deputy in the eye.

Dear God . . .

"Red," said Big Jim Ballard, "I need your help."

And Red saw it.

Finally, he saw it.

He looked deep into his deputy's eyes and wished to heaven that he hadn't.

Red could see the clandestine trips to Dr. Fenton in Lake Castor. He watched George Berry get chained to a tree in the darkness, down a desolate backcountry thoroughfare. He saw Ballard beating the bloody hell out of the Brown brothers. He saw all those things behind the eyes of his deputy, but what shook him most to his very foundation was . . .

Samantha.

Red's jaw hung on a hinge. He realized that he had prepared himself for anything, anything at all . . .

Except that.

"I . . . I really need your help, Red. Can you help me?"

Red backed away from the car. He could not tear his eyes away from those sunken orbs in Ballard's skull. That was not the face of his closest friend, his most trusted confidant. That was something entirely different. He searched and searched, but all he could see—

Poor, poor Samantha . . .

—was the narrowing of options. The window of time closing shut. The list of wrongs growing longer and longer and what little Red could do to end it.

Behind him, the sound of Billy Brown consoling his brother tore him out of his trance. *Yes,* Red thought to himself, *it all ends here.*

Red had forgotten he was holding the gun that had been used to kill Dane McGraw and so many others. It hung there in his hand, by his side. He gripped it tight as he walked across the gravel back to Billy Brown and his brother. He knelt beside them so he might talk to them eye to eye.

"Look at me, Billy," he said. "I need to know you're listening."

Billy knew the score. "Yes sir."

"You boys got kin in Florida—am I right?"

"Yes sir."

"You go see them." Red pointed down the road with the barrel of that gun. "You go now. There ain't nothing for you here."

"What about my mama?" Billy asked.

"Did you hear what I told you?" Red's tone left little room for questions. "I see you boys back in my county, and I'm going to finish what Big Jim started."

"But Cootie . . ." Billy swallowed thickly. "He's real hurt."

"He's going to be hurt a lot worse if you don't head south toot sweet."

Billy got the picture. He loaded his brother into their car, and they took little time turning around in the middle of the road and heading south. Red watched them until they had disappeared over a rise; then he let out a long, tired sigh. All the tension eased in his neck and shoulders but settled somewhere deep in his belly. He knew he'd better get used to it being there.

With one hand, he tugged an unlit Lovera from his shirt pocket and stabbed it into his mouth. With the other hand, he pulled back the hammer on that old .44 revolver, which had come to represent so much of his law and order in Deeton County.

Before heading back to Ballard's car, he stopped at his own. He leaned in and unhooked the two-way from his radio. He held the receiver to his lips.

"I got a ten thirty-three out here on FM 809, just past mile marker twenty-one," Red said. "I need all units toot sweet. It's Jim, dammit."

CHAPTER FIFTY-THREE

Dr. Christian Dean

Present Day

Careful to avoid the infamous sand trap between the tenth and eleventh holes, Dr. Dean stomped his way across the green at the Twisted Holly Country Club. The errant chips from nine irons nearly a hundred yards away came perilously close to nicking him, but the string of insults that followed never stood a chance of landing. He had an altogether different focus.

J. B. Baird, his longtime lawyer, rolled his eyes upon sight of the doctor.

"What's the big idea?" hollered one of Baird's partners. "Get off the green, you idiot!"

"Calm down, Russell," said Baird. "I got this."

Baird slipped his club into his caddy and cut the distance between himself and Dean.

"What gives, Christian?" he asked. "We're in the middle of a—"

"Why haven't you been returning my calls?" Dean wanted to know. "I must have left a dozen messages."

"I'm not exactly around the office much anymore. I've retired. I took care of that Hampton situation for you because of old times, but I can't keep—"

"They're at it again," Dean exclaimed. "They're out to get me. This time, they've made something called a podcast. It's a little radio show, and it's being used to slander me."

"I know what a podcast is," said Baird. "And I've listened to the one you're talking about. Quite frankly, I have to admit that it's compelling. They had the entire country waiting for the DNA results."

"What DNA results?"

Baird sighed. "Have you really not listened to it?"

Dean soured. "Between trying to sell my house and wind down my practice, I'm much too busy to listen to the radio."

"They got ahold of some of your DNA," Baird explained. "They tested it against the rope from the 1971 murders. There was a forty-five-day wait for the results, and in the episode that aired last night, it was revealed that there was not enough DNA to conclusively identify a suspect."

Dean thought that over a moment. "So that proves it wasn't me."

"Actually," said Baird, "it doesn't. All it proves is that the evidence wasn't properly stored and therefore degraded beyond the point of a positive identification. Technology improves every day, so it's possible—"

"What about the things they are saying about me?" Dean demanded.

From behind them, Baird's golf partners grew more impatient. "Are you going to chip or what, J. B.?"

Baird held up his hand. "To be fair," he said to Dean, "they used material recorded during an interview that you granted. I told you never to talk to the media. You gave her all the audio she needed."

"She tricked me!"

"It doesn't matter. Virginia is a one-party state." Baird selected the driver from his caddy. He stepped up to the tee. "The damage is done, Christian. There's nothing to do about it now but wait for it all to blow over. It always does. Now, if you'll let me—"

"We have to sue them."

"For what?"

"For . . ." Dean twisted up his mouth. "For . . . I don't know. I have to sell my house now, and the Lake Castor market still hasn't fully matured. Sue them for the money I'm not going to make on it. Sue them because I can't go to the supermarket or the gas station or anywhere in this county without having my picture taken. I don't know what all you can sue them for. That's *your* job."

"Not anymore, it isn't." Baird lined up his shot, then fired it over the bunker. He waited for it to drop nearly two hundred yards in the distance. "Look," he said, "the last thing you want is for this to go to court. Discovery would be horrible for you. Things might come up."

"What things?"

"Things." Baird leveled his eyes at him. "Things I'm sure you hope would rather stay buried. Things they've probably already uncovered but can't find a way to legally disclose yet. A trial transcript would certainly change that."

Baird's friends piled in the golf cart and drove it to within a foot of the two men. Baird signaled for them to wait.

"Trust me," he said as he climbed into it. "You don't want to go to court."

"Things will be different in Florida."

Phyllis spoke from the passenger seat of Dr. Dean's pickup truck. She used an upbeat, cheery tone, which sounded alien to her lips. When Dr. Dean did not reply, she turned her head from the window. She gingerly touched the edges of a dark bruise that had purpled beneath her eye. There was one that matched it just below her chin.

"You've been so stressed with retirement and the home sale," she said. "A little sunshine and relaxation will do wonders for you. You'll see."

Dr. Dean paid her as little attention as possible. Not because he'd gone silent again but because he had other matters on his mind. Not necessarily the hit his home equity had taken because he was selling it before the market matured or even the nagging issue of the podcast and how it affected his daily life. Mostly, his concern involved the black sedan that had followed them for the past ten minutes.

He'd first noticed it when he had turned off Pleasant Ridge. Later, on Westmoreland, he had still considered it a coincidence when he'd spotted it in the rearview. However, when the vehicle had followed him down Ash Lane, past the old high school, he'd grown certain that the occupants had nothing but nefarious purposes. They could be police, he thought to himself, or worse: more podcasters.

Still, Dean knew he had to keep his cool.

Phyllis, on the other hand, was oblivious. "We'll have to find you an entirely new wardrobe," she said. "It gets so hot down there. It's downright *tropical*. What with the humidity and all."

Dean turned right on Hammond. He checked his rearview. The car behind them followed. He gritted his teeth.

"Silk shirts. Rayon. You want fabric that can *breathe*. I know you don't like shorts, but if we bought you some of those—"

"Will you please *shut up*?"

Phyllis didn't flinch. Instead, she retreated into herself. Again she touched the bruise beneath her left eye. She dropped into a deep silence, which bothered Dean more than her speaking.

"You make me do this," he said. "It's all your fault. I try my hardest each and every day to do what is necessary for me to get into heaven. To be the man my father wanted me to be. You—and every other person who crosses my path these days—seem only to want to lure me off that path. Why must you const—"

Behind him, the car turned away. Dr. Dean could not believe his eyes. Perhaps, he thought, it was only his imagination. He leaned forward in his seat for a better look through the rearview mirror when—

First, he heard Phyllis scream. It was punctuated immediately by the crunch of shattered glass as he collided his pickup into the small Honda that had turned into the road in front of him.

"Goddammit."

Dean laid on his horn. He tossed aside his seat belt and threw open his door.

"Christian, don't." Phyllis reached for him. "It's not a good idea for you to—"

Dean spun on her so fast Phyllis could only snap her mouth shut. She shielded her face with both hands. Rather than waste his rage on her, however, he pushed himself out of the driver's seat. He pounded the pavement as he advanced upon the offending vehicle. He threw open its driver's side door.

"Lady," he growled, "I have half a mind to—"

Dean's throat seized. His mouth hung open.

"No . . . *it can't be . . .*"

But unless his eyes deceived him . . . it was *her*. The nurse. Not the nurse from 1971 but an older version of her. One who had been touched only by time instead of a rope at his hands. This one's mouth had not been twisted into a silent scream but instead—

"No . . ." His hand drew to his chest. "It's . . . it's *impossible*. You're dead. I made sure. You're—"

Dean took a step backward. He took another. He backed up farther still when the woman climbed out from behind the steering wheel. She stepped into the fresh air and appeared to breathe deep.

"You can't . . ." Dean's fist clenched and unclenched beneath his chin. "How the hell did you—"

The woman took a step closer to him. He backed up farther until he collided with someone behind him. He spun to find two corn-fed Virginia boys in overalls.

"Is this the man, Aunt Lee Ann?" asked one of them.

"It's him," came her reply.

Both boys reached for him.

Dr. Dean's entire world went black.

◆ ◆ ◆

When next Dean opened his eyes, all he could see was darkness. He took a moment to collect his consciousness, and when he did, he realized it was night.

There was a throbbing in the back of his head, and he could tell he'd suffered from a wound there. He brought up a hand to address it but realized he could not, as something impeded his movement.

His hands were bound together by rope.

In fact, Dean realized, his entire body was bound. He found his back pressed against a stiff oak tree, which towered above him and mingled with the treetops of an entire forest. He leaned back to better see, only to find a rope had secured him by the throat as well.

"Go ahead and scream," said a woman from the darkness. "No one can hear you."

"I have no reason to scream," said Dean.

"Go ahead and try it anyway."

Dean clenched his jaw. "I am not going to."

"This is the last time I will ask you nicely."

"I'll ask you to untie me from—"

The two Virginia boys emerged like lightning from the darkness. Each of them grabbed a hand and twisted back his index fingers until they snapped. Dean clenched down hard on his teeth. Pain shot through him like incandescent bolts, and it took everything he had not to cry out. Unsatisfied, the boys took hold of his middle fingers and did the same. They had selected his ring fingers when the woman said again from the shadows: "Now scream."

He did.

"Louder."

Dean screamed louder.

The woman stepped into view. Even behind the mask of several decades, he could tell she was the spitting image of the dead nurse. The reflection of how she might have looked, had she chosen a different cul-de-sac in which to park on that night so long ago.

That woman stood over him and did not break eye contact, even as she spoke to the two boys.

"Now shut him up."

One of them delivered a blow across his jaw. The other put a fist into the side of his head.

Dean fell silent.

"You see?" asked the woman. "No one can hear you."

"Christian?"

Dean recognized the second voice.

"Phyllis?" he asked. "Is that you?"

"Christian? What is happening to us?"

"Where are you, Phyllis?"

He felt the ropes tighten at his chest and throat.

"I'm right behind you," she said. "They've tied us to a tree."

Dean's eyes flashed as he stared up at the nurse's doppelgänger. "What do you plan to do?" he asked her.

"Do you know who I am?" asked the woman.

"I have no idea. No."

"My name is Lee Ann Thompson." She crossed her arms over her chest. "Linda Harris was my sister."

"I'm afraid I don't know wh—"

He would not finish that sentence, as he was subject to another round of blows from Lee Ann's nephews.

"What is it you want?" Dean demanded.

"Tell me what happened."

Dean blinked twice. "What do you mean?"

"That night," said Lee Ann. "I want you to tell me what happened."

"What night?"

"Christmas Eve."

Dean tried to shake his head, but the ropes held him taut. "You think I have something to do with what happened back in 1971? That podcast has people believing I'm the boogeyman. I know no more about what happened to your sister than—"

"If you don't tell me what happened," said Lee Ann, "then I promise these boys are going to make things even more painful for you."

"Christian," said Phyllis, from the other side of the tree, "maybe you better—"

"Shut your mouth, Phyllis." Then, to Lee Ann, he said, "I don't know what happened. So I can't poss—"

Lee Ann barely nodded. Her boys set upon Dean, and he washed the forest with a flood of his screams. Dean felt for certain that a rib had broken. He cursed the mortality of this aging body. If only he were younger, he might . . .

When they finished, Lee Ann crouched to eye level with him.

"Do you want me to tell you I did it?" Dean spit blood from his mouth and tried to wipe it with his hands—only they were broken and bound. "Fine. I'll tell you that. If it pleases you, I'll tell you anything you like. But you'll never truly know if I'm telling you the truth or simply trying to stop you from breaking more of my hand."

Lee Ann turned his face to hers. She gazed deep into him.

She knew.

"I want you to tell me what their last words were."

Dean saw little point in either resisting or complying. He reckoned his fate had been determined long before he'd found himself tied to that tree. Long before that night in 1971, even. He contemplated the futility of taking inventory of every deed that might have delivered him to that forest, if he could even remember.

It didn't matter.

"If you tell me," said Lee Ann, "then I promise to end it quickly."

"You'll let us go?" asked Phyllis.

Lee Ann sighed a sour smile. "I'll end it quickly."

"Christian, will you just—"

"Phyllis," he growled. "Shut your mouth."

Lee Ann's expression did not change.

"Did Linda cry out?" she asked. "Did she call for me?"

Dean shifted his vision and stared out over her shoulder.

"Did she cry out for our mama or daddy?"

The woods were dark and deep. He wondered briefly which side of the state line they were on. He wondered how long until anyone found him.

"Tell me: What were her last words, Dr. Dean?" Lee Ann's eyes burned like wildfires. "Tell me, or I promise you . . ."

Dean doubted he could even remember. His only recollection of the girl was the silence. Her and the boy both. How he had stood over them after they had expired, watched them, and marveled at their silence. How still they had been. How quiet they had remained, as he had begun to cover them with—

The rope at his throat tightened. He cut eyes toward Lee Ann.

"Tell me, Doctor."

He said nothing. The air filled instead with Phyllis's warbling.

"Don't do this," she whimpered. "You don't have to do this."

Lee Ann did not blink. The boys on either side of the tree slowly pulled at the knots until they constricted. Dean felt the heat clawing at his neck. He thought again of the girl's mouth, how her lips had retreated back over her teeth, as if to scream. Yet there would be no scream. There would be no sound. There would be no—

"This is your last chance," said Lee Ann. "Tell me what they said."

The ropes drew tighter.

Dr. Dean looked into Lee Ann's eyes for the briefest of moments, then returned his gaze into the dark of the woods.

He never uttered a word.

CHAPTER FIFTY-FOUR

Jess Keeler

Present Day

The office of Deeton County's district attorney had come a long way since the days of Nicholas Brandon. Gone was all the filibuster and flair. In its place was a bookish sort, more prone to precision than posturing. When Milton Eubanks had taken the office at the beginning of the previous decade, he had been considered by many to be a wonk. His most common criticism was that he tended to look too long before he leaped.

For that reason, he was skeptical. No matter how much Jess and Sheriff Worthy bucked, Eubanks didn't go for it.

"There are one hundred and one counties in North Carolina," he told them. "I'm afraid you picked the wrong DA to launch an investigation with so little evidence."

Jess Keeler stood from her chair and fought every urge to lean over his desk. "You said you would issue an arrest warrant if you had one of three things. You said physical evidence, like DNA or fingerprints—"

"Which you don't have," said Eubanks. "The rope did not positively ID him for 1971."

"Or a signed confession from the killer—"

"Which is not likely, especially with Dean in absentia."

"Or an eyewitness." Jess placed her hands on her hips. "Donald Riker positively ID'd Dean from a photograph and is willing to testify in court that Dean attacked him and Carrie Frederick that night in 1972. I don't know where you went to law school, but to me, that's an eyewitness."

Eubanks cut her a look that backed her away from his desk. He wasn't a big man by any means, but Jess knew he could make her life very hard if he so desired. Still, it required a gentle coaxing from Worthy before Jess returned to her seat.

"Even if I bit on this new information," Eubanks said as he consulted his file, "it does nothing to convince a jury of his guilt for the Harris-Hicks homicides in 1971."

"The hell you say!" Jess threw up her hands. "The story that Riker and Frederick told us provides a step-by-step guide on what happened with Linda and Steve. If he did one, he most certainly did the other."

"I'm afraid that's not how the law works, Ms. Keeler. Or juries either, for that matter."

"Okay, maybe not," Jess said, "but it puts him behind bars for *something*. We get him for '72, and he cools his heels in prison while we find something that conclusively nails him for '71."

"It's still not enough." Eubanks sighed. "Your witness is a man who listened to your podcast, then identified a photograph of someone he believes attacked him fifty years or so ago. It's shaky at best."

"But he said he'd never forget those eyes," Jess insisted. "He said the only thing different was the hair, but Dean had enlisted in the army, so he would have—"

Eubanks's decision was final. "Even if I rounded up the resources to locate Dean, who's been missing for . . . how long?"

"Four months and eleven days," Worthy said. "Just up and vanished."

"Even if we were to track him down," said Eubanks, "we wouldn't have nearly enough to extradite him back to Deeton County. I have a place I like to be before I pursue a conviction, and we're still a long way from that place."

Before Jess could say another word, Sheriff Worthy thanked the DA for his time. They gathered up their files and made for the door.

"I listened to the podcast," Eubanks said.

Jess stopped in the doorway. She didn't turn around.

"You did a good job," he told her. "It was a very well-researched and compelling story."

Over her shoulder, she said, "It needs an ending."

Eubanks returned to the papers on his desk. "I wish I could be the one to give it to you."

Since Jess Keeler had begun working on *Something Bad Wrong*, she'd come to associate the passions of storytelling with the sounds and smells inside the All-Niter diner. It was in those booths that she had first proposed the project to Dan Decker, and she had often written her scripts to the soundtrack of the antiquated jukebox in the corner. She had also developed a first-name relationship with the crew who staffed it.

"Hey, Jess, I got you set up right over—" Dotty, the second-shift waitress, caught sight of Jess's lunch companion. "Oh my goodness, Samantha, look at your hair. Did you just get it fixed?"

Jess's mother beamed shyly. "I think so."

"Well, it just looks grand." Dotty turned to Jess. "The sheriffs are waiting for y'all in the booth by the window."

Jess thanked her, then grabbed a copy of the free paper by the newsstand. Jess had already read it a dozen times; they had interviewed her after the last episode had dropped. She handed it to her mother.

"Let me find you a pen, Mom. You can do the crossword while I'm in my meeting."

"I've already done that one," Samantha groused.

"Yeah, but you won't remember all of the clues. It will be like doing it again for the first time."

Jess pretended not to see her mother flip her the bird. Instead, she zeroed in on Sheriffs Axel and Worthy, sitting across the table from one another. They both attempted to rise as she approached, but Jess stopped them.

"Howdy, Sheriffs." She smiled. "I hope you don't mind, but I brought my mother. She's having one of those days."

"And she's right next to you," Samantha said. "You'll be having one of those days if you don't stop talking about me like I'm not here."

"See what I mean?"

Axel did manage to rise from his chair. He made to remove his hat, but it was already resting on the windowsill next to him.

"It's always a pleasure, Ms. Bowen," he said.

Samantha's cheeks pinked. She thanked him and took a seat alongside him.

Jess set down her things. "So I'm excited to hear what you—"

"Excuse me?"

Jess turned around to find two young women, one with a baby on her hip. They both had wide eyes.

"Are you Jess Keeler?" asked one of them. "From the *Something Bad Wrong* podcast?"

"I am."

The two women exchanged eager glances. The one with the baby lit up. "I knew it. I recognized you from the interview you did on the TV news."

"Is there going to be another episode?" asked the other one.

"Not until they can locate the main suspect," Jess answered.

"Do you mean the doctor? OMG, my uncle has a friend who used to live down the street from his doctor's office, and he can tell stories about how Dr. Dean used to—"

It didn't take long for Dotty to butt in. "Y'all quit bothering these people so they can get back to the business of solving murders." She shooed away the two women, then filled four cups of coffee. "Sorry about that," she said. "I got busy filling up yonder sugar caddies and lost my focus for just a split second."

"They can be quick." Worthy smiled.

"It won't happen again."

"Don't worry about it," Jess said kindly. "I'm starting to get used to it."

It was true. Lately Jess couldn't go to the supermarket or fill up her gas tank without someone stopping her. The podcast was all anyone could talk about in Deeton and Lake Castor, as most people knew the many landmarks mentioned in the story or, in many cases, the players. Jess rarely minded it, unless she was with her mother. The story of those murders would always be high on the list of things that disturbed her, and Jess relished the moments her mother spent *undisturbed.*

For that reason, Axel waited until Samantha began her crossword puzzle before he dived in.

"My son served in the army," he told them. "He reached out to a couple of his old buddies. They helped move some things along. Of course, we're not allowed to disclose where we got this information, and therefore it cannot be used in your podcast."

Jess told them that she understood and no longer went to great lengths to convince them. She didn't have to. She had proved herself.

"Dr. Dean was honorably discharged two years after he entered the army as a doctor." Axel nodded to a manila file folder in front of him, which he did not open. "He'd been taken to court by a family who claimed he took nude photographs of their ten-year-old daughter."

Jess gritted her teeth. "What?"

Axel nodded. "It gets worse." He started to open the folder but stopped himself. "There were other families who came forward. None of the girls were older than fourteen."

Samantha glanced up from her crossword puzzle. She opened her mouth, as if to add something, but thought better of it. She lowered her head again to the newsprint.

"Why was he *honorably* discharged?" Jess wanted to know.

Worthy shook his head. "Let me guess," he said. "The bastard had a good lawyer."

"Not only was he honorably discharged," said Axel, "but they managed to redact it from his record. He went on to practice family medicine and pediatrics for several years before shifting to internal medicine."

Jess could not believe her ears. She was grateful for the silence between them for the next few moments, for it gave her time to contemplate the many horrible things she wished she could do to that man, if they could ever find him. She was still festering with that thought when the bell above the door rang, and in walked Lee Ann Thompson.

Jess noticed something was different about Lee Ann but couldn't put her finger on it. She couldn't decide if the woman now seemed detached—or was it *aloof*? When finally she put it together, she made room for Lee Ann on the booth bench next to her.

"You're alone," Jess said. "Where are your nephews?"

Lee Ann turned wistful. "I don't know where they are. I told them that I'll be fine now without them."

Axel repeated the information about Dean's army career. When he finished, Lee Ann turned her head to the ceiling.

"How many lives did this man upend with his evil?" she asked aloud.

"We may never know," said Jess.

"I have a theory," said Worthy.

Everyone at the table fell silent.

"I believe," he began, "that Christian Dean was a serial *rapist* but not a serial *killer*. Based on all the information we've gathered on him, I believe he never intended to kill Steve and Linda. He likely approached them same as he did Frederick and Riker, some months later. The only problem was that Linda would have recognized him. This means he could never have let her live to report him. He had to keep her quiet. So he killed them."

Lee Ann asked in a whisper, "So you don't think he targeted them?"

"No. I think they were in the wrong place at the wrong time."

The news seemed to unsettle Lee Ann. Jess believed because it signaled a change in the mindset the woman had fostered for over a half century. Before Jess could wander too far into the weeds on it, however, she noticed something that jarred her own attentions.

Samantha had lost herself in the crossword puzzle. However, it was not necessarily what Samantha was writing but *how*. Her penmanship had grown erratic. In some places, it shook; and in others, the pen merely wandered off the page. It was the first time she had seen her mother's handwriting deteriorate, but something about it teased loose a memory of something else.

Jess reached into her bag and retrieved her grandfather's notebook. She opened to one of the timeworn back pages—

GEORGE BERRY = GUILTY.

GEOOOORRRH RYRBY KLKED TME.

—and something clicked into place. Her eyes danced between the notebook and the crossword puzzle, from her mother's handwriting to her grandfather's.

"Oh my . . ."

"What is it?" Worthy asked.

Jess could not take her eyes off her own mother. Despite being caught up in the case, the tragedy of Dan Decker, and all the thrills of pursuing Dr. Dean, she shamed herself for not seeing it sooner. She played back every description of her grandfather's erratic behavior, his sloppy police work, his anger . . . all of it, over and over, and she realized in that moment that it would be forever impossible for any one person to know the complete truth of any story.

Lee Ann stood to leave. "I want to thank you."

"It's not over," Jess said as she rose from the table to meet her. "We'll find him. Dr. Dean can't hide forever."

"You tried your best," said Lee Ann. "You all did everything you could. You all went above and beyond. It's time for you to let it go."

"That's not going to happen," said Sheriff Worthy. "We don't believe these two incidents to be isolated. Rapes weren't reported back then the way they are now. And even if they were, I'm afraid law enforcement wouldn't have taken them very seriously."

"They used to blame the victim," said Axel. "Ask them what they expected to happen, out there in the woods all alone like that. Would turn them around, send them home, and tell them to be more careful."

"If he was a rapist," said Jess, "that means there are other women out there. They need to be heard."

Jess didn't know how to read the expression on Lee Ann's face. She wasn't certain if she was supposed to.

"One way or another," said Worthy, "Christian Dean is going to see justice. It may not happen until he's dead, but I promise he'll be judged."

"I don't believe you are ever going to find him," said Lee Ann.

"I've been told that before." Jess leaned back in the booth. "Somehow, I keep finding a way."

Lee Ann sighed. "I absolve you of any obligation to do anything further for me or my family. There's nothing more I need."

"I wish we could give you closure," said Jess.

"There's no such thing," Lee Ann told them.

"Of course. I mean . . . I guess I wish I could give you a better ending to this story."

"Sweetheart, you can't." Lee Ann put her arms around Jess and squeezed her tight. "Without Linda and Steve, there is never going to be a satisfying ending to this story."

ACKNOWLEDGMENTS

None of this would have been possible if it weren't for my agent, Josh Getzler; his assistant Jonathan Cobb; and the team at HSG Literary. Thank you all for believing in my book and for constantly fighting for it, even during the times when I had given up. I owe y'all one.

Many thanks to the team at Thomas & Mercer for helping me get this book into the best possible shape. I am grateful that Jessica Tribble Wells took a chance on me and thank the editing department—Charlotte Herscher, Rachael Herbert, and Mindi Machart—for their patience. I've been very fortunate to be in great hands with great professionals at every level from cover design, to marketing, to all of it and couldn't be happier with the experience.

The sincerest thanks to Tim Horne, Carolyn Spivey, and everyone who shared their stories with me.

Thank you to Charles and Natalie. Also to Piper, Tracey, Meredith, Paul, Geraud, Michael, and Jeffrey for your continued support.

A big thanks to everyone out yonder who supported me while I was writing this: Alexis, Paige, Christina, Bob Johnson, Sean and Lindsley, Jackie, Kenny and Jada, Katharine, Robert and Meghan, Jesse, DJ and Larry, Endless Will, Jeremy, Jim and Jaime, Sam Montgomery-Blinn, Brooke Cain, Wyatt and Jessie, Meg, Brandon and Mikki, John and Dorene and Kelsey, John K., Colin G., Sweet Johnny, Nick Singh, Lauren and Kiah, Dr. Lunchbox, and so many more than I could possibly list. And those back home: Emily, Melissa, Danielle, Emilie, and Sharilyn.

To the writers who kept me going and answered those late-night frustrated phone calls or sat with me while I puzzled through plot points: S. A. Cosby, Rob Hart, Todd Robinson, Nik Korpon, Jordan Harper, Katy Munger, Steve Weddle, Kathleen Kent, David Nemeth, and, of course, my Sunday-afternoon readers, J. G. Hetherton, Scott Blackburn, J. M. Rasinske, Phillip Kimbrough, and Russell Johnson.

But the biggest thanks of all goes to the woman who I'm still trying to impress, all these years later, who believes in me even more than she probably should: Thank you, Lana Pierce. Big time.

ABOUT THE AUTHOR

Photo © 2016 Alex Maness

Eryk Pruitt is a filmmaker, novelist, and screenwriter living in Durham, North Carolina. His films have earned top prizes at film festivals around the world, and his novel *What We Reckon* was a nominee for the Anthony Award. He can be found either at his desk, hard at work on another story, or mixing drinks at his bar, Yonder, in Hillsborough, North Carolina.